THE INFINITE HEIST

The Maverick Heart Cycle

Stephen Graham King

Renaissance.
Diverse.Canadian Voices
PressesRenaissancePress.ca

Also by Stephen Graham King

Non-Fiction
Just Breathe: My Journey Through Cancer and Back

Fiction
Chasing Cold

The Maverick Heart Cycle
Soul's Blood
Gatecrasher
A Congress of Ships
Ghost Light Burn

THE INFINITE HEIST

The Maverick Heart Cycle

This is a work of fiction. Any similarity to any events, institutions, or persons, living or dead, is purely coincidental and unintentional.

THE INFINITE HEIST ©2024 by STEPHEN GRAHAM KING. All rights reserved. No part of this book may be used or reproduced in any manner whatsoever without written permission except in the case of brief quotations in critical articles and reviews. For more information, contact Renaissance Press.

The author expressly prohibits any entity from using this publication for purposes of training artificial intelligence (AI) technologies to generate text, including without limitation technologies that are capable of generating works in the same style or genre as this publication. The author reserves all rights to license uses of this work for generative AI training and development of machine learning language models.

No part of this book or its cover art was generated by artificial intelligence.

First edition 2024

Cover art and design by Nathan Fréchette.
Interior design by Cassandra Pegg and Taylor Ash.
Edited by Alex Cuvelier, Alec Cimeša, and Max Emberley.

Legal deposit, Library and Archives Canada, September 2024.

Paperback ISBN: 978-1-990086-80-9
Ebook ISBN: 978-1-990086-83-0

Renaissance Press - pressesrenaissancepress.ca

Renaissance acknowledges that it is hosted on the traditional, unceded land of the Anishinabek, the Kanien'kehá:ka, and the Omàmìwininìwag. We acknowledge the privileges and comforts that colonialism has granted us and vow to use this privilege to disrupt colonialism by lifting up the voices of marginalized humans who continue to suffer the effects of ongoing colonialism.

Printed in Gatineau at
Imprimerie Gauvin
Depuis 1892
gauvin.ca

Dedication

For 'Nathan Smith,
who's been a member of the crew all along.

Keene has your gear. Ember needs your help planning a score. Vrick has your quarters ready. And Lexa-Blue poured you a drink. She doesn't know what it is, but it's green.

Chapter One

Galactum Year 152.5

"I would rather rub my face on an unshielded reactor core," Lexa-Blue said.

"Or go skinny dipping in hard vacuum," Ember added.

Keene scowled at them both. "Oh, ha ha. Very funny. I get it. I'm sorry I asked."

"Oh, no, wait," Lexa-Blue said. "I'd rather eat three helpings of that really disgusting, congealed…thing Paxt tried to get us to eat at that market stall on Bel Vie."

"Oooh, yeah," Ember said, grimacing. "The thing with the eyes."

"And the…" — Lexa-Blue made writhing motions with her fingers — "…things."

"And that smell. Like rotten vegetables baked in mould."

"And then burned. And then soaked in…"

"All right," Keene interrupted, his voice sharp. "I'll go by myself. I just thought it might make for a nice break. Scholus happens to be very nice this time of year."

"If you call being surrounded by a bunch of bookheads with no understanding of the real world all in the same place 'very nice,' then yeah, I guess so," Lexa-Blue said.

"Yeah," Ember agreed. "Didn't they make that whole planet one big campus just to keep them out of our hair?"

Keene walked away from them both. "Fine. Lesson learned."

"See, you learned something new, and you didn't even have to leave the ship," Lexa-Blue called after him.

"You're both awful," Vrick said. The ship's voice made es disdain perfectly clear. "He's been waiting for this conference for months."

"Oh relax, junkpile," Lexa-Blue said. "It's all in fun. He knows that."

She leaned back from the quisling board and stretched, cat-like, then ran a hand through the jagged crop of her blue-black hair. The light from the holographic game pieces glinted off the ebony sensor gem where her right eye had once been, stark against the warm, sandy tone of her skin. The vertical, stark white scar ran from forehead to cheekbone.

"I don't know," Ember said. "He seemed upset."

"Leave him be, squib. I've known him a lot longer than you have. He'll be fine. Besides, we have a game to finish."

She leaned forward over the tiers of the board again, already contemplating her next move. "And I'm winning. You owe me three pressure suit inspections and two of my dinner making shifts."

"Are you sure that's you winning? You've tasted my cooking."

"I'll take it if it means I beat your ass."

They played four more matches and Ember won back two of his shipboard chores, which, he realized, was the best he was likely to get. It was only then that he had noticed that Keene hadn't returned to the lounge. "Okay, I'm out."

"Come on, squib. You could still win the rest. One more hand."

"No chance. I managed to save a little bit of face. That's enough for me."

"Spoilsport."

Hearing her grumble behind him, he headed aft. He found Keene in their quarters, seated on the edge of the bed. He immediately saw that Keene's eyes were open but glazed over, unseeing — a telltale sign he was using the access node embedded in his brain to access Know-It-All. Long-time users of the still high-end tech got that weird, unseeing expression whenever they used their nodes. You could always spot a newer user by the way they shut their eyes tight when they fugued to use their nodes.

Ember entered their room quietly, figuring Keene was making final arrangements for his trip, or perhaps just reading some new tech journal with news about the latest advancements. The thought of the old, familiar habit made him smile.

Not wanting to disturb Keene for fear of aggravating any lingering tensions over their teasing, he busied himself while he waited for Keene to finish whatever he was occupied with. He emptied the laundry cabinet, folding and putting each item away with precise care.

"Hey," Keene said, coming out of his fugue. "It was my turn to do that."

Ember shrugged. "I'm not keeping score."

He hung the last shipsuit in the closet and came to sit beside Keene. "All set?"

Keene showed no surprise that Ember had intuited what he had been doing. "Yep. Room is booked, and I've got a seat on one of the shuttles running attendees from Hub to the conference."

Ember looked puzzled. "But I thought we weren't due on Hub until two days before the conference. It's at least a week and half travel time from Hub to Scholus."

Keene smiled. "Yes, if I was going via interspace. Scholus has a Gate now."

"Ah. That makes sense. I had no idea Sindel and her team were that far along in the implementation."

"Yes," Keene said. "Once we got rid of those resource embezzlers on Sound and Fury, things ramped back up again. Sindel even has Ophir and Initra running implementation teams."

Ember smiled at the memory of the whole Gatecrasher incident, something he could do now that time had allowed him to heal. Now that he'd found Malika again, his old partner in crime. Literal crime, as they had been running grifts on Weald when they'd gotten caught up in the whole mess. They'd been dragged along with the Maverick Heart crew to defend the first stable wormhole generating station, the prototype for those that were springing up around more and more worlds. And it had fractured their friendship until they'd found each other again on Sound and Fury.

Ophir Al Hirazi and Initra San Cristobal had been the original creators of the technology and had been neck-deep with them in keeping the tech from falling into the wrong hands. Now, Sindel Kestra, Lexa-Blue's on-again, off-again girlfriend, had brought a fresh drive to the Gate project, improving the basic design and accelerating the rollout.

"Do they mind working for Sindel now? I mean, she took the whole project over," Ember said.

Keene laughed. "Are you kidding? They're both the first to admit they were creators and not businesspeople. They were both thrilled, since Sindel actually runs her own successful tech company. Sindel says they drooled over her ideas and were thrilled to riff on them. The three of them are working really well together."

Ember nodded. He could imagine the three of them poring over designs and schematics in almost rapturous joy. But then he looked at Keene and saw... what? Longing? There was something there in his lover's expression. Something only he might have noticed.

"I'm sorry if we pushed your buttons back there."

"No, I'm sorry," Keene said, leaning into Ember's shoulder. He brought his hand up to touch Ember's sleek, silvery hair. The strands slipping through his fingers like soft, metallic threads, and the rich amber tone of Ember's skin seemed fair next to his. "It's not like we don't joke around like that all the time anyway."

"So, what's different?"

Keene was silent a moment, and Ember watched him search for the words he wanted to say. Ember knew that look, as Keene sorted his thoughts, ordering them as neatly and precisely as the gizmos or repairs he always had his hands in.

"I love being here," Keene said. "I love being here with you, Lexa-Blue, and Vrick. It's been a hell of a good life."

"Despite the constant life-threatening danger," Ember said.

"Yes, in spite of all that," Keene agreed, smiling. "This has been my home for a long time. And you're my family."

"But we don't speak your language," Ember said.

"Yes," Keene said, the word an exhalation of relief at Ember's once again sharp understanding of the human mind. "This conference is an opportunity to just let that tech junkie part of me out to run free. Dig into it and share with people who get it, who can both keep up with me and push me to think new things."

"Then why did you ask us to come along?"

"I don't know. I guess I'm just used to thinking of us as a unit. I can't remember the last time I did something on my own."

"It was probably the last time your life wasn't in danger," Ember said.

"It does seem to be a bit of a pattern for us, doesn't it?"

"It does, but at least it keeps us from getting boring."

"That, my little thief, is something we will never be. Though I sometimes wonder what it would be like if we were."

"Well, considering this conference you're going to, you get to be as boring as you want!" Ember said, ducking out of the way as Keene tried to shove him off the edge of the bed.

∞

The next several weeks were taken up with a delivery of machine parts to one of the newer colonies out on the Brink: a run that went so smoothly that they all started to get jittery as if catastrophe waited around the corner.

But despite their hypervigilance, once the supplies were offloaded and the payment had cleared, Vrick rose through the planet's atmosphere into the dark beyond. Even the trip back to Hub was calm, allowing them all time to relax.

Lexa-Blue took the time to strip, clean, and test all of her weapons, even giving Ember lessons on how to use some of the more exotic blades in her collection. Keene spent time at his virtual drawing board, working new designs for all kinds of stealth gadgets he knew would come in handy when the period of uncharacteristic quiet ended. Ember gleefully tested each one as it came off the printer, running every sim he could think of to push the designs to their limits.

They had plenty of time to indulge in sensies, read, and talk. Ember drew while Keene light painted; Lexa-Blue long ago resigned to modelling for them both. They were all old hands at filling their time during the long hours in interspace.

But then, as always, they emerged from the hyperacceleration back into home space above the densely populated capitol world at the metaphorical heart of the Pan Galactum.

"Has Greff checked in?" Lexa-Blue asked as the planet grew in the forward viewport.

"Yes, there was a message waiting as soon as we dropped out of interspace," Vrick said.

Lexa-Blue chuckled. "Just like him not to spring for tightline charge. He always was cheap."

"We still have to drop Keene off for his flight, so we can adjust if necessary," Vrick said. "And it's not like you can't find mischief to keep you occupied."

"Here's to mischief," Lexa-Blue said.

"Down, girl," Keene said. "Try not to make Greff angry before you have the cargo offloaded. Or no angrier than he was last time, at least."

"I've got this. You two go suck face and make moon eyes at each other at the shuttle terminal."

"Aww, don't go getting all mushy on us," Ember said. "You'll be getting yours with Si... someone soon enough." Ember recovered from the stumble but felt the heat of Keene's glare at having almost brought up the very sore topic of Sindel and Lexa-Blue's currently off-again relationship.

Something flashed darkly in Lexa-Blue's eyes at Ember's almost mention of Sindel. It was only there for a second, but she shook her head. "Nope, I've had enough of that kack for a while. I'm flying solo this trip."

"Solo?" Keene said. "You haven't flown solo since I've known you. How many other lovers do you have here?"

Lexa-Blue screwed up her face in concentration, as if pondering a deeply complex problem. "Only four. Regulars, that is. A few more semi-regulars. And then there's the occasionals."

"I'm imagining enough to fill your own private squish house," Ember said. "Men and women all ranked, colour-coded, and cross-referenced by preferences and degrees of kink."

"Hey, there you go," Keene said. "There's your retirement plan sorted."

"Don't think I haven't considered it," Lexa-Blue said. "But it's going to have to wait. First thing after the hold is empty, I'm heading to Textual Healing. After that, a nice meal somewhere. Then I'll see what trouble I can get into."

"You know you can just get books right on Know-It-All, right?" Ember asked. "Wherever you are?"

"Oh, now you've done it," Keene muttered to Ember.

"Of course, I know that," Lexa-Blue scowled. "But sometimes I just want to be around print books. And Neiru Birgen Smythe always makes the best recommendations."

"Yes, but surely you can get those long distance as well," Ember persisted.

"Just let it go," Keene said. "It's a thing she does."

"Listen to the man," Lexa-Blue said. "And don't question my ways. I want books, I want something other than ship's stores in my belly, and I want delicious, sweaty, endorphin-soaked sex with someone I will never speak to again once we're done."

Ember raised his hands in defeat. "I yield, O Fearless Star Pilot. Have at it."

"Oh, I will. Believe me," Lexa-Blue said. "Now get going, you two. We're landing in a few. You don't want to miss your flight."

Keene's bag was already packed and waiting by the main access ramp, so once they were settled in their docking berth and final entry clearances had been provided to the local tower, he just grabbed it up as he and Ember descended to the pitted hardpack of the landing pad.

They passed under the shadow of Vrick's hull, heading to the access point for the port's internal transport system. There, they found a map of the massive port complex. As they approached, the display came to life with a holo that emerged from the wall, awaiting input as to where they were headed.

"What terminal are you leaving from?" Ember asked.

Keene consulted his booking on Know-It-All and the designation flashed in the corner of his vision. Another thought sent the designation from his node to the map's system, requesting routing. "SS-23. They've got these Gate shuttles all running through the local departures locus."

"So... Over here," Ember said, pointing to an area on the map shaded pale blue.

"You have been assigned Capsule 421-Green," the map's interface said. "Please step through to the platform."

They walked through the pad's access hatch onto a broad, flat expanse of moulded ceramic abutting the transport tracks. A small cluster of capsules, like pearls on a string, whizzed past, splitting apart at the next junction as two continued on the same path, while the other three veered away to the right.

"Capsule 421-Green arriving in thirty seconds," a vox unit above them said. "Please prepare for boarding."

The smooth dark bubble of the transport capsule appeared far down the track, travelling faster than it could have with passengers, then decelerated and slid into place. As it came to rest, the side of the sphere unfurled like the petals of a flower hungry for sunlight.

They entered the capsule, and Ember sat right away while Keene stowed his bag in the rack in front of them. The hatch closed with a whisper, and as soon as Keene sat, the capsule accelerated away from the docking berth, switching off to a track on the left, then speeding up to join a trio of capsules ahead, obviously headed to the same terminal.

They didn't speak, merely sat holding hands as the port sped by. Their route took them past some of the larger landing pads reserved for bigger ships. They passed heavy-duty haulers, at least one Galactum Security cruiser, and even one of the big cruise ships that offered long, slow trips past nebulae and other stellar phenomena many didn't have the chance to see. And then they were in the area of the port devoted to local traffic that accessed the four corners of Hub and its massive populace. Finally, the capsule slowed, coming to a halt in the shade of the cantilevered roof of Keene's departure terminal.

Along the chain of transport capsules, the hatches spiralled open in unison, their passengers debarking on the paving stone entry to the terminal. The passengers moved as a mass into the gleaming glass and alloy structure, through the wall of doors, splitting off inside to head to their various departure gates.

"Which gate is yours?" Ember asked, craning his head to see over the mass of bodies to catch a glimpse of the Departures Board beyond.

"17-Violet," Keene said, his node confirming there had been no changes to his itinerary. "Down this way."

The gate was at the far end of the terminal, away from the many domestic flights scheduled for various destinations across Hub. The crowd thinned out substantially as they walked along the concourse, finally arriving to see a group of around twenty younger people in a knot conversing excitedly outside the portal leading to the Gate shuttle.

"Okay," Ember said in a low voice. "Those kids are even more excited than you are for this conference."

"They might not even be guests," Keene said. "They're probably just students heading back to Scholus after a term break or something."

"I don't know," Ember said, his tone light and teasing. "They look awfully squinty and tech-ish to me."

"Get out of here, you," Keene said, pulling Ember close to give him a kiss. "It's almost time for my flight anyway, so they'll be calling for boarding any minute. Go have some fun."

"Are you sure?" Ember said. "I can wait. The exhibit at the Museo Galacta is open all day, so there's no rush."

"We've been cooped up on the ship for weeks together," Keene said, kissing Ember again, this time on his forehead. "Go."

"Enjoy your tech stuff. We'll see you next week." Ember headed back toward the exit, turning back just once, his smile standing out amid the sea of people.

Of course, Keene was watching him go and smiled back just as brightly.

∞

"Power it up."

"Initiating system run up. Levels nominal. Ready whenever you are."

"Open it."

"Portal protocol engaged. Slight spike on grid three but well within normal range."

"Keep an eye on it."

"Yes, sir. Portal readings at maximum. Ready to connect."

"Do it."

"We have connection. Link stabilizing. And we're in."

"Send the probe through."

"Probe active. Manoeuvring to the other side and engaging sensor net."

"What are the readings showing?"

"There is a planet on the other side. Atmospheric readings coming through now. Mix is only .0072 off standard."

"Good. There are Galactum worlds with greater differences than that. No breathing gear required."

"Noted. Standard gear only."

"What about the lyonite?"

"Preliminary scans showing substantial readings. At least triple what we've seen from the other catalogued sites."

"Good. Initiate the secondary test."

"Initiating matter cohesion probe and sending it through. Initial readings look good."

"They looked good the first dozen times we tried. Don't read into it."

"Yes, sir. Sorry, sir. Signal dropout. Just like before."

"Bring it back in."

"Retracting the sensor probe now. Cohesion readings holding. Wait. I'm getting fluctuations."

"What's happening?"

"Damn it. Ninety-three percent molecular discordance. But it was close."

"Close won't get us there. Compile the readings and send them to me. I want to review everything. What about the acquisitions team?"

"Mission successful. All materials found and brought in."

"Good. Get them ready for their next target."

"And what about the discordance issue, sir?"

"Always have a backup plan. I've sent it to you. Recalibrate the system and prepare to activate. It would seem we need assistance. And I know just where to get it."

∞

Sindel Kestra dropped into the seat of her two-person pod, exhausted from a long day of meetings with the implementation team at the Weaver's Willow Gate. Everything was on schedule, and the new Gate was fully operational and ready for public use. All of the final test flights had gone off exceptionally well, with some of the highest performance results of any particular site so far. And she had gone over everything herself to ensure nothing had been missed.

It had all gone so well that she was leaving a day ahead of schedule. She hadn't even let her second in command, Hetri, know she was coming home early.

Maybe I can have the night to myself.

One thing that had become abundantly clear to her on this trip was that the schedule was wearing on her. As much as she trusted her teams, she never let any Gate come online until she had reviewed all the final testing data and given the okay herself. And with the continuing pressure from the Pan Galactum Council to forge ahead and link all of the member worlds to the Gate network, the mountain of information she was responsible for was constantly growing.

Not to mention the toll it was taking on her personal life.

The thought of Lexa-Blue made her chest constrict. They hadn't seen each other for months. The last time they'd shared anything meaningful was when she'd taken Sindel out for dinner on the anniversary of the genetic alignment that had been the final step in her gender confirmation. But that seemed like the last truly happy moment they'd shared. Since then, it had been one missed or cancelled date after another. And the tone of sharp unhappiness that had begun to permeate their conversations had just made them both even less willing to make the effort to call.

Enough. There was nothing to be gained by going down that path. Not now. With the yawning black hole of her schedule sucking in all light from her surroundings, there didn't seem to be much she could do about it. With more force than she intended, she stabbed the commo and opened a channel to the hangar deck's controller.

"This is Pod 37 requesting departure clearance and Gate transit confirmation," she said in a clipped, efficient tone.

"Clearance granted," said the voice from the control room. "And your transit coordinates are locked in for transition back to Hub."

A glance at the pod's control interface confirmed her simple parabolic course from the bay to the Gate's glide path was set and ready for her, requiring no actual piloting on her part. *Which is a good thing, considering how bad a pilot I am.*

She touched the Limited Intelligence pilot's activator, and the metal ball of the pod lifted from the deck of the hangar bay, then flowed smoothly forward. The atmospheric field flashed as she passed through it, and then the pod was on its way.

There was nothing to do but sit back and enjoy the ride.

Despite the number of Gates she had supervised and visited, this never got old. The pod arced out from the bay in the massive Gate station's rim into glittering studded black. She felt only the slightest inertial pull as the pod shifted course to bring it into position for Gate transition.

She enjoyed this part, liked seeing it confuse and confound those with little off-planet experience.

For those on the Gate itself, the massive structure's orientation was that of a massive metal ring lying flat on a floor, its circular decks traversing the entire circumference.

But to transit the Gate required a change in that orientation. For vehicles traversing the Gate, the structure became a ring perched on one point of a long radius. Anyone readying themselves for transit of a Gate found themselves at a ninety-degree angle to the plane of the Gate itself, the vast eye of the wormhole now yawning before them.

No up, no down. The reminder of the vast, directionless void of space sent a chill down her spine.

The LI jockeyed her pod into final position, dead centre of the sheet of milky, opalescent energy that stretched across the Gate's mouth, awaiting the final signal to open the stable wormhole at its heart.

"Pod 37 in position," Sindel said, leaning forward in her seat in anticipation.

"Gate energies at maximum, destination coordinates ping back clear," the controller said. "Whenever you're ready, director."

The pod glided slowly forward, and Sindel thought of getting to sleep in her own bed again, as the universe turned white.

High above the surface of Hub, the Gate flared to life, and a tiny pod exited the wormhole on a perfectly set trajectory to the complex that housed the main research locus for the Gate project. The very same location it had set out from early that morning.

Pod 37 descended through the drifting clouds over the complex, homing in on its base. With exacting precision, it located its landing berth, sending a ping to the complex's AI that it required charging and receiving a reminder from the AI that its routine maintenance cycle was only days away. Accepting this information, the pod's LI pilot positioned the pod precisely over the landing pad and dropped to the surface. Its landing struts bent slightly, then came to rest. One final release of heat from atmospheric friction as a puff of steam, and the pod's hatch folded open.

As its engines cycled down, Pod 37 sat in silence, its hatch open.

For there was no one on board.

Chapter Two

Textual Healing stood out against the avenue full of stores. But it would have stood out pretty much anywhere.

The bookstore's facade was three storeys tall, bevelled like an inverted pyramid, each storey larger than the one below it. Along the street-facing exterior walls, holos danced across the emitter panes, projecting book covers that came to life, characters springing forth into the air above the street.

As Lexa-Blue approached, she saw the Irian Queen leap from the back of her horse into the air above the sidewalk to battle the Knave of Fire, their lances clashing in a thunderous roar.

It made her smile, seeing these characters from one of her favourite childhood stories locked in battle as they had been in her imagination. It took her back to the time of her family and their massive ship. To the time before Vrick and Keene, before life had changed so completely.

Her scar itched suddenly, and she rubbed its fine white roughness. The involuntary movement of her hand made her scowl at what it revealed, and she shoved her hand into a pocket of the long sleeveless vest she wore over her shipsuit.

That's enough of that.

She strode toward the store's door and pushed it open, inhaling the remembered scent deeply. It was a mix of old paper and history, books that had been carried and stored for years. But mixed in were the scents of baking and coffee, heady and sweet, along with spices and incense. She'd never smelled anything like it on any other world in the Pan Galactum, and it always felt like home.

Her second impression of the store was always the sound, hushed and reverent, even from the back of the store in the café, which was pretty much always at capacity day or night. She'd spent many an hour back there herself, deep in discussions of character and plot with anyone willing to talk to her.

Even though her life had taken such a drastic turn into what seemed like constant danger and action, she'd never lost her love of books. The memory of her childhood room on her clanship came to her: there were books wedged into every corner, and her family so often found her absorbed in a book, her body contorted to fit into some secluded nook.

Though the massive family-crewed trading ship with her book-filled room was gone, and her clan had been lost to pirates all those years ago, the stories remained. She didn't keep any physical books anymore. Space on the Maverick Heart was at a premium, though she knew Vrick would accommodate her in any way ey could. When she'd lost her family, she'd shed a lot, wanting to move through the universe lightly, swiftly, with as little tying her down as possible. Now, books made their way to her innernet or to an external reader when she felt the need to hold the story in her hands.

And every time she returned to Hub, she came here, to the one place new stories always waited for her.

She scanned the main floor of the store, the racks of books and sensies converging at the perspective point far at the back of the building. She'd checked Know-It-All and found he was working today. Visits without him were never the same.

Finally, she saw him towering over a customer, sweeping his hands dramatically as he described who knows what. The fiery ginger of his thick beard was shot through even more with white, and it brought her up short a moment. *Has it been that long?*

He looked up and saw her, then excused himself from the conversation and came toward her. When he reached her, his finger came up in a gesture of warning.

"No," was all he said.

"Oh, come on, Nei," she said, grinning. "You know I'm your favourite customer."

"You started a brawl," Neiru Birgen Smythe said, the words drenched in disdain. "In a bookstore."

"Once. It happened once. And it was a long time ago."

"Once isn't enough?" His scowl deepened, then suddenly broke into a grin as he opened his arms wide to embrace her.

She moved into his arms and crushed him to her, her chin only just coming to his shoulder. He released her and held her at arm's length, his hands on her shoulders.

"You look different," he said, eyeing her critically. "Less... destructive, somehow. What's going on?"

"That is a terrible thing to say to someone. I can mayhem every bit as violently as I used to, I'll have you know."

"As long as it's not here," Nei said.

She raised a hand as if taking an oath. "I swear by... whatever will make you believe me."

"I guess that will have to do," he said. "Since you're not here to start a fight, I assume you need to stock up?"

"Yes," she said, drawing out the sibilant in a purr of anticipation. "I need more to read."

"You know you don't have to come here, right?" Nei said. "You don't take anything in hard copy anymore. I can just have things uploaded directly to you. It's not like I don't have a pretty good idea of your tastes by now."

"You've never steered me wrong yet," she said. "But I like coming here. I like wandering the aisles. I like picking the books up and feeling them in my hands. And I especially like sitting with you while you talk me through the titles you've picked for me and hearing you tell me why."

"How can someone so destructive be so sweet as well?" Nei asked with a smile that lit his face.

"Lulls people into a false sense of security," she said. "Makes it so much easier to take them down."

Nei rolled his eyes. "I should have known. Well, before you decide to injure anyone, let's get you stocked up."

She saw him close his eyes, and the fluttering motion under his lids told her he was accessing the store's system, calling up the preset list he kept running for her, as he did for many of his clients. She knew he added to it whenever he saw something he thought she would like.

He opened his eyes and beckoned her toward the back of the store and one of the small private salons attached to the café, where he or the other booksellers could meet and discuss personalized recommendations. "Come on. Zali will meet us with the titles I've chosen for you. And a bottle of Tanisian port."

"Oooh," she said, "my favourite. And by favourite, I mean, anything with alcohol in it. Lead on."

∞

Where to now? Ember asked Vrick through his node. They'd been sharing the trip to the museum as they had done on many other worlds.

You choose, Vrick said. ***I'm just along for the ride.***

Ember scanned through the gallery's directory, a pane of virtual information available through his node. The names of the various exhibits scrolled by, flashes of imagery expanding in his vision as he called them up. So many things to choose from. The Planetary Gallery spanned several acres, having grown and spread over the Pan Galactum's history, to encompass as many forms of art as possible, both old and new.

Well, there's the Gallery of the Ancients, Ember said. *Or there's the new exhibit of monochrome street holography that just opened last week.*

I leave it to you, Vrick said. *You're driving.*

Let's try the holography, then, Ember said, checking the directory for the route to the exhibit.

Their path led them along an arcade of glass and wooden beams that slowly curved upward to the next floor where they could access the wing next door.

Are you sure you want to tag along with me? Surely you can access the gallery's archives and their security cameras and pretty much every record of every piece that they've ever had on display?

Vrick's tutting sound ricocheted through Ember's node, a light, feathery touch in his mind. *Of course I can. I can see the art any time I want. But I want to see it with you. Hear which pieces you love or which ones you don't get. Being here with you, I get to see the works through your eyes. I can use the medical sensors in your node to experience how your body reacts to the work, even in the ways you may not even consciously realize you're doing. But most importantly, I get to share it with my friend.*

Don't go getting all mushy on me, you rusty old ore hauler, Ember said. *We've got art to see.*

He found the correct section of the gallery, the artist's name in a swirl of silvery grey mist above the coved archway leading in. A shimmering veil of light gave way to admit him, and he stepped through into another world as the exhibit's entrance led directly into the first work.

It was twilight, with the setting sun just dropping below the buildings in the distance. Shadows stretched along the street, cast across the pedestrians frozen in time, on their various trajectories as they passed each other, each on their own private errands. There was no colour, only greys and blacks limned in white where the sharpest, brightest light hit. As the artist before him, Ember knew nothing about them other than what his eyes could see. They were mysteries, their lives untold, caught in the moment of the holo. A smile here, the crease of a frown beginning there. There were couples, groups, arranged with only body language and expression to tell the story.

Ember found himself stepping around them, navigating between the monochromatic figures as if they had physical form, even though he knew that the figures would melt into mist and reform around him if he collided with them. It didn't feel right to disturb them in their silence.

There were more tableaux further into the gallery room, the holos shifting and blending, combining dozens of locales and worlds into one winding avenue. There were scenes barren of all but one person, and scenes of throbbing, pressing crowds. There were images that shifted from black and grey to ranging tones of a single colour, as well as images in greyscale with only a single colour highlighted where it touched the myriad components of the scene.

Ember walked the exhibit for the better part of an hour.

You should take a break, Vrick said. ***Sit down for a bit.***

Are you spying on my biomonitor again? Ember asked with a smile.

Someone has to. The three of you never take care of yourselves.

All right, all right, Ember said. ***You win.***

He didn't want to admit it, but he could already feel the beginnings of prickling fire in where the experimental, one-of-a-kind prosthetics connected to his body. He knew that part of the problem was that he had them set to mimic his skin tone rather than their default black. That always aggravated the linkages.

But it was a beautiful day, and he'd wanted to wear his favourite sleeveless shirt along with the new asymmetrical skirt, and the outfit showed almost all of the black prosthetic flesh. It revealed where it twined down his arm to his two replacement fingers and the full black of the left leg.

And he'd just wanted to wander among the art, unnoticed, with no eyes wondering what had happened to him. Why he looked the way he did. Maybe it was too many years wearing identities at will, fading into the background, moving among his targets unseen. Sometimes he just wanted to go unnoticed.

He knew he could bypass the sensations if he had to, but that came with its own cost, so he saved that little trick for when he really needed it. He knew it would be better to just sit down and rest a bit, so he left the exhibit and found the nearest rest area: a long, arched passage with seats arranged down the centre. He found a space on one of the benches and sat. The neural connections between skin and tech eased right away, murmuring rather than shouting as they had threatened to. He actually sighed out loud with relief, managing to keep it quiet enough that the other patrons in the salon didn't notice.

You don't have to push yourself so hard, you know, Vrick said. *We're here for a couple of days.*

I know, Ember replied. *And I'm resting, aren't I?*

Grudgingly, I can tell. You don't have to keep it from us, you know.

I don't, Ember said. *At least, I don't mean to. It's just... there, you know? There's nothing we can do about it. And most of the time, it's manageable. Like now. This is me managing it.*

I know, Vrick said. *I could try to manipulate your pain receptors again. I think I know what went wrong last time.*

Ember smiled at Vrick's eagerness to help. Through their nodes, ey could monitor their physical well-being, and even, in emergencies, manipulate their biochemistry to a certain degree. But the persistent neuropathy his prosthetics had created required greater manipulation and monitoring than the limited interface was meant to provide. The one time Vrick had attempted it, ey had unwittingly caused a cascading set of alternative health issues that had made everything worse.

Let it be, my friend, Ember said. *I'm managing just fine. I can even keep up with Keene and Lexa-Blue when things get... like they always get.*

I know you can, Vrick said. *I just wish you didn't have to.*

What do you think of this? Ember asked, seeking to steer the subject away from his disability.

The walls of the room arched up and over his head, as if he were in a long tube. The surfaces around him were an art piece unto themselves, the walls embedded with colour. As Ember watched, the broad, bold swaths of colour softened and moved. What had been primary colours softened, shifting through different tonal values, contrasting, then complementing, then blending before changing again. What had been strokes of a physical brush became holographic, going from two dimensions to three, as if expanding back through the salon's wall itself and taking on a holo-realistic depth that made Ember feel like he was teetering on a precipice, about to literally fall into the artwork itself.

What the artist has done with holographic pigments is quite remarkable, Vrick said. *Even seeing it through your limited human visual acuity.*

Alas, these fragile little orbs are all I have to offer, Ember said good naturedly.

Hush, you, Vrick said. *It's not your fault you're just a fragile meatsack.*

Ember laughed out loud at that, earning him a disapproving glance from a dour, overly serious patron off to his left.

They watched in silence as the painting cycled through the rest of its loop and back to the beginning.

With his leg now only a murmur of numbness, Ember moved on to the next painting along the wall, catching it just as it exploded into colour, timed to coincide with the one he had just passed.

∞

Well, it's not the worst place I've ever woken up.

Sindel paced the room again, taking in the details, though she had lost count of how many times she'd done the exact same thing in the two days since she'd arrived.

The room was featureless and practically empty; no decoration on the walls, with only a small table, two chairs, and plainly dressed beds against opposite walls. A small refresher cubicle contained a tightly packed shower, toilet, and sink. Everything was cheap, sturdy ceramic composite. And all of it had been well used before her arrival.

A slot in the door had opened at what seemed to be set mealtimes, though she had no way to gauge the amount of time she'd spent here. The holo window seemed to go through a day/night cycle, but she had no idea how regular it was, or what planet's rotation it was set to emulate. It did seem to mesh with the approximate times food was provided.

The desk had an old-fashioned terminal, but it had taken her mere minutes to discover that, though it had a prodigious database of books and music, it had no connection to Know-It-All either, nor did it give any indication as to where she might be.

There was one "window" over the bed showing a vast tract of empty land, pastoral and green. She'd almost believed it was real, but she'd seen enough holos in her time to recognize the telltale signs most missed. *Almost convincing. But not to me.*

Nothing gave her any indication of where she might be. The holo might have been an actual representation of the world outside, but it seemed more likely to be a misdirection. For all she knew, the building was surrounded by factories. Or glaciers.

I could literally be anywhere.

Ordinarily, her node would have told her where she was down to the exact planetary coordinates with the local time and a smattering of planetary history thrown in. Instead, her node remained silent, the void in her mind where her access to Know-It-All usually resided nauseatingly blank. Having lived her entire life with that kind of access, being cut off ached in a deep and penetrating way, unlike any sensation she had ever experienced before.

All I have is what's in my own brain. Lucky for me I'm so goss-damned smart.

Again, she went over in her mind the sequence of events she could piece together.

Everything was clear until the moment her transport had entered the Gate. The pod programming its course, the light of the Gate's transition energy filling the transport's cabin.

But every other time she had transited a Gate, she'd felt a moment of dislocation, of being everywhere and nowhere before returning to reality in a heartbeat, and that moment never came.

Instead, it felt like the universe had torn down the middle with her at the locus of the tear, reality sundering around her. Everything was fire as her body was turned inside out, restored and dropped back into what she had hoped was the world she had known.

Light pried its way past her eyelids, burning into her skull, nauseating her. Sound, raw and formless, pounded in her ears. Every sense provided nothing but garbled gibberish. Instinctively, she'd reached for Know-It-All to get her bearings, recoiling at the emptiness where it had been.

She'd been dragged, retching. Down a hall? What little she could recall of those initial moments led her to believe that still seemed right. Dimly, she remembered a line of doors to her right. The next thing she knew she was gradually coming back to her senses, curled in a ball on the floor of this very room.

When she'd finally been able to think again, she managed to rise to a seated position, her back against a wall, and take an inventory of the space. The lights were low, and she was struck by the consideration on the part of whoever had taken the time to make this small concession to her discomfort. Whoever had lowered the lights had also left her a bottle of water and two familiar anodyne patches she had applied away, sipping the water greedily.

Her head pounded in those early hours, her quiescent node leaving her weak and unnerved. But her faculties had returned. Whatever had happened to her seemed to have no long-term effects.

And that had been that. She'd been here in this minimal room since.

So there had been nothing to do but wait. She'd set the music library for random instrumental and spent her time reading random texts from the terminal and eating when food presented itself.

Which led her to where she was now. In the exact same spot she'd been for the last three days.

The "window" showed it was morning, so she'd showered, dried, and dressed. And gone back to pacing the room, searching for any clue she might have missed.

She recognized the sound of the door, but this was not the sound of the meal slot being opened. She moved away from the door, as far as she could get, and watched, wary of what might be coming next.

The door expanded to a space wide enough to admit three people walking abreast, one just a pace in front of the others. They were all wearing blurs, every recognizable feature dissolved into swirls of faded, twisting colour. She couldn't tell anything about them other than the fact that they were bipedal and human. But she knew that formation anywhere. One slightly ahead, the other two a step behind and one on each side, covering the room She'd been to enough official government engagements to recognize that whoever was in the middle of that formation was important to whatever was going on. Whatever it was that had resulted in her arriving here with her guts turning inside out. And those two flanking? Those were bodyguards. Even hidden behind blurs, she could see they were taller, wider than the leader.

Frightened of little old me? I'm flattered.

None of the three spoke for a moment, then the middle one took another pace toward her. When they spoke, their voice was distorted by the blur, giving no indication of gender or accent. "I trust you have recovered from the unfortunate side effects of your arrival?"

Sindel eyed them warily, then nodded curtly. "I have. As much as can be expected, I suppose."

"Forgive me," the other said. "Needs must, as they say." They turned to the bodyguard on their right. "Bring her another dose of the anodyne."

The vaguely human shape turned in a swirl of hues and left them.

"Now, I'm sure you have questions."

"You think?" Sindel said with a snort. "I'd say you're smarter than you look, but it's hard to say. Maybe drop the blur so I can form an empirically solid opinion."

The shape chuckled, the sound metallic and hollow through the blur's distorter. "Perhaps not quite yet. There is more to discuss first. I need your help."

"Colour me shocked to my core," Sindel said. "It was either that or you were planning to ransom me to the highest bidder. Only I'm the wealthiest one in my family, so it would be stupid to ask for a ransom from them. And if you're trying to stall the Gates, all aspects of my work are public domain through the Gate Implementation Project, so even without me, they can go on. So, that leaves me wondering just what you need me for."

It was hard to tell, but she got the impression the shape was smiling behind its disguise.

"You were always one of the greatest minds in the Pan Galactum, Sei Kestra. You do not disappoint."

"You have no idea how happy that makes me," Sindel said, her tone biting. "But it's a little hard to take you seriously when you're hiding behind a blur."

"It's early days," the shape said. "And for all my need, I am… cautious."

"So, what now?"

"Perhaps you'll allow me to… make my pitch, as it were?"

Sindel paused a moment. *Whatever it is, I'm stuck here for the time being. May as well find out whatever I can.* "Go on."

"Perhaps you will allow me to speak to you in a language you'll understand. The language of science. Of innovation."

The shape held out its hand and the blur faded, pulling back to the wrist. Sindel observed the hand intently as it extended to her. Fingers up but tightly closed around something. Male, if the dark hairs and thick fingers with their bluntly cut nails were any indication. Smooth skin with no calluses. But then she saw what it was holding: a bit chip.

Out of sheer spite, she stayed exactly where she was, willing him to bring it to her.

"What is it?" she said.

"See for yourself," he said, refusing to be baited by her. When she still didn't move, he tossed it at her feet and gestured at the terminal behind her. "My work. And, perhaps, yours too. If you join me."

He turned abruptly and was out the door in a swim of colour, the bodyguard following. The door hissed shut behind him. She didn't have to check it to know it was locked again.

Scowling at the door, she finally bent to pick up the chip. *Whoever he is, I don't like him. And I have a feeling I may like him even less after I look at this.*

She turned to the terminal and inserted the chip in the reader, closing the book she had been reading with a wave of her hand. Data blossomed in a holo above the terminal, filling with colour and text, and it was clear immediately why her nameless captor had sought her help. It was somehow related to her own work with the Gates, as well as the theoretical and engineering work of Ophir Al Hirazi and Initra St. Cristobal who had developed the initial hardware for the first Gate.

There were holos of initial tests, discs of swirling, opalescent energy so similar to the those produced by the Gates themselves. But there was nothing to indicate the scale. They could be the size of a tabletop or the size of a planet. Whoever had compiled this presentation for her had carefully scrubbed that information.

But this was... different somehow. It was definitely based on her work, but the energy looked wrong. She doubted anyone else would have been able to tell. But it stood out to her as if in contrasting colours.

She gestured, opening up the accompanying documentation, digging further into the specifications of the hardware that had produced this particular twisted version of the Gate energy. She skimmed as much as she could as fast as she could. As it was, it was almost fifteen minutes of technical specifications before she found it in the resonator specifications.

The numbers were all wrong. The resonance frequencies that allowed the Gates to access the interspace substrate to open a bridge between one location and another were very specific. And this wasn't even close at all. She ran the calculations in her head, taking the listed frequencies and extrapolating from the data given.

When she saw it, her blood ran cold. It couldn't be. No one would dare. Not after... She ran the numbers in her head again, just to be sure. She was right. Her still unsettled stomach twisted in on itself.

No.

∞

Ohlia Joi deliberately selected a seat as far as she could from the raucous crowd of students on her flight. She tried so hard to guess which of the flights might be filled with fewer students and more fellow attendees of the Flow of Ideas conference itself, but as usual, she'd made the wrong choice, and it festered a little, deep in her chest.

At least it would be a short flight, and the thrill of what was to come overrode any lingering dissatisfaction with the other circumstances of her trip.

She pushed past the boisterous knot of students, all jocular and jostling as they found their seats and stowed luggage above their heads.

As she'd waited for the flight, her heart had sunk as she saw and heard the rumbling chatter of the large group. She'd been so displeased she'd used her Link to log in and change her seat assignment, not caring about the extra fee.

It was a standard suborbital shuttle, relatively short range. It didn't even have interdrive, not that they'd need it for this jaunt.

The frisson of excitement bubbled up again. Though the thought of the conference itself was exciting, it was this two-hour trip that really caused the butterflies in her stomach. Or rather it was the thought of those few moments in the middle.

Her first trip through a Gate. Excitement thudded through her at the mere idea of it.

As a First Level Engineer with Moebius Shipwrights, she'd followed the project from the early days, when the first information had been made public. Her specialty was testing and prototypes of hull materials and construction, so she'd needed a more than passing knowledge of interspace drive theory as a grounding for her work. She understood enough to be fascinated by the idea of stable wormholes eventually orbiting every planet in the Pan Galactum.

She'd watched in fascination as the first Gate had been ported into orbit over Hub, her heart skipping as the empty, starry dark had rippled for barely a second before the massive structure was suddenly just there, hanging over Hub as if it always had been.

Oh, how she'd wanted to travel through it, to go somewhere. Anywhere.

But, like all advances, the creation and the deployment of the Gates into a network had taken time. Even now, with manufacturing facilities working around the clock, only six had been completed and linked—a small network connecting only a handful of worlds, none of which she had reason to visit.

Until now.

She found her seat and stowed her weekender bag in the overhead bin. She'd chosen to be near the rear of the cabin in a window seat, not that she expected to see much other than the trip across the continent to the Gate's orbital position, and then the descent into Scholus. But if there was anything to see as they transited the Gate, she intended to see it.

As she settled into her seat, she decided the student group was far enough up near the front of the cabin that she could endure their presence. And there was a comfortable expanse of empty seats in the double rows that lined the outer walls of the cabin. She thought she might even get the rear of the cabin to herself.

No such luck.

A tall man was already moving toward her down the aisle towards a seat in line with hers. Not that it would be unpleasant sitting near him at all. He was definitely handsome, broad shouldered, and he moved with an ease, a comfort in his skin she both admired and envied. Just the sight of his easy stride and confidence made her feel ungainly even though she was sitting still.

The man ended up in the window seat just across the aisle from her, and he smiled as he settled in, his teeth dazzlingly white against the deep umber of his skin.

He made for a nice distraction from her nerves, but she couldn't just stare at him the whole trip, so she looked back out the window at the port beyond. *How much will these places change,* she thought. *What happens to our worlds, to our industries, to our culture when we don't have to spend weeks or months in interspace just to travel from one world to another?*

She'd already seen it at Moebius. Projects had been shelved as their viability and utility came into question. There'd been rumblings among the higher-ups already. She didn't think she'd be hit. With her specialties in metals and design for vacuum environments, she'd be in demand for whatever types of vehicle or habitat construction eventually became needed.

But none of that changed how deeply their society was changing.

"First time?" His voice was deep and resonant, everything she had thought it would be.

"I'm sorry?" she said, flustered.

His smile was understanding as he nodded toward her legs. She looked down and saw her left leg vibrating in a nervous rhythm, her hands clenched in the fabric of her trousers. She felt rosy heat flush to her cheeks.

"First time through the Gate?"

"Pretty obvious, I guess, eh?" Ohlia said, chuckling at herself.

"I remember the feeling well," he said, leaning over to offer his hand. "I'm Keene."

"Ohlia," she said. "You've done this before, I take it?"

"A couple of times," Keene said. "I know some people who work on the project."

There was something about the smile when he said that that she noticed. *There's a story there.* And she yearned to hear it.

"What's it like?" she asked.

"Honestly, there's no way to describe it," Keene said. "And I don't want to spoil it by trying. You'll know for yourself soon enough."

She smiled, liking this man and his earnest, open manner.

The pilot's voice came over the speakers, letting them know they were ready for takeoff.

They lapsed into silence as the shuttle gently lifted from the pad and arced onto its path to high orbit. Once they were in the air, they chatted easily, ignoring the noise from the fore of the cabin.

"Are you heading to the conference too?" she asked. "You don't look much like a student."

"I'll take that as a compliment," Keene said. "Yes, my student days are long gone. I've been looking forward to this conference for a while now. Arranged my work schedule just so I'd be able to attend."

"Same here," Ohlia said excitedly. "I'm dying to hear Lisner's paper on the new hyperconductors he's been experimenting on."

"Yes," Keene said, his voice just as excited as hers. "If he's worked out how to stabilize the external matrices then the practical applications in manufacturing alone would be staggering."

They launched into volley of technical jargon that kept them occupied until the pilot announced their final approach to the Gate. Even the brassy loudness of the student group lulled as the final numbers counted down.

Ohlia felt her mind blur and expand, feeling suddenly like she was filling every corner of reality itself, her vision exploding in a brightness that whited out the interior of the shuttle completely. Then, just as quickly, she felt for a second that she was nowhere at all, the stars and worlds around her having vanished.

And then, it was over.

She sucked in a sudden breath of air, her body deceiving her into thinking she hadn't inhaled in aeons.

"Wow," she said, turning to Keene. "That was..."

But his seat was empty.

She frowned, looking up and down the aisle. *How odd. He must have... gone to the restroom or something. I mean, it's not like someone can just disappear off a shuttle in flight.*

Right?

∞

White.

The universe was white.

Pervasive and pure, the light seemed to come from everywhere, singing deep into his very cells.

The light filled him. For an instant and forever.

And then it was gone, reality rushing back in and the first thing he became aware of was the ache of his hands gripping the armrest of his seat. Finally, unwillingly, he opened his eyes. There, outside the skiff's main port, was the dark of space once again, dusted with the distant stars. When he lowered his eyes, he saw the massive curve of the planet that was their destination, verdant with rich and growing nature beneath its clouds. It all seemed disappointing somehow, as the memory of that sumptuous, all-seeing light faded.

"Are you all right?" asked the man at his side.

Rogan turned to his travel companion, an elegantly dressed man in a formal suit, the jacket and straight cut skirt impeccably tailored. He was younger than Rogan, by a good quarter of a century, leaving him somewhere on the verge of his forties. Where Rogan's hair had passed from steel to snow now, the other man maintained almost all of his coppery ginger colour. Just those distinguished intrusions of grey at his temples now.

What am I doing here? Here in this vessel with a member of the Galactum Council. The Technarch of Brighter Light. Practically a king, if kings were chosen for their intelligence and not their bloodlines. The head of a city state responsible for most of the technological advances today. And now, my friend.

Daevin Adisi smiled, and his usually stoic and professional face took on a softness, a warmth that Rogan knew was reserved for only a select few.

"So there you go," Daevin said." Your first trip through a Gate. How was it?"

Rogan opened his mouth to speak, but any words he tried to compose wedged at odd angles and wouldn't come out.

Daevin merely nodded. "I get it. I have never forgotten the first time I went through. But it must be different for you. You had the drop drive in your universe for decades, even before you and your crew set out on your voyage. Surely, that's comparable somehow?"

Rogan shook his head. "Yes and no. That was more a sensation of falling, of literally descending from one place to another. This was… light. But something purer than that. I remember white. The purest white I'd ever seen. And then I… felt I was somewhere else. It was exactly the same. But completely different. Which I realize doesn't help at all."

Daevin laughed, but the sound was subtle and dignified. "Considering how badly I mangled my words when I tried to describe it, you'll hear no judgement out of me."

"Entering Scholus's outer marker," the skiff's AI pilot announced. "We will be landing in 23.47 minutes."

"Thank you again for inviting me to the conference," Rogan said. "There's still so much to learn about the Pan Galactum. About its history, its technology. This will be a good chance to see what's going on."

"You're very welcome," Daevin said. "I love this symposium. I come every year. The topics are always fascinating, and the organizers are a joy to work with. I may head one of the foremost innovators in the Galactum, but it's good to learn what people are working on. To see the ways we can work together, so our respective projects and discoveries can come together into even more ideas and projects."

"And it's good to get away," Rogan said.

Daevin returned his smile. "And it's good to get away. Not to mention see Keene. It seems to be happening ever more rarely these days. He spends more and more time out among the stars and away from me."

"And getting into more and more trouble," Rogan added, still amazed Keene, Lexa-Blue, and Ember hadn't managed to get themselves killed yet.

"There is definitely that," Daevin said.

They felt the skiff bank, with only a brief mutter from the engines and a slight lurch from the inertial compensation system, taking them lower into Scholus's atmosphere. Through the ports, they saw vacuum change to atmosphere, the skiff's fields glowing as they diverted the atmospheric friction away.

"So, how is the drop drive reverse engineering project going?" Rogan asked.

His ship and its complement had fallen through a spatial rift from an alternate timeline, where a voracious alien race called The Flense had driven humanity almost to extinction. Once Rogan and his fellow passengers from the Spearhead had been integrated into Galactum society, Daevin had approached him with a proposal. The Spearhead's drop drive was like nothing that existed in this universe, and Daevin and his people saw an opportunity to study and possibly adapt the technology.

"It's... going," Daevin said.

"That good, eh?" Rogan said. "But you have interdrive, right? And now, you have the Gates. It's not like you need it to work."

"Interdrive is still relatively slow by comparison," Daevin said. "And the Gate network takes time to implement and build. Even with the influx of construction material from Sound and Fury, the network won't be complete for years."

At the mention of Sound and Fury, Rogan couldn't help but shudder. The Maverick Heart crew had told him of their adventure in that broken system. The thought of that massive, shattered planet, with its tiny, only barely habitable partner, had chilled him. In his own universe, he had seen too many worlds like that. Too many planets broken and discarded by the Flense. And though he knew in his head that Fury had been uninhabited when disaster had struck it, all he saw were ghosts when he looked at it.

"So, your drop drive is kind of like a backup plan," Daevin was saying, not having noticed Rogan's momentary distraction. "Even if we don't replicate it exactly, it will open up all kinds of pathways that have either never been thought of here or were abandoned for whatever reason."

"Landing beacon locked," the skiff told them. "Arrival at Scholus Port in two minutes."

As the clouds parted below them, Rogan got his first glimpse of the campus below, and it made his breath catch. When he'd researched Know-It-All for more information on Scholus, it had astounded him to find out there were more than seven hundred thousand students enrolled at the moment. And that wasn't counting the instructors and myriad of support staff.

Even before the Spearhead had begun its long voyage, none of the human habitations in Rogan's universe had but a tiny fraction of that many citizens. And now, to see the sprawl of buildings and parks that made up the campus left him in a kind of semi-paralyzed awe.

Like most of the other members of the Spearhead's community, once they had been free of the ship and given land and a fresh start on Daevin's world of Orb, he had spent most of his time in their new community, working to make a new life. The nearby corporate city-state of Brighter Light had been a destination only a few times, its grandeur and size feeling too strange for them all.

And this campus, devoted just to education in any discipline from arts to sciences, wasn't even the only such world in the Pan Galactum. Still, Rogan struggled to believe in the network of worlds he and his people now called their home.

As befitted a guest of Daevin's stature, they were given a prime berth in the main port servicing the campus, and the skiff dropped into the opening of the shaded landing pad before settling with only the slightest give of the landing struts.

"Shall we?" Daevin said, standing. As he walked toward the skiff's ramp, four security drones hummed to life and surrounded him, floating just above his head. Rogan saw the flicker of a grimace on Daevin's face. He couldn't imagine having to live as the Technarch and a member of the Galactum Council, behind a barrier of protection in even the simplest activities. "Don't worry about your bag," Daevin said when he saw Rogan reaching for it. "The porter LIs will have them in the suite before we even manage to check in, I'm sure."

Despite how wrong it felt to leave it, Rogan put his bag back into the luggage rack and followed Daevin out of the skiff.

A limousine waited for them, of course—another bizarrely alien experience for Rogan, but he couldn't help but gawp at the streets of the campus outside, crowded with students and faculty as they went about their business. Even though it reminded him of the hectic streets of Brighter Light, it had a different energy, an altogether different character to the new world he saw out the windows.

The hotel was another luxury, sumptuous and obviously up to the standards of a guest of Daevin's stature. And as surely as Daevin had predicted, Rogan's bag had been delivered to the room and carefully unpacked when he opened the door from the main room of the suite.

"I'm just going to let Keene know we're here," Daevin called from his own room. "I was thinking the three of us could have dinner together. There's an excellent restaurant close by."

"That sounds fine with me," Rogan said. It would be nice to see Keene again. It had been months since Keene's schedule had brought him back to Orb, and Rogan liked the charming young adventurer. And any restaurant recommended by Daevin was bound to be well worth a visit.

As Rogan went to the closet to choose something to wear to dinner, Daevin was silent in the other room. He assumed Daevin was communing through Know-It-All with the hotel's system to connect to Keene's room. Then he heard Daevin speak aloud.

"That's strange."

And something in the way he said it made Rogan stop and turn away from what he was doing.

∞

Vrick's long range tightline array lit up with a packet of information that let em know instantaneously the source of the call, the planet of origin, and the identity of the caller on the other end. As the information flashed through es consciousness, ey experienced an instant of consternation. While it was not unusual for this particular individual to contact em, ey was never the actual target of the calls. And the target of this person's calls was supposed to be there with him.

"Technarch," Vrick said as the tightline connection blossomed. "This is a surprise."

"Hello, Vrick," Daevin said. "When are you going to call me Daevin like the others do?"

Vrick chuckled. "I'm afraid I just enjoy the sound of the word Technarch. I hope you don't mind indulging me."

"Of course not," Daevin said. "Considering how much I and my people owe you all, I can make allowances."

"To what do I owe this pleasure of your call?" Vrick said.

"I was wondering if I could speak with Keene?"

Vrick's consternation bubbled higher. "Is he not there with you?"

"He hasn't checked into the hotel here," Daevin said. "I haven't gotten his itinerary wrong, have I?"

"No," Vrick said, Keene's travel plans appearing to em in a blink. "His flight landed just under two hours ago. He didn't indicate anything to me about any plans other than going straight to the hotel. I know how excited he was to take part in this conference. And to see you, of course."

Daevin smiled at the polite fiction that even he could have distracted Keene from the slate of sessions he planned to attend. "It could be anything. His flight might have been delayed. For all we know, he may have just been distracted by someone or something shiny on his way."

To Vrick's ear, Daevin didn't sound convinced. And ey shared that sentiment.

"Anyway," Daevin said, obviously tamping down worry. "I'm sure it's nothing. I'll check with the port about his flight. I'm sorry to have bothered you."

"Not at all," Vrick said. "You know you're welcome to call any time. Even if the others aren't here. Enjoy your conference. If I hear from Keene, I'll let him know you're looking for him."

"Thanks, old friend," Daevin said. "Be well."

As the tightline disconnected, shunting a record of the call into Vrick's comm storage, ey was already opening several lines of research. A thought opened the local port's public arrival and departure information. Keene's flight had departed almost exactly as scheduled, barely a minute and half late.

Vrick dived deeper into the local emergency grids. No reports of forced landings or crashes. Relief coursed through em at that nugget of information. Ey knew Keene's transport had left the port more or less on time and had not reported any emergency conditions as it lifted for the Gate.

Ey brought up the bio-tracker system and checked for Keene's bio-signature. He was not on planet, and the historical record showed the signal following exactly the trajectory it should have, up from the port to the Gate's orbital position, before winking out at exactly the time recorded by the port for the transport's transition through.

Next, ey dug into Know-It-All for similar conditions at Scholus. Tightline relays kept the various worlds of the Pan Galactum in contact with each other constantly, allowing for virtually instantaneous communication and local news, even at the greatest distances. Keene's transport had arrived on time and without incident.

Well then, that exhausts the legitimate public channels. Time to dig deeper.

Es first stop was the entry office on Scholus. Reactivating the tightline once more, ey sent the routing code that would bypass human interaction and send em directly to the automated record system. A cursory examination of the entry records for the time and transport in question elicited a stream of invective from em in a long forgotten Cintrian dialect. With the sudden influx of visitors for the conference, the system was running only cursory checks on incoming passengers. Keene's transport had arrived without incident but showed no detailed passenger manifest of travel document check.

Another thought brought up the public interface of the Gate network, with its flood of PR hype, map of currently Gated systems, projected roll-out schedule, and the public transit request booking system. Ey bypassed it all, using es cadre of sophisticated slicing tools to dive straight through the system's defenses. Not exactly on the up and up, but ey was sure Sindel would forgive em given the circumstances.

There was next to no information available, though. Sindel had not scrimped on the security protocols of the Gate network. Despite several hours of subjective time—mere seconds in the physical world—Vrick could find only that the Gate had activated at the specified time, allowing the transport to transit. The origin and destination world of the transit were recorded, as was the fact that the transit had been successful, and that the Gate had cycled back to its default state and reset coordinates for the next transfer. If there was any further data available, it was buried so deep in the Gate's operating code that ey didn't think ey could reach it without bringing the whole network down.

So, what do we know?

Keene had left the ship with Ember and travelled to the port, saying goodbye and boarding his transport, which departed as scheduled. Every possible record confirmed that. The ship transited the Gate as it was meant to and arrived on Scholus at its scheduled time. But that's where the chain of evidence ended. Scholus was more than forty light-years from Hub. Even with Know-It-All and the tightline, only so much information was available. There was no way for em to slice into any local feeds from the university's port or any local records beyond what ey had already found out from the port's public facing system. Basic arrival and departure data was synced, but specific passenger data would only be available at the source.

Still, Keene might have made some kind of plans that delayed his arrival and check-in at the hotel. But that wasn't like him. At all. He lived for the details, both in his tech abilities and in his art. If his plans had changed, he would have let someone know. If not Vrick, then Daevin there at the hotel on Scholus. There was no way that he would have just gone off on his own without letting anyone know. Even if he was on the fly somehow, he could and *would* have let em know that something was up.

The chain of evidence and supposition left Vrick deeply concerned. And ey had done all ey could with the information ey had, and as much as ey could do alone. Ey accessed es dedicated local comm grid and opened a channel.

You two need to get back here, now.

∞

At some point, the bodyguard or henchman or whatever came back with another dose of the medication for the lingering queasiness she still felt from her journey. She was sitting when he returned, not even on a chair or the bed. Just there on the floor where she had slid down. The data from the chip still floated over the terminal, untouched. Lost in her thoughts, she dimly recalled the blurred shape holding it out to her, then just tossing it onto the bed when she refused to take it.

She now understood with cold clarity what had brought her to this bland, featureless cell. Deep in the data she had read was more than enough information to piece it together. And it chilled her to the bone, her mind reeling as she tried to figure out some way to halt it, to mitigate what would surely come if this plan ever came to fruition.

No. I can't think like that. He hasn't worked it out. Not yet anyway. And there's no way in hell I'm going to help him do it.

Feeling her energy renewed, she pulled herself up from the floor and headed to the refresher to splash her face with water. The bracing coolness woke her and pulled her back to the present, banishing the last vestiges of the malaise from her body.

So, what now? He must want this very badly to bring me here. What exactly is he willing to do to get me to help him?

As if in response to her thought, she heard the door whisk open once more, revealing the disguised triad that had visited her before. She returned to the main room and stood, facing them down.

"Here we are again," the leader said through the vocal distortion of the blur.

"Yes, we are," Sindel answered. "But not quite on the same footing as before."

It was hard to tell through the blur, but she thought she saw the leader tilt his head. She'd struck a nerve. He wasn't expecting that from her.

"It would seem not. I should have known you would figure it out from the data I provided. They say our research and documentation styles can be as identifiable as fingerprints to the right observer. Especially to a mind like yours."

"Flattery?" she said, her disdain for him plain. "Is that your angle?"

"When one has a goal in mind, one must be prepared to use whatever means one can."

"You can dispense with the disguise, Sei Ckurahris," she said. "I think we're past that now."

He hesitated for a moment, then reached for his waist where the blur's controls were. The swirl of colours folded in on itself, revealing the man responsible for her captivity. He was a shade taller than her, the lean angles of his body accented by a tailored but casual suit. But his eyes were flinty and hard, appraising her above a smile that never quite reached them. When he spoke, his voice was silky smooth, but with a faceted, gem-like hardness beneath it.

"Astel, please."

"What is it you want with me, Sei Ckurahris?" she said, ignoring his overture of familiarity.

"Oh, I think you know," he responded, his smile never flickering for even a moment.

She tried to hold back, make him explain it. Make him justify it. But her words burst forth from deep inside.

"What you're planning is obscene. It's potentially the most dangerous thing anyone could attempt."

Ckurahris shrugged. "Is it? More dangerous than to tear holes through spacetime and connect them together? Once upon a time, I'm sure those words were used to describe your life's work."

"That work was created by two of the greatest minds the Galactum has ever seen. Who happen to also be the most conscientious, responsible scientists I've ever met. I can't say the same about you. What you're attempting is thousands of times more dangerous. Trust me. I've seen it happen."

"Ah, yes," Ckurahris said. "The Spearhead Incident, I believe they call it. You were indeed there. The data you recorded was invaluable to my initial research. You call it dangerous, I call it… proof of concept. Think of it. An infinite variety of universes waiting to be discovered, to be accessed."

Something in his tone provoked a sudden insight. "You mean, to be exploited."

Another shrug.

"Semantics," he said, and his eyes flashed with a real, sudden passion. "Think of it. Resources untold. Rare elements that could elevate humanity and bring about a new age for the Pan Galactum."

"Resources that you control."

"Someone has to. Someone with vision. Someone ready and willing to do what must be done."

"You're talking about ripping through the walls of reality itself," Sindel said. "You have no idea what that could do. What might be on the other side."

"Sacrifices must be made if we are to progress."

"Sacrifices by others, you mean."

"We stand on the precipice of the most incredible advance in science ever conceived. All I need now is your help," Ckurahris said. "To make one small step sideways."

"You are…" Sindel said, stunned at the immensity of the peril that spread before her. "You have no idea what you're trying to set in motion. There is no way in all the hells I would ever help you."

Ckurahris looked at her pityingly, as if at a truculent child. "I was afraid you would say that."

He gestured at the bodyguard on his left, nothing more than a blasé flick of his fingers. The guard turned and left. Sindel watched the guard go, suddenly alert, unsure of the next move.

"You are a very intelligent person, Sei Kestra," Ckurahris said. "But so am I. And you are also predictable. Your resistance does not come as a surprise. Suffice it to say, I made arrangements."

The guard returned, half dragging someone along. Someone barely conscious by the looks of the limp, boneless way he stumbled along. His head lolled, lost in the same malaise that had afflicted her when she'd been brought here. But she recognized him instantly. The tight cropped black curls of his hair. His beautiful skin the exact shade of coffee that has been kissed just lightly with milk.

"Keene," she said.

"Indeed," Ckurahris said. "I had hoped for Sei Lexali Blu-Sahn, but this one fell into my hands instead. And I know you care for this one as well."

Sindel sent a quick thanks to the universe that Lexa-Blue was safe. But Keene was here in her place, and that wasn't all that much safer.

Ckurahris nodded to the guard holding Keene upright, again the barest of subtle, economical motions.

It all happened before her mind could register the order of events. The sharp, sickening crack of bone. Keene's scream of agony as he sagged almost to the floor. His forearm suddenly bent at a horrifying, unnatural angle.

"Now," Ckuhraris said. "I will ask you again."

Chapter Three

"Tell me again," Lexa-Blue said, pacing the common room, her body tight as a wire.

"Vrick has already gone over it," Ember said, trying for a calm tone and only just succeeding.

Lexa-Blue stopped and fixed him with a glare as cold as vacuum. When she spoke, each word was clipped and tight. "Walk me through it again."

Ember held his hands up in a gesture of defeat and remained silent.

"What we know," Vrick said, "is that Keene got on his transport, which took off and made its appointed transit at the Gate. That's the last I can find of him."

"Do we know he made it on board?" Lexa-Blue asked, her brow furrowed in concentration. "Could something have taken him off again?"

"I saw him go through the departure gate," Ember said. "I didn't wait for the transport to depart, though. So, it's possible he got off for some reason after I left the port and I wouldn't have known."

"Except for one thing," Vrick said. "His bio-signature is nowhere within range, which means nowhere within Hub's planetary system. Also, the trace records show him on the transport up until the moment it transits the Gate."

"Could someone have spoofed the signature?" Ember asked. "Taken him off the transport at the last minute and just made it look like his bio-signature was still on it?"

"It's... possible," Vrick said. "But the level of sophistication for something like that would test even my limits. When I dug into the port's security feeds, they show Keene going through the gate and onto his transport. So, not only would someone have to fake his bio-signature, but they'd also have to fake those recordings."

"Which seems unlikely," Ember said.

"And there's no record of him arriving on Scholus?" Lexa-Blue asked.

"Their system isn't nearly as sophisticated as the one here," Vrick said. "Hub is the capitol of the Galactum. Scholus is one of several university worlds. Their system shows the arrival of the transport, but their entry office doesn't track or confirm passenger manifests. It's like that on a lot of the smaller worlds. Someone gets on a ship, where are they going to go? People usually notice when passengers get tossed out of airlocks."

"And you can't register Keene's bio-signature from this distance?" Lexa-Blue asked.

"No, the range of the sensors is too limited."

"So, we go there and check for ourselves," she said. "Once we're on planet, you'll be in range and can scan properly."

"There's no need," Vrick said.

"No need?" Lexa-Blue said sharply. "Our friend is out there somewhere, and we have no idea where. He could be lost. He could be.... I'd say there's a rucking need."

"If you can stop ranting for a moment, meat," Vrick said, "I can explain. It just so happens we already have a presence on Scholus looking into things for us."

"Daevin," Ember said.

"And Rogan," Vrick added. "I've already tasked them with looking into things on their end. Daevin more than understands the urgency. He has a stake in this too. I've already sent them Keene's bio-signature data."

Lexa-Blue said nothing, still for a moment, and then lashed out at a nearby bulkhead, her punch a concentrated expression of her frustration. Ember winced in sympathy as he heard her fist connect. Luckily, the section of the common room's wall was padded. She hissed breath through her clenched teeth and shook the hand out.

"Are you done now?" Vrick asked, already aware through her bio-signature that the hand was just bruised.

"Maybe," she said, sullen. "We need to do something."

"Lexali," Vrick said, es voice soft. "Do you think I haven't already done everything I can? I've checked and re-checked. I've gone over the data, over and over. I contacted Daevin and gave him what he needed to search on his end." Ey paused before continuing. "I'm as worried as you are."

"Okay," Ember said. "Everyone just take a breath. As much as I hate it, we have to wait for whatever Daevin and Rogan find out. It's lousy, but that's the way it is."

Lexa-Blue tried to expel or at least control her frustration. She winced and shook her hand again. "Damn it, that hurt."

"You've no one to blame but yourself," Vrick teased affectionately. "I've told you before, hitting me only hurts you. You're lucky I'm so even tempered."

Lexa-Blue snorted with laughter. "You're a rucking saint."

"It's true," Vrick said. "You really don't deserve me."

"I need to hit something," Lexa-Blue said. "I'll be in the gym. Are those animates working?"

"I had them repaired after your last tantrum," Vrick told her. "But be careful of that hand."

"I'll prime the auto-doc," Ember said. "Just in case."

"I heard that," Lexa-Blue called from the corridor leading back into the ship.

∞

The limousine hummed to a stop outside Scholus's main Galactum Security station. The building's architecture was bland to the point of inoffensiveness, and Rogan couldn't see how the security force housed in it could possibly maintain order among so many students and faculty.

"Follow my lead." Daevin's tone was even and formal, seeming almost cold, but Rogan had seen him use this same tone before, on the Council floor as well as in his dealings as Technarch of Brighter Light. Having seen the younger man both chair contentious council meetings and host raucous, relaxed parties, the change in his demeanour was no surprise to Rogan.

The door of the limousine slid open, and Daevin stepped out, Rogan following. It was then that Rogan perceived the full effect of the transformation from Daevin his friend, to Daevin the formidable politician and leader.

Daevin was wearing the most formal suit he had brought with him on the trip, one he'd originally intended to wear to the opening reception. He'd ornamented it with his sash and medallion of office, identifying himself immediately as a member of the Council that guided the Pan Galactum's democracy. But it was more than that.

As Daevin stepped from the car, his entire mien changed, not stiffening exactly, just drawing himself up to his full height, reflecting the tone in his voice with his entire body, letting all and sundry know that, while he was listening, he was definitely in a position of power and someone to be reckoned with.

Rogan fell into step behind him, trying to pull on his own past experience as the head of the Spearhead's Citizen Advisory Council, reporting to the ship's last captain, Mirinda Clade.

The ache was softer now, the pain of the captain's loss merely another in a long list that had occurred over the many years of the Spearhead's journey to the new home none of them could have foreseen. It had been six of Orb's months since Mirinda had died, and the sudden knife thrust of grief to his heart brought him up short. Helpfully, his Link flashed the conversion of Orb's months to Galactum standard across his scleral displays and he blinked more vigorously than necessary to dismiss the information, still getting used to the technology. But at least the sudden awkwardness pushed away the ache of loss.

Am I ever going to get used to this place?

He hoped his distraction hadn't shown on his face as they entered the main atrium of the security depot. He took in a deep breath as discreetly as he could and focussed on the determined set of Daevin's shoulders.

He knew from the plan they had discussed that Daevin had sent his credentials ahead, requesting a meeting and assistance. And also that Daevin had contacted the depot's innernet to announce their arrival as soon as they had stepped from their car.

From somewhere off to the left, a door opened, and a woman came toward them. Rogan took her in with a steady gaze, recognizing in her a different version of the stance and attitude Daevin had adopted for himself. While Rogan didn't know how to read the rank insignia on her charcoal grey uniform, the way she carried herself made him quite certain she was in charge of this building and all who worked within it.

"Councillor Adisi," she said, extending her hand. "Security Chief Rethe Edneia. I was surprised to get your message. What can we do for you today?"

Daevin took her hand and gave it one simple shake, then released it. "I have need of your sensor arrays."

Rogan saw the chief widen her eyes in surprise. Even he knew how unusual a request this was. "That is…an *unorthodox* request, Councillor," Edneia said.

"Do I seem like the kind of person who would make such a request lightly?" Daevin asked, sharply, then visibly pulled himself together. "Apologies, Chief. Believe me, I know just how unusual this is. And I would not be asking if it wasn't important to me."

"To you," Edneia pressed, picking up on the pronoun. "Not to the Council."

"Yes. And I know I am stretching all bounds of my position to be here, but a friend is missing and may be here somewhere on Scholus."

Chief Edneia paused a moment, obviously weighing the decision. "I'll do what I can to help. This way, please."

She turned, leading them in the direction she had come from, and Rogan fell into step behind Daevin again.

"What do we know about the disappearance?" Edneia asked as she led them to a junction and then right down a subcorridor. "What makes you suspect the person is here?"

"He was due here for the same conference I'm here for," Daevin said.

Edneia nodded. "It's been a logistical nightmare here, what with the influx of people and the various private security forces some have felt compelled to bring along with them."

"I can imagine. Part of the reason I kept my own detail small."

"And for that, I am grateful, Councillor," the Chief said. "Where are they, by the way?"

"With the car," Daevin said. "I did my homework on Scholus and you before I even left Orb. Your record, and the record of this unit since you took it over have been exemplary."

"Thank you, Councillor," Edneia said. "But it isn't exactly the most challenging position I've ever held. This is a university, after all. A large one, but still a university. The most challenging thing we usually deal with is breaking up a disruptive party. I'm not sure how much good our system is going to be to you."

She led them through a set of double doors into a data centre that looked small and woefully inadequate even to Rogan's untrained eye.

Curved racks of barely two dozen consoles surrounded a main holo display where various panes of information floated at different angles. Barely half the consoles even had anyone seated at them.

Rogan saw the fleeting crush of disappointment play over Daevin's face, then disappear.

"How wide is your sensor net?" Daevin said.

"It's rudimentary," Edneia said. "This isn't Hub. There's not much crime here and policing here is pretty simple. The board made sure extensive mental health resources were built right into the university's charter. They modelled it after the Galactum's own policies, only shrunk down to smaller scale. We barely even have a traffic monitoring system. You're welcome to use what we have, but I don't know what good it will do you."

She waved a hand and a pane detached from the main display, moving to the air in front of them. Rogan felt the security depot's innernet opening a data portal to them. He felt the moment when Daevin transferred Keene's bio-signature through the portal into the security network.

For a moment, they felt the system working, but then the pane flashed red, the pattern embedded in its light broken and fragmented.

"I'm sorry, Councillor," Edneia said. "We just don't have the street level sensor coverage for a job like this. Your friend isn't in any of the areas served by our current net. And that doesn't take into account areas of the planet we can't see."

"What about your emergency medical system?" Rogan said, the idea springing from the mass of information he had taken in about this strange new universe he'd found himself in.

They looked at him for an explanation.

"Aren't all worlds in the Galactum required to maintain a satellite and sensor network to register medical emergencies? With planet-wide coverage?"

"Of course," Edneia said. "But how does that help us? That system detects extreme changes in human bio-signatures from illness or injury. It's activated by calls to the emergency system to provide further data to medical teams."

"All we have is Keene's baseline bio-signature," Daevin said.

"That may be so," Edneia said. "That still doesn't help us. If your friend was in distress, the system would have picked it up already."

"True," Rogan said. "But is there some reason we can't adjust the system to function in reverse? Recalibrate it to see the bio-signature file as the signs of someone in distress? It means taking the system offline, but from what you've told me, not much is going on."

Endeia paused, and Rogan could tell she was thinking about the possibilities. "You know, it might work."

Daevin shook his head. "I can't authorize this risk. Even for Keene. If something were to happen to someone because of the system being ret-asked…"

Rogan could see how much it agonized Daevin to say that, and Rogan's mind raced to find a solution.

"No, I think it can work," Edneia said. "We don't have to take the whole system offline at the same time."

Her eyes unfocussed and Rogan knew she was accessing her systems through Know-It-All. After a moment, she focussed again and looked at them. "We do it as a rolling sensor cascade. Rather than everything at once, we do it in sectors. First the areas outside the campus, leaving everyone within protected. Then, as we roll through the various sections on the campus, we keep the EM teams monitoring those regions on high alert while the system is tasked elsewhere."

Daevin considered it, then nodded sharply. "If you and your people are willing, and the risk is low, do it. Please."

Edneia showed Rogan to a console. "My team is at your disposal."

Suddenly on the spot, Rogan took a seat at the console and looked at a set of controls that looked like nothing he'd ever seen, just smears of light.

"You have control," Edneia said, and he felt his Link connect to the depot's system. Helpfully, Know-It-All began translating the meaningless patterns into terms he knew, overlaying them with clear terminology he understood. With a deep breath, he moved his hand forward into the pane, took hold of one particular pattern of light and set to work.

∞

"Nothing?" Lexa-Blue asked, still in her workout clothes. Ember caught a pungent whiff of her sweat and fear.

The holo of Daevin shook his head in frustration. "Once Rogan had calibrated the system, it was nothing to run Keene's bio-signature through the local innernet and check the whole planet. The sensor cascade showed no sign of him anywhere."

"Maybe Rogan made a mistake," Lexa-Blue said. Ember heard the desperation in her voice, for it mirrored his own doubts.

"We triple-checked every aspect of the process, and the local AI confirmed the data," Daevin said. "There's no doubt about it. Keene is not on Scholus."

Ember hissed sharply. "Not now, but could he have been removed as quickly as he arrived?"

"Yes, yes," said Lexa-Blue, nodding enthusiastically at Ember's idea. "Maybe as soon as he hit the ground, whoever took him hustled him back off world?"

"I'm sorry," Rogan said gently. "Once I had the calibration down, I was able to review the EM network's records back to the time Keene's transport was due to arrive. The historical records show no sign of his bio-signature at any time since then. Not even as the transport came through into Scholus orbit."

"That makes no sense at all," Vrick said. "My own records clearly show him on that transport transitioning through the Gate into Scholus local space."

"The records are fake," Lexa-Blue stated, as if merely voicing the words made them true. "He was removed from them somehow."

"We ran them through every authenticity check we could," Daevin said, Rogan nodding at his side. "And for good measure, we transmitted the entire dataset to Vrick for review."

"I see none of the usual artifacts that slicing leaves," Vrick said. "There's no data shimmer, no info ghosting, and not one of the usual indicators the data has been altered in any way. I'm not saying it's impossible, but data manipulation on that kind of scale, in that short a time, should leave some kind of trace behind."

"So, we're left with only one conclusion," Ember said. "Keene got onto his transport, went through the Gate, but wasn't on the transport when it came through the other side."

"That's inconceivable," Daevin said, shaking his head again.

"And yet, it seems to be the only conclusion available to us," Vrick said dryly.

"What about the transport itself?" Ember said, seeing Lexa-Blue pacing again, her fists tight at her side. "Can we get access to it? There might be some evidence on board of what happened. Something in the flight logs or the internal scans."

"That was the first thing I checked on this end once we knew Keene wasn't here," Daevin said. "According to the port records, the transport was groomed and back in service within the hour for its next trip. And has been in service making regular trips ever since then. Because it's a Gate shuttle, it's little more than a pressurized can with thrusters and comfortable seats. Internal sensors are minimal, as are guidance and trip logs. There is next to no usable information, and any physical evidence would be gone by now anyway."

Lexa-Blue growled in frustration and drew one of her balled fists back as if to deliver a blow. She then froze in place, the cords in her neck straining against whatever force held her still. Ember knew before Vrick spoke that ey had encased her in a tightly focussed crash field.

"Don't hit me again." Vrick's voice was tight with es own depth of emotion. "Not one person here is any less concerned or upset about this than you are. But we all need to think clearly and as calmly as we can manage. Am I clear?"

Lexa-Blue grunted and gave a short, sharp nod.

"Are you going to behave?"

Another nod. And then she relaxed, her shoulders sagging in surrender. Ember went to her and reached for her, but she shied away.

"I'm sorry I can't be of more help," Daevin said. "I'm already getting pressure from the Council to get back to my duties here. I've already missed a big part of my schedule of appointments here at this conference, and the Dean is expecting me."

"It's all right," Ember said. "Go. We've taken advantage of you enough already."

"Not at all," Daevin said. "You know I would never hesitate when it comes to helping Keene."

"I know," Ember said, as he and Daevin, Keene's lovers, shared a rare moment of understanding. Despite their love for Keene, they were still only hesitant friends with each other.

"There is one more thing I am going to do before I have to get back to the conference," Daevin said. "The head of security is going to interview a witness from the transport that remembers talking to Keene in flight. Everything points to her being the last person to see him. It's a long shot, but Rogan and I will see if she has anything useful she can tell us."

"We'll take whatever we can get. Let us know what she has to say," Ember said.

"I'm here for another few days for the rest of this conference," Daevin said. "Let me know if there's anything else you need. I can fit it in."

"We will, Daevin," Vrick said.

The holos of Daevin and Rogan disappeared as the long-range tightline connection was cut.

"So, as inconceivable as it sounds," Vrick said, "we are left with all evidence pointing to the conclusion that Keene disappeared from his transport as it transited the Gate."

"But how?" Ember asked. "There are so many failsafes built into the transition buffers, redundancy on redundancy on redundancy. There should be no way for that to happen."

"And yet it did," Lexa-Blue said, her voice only slightly calmer. "The question is, how?"

"I've studied all of the material available on the Gate network," Vrick said. "But a bent for that kind of displacement physics was not in my original matrix. I can grasp the basics, but the deep-dive stuff is beyond even me."

"But it's not like we don't know someone who does get it," Ember said. "Someone who's pretty much responsible for making sure it all works."

"My thoughts exactly," Vrick said.

"Sindel," Lexa-Blue said, as though the name was hard for her to say.

"I know things have been tense for the two of you lately…" Ember said. Lexa-Blue's snort cut his sentence off.

"But we need her," Vrick said.

Lexa-Blue's body language shifted, showing her assent, and Ember knew how much it was costing her.

"Fine," she finally said. "Make the call."

∞

It was one of those days when all Hetri li Ffiann wanted was one of those huge desks he'd seen in old holos, covered in papers and office supplies—for no other reason than to sweep one of his chair's manipulator arms dramatically across the desk's surface, sending everything crashing to the floor. He imagined it would be an immensely satisfying, if childish, gesture.

But one of the first things he had done when he had taken the job as Sindel Kestra's project manager and attaché was have the desk removed. There was no real need for it, and with most of the data related to the Gate project stored in Know-It-All and accessible through his own innernet, he couldn't understand why so many of the others maintained the vestigial furniture as part of their office layout.

He'd maintained two chairs for visitors to his office, having the most rudimentary Limited Intelligences installed in them so they would return to their places if anyone still forgot to move them out of his way when they left the room.

Other than that, he'd had more powerful holo emitters added to the space, as well as layered all of the walls with screenfilm that allowed him to put any of the surfaces to use. The space was his and his alone, and he'd made sure it reflected his own needs above all else.

But still, the thought of the big, dramatic desk sweep appealed to him on a gut-deep level. Especially on days like this.

He turned his attention back to the standard array of holo panes that floated around his chair in the centre of the room — his favourite position for the best access to whatever data he needed during his day.

The shapes of light floated around him, data funnelling and spooling through the various feeds. Today, the problem seemed to be Bernohr in the materials division. Ever since the difficulties with the supply chain out of Sound and Fury, Bernohr, who was prone to worry at the best of times, panicked at the slightest delays in delivery of any shipments of construction materials to the newer Gate locations still in the earliest stages of construction.

Despite Hetri telling him over and over that the margins built into the logistics schedules were designed specifically to accommodate and adjust without affecting the overall construction schedule, it had taken most of the morning to review the schedule in minute detail to allay Bernohr's fears. Once that had been done, there was a minor scuffle with the micro-component team responsible for fine-tuning the singularity generators before they could be used to open the nexus points.

And with Sindel on Weaver's Willow for meetings with the team there that was about to bring the Gate in that system online, Hetri had been left to cope on his own. He'd been this close to resorting to, 'Just you wait until the director gets home', but thankfully it hadn't come to that. He had his pride after all.

So, in the end, he'd merely thought the command to close his commo channels all down, leaving everyone with a busy signal for ten minutes. And his manipulators had stayed snugly folded into the arms of his power chair. No desks had been cleared or overturned in rage.

With one last deep breath, he accessed the commo net again, and it was actually quiet at the moment. Except for one call.

Hetri rolled his eyes. This was on Sindel's private channel, and he recognized the call code immediately. *Are they on-again or off-again at the moment? I can never keep track.*

With Sindel on the other side of the sector and, by extension, out of range, the system naturally rerouted the call to Hetri's message queue. He hesitated before responding to the call, hoping it wasn't just some new emotional upheaval between the two of them. He had a very strong hunch that both of them enjoyed the drama.

He flicked his attention to the corner of his vision where the commo interface blinked steadily to indicate the incoming call. An impulse along his neural interface opened the channel, and he accepted the call.

He had to admit, she was definitely striking, even without that scar bisecting her right eye and the jet-black sensor that replaced the eyeball. From all that he knew of the exploits she and her crew got up to, he knew just the type she was. And he had no trouble at all picturing her and Sindel both loving each other and being at each other's throats.

"Sei Lexa-Blue," Hetri said. "What can I do for you?"

"Sei li Ffiann," Lexa-Blue said, frowning. "I called Sindel's office code. Is she there?"

"She's offsite with the team on Weaver's Willow going over their final implementation schedule, so her calls are forwarding to me. But I expect her back tonight. Is there anything I can help with?"

Lexa-Blue hesitated, and Hetri got the feeling something deep and difficult was in that silence. "No, thank you."

"Shall I ask her to call you back when she gets in?"

"Yes, please," Lexa-Blue said. "And then you might want to duck."

Hetri grinned. *Yes, I can definitely see what Sindel sees in her.* "I'll make sure I'm out of arm's reach."

Lexa-Blue actually laughed at that. "Thank you. Please let her know… that it's important."

"I will," Hetri said, understanding that whatever it was, it actually was important. "As soon as she gets in."

Lexa-Blue nodded her thanks, and the image shrank to a point and was gone.

∞

Through a sick, throbbing haze of agony, Keene heard Sindel's voice, constricted as if her throat was closing around the words.

"Stop," she said. "Please."

Keene felt the sudden release of pressure on his broken arm and swooned from the momentary relief from the grinding agony of the fractured bones rubbing against each other.

"I'll do whatever you want. Just don't hurt him." Sindel's voice echoed as if from far away as Keene's vision greyed around the edges.

Through the haze of pain, he heard a man's voice, the sound like velvet around stone. "That's better. Remember I am a reasonable man. Give it to her."

Keene heard something hit the floor and felt Sindel scramble for it, jarring him in the process. Electric agony shot through him.

"I will be back later. Tend to him," the silky voice said, and Keene registered the hiss of the door.

Sindel's face swam into view, holding something in her hands. With effort, he focussed on it.

Field dressing and splint. Good. That will help.

"I have no idea how to use this," she said, her voice rising.

"Open. Package." The words jammed sideways in his throat. "Get my sleeve out of the way. Then just put it on... the arm."

He heard his sleeve torn open, causing a new starburst of pain from his arm, but then he sucked in a sudden hiss of breath as the cool splint pack slid across the skin of his forearm. The sensation of the splint seemed to both crawl like something alive and flow like a liquid.

He'd been on the receiving end of one before, and he knew it was pumping him full of pain meds as it reset the bone. After one last sharp wince of dulled pain, his forearm was numb.

"Who's your friend?" Keene asked, hearing his voice grow steadier. "He sounds fun."

Sindel scowled up at him. "So much fun. How's your arm?"

"I'll live. This thing is at least pumping some vague attempt at painkillers into me. Now I just need the room to stop spinning."

Sindel knelt beside her new roommate, recognizing he was in the same state she had nearly recovered from. *Doesn't take a genius to recognize that mode of travel.* She handed him the restorative the bodyguard had brought her earlier. "Here. You look like you could use this more than me."

"You're okay?"

"Well, that last shot of adrenaline seems to have burned away the last of the aftereffects. Funny how that works."

Keene took one of the patches from the pack she offered, peeled it, and then slid it under his open shirt and affixed it to his skin.

"Easy," Sindel said. "Easy. It will pass. Just try to breathe and let it take its course."

Keene winced at the sound of her voice, but seemed to calm slightly, his breathing becoming more regular.

"That's better," Sindel said, rubbing his back. "Take it easy."

His groan changed, mixing with the sound of fresh retching convulsing his torso.

"Oh, okay," Sindel said. "Not good."

She wrestled him up and managed to get him moving to the refresher and over the toilet just in time. He heaved, though nothing came up. She stayed there, holding him until she felt his body relax against her, and then she eased him into a sitting position against the wall of the shower enclosure.

"Hang on," she said, reaching toward the sink. "I'll get you some water."

She filled a cup and held it to Keene's mouth. He took a gulp but spluttered, a dribble running down his chin.

"Easy," she said. "Take it slow. It will pass. Trust me on this one. I've been there."

Slowly, his laboured breathing evened out, and he was able to open his eyes a bit, squinting at her through the visual aura she knew he must be experiencing if her own arrival was any indication.

"Thank you," he managed to say, his voice still weak. "But what the fek-knaa is going on?"

"That is a long story," she said. "Can you stand?"

His nod was weak, but he began to stand on his own, his limbs still rubbery and unstable.

"Hey, wait for me," she said. "Let me help. Just rest," Sindel said. "There's not much else to do. Trust me, you should feel better in an hour or so."

She leaned in to get a closer look at the splint on his arm. "Let me see if I can get this thing to dose you with some more painkiller for this arm."

It turned out to be a simple adjustment of the splint's controls, and she saw the creases of pain on his forehead smooth. "Better?"

"Much," he said, the ragged edge of pain and nausea fading.

"Chair or bed?"

"Bed. Just in case," he said, pointing with a feeble gesture.

She lowered him into a sitting position on the bunk opposite the one she had been sleeping in, then she helped him slide back until he was leaning against a pillow she propped against the wall behind him. His sigh of relief seemed to come all the way from his toes.

He sat a moment, just breathing, his chest expanding and contracting in a slow, even, almost meditative rhythm. Sindel pulled a chair from the table and sat, just letting his symptoms ease.

"So, how long have you been here?" Keene asked eventually.

"Three days, maybe?" Sindel said. "The fake window goes through a day/night cycle, but it could be set to any rhythm. Doesn't give any indication of where we might be."

Keened studied the window, his face screwed tight with concentration. He examined the scene the holo presented, then did a close examination of the holo frame itself. When he finished, he lay back on the bunk. "Nothing. Even if that planetscape was real, it could be anywhere."

"Yep," Sindel said.

"You checked it yourself, didn't you?" Keene said with a scowl.

"First thing I did when I stopped puking."

"So, why did you let me go through the whole thing again?"

"Would it have stopped you?"

"Not even slightly," Keene said with a wry smile. "So, what do we do to amuse ourselves until our charming host puts us to work? Want to play a game?"

"It's not like we have anything else to do at the moment."

"I spy, with my little eye, something that rhymes with dingy prison cell."

"That is not how that game is played," Sindel said, laughing.

"I make my own rules."

"Gee, I wonder where you get that from," Sindel said. Keene heard the undertone of bitterness in her voice. "I'm sorry. That was a cheap shot."

"Oh, I get it, believe me. I've known her a lot longer than you have. No one has to tell me what a complete pain in the ass she is."

"I wish I could say it was all her fault. I'm not exactly the easiest person in the world to get along with."

"Really?" Keene said, mock serious. "Hadn't noticed."

"I'd hit you, but it would make me throw up again."

"Better for both of us if you don't then."

Sindel paused, turning away from him to concentrate on the fake pastoral scene in the holo. "I do love her."

"I don't think there was ever any doubt about that," Keene said, "but it's one of those things that only gets you so far. Only means so much. Relationships are hard. No matter who's involved or what kind of relationship you're having."

"How do you, Daevin, and Ember deal with it?"

"Carefully," Keene said. "Very carefully. Like hopscotch through a minefield carefully. Daevin and I know our worlds don't intersect. And haven't for a very long time. But we get to be the best of friends, and we sleep together when we're able. And Ember and I found a way to have our lives follow along the same path. But he knows what Daevin means to me and that I'm a better person when Daevin is present in my life. Maintaining my relationship with Daevin makes me a better partner to Ember. And vice versa."

"You make it sound so simple," Sindel said.

"Hardly. But I'm not Lexa-Blue. She's always been… like some volatile compound that explodes if you shake it too hard."

Sindel snorted a laugh. "And I got caught in the blast radius."

"Something like that. But you said yourself you're not the easiest person to reach. You're one of the smartest people I've ever met. And the connections you make from the simplest of data are incredible. It's hard not to be intimidated by that. For all her bravado, Lexa-Blue is pretty uncomplicated. She likes to drink and squish and beat up bad guys. Even as much as she loves Vrick, she hates not having a set of piloting controls in her hands. She never really got over losing her family, and I sometimes think she keeps us around only as long as we don't demand too much of her."

"That sounds... remarkably accurate."

"She's always been one to handle with care," Keene said. "And in your own way, you are too. You built your company only to have it stolen away from you by those assholes who eventually tried to steal that first Gate, too. It was only then that you were able to start building yourself back up again. You've taken the Gate project in directions that Ophir and Initra couldn't have even imagined. But that fierce drive can sometimes leave people behind."

Sindel was quiet a moment. "I miss her."

"I know you do. And in her annoying, complicated way, she misses you too."

Keene thought he saw tears threatening to well in her eyes, but she turned her face away from him while leaning into him. "It's good to see you."

"Even while trapped in a random beige prison cell?"

"Yes," she said. "Even now."

"So, any idea at all where we might be?"

"Honestly, I have no clue," she answered. "One second I was piloting a pod home through the Gate at Weaver's Willow, and the next I was on the floor in this plastic jail cell bortching my guts up."

"Sounds about the same for me," Keene said, "except it was a transport, not a pod. I hit the Gate over Hub, heading for a conference on Scholus, and then was here, puking my guts out."

"Same," she said. "I'm never using that travel service again."

He chuckled, then winced as the laughter seemed to hurt. Though he was still wan, she could see some of his old self coming through as the sickness faded.

"It would seem that, somehow, someone managed to divert us as we went through the Gate," he said. "Is that even possible?"

"Well, it would seem so," Sindel said. "Since it's happened to both of us."

"But what I mean is, that should be impossible, shouldn't it?"

"Not necessarily," Sindel said, looking away from him.

"I'm sorry?" Keene said. "You never thought to mention it was possible to disappear people from the middle of a Gate transfer and drop them" — he gestured at their surroundings — "wherever?"

"It's always been theoretically possible," she said. "With all the manipulations of spacetime, there were always other hypothetical ways of using the underlying tech. We just focussed ourselves on a specific avenue of that research and implemented it."

Keene was silent a moment, absorbing the implications of what she'd said. "Okay."

"Remember what happened with the Flense," Sindel said. "I set the Gate we positioned there to slag any Flense tech that tried to come through. Anything else had safe passage.

"I set the matter discriminators to do that. Those same filters could theoretically be used to filter out matter patterns of a specific person and keep them from going through a Gate."

"Okay, setting that disturbing thought aside for a second," Keene said. "Why are we here instead of floating through space as a pack of random atoms?"

Sindel frowned in frustration. "That part, I don't know. As we were adapting the original Gate designs when I took the project over, there were all kinds of avenues of other research that had been acknowledged as possibilities but either abandoned as irrelevant to the specific work we were doing or were locked away as not worth the risk. It's always been possible to use the tech in other ways for other types of travel, but we never pursued them."

"But by the looks of things, someone else has," Keene said. "And the question is why." He held up his broken arm, the splint humming faintly. "I mean, judging from this and what I remember of that conversation, I'm here as leverage to get you to help in whatever it is."

"You win a prize," Sindel said. "He tried the carrot. And when that didn't work, you became the stick."

"Lucky me. What does he want?"

Sindel returned to the room's terminal, angling the holo so Keene could see it. Swirls of opaline light formed alongside the streams of theoretical and tested data. "Look at this. It's almost exactly the same energy pattern as the rift that opened up and brought Rogan and his people here."

"No," he said, shaking his head. "No. He can't be planning to open another tear like that. On purpose?"

"Oh, he is. And from what I can see of his theoretical modelling, he's close. Too close."

"But why would he even consider it?" Keene said. "That rift just about destroyed that whole system. And us along with it. Not to mention it almost let the Flense through en masse."

Sindel sighed, the sound coming deep from her core. "What's usually the reason for people using innovations irresponsibly? Greed. Think about it. Think about the rarest, most valuable commodities in the Galactum. The ones we need the most, the ones that we have the least of. The ones that would give us a quantum leap in progress if we just had enough of them. Think what we'd pay for those if we could find them. Only there is hardly any of them in this reality."

"But if you weren't limited to this reality," Keene said.

"Exactly. You could take as much as you want from wherever you wanted."

"That's..."

"Diabolical? Utterly irresponsible?"

"All of the above," he said, "but also kind of brilliant in an utterly amoral kind of way."

"I'd agree with you if it wasn't for the fact that those barriers are not meant to be crossed. Who knows what that could do to the fabric of our reality, let alone all the others."

"And that's how he got us here?"

"Sort of," Sindel said. "In the same way I was able to program the Gate we left there as a filter, he managed somehow to set up a way to pull us right out of the transition energies and bring us here."

"Such as the trip was."

"Yes, well those side effects are nothing compared to what's coming if he actually manages to perfect it and use it the way I think he plans to."

"If you help him perfect it, you mean."

"Yes," Sindel said, her voice flat.

"Which is where I come in. On the wrong end of that stick. What are you going to do?"

"The only thing I can do. Play along until a better option comes along."

∞

A thin film of sweat broke out on Ohlia Joi's skin. She had seen rooms like this far too many times on holos and sensies, never in person before this. But she recognized the stark table, with one seat on her side and two on the other side. And facing her was a mirror, reflecting her wide-eyed anxiety back at her. She knew she was likely being watched from the other side of that mirror and that any number of recording devices and sensors were focussed on her at that very moment.

What could they want with me? She wracked her brain for any infraction that could have sent the local security force to the door of her hotel room requesting that she come in to 'assist with their enquiries'.

What does that even mean?

She shifted in her seat uncomfortably, growing even more anxious as she waited. Wringing her hands, she kept looking over at the door to the left side of the mirror, waiting for someone to enter.

When it finally did open, Ohlia bounced in her chair with a small squeak of surprise. Feeling her face redden with embarrassment, she tried her best to cover the startled sound with a cough, and then composed herself as best she could.

Three people entered: a woman in a security uniform and two men, both reasonably well dressed. One had spiky silver-white hair, while the other's was a deep auburn. Ohlia leapt to her feet when she recognized the second man's face. She wasn't sure what the protocol was, but she made an awkward sort of half bow before her brain even registered it probably was completely inappropriate.

"Councillor Adisi," she blurted, recognizing him from the newsfeeds from Hub. And from her own interest in the work Brighter Light was known for. "It's a… I'm honoured."

She saw the corners of his mouth turn up slightly, which only made the embarrassment even worse.

"Please, Sei Joi," he said. "Have a seat."

He sat to the woman's right, while the other man sat next to him.

"Interview commences, Security Chief Rethe Edneia, voiceprint check," the woman said.

"Recording engaged," another voice, presumably an AI, said.

Interview? Security chief? What have I gotten myself into??

"Now, Sei Joi," Chief Edneia said. "Let me be clear. You're in no trouble here. We just need your help with a missing persons case that we're investigating."

"Me?" Ohlia heard the squeak in her voice again and cleared her throat, her cheeks reddening even more.

"You're not in any trouble," Councillor Adisi said. "My friend is missing, and we believe you are the last person to see him."

"Of course, I'll help however I can," she said.

"Do you recognize this man?" Chief Edneia gestured and a holo appeared over the table.

Ohlia recognized the face immediately. "Oh, yes. He was on the transport from Hub for the conference. We talked about the Gate. He's missing? I didn't see him after we came through. I wondered what happened to him, but I got distracted..."

"Please, take us through it, Sei Joi," Edneia said. "Step by step, if you don't mind."

Ohlia collected herself a moment, feeling the sudden weight of being the last person to see someone before they disappeared. "At first, I was too excited to notice much of anything. It was my first time through a Gate, and I was so absorbed in taking it all in. Even just sitting there waiting for the transport to lift off was thrilling. But I noticed him. I mean, come on. Who wouldn't?"

She nodded at the holo of Keene and blushed pink at her own words.

"Anyway. Everything was completely normal. The transport lifted off on schedule. The airspace was clear. There was nothing noteworthy about it at all until we left atmosphere, and I could see the Gate in orbit as we approached. I couldn't take my eyes off it the entire time we were flying toward it. That's when we started talking. He was very kind. We talked about it as we made the final approach. Then, once we transited the Gate, I turned to talk to him again, but he wasn't there. I figured he'd just gotten out of his seat to use the refresher or something. I could tell he wasn't as excited as I was, that he'd done it before. I didn't think anything of it.

"Then, when my Link reconnected with Know-It-All, I received the message about my hotel room and spent the rest of the descent to Scholus port trying to sort it out."

"Thank you, Sei Joi," Edneia said. "Can you remember anything unusual about the trip at all?"

"Like I said," Ohlia said, "the trip to and from the Gate was like any other flight. And the transition through the Gate was completely new to me, so I wouldn't know if anything was unusual."

"I'd like to try something, if I may," Councillor Adisi said to the security chief, then focussed on Ohlia again. "With your permission, of course."

Ohlia nodded. "I'd like to help if I can."

"I'd like you to describe the moment you transited the Gate," Adisi said.

"What you saw, what you felt, what you heard. You may not have experienced it before, but if you describe your own sensation of the experience, it might provide us with some clues."

"It was so fast," Ohlia said doubtfully.

Adisi smiled at her. "But it was the first time. You'd been waiting for it for a long time. Anticipating it. The moment had finally come. What did it feel like? To finally experience something you had been waiting for?"

His voice was so soothing, so calming. She understood his authority, why he had achieved what he had. Ohlia closed her eyes.

"It was so bright. This incredibly bright white light flashed for just a moment. It was like they always tell you in science, that white light is actually all the colours. That was what it felt like. All the colours at the same time. And that moment of light felt like forever somehow."

"What else?" Adisi's voice was calm and even, and Ohlia felt it drawing her out, gently urging her toward memory. She closed her eyes a moment and it was there, the thing she'd forgotten.

"The sound," she said, as she suddenly recalled the detail. "There was a sound. Just as the light bloomed all around me. It was like… a pop. Like a bubble bursting, and I felt it in my ears, like air pressure changing."

He didn't respond, so she opened her eyes and saw his furrowed brow, the concentration on his face directed not at her, but off into the distance somehow.

"What is it?" Ohlia asked. "Did I say something wrong?"

Councillor Adisi focussed on her and flashed the comforting smile she recognized from the newsfeeds. "Not at all. You've been very helpful. Thank you. If you'll excuse us."

He stood, and the other man and the security chief followed suit.

"I'll arrange for someone to take you back to your hotel," Chief Edneia said. "You have our gratitude."

They all strode from the room, and Ohlia was left alone again, unsure of just what she'd done.

∞

"What was that all about?" Chief Edneia said outside in the hall.

Daevin stopped and turned to face her, raising steepled fingers to his lips. "Chief, before I was named to the Council, I was heavily involved in the Gate Project. Brighter Light still is, though now more and more of the day-to-day involvement is handled by my team rather than myself. I still oversee Brighter Light's contributions as closely as my other duties allow. I've also travelled by Gate any number of times. You could say I'm very familiar with the whole process."

He turned to Rogan. "Did you catch it too?"

"I did," Rogan said. "She got the description of the light perfectly. And granted I've only travelled by Gate once or twice, but there was definitely no sound or pressure shift like she described."

"Exactly," Daevin said. "I'd have to confirm it against the records, but I don't remember hearing any evidence of that being a transition effect."

"But what does it mean?" Edneia asked.

Daevin made a low, frustrated sound in the back of his throat. "I wish I knew. But a specific, anomalous effect at the exact moment Keene disappears from a ship transitioning through a Gate may be our first clue as to what happened. We need to get this information to Lexa-Blue and Ember."

Chapter Four

Their captor returned eventually, though without their nodes, they couldn't tell how long it had been. He stood near the door, backed by the two guards in their blurs, hulking masses of colour.

"There now," he said. "How are we feeling?"

Sindel stood up like a shot, putting herself between him and Keene.

"Just stellar for someone with a broken arm who recently had his insides scrambled," Keene said. "How about we skip the fake politeness and get to it."

"What you're planning is obscene, Astel," Sindel said, her voice a roil of disgust. "You can't possibly think it will work."

Keene stood at Sindel's side on his own, still a bit shaky, feeling her arm go around his shoulder.

"You saw the data. He wants me to help him rip holes in reality," Sindel said. "Because he hasn't figured out how to make it work yet."

"But what for?" Keene asked.

"That, I don't know. But I'm pretty sure it's not out of the goodness of his heart."

"What I want is for you to help me with the greatest technical achievement in the history of the Pan Galactum."

"Spare me the hyperbole," Sindel retorted. "I build wormholes, remember?"

"Wormholes. Your wormholes are a nothing you inherited from the true innovators that did all of the real creative work. You're second-string."

"And yet here you are, breaking my friend's bones to get me to help you."

"Needs must," he said. "You may be second rate as an innovator, but your technical expertise at refining the work of your betters is exactly what I need right now."

The Infinite Heist

"Would someone," Keene said through a rush of dizziness, "please tell me what is going on here."

"What is going on here is that I am on the verge of a breakthrough that will rewrite the face of reality itself."

"So, no delusions of grandeur, then," Keene said.

"I assure you, Sei Ota Chiaro, I have no delusions. It was my work that brought the both of you here. And that was merely a taste of what is to come. My name is—"

"Oh, stop with the melodramatics, Astel," Sindel said. She turned to Keene. "His name is Astel Ckurahris. And yes, he did work for me on the Gate Project until he began using our resources for unauthorized research and experimentation. So, I fired him. And deleted all of his data from our primeframe. Stupid me, I thought that would be the end of it."

Ckurahris laughed, the sound brittle as cracking ice. "You did indeed. And I want to thank you for that. You gave me a new purpose in life. Because you see, I had already copied all of that research material elsewhere. And I have focused my energies on other ventures now."

He turned his fiercely cold gaze on Keene again. "Welcome, Sei Ota Chiaro. You are now part of something that will change the universe forever."

"You'll forgive me if I don't shake your hand," Keene said. "I'm allergic to being kidnapped."

Ckurahris let out a wintry chuckle and shrugged. "Exigent circumstances."

Keene took a good look at him. He was about half a head shorter than Keene, dressed in simple trousers and a tailored shirt, fairly nondescript if Keene was honest with himself. He could easily see Ckurahris amongst the many teams of scientists and engineers in the various divisions of the Gate project until he looked into the other man's eyes. There was something hard and calculating there. Something penetrating that made the hairs on the back of Keene's neck stand up.

"And that little trifle I used to bring you here?" A grin spread over Ckurahris's face. "It's a mere prelude to much greater things."

"How can you even consider this?" Sindel asked. "You saw the results of those experiments. You know what could happen."

"Which is exactly why the two of you are here. Don't you trust me?"

"Well, considering the kidnapping and all," Keene said, "no."

"A fair point. I took the liberty of arranging breakfast for you. Nothing fancy. I'm afraid our current circumstances don't allow for much beyond the basics."

He waved a hand, and the blurred bodyguards brought forth a trolley of food.

"I arranged for coffee and sustenance," Ckurahris said. "I hope that is acceptable. I know of Sindel's preference but was unsure of yours."

"Coffee is fine," Keene said, feeling a pang of hunger at the sight of the rations. He wanted to reach for at least two but hesitated, considering the source. *When did I eat last?*

"No need to be concerned," Ckurahris said. "I would hardly have gone to the considerable effort to bring you here just to poison you with tainted ration bars."

"Poison, no," Keene said, "but you could have added any number of other options. Psychoactives. Autonomy inhibitors. Truth drugs. Are you catching my drift here?"

"Fair enough," Ckurahris said. "Whether you choose to believe me or not, I have not altered the food or the beverage in any way. Just be aware that excessive hunger will reduce your usefulness to me and the project I am undertaking." He narrowed his eyes. "And I would not like that."

Keene looked into his eyes for a moment, seeing just how deep the emptiness there went.

"At a convenient time, once you're both rested, you will be taken to my facility where your expertise will be put to use. There is much to do."

"Astel, how did you manage this?" Sindel said. "What you're planning would take a facility comparable to several departments I have back at the Gate Project. Who's funding all of this?"

"I am," Ckurahris said.

"You stole it all, didn't you?" Sindel said, then turned her attention to Keene. "Our generous host used to think nothing of appropriating what he needed from other departments whenever it suited him."

Ckurahris shrugged again. "I did what I had to do to advance my research."

"And the projects he was researching were foolhardy at best and incredibly dangerous at worst."

"My work was visionary," Ckurahris said. "You were too preoccupied with your own goals to see it."

"*My* goals? You make it sound like it's some kind of hobby project that I ran from my bedroom."

"It might as well have been for all the vision you lacked," Ckurahris said, his voice rising. "My research held the key to far more than you and your 'Gate Project' could even conceive. As you've already seen."

"Your project built the portal that brought us here, right?" Keene interjected, trying to defuse the growing tension between the other two. "How?"

Not to be deterred, Sindel kept on. "Because he stole and perverted the research behind the Gates in ways it was never intended to be used."

"Research you didn't even have a hand in," Ckurahris said.

Sindel was so deep in her argument that she didn't notice the door to the room opening, or the two solidly built associates of their captor that entered the room and approached her. But Keene did. And he noticed the heavy pistols at their waists.

"Sindel," he said, his voice a sharp hiss. When she shifted her attention to him, he flicked his head at the new arrivals. "Maybe this isn't the time?"

He saw Sindel pull herself together with effort, though she still stared daggers at Ckurahris across the room. Even though she remained silent, Keene saw the two new arrivals split up, one taking a position at Sindel's left shoulder while the other came directly to Keene, coming to a halt a bit too close for Keene's comfort.

"Now," Ckurahris said, his tone as pleasant as if they had merely bumped into each other on the street, "perhaps you'll have something to eat, and we can discuss my... proposal like civilized humans."

Keene saw Sindel about to open her mouth to argue but managed to warn her off with another look. Satisfied for the moment that they weren't in immediate danger of being vaporized, he turned and helped himself to a ration bar and poured a cup of coffee for himself. After a moment's thought, he put his cup down and poured another for Sindel, who was alternating her scowl between Ckurahris and her new shadow. Thankfully, the furrows of her brow eased when she took the cup and thanked him. He pulled out one of the chairs at the table and sat, tearing open the ration bar. As flat and artificial as it tasted, his mouth watered with the first bite. Even the coffee, though it was reconstituted, was heaven after the last few days.

"Now, isn't this more civilized?" Ckurahris asked.

Keene felt Sindel tense beside him, but she said nothing. Though Keene was certain he could hear her chewing her ration bar more intensely.

"Well, we're here," he said to Ckurahris. "Care to tell us why?"

Ckurahris paused a moment, as if choosing his next words carefully. "Would you happen to know what the most valuable substance in the world is?"

"Tell me you did not take us hostage to take part in a pub quiz?" Sindel snapped.

"Indulge me."

"Well, it depends on the markets and what's—"

"Lyonite," Keene said.

Sindel looked at him sharply, both at being interrupted and at his answer.

"Sorry," Keene said. "When Blue and I aren't in the middle of whatever latest crisis has unfolded around us, we're traders and cargo haulers. We have to stay on top of market demands all across the Galactum to be competitive."

"A gold star for you," Ckurahris said. "It is, most definitely, lyonite. And do you know why it has become so valuable?"

"It's the perfect combination of being both incredibly rare and incredibly versatile in the ways it can be used," Keene said. "It has hundreds of practical applications where it outdoes the other options. And we've practically mined out any of the deposits we've managed to find."

Ckurahris sat back in his seat and clapped his hands together in satisfaction. "You go to the head of the class. An incredibly rare material with an extensive number of practical applications. You can see why it is so highly valued."

"Fine," Sindel said, biting off the word. "Consider me educated. What's your point?"

"My point, dear Sindel," Ckurahris's voice went cold. "Is to ask you both what would happen to the person who located a new and inexhaustible supply of the most valuable metal known to human civilization?"

"That person would be richer than anyone in the Galactum," Keene said. "But all indications are that to find any lyonite, you'd have to travel far beyond any planet human technology could even reach. And even then, there's nothing to indicate any of those planets would even have lyonite ore to mine."

"Oh, we don't have to travel nearly that far," Ckurahris said. "All it will take is a step sideways."

Keene heard Sindel gasp and turned to face her. Her eyes were wide with shock, and her face had gone pale and chalky. "Sindel, what is it?"

Her throat worked a moment, as if she was struggling to form words, but eventually, she said, "Astel, you can't."

"If you think back to how you both came to be here," Ckurahris said. "It shouldn't be much of a leap to understand what I have already accomplished."

"Are you joking?" Sindel said, her voice rising. "Ripping space apart so you can get around is foolhardy enough, not to mention dangerous."

"Do you not see the irony of that statement?" Ckurahris asked.

"That's completely different. The Gates are built with hundreds of safeguards around naturally occurring features of spacetime. They are the product of intense research and safety protocols. Ripping open portals on the scale you're talking about in whatever random location is bad enough, but you're talking about doing the same thing between dimensions. The results could be catastrophic. *Will be* catastrophic."

"Wait," Keene said, stunned. "Between dimensions?"

"Think about it," Sindel said, turning to him. "No lyonite on this planet. Step through to another dimension where there's plenty. Set aside the ethical considerations of looting other realities on a whim, which are considerable, and just consider the potentially irreparable damage that tearing through dimensional barriers might cause."

"One does what one must," Ckurahris said, his voice steely.

"Why are we here, Astel?" Sindel asked. "You seem to have your grand plan worked out. Why do you need us?"

"Because things aren't going as planned, are they?" Keene said. "There's something that's not working. You need our help."

"Help you?" Sindel was incredulous. "I would never help you with this. It's preposterous."

Ckurahris barely moved, nothing more than a flicking motion of a finger, and the man standing behind Keene moved forward with a speed surprising for someone of his bulk. In a flash, he was at Keene's side, one hand clamped like a vise on one shoulder. In the other hand, he held a heavy, vicious looking pistol. The man rested the barrel against Keene's temple, and he heard the slight whine of the gun's power coming alive. In barely a second, he felt the heated metal burning his skin, but he gritted his teeth against the sudden sear of pain.

"Stop!" Sindel cried.

Keene felt the gun barrel move away from his head, and he let out a sharp exhalation of breath.

"Are you all right?" Sindel said, reaching across to lay a hand on Keene's arm. Through the throbbing of the burned skin, he nodded.

"What do you want me to do?" Sindel asked, turning her attention back to Ckurahris.

"I need your expertise," Ckurahris said. "You used a Gate to stabilize that dimensional tear that opened out in the Brink, filtering out any technology from that alien race. What were they called again?"

"The Flense," Sindel said. "How do you know about that?"

"Don't be naïve," Ckurahris said. "I was still working for you at the time. I had access to your files."

"You had access to files related to your own projects. Those files were code locked."

Ckurahris shrugged. "Until they weren't anymore. I managed to adapt that filter algorithm for my own purposes. However, there are still issues with the interdimensional stabilization routines." Ckurahris flicked a hand and a holo pane appeared over the table. The swirl of light flared, revealing a figure in a containment suit. The suited figure stood a moment, then collapsed, almost in slow motion. As the helmet hit the floor, its faceplate shattered, and a viscous ochre substance oozed out. Within a second, the suit's seals gave way as well, sending more of the ooze out onto the floor, deflating the suit completely.

Keene's stomach lurched.

"We've made progress since then," Ckurahris said, "but there are still concerns among my team as to whether we can proceed with the plan on schedule."

"You think?" Sindel said. "Let me look at your files. I'll need to see everything you have."

"Excellent. I'll have the data unlocked for you and your" — Ckurahris turned to Keene — "assistant. In the meantime, please enjoy your breakfast while I make the final arrangements for the next phase of our work."

∞

"I have a transmission coming in on the local commo network," Vrick said "It's not from Sindel."

Lexa-Blue looked at Ember and felt a surge of hope go through her, mixed just as equally with trepidation. "Put it through, please."

The holo that formed showed the florid, enraged face of Hetri li Ffiann. "Okay, just what in the zyx is going on?"

"What's happened?" Lexa-Blue asked.

"Well, I have an empty pod sitting on the landing deck upstairs," Hetri said, biting off the words. "A pod that took off from the Weaver's Willow Gate with Sindel in it. Only Sindel wasn't in it when it landed."

"Where is she?" Lexa-Blue asked, her throat constricting.

"That's exactly what I want to know," Hetri said. "And I didn't just fall off the transport hauler yesterday. Right after you call me, practically slavering to speak to her, I find out she disappeared. From a transport pod. In transit. A pod that sat on its pad for three days before anyone figured out it shouldn't have been empty. I played a hunch and called you. And judging from the lack of surprise on your faces, you know more about this than you let on before."

Tell him, Vrick said. ***All of it.***

Lexa-Blue filled Hetri in on Keene's disappearing in almost exactly the same way, while Vrick sent all of the data they had regarding it. They watched as Hetri's eyes looked away from them to one side, skimming over the information before looking directly back into the holo.

"That is not possible," Hetri said.

"Twice," Ember said. "Impossible, and yet it's happened twice."

Get him to sequester that pod before anyone can get into it to destroy evidence, Vrick said to Lexa-Blue and Ember through their nodes. As far as Hetri knew, the humans flew an AI piloted ship rather than living with an Artificial Sentience. Ey always opted for discretion whenever possible. ***And get us access to it. Whatever you have to do.***

"Sei li Ffiann, I have a very big favour to ask of you," Lexa-Blue said. "Please quarantine that pod until we can have a look at it."

"Do I look like a null to you?" Hetri snapped, then visibly took a moment to collect himself. "Forgive me. When impossible things happen, it offends my sensibilities. I had the pod moved to a secure hangar as soon as I could. To the best of my knowledge, the interior has not been touched. With Sindel away, I'm in charge of the facility. Here are the coordinates of the hangar and visitor passes for the facility."

I have them, Vrick said. ***And a car is on the way. Five minutes.***

"We're on our way," Lexa-Blue said. "Thank you."

With a curt nod, Hetri cut the connection.

"I'm preparing a scan kit for you," Vrick said. "It's got everything I can think of that you might need to go over that pod in minute detail."

"Yeah, but who's going to use it?" Lexa-Blue said. "This is Keene's thing. He's the one who handles the gizmos. Not me."

"Me either," Ember said. "I mean, I have some basic knowledge, but this is going to require a pretty specific skillset."

"Which I happen to have," Vrick said. "Nothing personal, but I'm the brains on this one. You two get to be my hands. I wouldn't trust you with any of this if I didn't have to. But we have to. And one more thing. I need your eye."

Lexa-Blue's hand moved to her right cheek where the scar stood out against her skin. "Whoa, whoa, whoa. I'm not giving it back."

"I'm going to need to install some extra processing subroutines into it," Vrick said. "And I don't need it back to do it."

"I was joking," Lexa-Blue said.

"I know you think so," Vrick said. "If I may?"

Lexa-Blue nodded her permission, then bent in a sudden wince that made her cover her eye socket with her entire palm.

"Holy ruck," she said, rubbing her eye as the sudden lance of pain subsided. "You didn't say you needed to install it with a jakta knife."

"I'm sorry, Lexali," Vrick said, es voice contrite. "I'm worried."

"We all are, Vrick," Ember said.

"I don't like impossible things," Vrick said. "I like my laws of physics inviolable, thank you very much."

"Same. Especially when they're happening to people I love," Lexa-Blue said.

"Your car is here," Vrick said. "Go. I'll guide you with the tools once you're there."

∞

The Gate Network Implementation Project complex had slowly expanded to take up an area bounded by several city blocks, eating up more and more space as the network had grown under Sindel's guidance.

The main portal onto the grounds read their passes as the car approached, swinging the high gates open soon after. The car took them right to the main building of the complex: a massive edifice of stone and 'crete, its moss-covered facade studded with terraces of verdant foliage that twined up and along the surfaces.

As soon as they entered the building, guide strips overlaid their vision, leading them to a bank of lifts that went up to the pod hangars on the roof. Bands of light flowed up from the lift car's floor to its roof as they rose through the massive building.

When the car finally stopped, the doors opened to receive a travel concourse that curved along the edge of the building and opened onto a wide, flat staging area for the various transport pods and larger tugs used to access the Gate in orbit above their heads. Their guide strips arrowed across the deck to the set of hangars on the other side.

They crossed the roof, still feeling the day's heat radiating up from the surface below, and saw Hetri waiting for them, the deck's landing lights glinting off the metal of his power chair.

"I want to help," he said as they approached. "I have no idea what's going on, but I don't think you do either, so I figure we all need whatever help we can get."

"Lead on," Lexa-Blue said. "None of this is our specialty at all, so we'll take whatever is on offer."

Hetri led them into the hangar, where the pod sat, alone in the harsh overhead lights. "I've confirmed with the ground crew that no one has been inside. They knew Sindel was due back on that pod, and the moment they saw she wasn't on board, they sequestered it and contacted me."

"Good," Ember said. "We lost our chance at any evidence that might have been on the larger transport that Keene travelled to Scholus on. I'm not willing to let this out of my sights at all."

As Hetri approached the pod, its access hatch opened, and the interior lit up. "I've set up an innernet in our primeframe for you. Here's the access to link you and your devices to it."

The access code flashed to their nodes, and through them, back to Vrick, and they all felt the innernet open, and then code to them.

"It's only a two-person pod," Hetri said. "So, limited room. I don't mind waiting out here, but if you don't mind…"

One of his chair's manipulators extended from the back and dipped into a compartment under his right arm. It emerged with a scan module and held it out to them. Ember took it, feeling it hum to life in his hand.

Lexa-Blue and Ember ascended the ramp into the pod's interior, where Lexa-Blue set the case of scanning tools down and opened it. Ember heard a tone from Hetri's scan module and opened his hand. The module lifted into the air and took up a position near the pod's ceiling.

"Okay, let's get on with this," Lexa-Blue said, and she blinked her eye several times in rapid succession as the new scan subroutines booted up.

"You okay?" Ember asked, taking out the scanning wand Vrick had instructed him to begin with.

"Other than feeling like I have bugs crawling around the inside of my eyeball," she said. "I'm just rucking ducky."

You are such a baby, Vrick said.

*What do you know, junkpile? You don't even *have* eyeballs.*

No, but I'm smarter than you and know more about them than you do. Now be quiet and do as you're told for once in your life.

Instructions flowed to their nodes regarding the various scanning tools and procedures Vrick needed them to complete. While it was incomprehensible to them in the moment, they felt the viscous, silken flow of data from the pod's interior to their devices and through them all to both Vrick and their specially partitioned innernet.

They kept at it diligently for the better part of three hours, scanning and rescanning every possible corner of the pod, sucking up anything and everything they could glean about the tiny empty vehicle.

∞

"Run it again," Lexa-Blue said, and Ember saw the tension in her as she rubbed the back of her neck.

"We've run the data three times already," Hetri responded. "What makes you think that anything else is going to come up that we haven't seen already?"

"I don't know," Lexa-Blue said through gritted teeth. "But my best friend has gone up in smoke. My best friend *and* my… And I am not stopping until we find them. Are we clear?"

"If he'd gone up in smoke, at least there'd be a trace of it," Hetri muttered.

"Is that supposed to be funny?"

"It's better than crying, which is what I feel like doing," Hetri said.

"Let's all just take a breath," Ember said. "We're all exhausted, and it's the middle of the night. Have a drink, have a coffee, have something to eat. Go for a jog around the floor. Just step back and take a break."

Lexa-Blue muttered an inarticulate sound of frustration and strode to the cart of food and drink Hetri had brought in after the second time they had reviewed the sensor data they had collected from Sindel's pod. Ember saw her rummage through the collection, roughly pushing the bottles and food packs aside. He knew exactly what she was looking for.

"There's nothing here," she complained.

"What do you mean?" Hetri said. "I had the commissary send up a full selection."

"She means there's no alcohol," Ember said. "For some strange reason no one can figure out, she thinks better when she's had a few."

"That makes no sense at all," Hetri said, and Ember saw his eyes flicker in a pattern of motion that made him believe their host was accessing the commissary. "But who am I to argue with the thought processes of a lunatic."

"I am still in the room, you know," Lexa-Blue said, but Ember could tell that the ribbing had helped at least partially crack the wall of her frustration.

"I've ordered a selection for you," Hetri said. "Along with sober up meds. Just in case."

"Good call," Ember said.

"Sindel tells me things," Hetri said, then paused. "Sorry. I shouldn't have said that."

"It's okay," Lexa-Blue said with a sigh. "It's… complicated."

"Trust me," Hetri said. "I've worked with Sindel long enough to know she's not an easy woman to deal with sometimes. And though I haven't known you long, you make a pretty strong impression. Also, I have plenty of experience dealing with volatile substances."

"It doesn't take much imagination to picture the fireworks," Ember said. "Seriously, they need warning signs."

He ducked when Lexa-Blue swung her arm to cuff him in the shoulder.

A melodious chord announced the arrival of Hetri's new delivery, and the door to his office slid open, admitting a squat, boxy, LI-driven delivery cart. Neatly arranged on the top tray was an impressive selection of bottles in different shapes and sizes.

"Now, this is what I'm talking about," Lexa-Blue said, opting for a tall sinuous bottle whose contents were fluorescent pink. She poured a generous glass and downed it.

"What is that?" Hetri asked, his nose wrinkled in disgust.

"Not a clue." She poured another and offered it to Ember.

"Oh, sure," he said, accepting the glass. "What the hells."

"You are a braver being than I am," Hetri said.

"Oh, come on," Ember said. "All your friends are doing it."

"You two are very bad influences," Hetri said. "Oh, all right. Hit me."

His right manipulator extended from his chair to take the glass, then contracted back to hold the glass to his lips. He sipped delicately and made a face. "Well, that is… unique."

"It tastes pink," Ember said.

"The taste actually glows in the dark," Hetri said, holding the glass as far away as he could, as if it might be radioactive.

"It burns," Lexa-Blue said with a grin. "It burns real good." She put her empty glass down and smacked her hands together. "All right. Let's get back at it. What are we missing? There must be something we haven't thought of. If there's no evidence in the pod, could there be evidence in the Gate itself?"

"See?" Ember said to Hetri. "It's the oddest thing. Never before have I seen anyone get smarter after drinking."

Hetri took a cautious sip of the pink concoction and winced, moving to put the half-full glass on the table he'd had brought in for them. His manipulator froze in mid reach. "What did you just say?"

Ember and Lexa-Blue froze, looking at him curiously.

"I've never seen anyone get smarter from drinking?"

"Not you," Hetri said. "You."

"Evidence in the Gate itself?" Lexa-Blue said, confused by Hetri's surge of excitement.

"Yes!" Hetri shouted. "That's it."

A flurry of information panes erupted around Hetri, then flew outward, passing through Ember and Lexa-Blue to rest in the screens embedded in the walls. Data scrolled through the wall screens, numbers, text, and image swirling in patterns too complex for them to even follow.

Are you getting this? Lexa-Blue said to Vrick through her node.

Every last luscious top secret bit of it, Vrick said.

"What are we looking at?" Lexa-Blue asked.

"This is the deepcore data from the Gates themselves," Hetri said, distracted by the heavy flow of information. "If my hunch is right, what we're looking for will be in the matter discriminator sub matrices."

"In Standard for the non-genius, non-drunk folks in the room?" Ember asked.

"Every Gate has a set of matter discriminators built in," Hetri said. "When we send a ship through, they track what's going through in terms of what is organic and what isn't. There are slight differences in terms of how the Gate's singularity affects organic or inorganic matter. The discriminators track that and ensure the artificial transit effect applies properly to everything that goes through."

"Which means?" Ember asked.

"That there might be some evidence in the discriminator logs that can help us," Hetri said.

The information flashed across the office's walls in a furious, clashing glare of colours, until finally Hetri cried out in triumph.

"There!"

The displays froze, the sudden cessation of motion dizzying in itself. On the wall screen before them, two specific columns of information pulled forward while the rest receded. In each of the columns, one specific line of data glowed red, pulsing steadily.

"That's it," Hetri said. "Both your friend and Sindel went into the Gate with their ships but didn't come out the other side. Somehow, the destination coordinates for them were changed. The ships they were on came through exactly as they were supposed to. But the Gate sent them somewhere else."

"Somewhere else?" Lexa-Blue said, the two words clipped and sharp. "Are you telling me it's possible for people going through a Gate to be rerouted?"

"Theoretically," Hetri said. "The possibility was always there, but it wasn't something we wanted to advertise. And the Gate's original designers and builders added so many fail-safe subsystems that it can't happen."

"And yet it did," Ember said.

"Yes, well, I think we've already established that whatever happened isn't possible," Hetri said. "But here we are."

"So, somehow," Lexa-Blue said, "the Gate just sent them somewhere?"

"Trust me," Hetri said, "I'm no happier about it than you are."

"And where did they end up?" Ember asked.

"That's one question," Hetri said, "but there's another one. If I'm reading this right, this isn't some random glitch. There's design here. Two people who know each other were taken from separate points of origin and put somewhere else. But I don't know where because whatever took them was designed to cover its tracks. This was no accident."

"Someone took control of the Gate's system, overrode every safety protocol you have in place, and took our friends," Lexa-Blue said, cold fury in her voice. "And that is a big mistake."

"But I have no idea how to track them or where to even start looking," Hetri said.

I think I can help with that, Vrick said. ***I think it's time for an introduction.***

∞

"You're…. I mean…." Hetri said. "I've never met… I thought you were all…"

"Breathe," Vrick said, having been patched directly into the room's communications array. "I'm just another type of being. Just like you."

Except with way more attitude, Lexa-Blue sent privately through her node.

I can't help my natural superiority, Vrick said with tart good humour.

"This is… a lot to take in," Hetri said. "I mean, does anyone even know you exist?"

"More than a few," Vrick said. "Probably more than I'd like, but it's hard to avoid considering the circumstances we usually keep finding ourselves in. These ones need my help more than they'd like to admit."

"We would be lost without you, Vrick," Ember said. "And we all know it."

"Speak for yourself, squib," Lexa-Blue said. "I do just fine without em."

"Should you really talk to him…them… like that," Hetri said, his voice quiet and constricted as if he was trying to keep Vrick from hearing.

"My pronouns are ey, em, and es," Vrick said, and only Lexa-Blue and Ember could hear the ripple of quiet good humour in the words. "Just like any of the AIs you deal with."

"Of course," Hetri said. "Thank you."

"Now, if you don't mind," Vrick said. "Is there a way for me to get access to this data straight from the source? It will be a lot easier for me to run some analytics and data mapping if I can connect right into the systems themselves."

"That's a complicated request," Hetri said. "We're talking about the systems that pretty much run the routing of the entire Gate network. This project is the biggest undertaken, and there are hundreds of companies and as many, if not more, worlds involved in running it. And every single one of them has a tremendous amount at stake. You're asking me to hand over access to enough sensitive information to pretty much crash the Galactum."

Give me strength with this one, Vrick said, then continued out loud. "Forgive me for being blunt, Sei li Ffiann, but if I put my mind to it, I could slice my way into your systems and copy everything I find for myself. But that would take time. My crew and I are directly responsible for keeping this project out of the hands of a corp that wanted control of the tech in their own greedy little hands. I happen to be responsible for nudging your direct employer, Sindel Kestra, in the direction of this project and the job she has demonstrated time and again to be so good at. She has probably shared more about this project in discussions with me than she ever has with you.

"And in the time it took me to speak those sentences, I have designed and written the code for enough subroutines to examine, cross reference and analyze every scrap of data I am asking you for access to. Every moment you spend twiddling your thumbs means my friends may be in danger. I would advise you not to impede my investigation into this any further. Do we understand each other?"

The Infinite Heist

Hetri sat, eyes wide and face pale, silent in the face of Vrick's speech.

I think you broke him, Lexa-Blue said.

If it gets us what we need, I'm fine with it.

"I know we're asking a lot," Ember said, his tone even and calming, "but we can be trusted. And with Keene and Sindel missing, this is urgent. If Vrick says ey has the ability to go through this data and get us some leads, I believe em. This is exactly the kind of mess we usually find ourselves in, and we have the experience needed to see it through. But we need a place to start."

Hetri weighed the decision, and to Vrick's heightened time sense, it felt far too long. Finally, he nodded. "All right. The board will have my head if they ever find out about this."

"Relax," Lexa-Blue said. "We'll keep your name out of it."

"My name will be all over it," Hetri said. "With Sindel gone, any kind of access authorization falls to me. You'd better not mess this up."

"Us?" Lexa-Blue said. "Not a chance. This is my best friend and my… And Sindel. I will not stop until I find them, and I will tear through anyone that gets in my way."

"As will I," Ember said.

"Are we clear?" Vrick asked. "Good. I'm sending you the encrypted commo tunnel coordinates now."

Vrick watched the glacial human slowness of Sei li Ffiann as he made the connections that would allow em access to the deep layers of Gate data that ey needed, then performed the multiple verification protocols that allowed the human to be comfortable with the level of access he was providing.

Meats are so slow.

When the encrypted tunnel signalled the incoming access, Vrick had a sudden sensation that beyond that door ey was about to open was a collection of data unlike anything ey had experienced, like a torrent held back by one tiny dam. For an instant, about as long as that of a cell dividing, ey hesitated, uncertain of what ey would even do with that much information, how to parse any of it. Even wondered if any of it would be of use in finding Keene and Sindel.

But this was their only lead, the one scrap of hope in locating their friends.

Ey accepted the connection.

And in that nanosecond, ey realized even es wildest imaginings could not have pictured the astonishing amount of data stored in the Gate Network's regulatory systems. But rather than a dam, it was more like an ocean, its surface still as glass as far as ey could sense. As ey perceived it, ey saw the surface flash with light, spheres of data bursting to life and then connecting into a lattice of interconnected information.

It was more raw data than ey could have conceived, despite es astonishing data handling capacities.

Is this what humans feel like around me?

Ey reached out and touched the sea of information and was suddenly slammed with what felt like a billion, billion voices announcing their presence at once. Ey was rocked back by the sensation and had to take almost two full seconds to steady emself and prepare for whatever path this data might lead em on.

Gearing emself up, ey reached out to the data once more, holding firm against the sheer dizzying volume of it. This time, the vertiginous feeling of standing on the edge of infinity clearly decreased. And in the massive ocean of information, ey could see that what initially had looked like one cohesive mass was also thousands of thousands of subsets, each with its own colour, flavour, appearance, texture, and sound. And in among those physical analogue sensations were a dozen more, undefinable in any physical world way.

Ey realized ey could see the mass of data as either a whole or as an interconnected set of smaller datasets just by choosing es point of view. Taking es time, ey allowed emself several more seconds to grow accustomed to the size, shape, and file structure of the infomass before em.

Then, decisively, ey selected one of the smaller of the inlets of pulsing, quiescent data, testing es access. The information subset blossomed out towards em in all directions, filling the universe of Vrick's mind.

Ey recognized it as the site log of the Gate Network itself, all of the fully functional locations currently operating. Ey "turned" the information slightly and the dataset expanded outward to locations under construction, and further to the next planned locations where construction had not yet begun. Then, deeper examination showed how this one particular set connected to all of the others in the dense web needed for the network to function.

Taking time to acclimatize emself, ey examined the other datasets making up the gestalt: nexus point coordinates and mapping, interspace cross-referencing, quantum tunnel generational matrices, and the swollen, prodigious knot of the processing system needed just to simply open the bridge between one Gate and another.

Feeling as comfortable as ey could in the face of so much information, ey narrowed focus, selecting two specific Gate locations, Hub and Weaver's Willow, where, respectively, Keene and Sindel had disappeared. Then ey added the prospective destinations to those two individual subsets: Keene to Scholus and Sindel back to Hub.

The remaining information faded back as the selected information came forward in es mind, while a second set of instructions from em called forth all the interstices of data connecting those locations, on those dates, at those specific times that the Gates somehow allowed Keene and Sindel to be taken.

There. Captured by the web of information stored in the immense, heavily redundant data cores buried under the Gate Network complex, were the exact instants that those two Gates had called on their power generators with their interlinked AI cores and spun up to delicately bring the two sets of spacetime coordinates into contact with each other and open the Gate.

And from those two specific moments, Vrick saw a tangled forest of data that spread before em through the whole collective ocean, still the equivalent of an entire solar system.

This could take a while.

∞

"By the stars and moons, I have such a… what do you meats call it? A headache, that's it."

Ember and Lexa-Blue were back in the Maverick Heart's lounge, having left Hetri li Ffiann's office while Vrick began es work on reviewing the data now available to them

"You don't even have a head," Ember said to Vrick.

"Not the time, squib," Lexa-Blue snapped. "What did you find out?"

"Look," Ember shot back before Vrick could respond. "You're upset. So am I. So is Vrick. We all have something big at stake here. Save it for whoever is responsible for this. Don't take it out on me."

Lexa-Blue balled her hands into fists. "Why, you…"

Before she could finish, a shrill klaxon blared from the walls around them, shutting them both up.

"Enough," Vrick shouted, pitching es voice exactly at the right tone to make them both wince in pain without causing any permanent hearing loss. "Stop it, both of you, or I swear on my processor I will space you both and go looking for Keene by myself."

Both Ember and Lexa-Blue were silent a moment, before she spoke again, her tone subdued. "Oh, sure. But who's going to get shot at for you?"

"I could send a couple of those animates you're so fond of beating up in the gym," Vrick said. "Or maybe the bots that clean up after you. They're certainly more well behaved than either of you."

"Okay, okay. Message received. I'm sorry," Ember said, then looked at Lexa-Blue for her agreement. "We're sorry."

"All right, I'll behave," she said, her hands up in surrender.

"I've heard that before," Vrick said. "Tread carefully."

"What have you found out?" Ember asked.

"Well, I had to dig deep into the transit records," Vrick said. "And there are a lot of them. I started by confirming what we already knew. The bio records confirm Keene was on the transport when it entered the Gate but gone when it came out at Scholus. Same with Sindel. The discriminators that read the bio signatures of the passengers of any ship that transits a Gate show without a doubt that both of them were somehow taken in that moment of transition."

"Which, we know, should be impossible," Ember said.

"Well, yes and no," Vrick said. "You probably don't remember what happened at the Rift, as you were incapacitated at the time."

"That's one way to put it," Ember said. He'd been grievously wounded during the last part of their raid on the Flense ship, barely held together by his armour's emergency systems. Only a radically experimental prosthetics technology had been able to replace the swaths of ruined flesh on his leg, side, and hand. He rubbed his thigh reflexively. "But Keene filled me in after I'd healed."

"Indeed," Vrick said. "The same systems Sindel used to block the Flense from coming through don't have to be used only to reduce an unwanted guest into vapour. If you can set it to filter them to nothing, you can filter them for some other reason and do something else with them."

"I do not like where this is going," Lexa-Blue said.

"Me neither," Ember agreed.

"On a purely intellectual level," Vrick said, "it's fascinating. From what I've gathered from my deep-dive into their system, one could fine tune a particular Gate's coordinate targeting system to send a ship to one place and its occupants to another."

"Fascinating unless the occupant being sent is one of your friends," Lexa-Blue said.

"And they're sent there without their consent," Ember said. "Were you able to figure out where they were sent?"

"That's the hard part," Vrick said. "There are, if you'll pardon the expression, an astronomical number of possibilities."

"Why so many?" Lexa-Blue asked. "There are only…what? Twenty-three Gates operational?"

"True, but that isn't the whole picture," Vrick said. "A Gate isn't restricted to just connecting to another Gate. They can actually transit a complete Gate to a location on its own. And could, if they wanted to, send someone anywhere. It's not practical, because you still have to get back from wherever they send you."

"So, Keene and Sindel could be on any planet in the Galactum," Lexa-Blue said.

"Even worse," Ember said.

"Exactly," Vrick said. "The Gate database has the entire Galactum map in it."

"Right, so all the planets," Lexa-Blue said.

"No," Vrick said gravely. "Everything. Planets, moons, and everything in between. With the active positioning system, whoever has done this could conceivably calculate a set of coordinates so exact they could have dropped them literally anywhere in the Galactum, on planet or off."

"So, whoever did this could have dropped them off in hard vacuum?"

"I doubt it," Ember said. "Something like this would take an amazing amount of effort and energy. If they wanted Keene and Sindel dead, why go to all that effort? Just shoot them or poison them or any of the dozens of easier methods."

"I have to agree," Vrick said. "It seems like a ridiculous amount of difficulty for a simple revenge plot."

"Whoever it is," Ember said, "wanted to take them somewhere. For some specific reason."

"Somewhere they could control," Vrick said.

"That is some completely rucked up shit," Lexa-Blue said.

"It's pretty next level," Ember said. "Whoever this is has some big plans."

"And even more frightening," Vrick said, "seems to have the potential to pull them off."

"One problem at a time," Ember said.

"Agreed," Lexa-Blue said. "We can burn that supernova when we come to it."

"Let's try and avoid blowing up any star systems, all right?" Vrick said.

"Okay, just this once," Lexa-Blue said. "So where do we start?"

"I think I have at least a basic handle on the resources at hand and what I can do with them," Vrick said. "I've called Sei li Ffiann and have the time booked on their systems to run some datasets. You both might want to sit down for this."

Ember and Lexa-Blue took seats, looking forward to the main port, which faded from the view of the surrounding landing area into a swath of black punctuated by stars. As they watched, the star pattern coalesced, resolving into the familiar boundaries of the Pan Galactum itself.

"Now, we're here," Vrick said, and one of the stars glowed brighter, Hub's name appearing beside it. "Where Keene disappeared."

Another star brightened and labelled itself. "And this is Weaver's Willow, where Sindel disappeared."

"That is a long way off," Lexa-Blue said. "Still hard to get my brain around her just popping three sectors away for a meeting."

"Brave new world," Ember said.

"Many of them," Vrick said. "All right. A lot of this is guesswork, but from our conversation, I think it's as sound as we can make it."

A spray of bright blue circles appeared in the display.

"These are the worlds with existing Gates, the ones already completed. And these…"

Another set of locations highlighted itself, this time in two shades of bright green.

"…are the projected locations for the next phase of the rollout."

"So, unless our initial assumption is off…" Ember said.

"Which it very well could be," Lexa-Blue said.

"Which it very well could be," Ember said. "We can take the existing Gates off the list, because if our nemesis sent Keene and Sindel there, then they'd come out the other side into vacuum and die."

"Somewhat counterproductive," Vrick said dryly. The locations of the Gates faded to grey in the display.

"Great," Lexa-Blue said. "That just leaves us with 99.999 percent of the Galactum to search."

"We're not done yet," Vrick said. "One of the little nuggets of information Sei li Ffiann opened up for us is the routing commands and the biosignature records used for those two specific transits."

The Infinite Heist

In the display, the glowing star that indicated Hub expanded into a new pop out pane, showing the planet. A time stamp formed, showing the exact temporal coordinates of Keene's aborted trip to Scholus, which expanded out of the display as well. "As you can see, the Gate coordinates functioned exactly as programmed, linking Hub's Gate with the one at Scholus."

Weaver's Willow came forward as well, showing the same information for Sindel's trip back to Hub.

"No surprises. The information in the system shows the transits completed successfully," Vrick said. "But this is where it gets interesting."

A new pane of information opened up, with two columns of glowing pink characters in flowing lines.

"This is the biosignature data," Vrick said. "This column is Keene's transport when it took off from Hub."

The column on the left brightened, showing a set list of about twenty individual entries. "Each of those specific strings of coded letters and numbers corresponds to a passenger or crew member."

The much shorter list on the right brightened, showing only one item. "And that is the entry for Sindel's pod. Now watch what happens when we cross reference them with the transit log."

A time stamp and departure data appeared beside each of the columns and proceeded to count down to the moment of transition through the Gates. As the time stamp clicked to zero, one line of letters and numbers in the list on the left disappeared. And the pane on the right was now empty.

"Which proves how it was done," Ember said, "but not why or where they were taken."

"Correct," Vrick said.

"How is it that their system didn't raise seven kinds of hell when two of their passengers disappeared off ships going through Gates?" Lexa-Blue said, incredulous. "You would think some part of that gigantic pack of AI brains that run those things would have noticed, even if a human didn't."

"You overestimate their capabilities, as usual," Vrick said. "Those AI cores were grown for one thing and one thing only, which is the immense number of calculations required to make a single jump, let alone all jumps. From what I can see, the designers put in failsafe codes to prevent this from happening. The system is set up to not allow it to happen. And the AIs were made to not recognize this thing that should have been impossible if it actually happened."

"So, how did it happen?" Ember said.

"Now that I'm in their system, I can dig deeper into their records to see their changelogs. They've been cleaned, but not well enough to hide that someone injected a codeworm that enabled them to bypass the safeguards and allow them to use those bio-signature discriminators to pluck Keene and Sindel out of their ships and reroute them."

"Now I have a headache," Lexa-Blue said.

"Okay, back to my point," Ember said. "We have proof it happened, but we still don't know where they were sent."

"Have a little faith, junior meat," Vrick said. "If I take those bio-signature tags and translate them into the Gate's own language…"

The display blurred again, the transit information for those two trips replaced by single lines of code that represented Keene and Sindel at the moment they passed through their respective Gates.

"… and I bypass the blocks on transit routing code subroutines, I should be able to reference the energy signature even though our slicer has redacted the coding in the logs."

In the display, panes of information flashed into existence and then disappeared, colours blurring and blending at a dizzying pace as Vrick's own algorithms sifted through the incalculable amounts of Gate data. In the map of the Galactum that formed the backdrop for the data, lines and arcs formed between worlds and disappeared just as fast, illuminating an infinite number of possible courses and destinations.

Minutes passed as Vrick sifted through the mounds of data coursing from the Gate's memory into es mind, before the shifting patterns finally calmed into two intersecting lines, one from Hub and one from Weaver's Willow, both intersecting at the same point. And at that point, information bloomed about one small unnamed planet.

In the final pane of information that formed, they saw its planetary designation from the Galactum's roster of charted worlds: PD-785.3.

"It's nothing," Lexa-Blue said, reading through the planetary data that appeared beside the rocky brown planet. "Just a hunk of rock in far out orbit around a half-dead sun."

"Is there anything there?" Ember asked.

"Records show a small hab dome was set up for a research team," Vrick said. "There were initial indications of lyonite deposits in the outer layers of the planet's crust, but they didn't pan out. It was mined dry and then abandoned."

Lexa-Blue whistled in appreciation. "Lyonite? That would definitely have been a score for the ages. There's hardly any left anywhere these days. And even when there was some, there wasn't much."

"What there is in circulation trades for about seventy thousand standard an ounce," Vrick said. "It's still the best semi-conductor and insulator used in ship field generators. Lasts ten times longer than the erlanium used nowadays."

"Any one onsite these days?" Ember asked. "You said there was a hab dome."

"Records say it was abandoned after the research team left, but it was never decommissioned. It could very well still be up and capable of supporting squatters."

"Like someone who doesn't want to be found," Lexa-Blue said.

"Exactly," Vrick said.

"Which makes it our first port of call, if you ask me."

"But look where it is," Ember countered. "That's a two-week trip, even at Vrick's top interspace speed."

"That is, if we travel that way," Lexa-Blue said and saw the understanding in Ember's eyes. "Vrick…"

"Sei li Ffiann has already provided us with clearance and a top priority Gate transit slot. We leave in one hour."

Chapter Five

"We're through," Vrick said. "Going full stealth. Chameleon field and transponder masking at full."

"That was… different," Ember said.

They had all transited Gates before, and that sensation of dislocation and reintegration was familiar. But this time, the Gate had not sent them to and through another Gate but rather had deposited them in empty space just outside the local zone of the empty planet.

"Right?" Lexa-Blue said. "It's like I'm still waiting for the other shoe to drop. Like something's missing."

"I can see why people don't do this very often," Ember said.

"Jumping from a Gate to empty space is definitely a different experience from Gate-to-Gate travel," Vrick said. "The sub-quantum resonances taste completely different. I'm going to have to study my readings in detail."

"Okay, brainbox," Lexa-Blue said. "Wrong audience. Save it for when Keene gets back. I'm sure he'll be fascinated."

Vrick harumphed at them. "We need to get Keene and Sindel back just so I have someone slightly smarter than one of deck plates to talk to."

"Hey, I'm at least as smart as a repair drone," Ember said. "More than her anyway."

"Well, let's focus on getting them back so junkpile doesn't get lonely," Lexa-Blue said. "Any readings from the planet?"

"I'm getting a lot of signal chaff from the location of the dome, but I can't be sure if it's active jamming they're generating now or if it's residue from jamming particles they were using when they were here. I'm trying to punch through it, but it's going to take time."

"Which means they could be down there waiting for us," Ember said. "Armed to the teeth."

"Less than ideal, yes," Vrick said.

"Doesn't matter," Lexa-Blue said. "If there's a chance Keene and Sindel are down there, we go in."

"Guns blazing?" Ember asked, his tone making it very clear how little he thought of that idea. "If we don't know what we're getting into, we could end up getting Keene and Sindel killed, not to mention ourselves."

"At least we'd be doing something," Lexa-Blue shot back.

"Something not only dangerous, but potentially pointless as well."

"If anyone's interested in my opinion," Vrick said. "I would stake my life on my own stealth systems to get us down to the surface undetected. Yes, I am just that good. There's some natural cover from the ridges to the north, and once we're down, I can also do some reconnaissance with my drones. See if there are any visible signs of activity from the dome. Then, you can make the decision as to whether you want to go in. It means you two having to suit up and go overland to the dome itself, but it might improve your chance of taking them by surprise."

"If they're even still there," Ember said. "But you're right, there's no way to know if they're there or not."

"It's a gamble, I know," Lexa-Blue said. "But if they're there, we need to get in and get them out as soon as we can."

Ember nodded, but his reluctance was plain.

"Look, I agree that you need to go in, but that doesn't mean you go in unprepared," Vrick said. "I promise, Ember, I'll get you as much information as possible to formulate your plan of attack."

"Thanks for that," Ember said. "I'm not sure I'll ever get used to the way you like to barge in, guns blazing. But this might be a special case."

"I don't like waiting," Lexa-Blue said, "but I guess it wouldn't hurt us to gather intelligence first before we go in and get our heads blown off."

"Okay, now I have officially heard it all," Vrick said. "This one expressing a desire for caution. Decommission me and send me to the big junkyard in the sky. Melt me down for scrap and send me on my way."

"Can it, you," Lexa-Blue said. "I'm as careful as the next person."

"If the next person has no impulse control," Ember said.

"Oh, that's good," Vrick said. "I need to shake your hand."

One of the internal repair drones emerged from its charging niche and rolled over to Ember, extending one of its manipulators to him. Struggling not to laugh out loud, he bent down and shook it with great formality.

"You are one cold hearted garbage scow, junkpile," Lexa-Blue said, though she was struggling not to laugh herself. "After all we've been through. Don't you have flying to do?"

"Optimal landing site already chosen, and we're on our final approach to the planet," Vrick said. "I had the Gate drop us on the opposite side of the planet, and I've been tracking its rotation. At least they won't see us coming in. Can't say the same for their sensor net if they've taken precautions."

"We'll just have to take the chance," Lexa-Blue said.

In the main viewport, the dull, rocky surface of the planet grew steadily, only the faintest ghost of an atmosphere to soften the flat greyness of its surface. As Vrick descended from the black of space to the pale unbreathable atmosphere, the scarred and jagged surface rendered itself in greater detail. Patches of frozen gases glinted weakly up at them from the bleak surface.

"Well, now. Doesn't that look inviting?" Lexa-Blue asked.

"Reminds me of home," Ember said.

Lexa-Blue looked at him, confused. "Weald is nothing like this."

"Weald is where you met me. Not where I'm from. And it was definitely a step up, believe me."

"I'm setting down there," Vrick said, crosshairs highlighting a notch between two rocky ridges in the main port display. "There's a path out from the landing site that will get you onto the plain leading to the dome. It won't be the most pleasant walk, but it will get you there."

"The exercise will do us good," Ember said.

"And by exercise, I hope you mean busting some heads," Lexa-Blue said. "Because I have some frustrations I need to vent."

"Try to leave a few of them alive this time," Vrick said.

"No guarantees."

"Be that as it may, I'm taking us down," Vrick said.

As gently as a ballet dancer on pointe, Vrick set down in the secluded cleft in the rocks, the stone rising on all sides to shelter them. "Okay, we're down. Releasing a stealth drone to do a flyover of the dome."

In the viewport, they saw the small sphere leave its niche on Vrick's hull and head away from the ship before disappearing as the camouflage systems took over. The view in the main port then changed to show the sensor drone's point of view.

"Not a particularly hospitable place, is it?" Ember asked as the barren, dimly lit terrain raced by in the drone's visual sensor.

"Between how small it is and there being no magnetic field to speak of, there was pretty much no chance of it holding any kind of breathable atmosphere," Vrick said. "And it's so distant from its star, I'm having to compensate for the lack of light."

"Good place to hide out if you don't want to be found," Lexa-Blue said. "Who'd think to look for anyone out here if they didn't have insider information?"

"Coming up on the dome," Vrick said.

The hab dome grew from the rock like a pale, sickly blister, struggling to reflect the light from the stars above. As they watched, the drone made a wide circle around the structure and data flowed across the port as its sensors came online.

"There's still a lot of interference," Vrick said. "It looks like it's from the remnants of the old reactor core used for the initial mining assay, but it could be intentional jamming."

"Convenient," Lexa-Blue said.

"Isn't it just," Ember agreed.

"Wait," Vrick said, highlighting one set of data in the port. "I've got what could be some heat signatures from inside the dome. Hard to get a firm fix on it, but I think we have some people in there."

"I just thought of something," Ember said, and Lexa-Blue looked at him questioningly. "Look at that dome. What do you see? Or better yet, what don't you see?"

Lexa-Blue peered at the image of the hab but shook her head, unable to see what he was referring to.

"There's no ship," Ember said. "If they're in there, how did they get here? I mean, they could have been dropped off, but would anyone want to be left here with no way out if something goes wrong?"

"Good catch," Vrick said. "The drone hasn't seen anything, and any ship big enough to get here would be big enough to register some kind of mass or energy reading. Unless they powered their drives completely down."

"No one does that," Lexa-Blue said. "A drive that cold would take a couple of days to spin back up for flight or even just for basic life support. That's incredibly risky on a planet with no atmo at all. Especially if your only other shelter is a decades-old abandoned hab."

"So, if they're here, how did they get here?" Ember asked.

"And how do they plan to leave?" Vrick added.

"Only one way to find out for sure," Lexa-Blue said. "Come on, squib. Time to go for a walk."

Ember followed her to the pressure suit lockers, where they began to strip down and prepare their suits to leave the ship.

"So, do we have a plan?" Ember asked.

"The plan is to beat them until they give our friends back."

"I'm there with you on the broad strokes," Ember said. "It's more the fine details I'm concerned about."

"Look, just follow my lead, okay?" she said. "We don't even know if Keene and Sindel are in there. Or if anyone is. We know exactly nothing about what we're walking into. But I want my friends back."

"Okay, okay," Ember said, backing off at the harshness of her tone. "I want the same thing. We'll figure it out as we go along."

Lexa-Blue yanked at the closures of her shipsuit and pulled it off, throwing it into the storage locker. Grabbing at her scarlet red steelskin environment suit, she roughly hauled it on, slapping at the pressure seals.

"Easy there, champ," Ember said, helping her even as she shoved his assistance away. "Hey, you've got your seals misaligned. You go out like that, and you'll be dead in about a minute. Let me."

She was rigid a moment, then she huffed out a breath as she went still. Ember realigned the seals of the suit, then punched up the diagnostic menu on her suit's chest plate to confirm everything was in place. When all the telltales were green, he stepped back.

"There," he said. "That should keep you alive so you can wreak some mayhem when the time comes."

This actually brought a smile to her face.

"I'm on your side here," Ember said. "Don't forget that. I want them both back as much as you do."

He turned away before she could say anything and finished putting on his suit, as rich and vibrant a purple as hers was red. When he'd finished and all the seals showed green, he reached for his helmet and locked it into place. Then he picked up the sensor packs Vrick had prepared for them and slung the strap of one over his shoulder as he handed the other to her.

The inside surface of the visor came to life with a heads-up display showing all of his suit's diagnostic data and a glowing icon for the visual augmentation they would need out on the planet's dark surface.

"Confirm suit inputs and go status," Vrick said.

"Confirmed," Ember said. "All green."

"Same here," Lexa-Blue said. "Let's go."

"Internal atmosphere field at maximum," Vrick said. "Depressurizing now."

Through their suits' audio links, they heard the hiss of internal atmosphere emptying from the airlock, as an indicator in their HUDs showed the lock pressure steadily lowering to equal the dead planet outside.

"Pressure equalized," Vrick said. "Opening the lock and lowering the ramp."

Lexa-Blue was already moving as the ramp lowered to meet the planet's rocky surface, but her pace wobbled as the ship's internal gravity sim gave way to the microgravity of the tiny planet itself.

"Easy there, champ," Ember said, reaching out to steady her. "Bit of a gravity differential going on. Give your suit field a moment to compensate."

He saw her regain her footing, grumbling. "Rucking dirtball."

"I told you you should play more ZeroBall," Ember said. "Gets you used to varying gravity levels."

"I hate that damn game," she said, walking more carefully now.

"Oh, I know, believe me," Ember said.

"Give me real gravity or no gravity," she said. "It's this in-between cark I can't handle."

"Just take it slowly," Ember said. "Too much spring in your step, and you'll end up in orbit."

But as if to tease her, he leapt ahead to bound down the ramp, his formidable ZeroBall skills evident in his graceful landing at the foot of the ramp.

"Show-off," she said but seemed surer footed as she descended to stand beside him.

The bleak emptiness of the small planet spread before them, rocky and desolate. As they took the vista in, their HUDs adjusted and enhanced the scene so they could see where they were going.

"Wow. It's even more awful up close," Lexa-Blue said. "Come on, squib. Let's get moving."

Attempting to mimic Ember's confident stride, she started off in the lead. "I figure if I start to achieve liftoff, you can at least grab me back down if I'm ahead of you."

Her suit's field took only a few minutes to adjust for the negligible gravity, and soon they were making good time across the surface, guided by the augmented view of their route.

They moved through the pass hiding the Maverick Heart, sheer rock walls rising above on each side, and a craggy vee of stars ahead of them where the rocks gave way to the dusty plain beyond. Within minutes they were free of the cliff faces and on to the sheer emptiness beyond.

"There it is," she said, her HUD indicating the dome in the distance. With a thought, she shifted to an unaugmented view and was just able to make out the slight colour difference in the smooth hab dome in the distance.

"And here's hoping they don't know we're coming," Ember said. "Anything on the scans, Vrick?"

"Nothing so far," ey said. "It's drawing power still, but I can't be sure if that means anyone's there. The dome's standby mode should be good for years yet, which would have kept the baseline systems running. That might be what I'm seeing."

"What about any emissions?" Ember said. "If there was someone there, wouldn't the dome be venting CO_2 or something?"

"It's possible," Vrick said, "but this kind of isolated dome would likely be designed to recycle everything. The specs show the atmosphere scrubbers are designed to filter the carbon dioxide, convert what it can, and then put the rest back into the basic recyclers."

"That's a whole lot of nothing you're telling us, junkpile," Lexa-Blue said.

"And it's not something I'm at all happy with, believe me," Vrick said. "I am not fond of you having to get that close to find out whether anyone's there or not."

"Can't say I'm thrilled with it either, Vrick," Ember said. "But here we are."

"Looks like you'll be there in about twenty minutes," Vrick said. "Be careful."

As they walked, Lexa-Blue kept her hand near her guns, which were strapped to the suit's external holster mounts. Her suit read the motion and let her know that both were fully charged and ready.

∞

"You can't seriously be planning on helping him?" Keene said.

Sindel was hunched over the room's terminal, Ckurahris's data flowing from its memory.

"What choice to I have? If I don't help him, he'll keep hurting you until I give him what he wants. I don't have to tell you how many bones you have in your body. Not to mention vital organs. And I think we've established how far he'll go to get what he wants."

He had no response to that. While the telltales on the splint's surface indicated he was properly dosed with pain medication and his arm was healing properly, a dull ache still echoed all the way up the arm to his shoulder. Even with proper medical technology, he didn't relish the thought of going through this repeatedly. Or even again, really.

"Besides," Sindel said. "Even if you can withstand repeated torture, Lexa-Blue will never forgive me if something happens to you." She looked up from the data display with a crooked, sardonic smile.

"Well, yes," Keene agreed. "There is that." He was quiet again a moment, mulling the sour array of possibilities that lay before them. "There has to be something we can do," he said finally. "Can you sabotage the system from the inside somehow?"

"Ckurahris is way too smart for that," Sindel said. "He'd see through anything I could come up with on the fly. And I don't have time to truly gum up the works. Not to mention, he may be arrogant and unconcerned with who his plans hurt, but he's also incredibly meticulous. He tests everything repeatedly."

"Can he actually pull this off? Can he do what he says he can? Break through the dimensional barriers and pull off this… interdimensional heist he has planned?"

Sindel sighed and shook her head. "For as truly bizarre as this may be, his theory is sound. We saw all the basic principles in place already when the Spearhead came through from Rogan's dimension. All of the data suggests this could work. Not as it stands now, because there's something fundamentally flawed in the execution of the theory. The hardware is just not where it needs to be, but it's close to working. Too close."

"And that's what he wants you for," Keene said.

"Exactly. And the frightening thing is, if I'm reading this right, I actually can fix it."

Before either of them could speak again, the door slid open. Two human shapes, once again hidden behind a blur, entered, a heavy, wide-range stun baton extending from the shimmering edges of the cloaking field and aimed in their direction.

"Both of you, move. Now," one of them said, and the words were flat, distorted but still more than a little threatening.

Sindel helped Keene up, for he was still weak from the Gate hijack. Despite the pain from his arm and the residual nausea, he managed to stand and took up a spot at her side.

One of the shapes came at them, and the one on the left grabbed Sindel's arm to pull her toward the door, the blur's shield energies itching against her skin.

"All right," Sindel said, her temper rising. "We're coming."

The two disguised beings dragged them into the corridor, pulling them to the right. Keene was able to see for the first time the wall opposite their room curved in both directions. Not missing a step, he turned to take it all in. The walls were indeed blank; his memory had served him well on that count, at least. There wasn't a single marking or image in either direction, though the scuffed and uneven finish on the wall suggested to him those blank walls had been scrubbed of identifying marks at some point in the past. And there was something flat and stale in the air. He could tell wherever they were was old and none too clean. As they were half-dragged along the corridor, he pushed against the last of the fog in his brain and tried to identify why it smelled familiar.

Finally, he had it. Air recyclers. That was it. And they hadn't been serviced in a long time. There was dust and neglect in the air. Recyclers meant they were on a ship, most likely. Or possibly on a planet where the outside air wasn't human breathable. *Narrows it down*, he thought. *But not enough*.

After a few moments, the corridor emptied into a large open space. They were hauled forward, Sindel stumbling into Keene's side as they were pushed aside.

"Don't move," one of their captors said as it stepped away, the modulated voice echoing even more oddly in this larger space.

Trying to be discreet, Keene took the room in. The other guard stayed to watch them, menacing as a spectre behind the swirling camouflage of the blur. Keene looked past them to the five others in the room, all of them hiding behind blurs as well. There was also a pile of unfamiliar equipment and apparatus. From what he could see, it was all portable, and most of the blurred figures were deactivating and closing the cases up, then loading them onto a small grav sled that hovered on pale green energy, preparing for something.

Though he couldn't read their body language through the blurs, his gut told him they were in a hurry. They were bugging out. Whoever they were and whatever they wanted from him and from Sindel, this was no longer the place to accomplish it. Not even the adaptive body camouflage could hide the urgency of their movements as they packed away the equipment and loaded it on the sled.

Only one was not hidden by the personal cloaking fields.

Ckurahris.

And he's pissed.

From where he and Sindel were being held, he couldn't hear the instructions being lobbed back and forth, but what little he could catch was muddled by the blurs into a thick, urgent mud of sound.

If only I had a way to listen in. Oh, wait. I do.

They may have cut off his access to Know-It-All, but that didn't mean he was helpless. His node implant wasn't just an off-the-shelf standard model. He and Vrick had made some very useful modifications over the years, as needs dictated. A little software upgrade here, a little nanosome upgrade there, leaving him with some very useful skills when it came to the crunch.

And it doesn't get any crunchier than this.

He thought the command that activated his node's surveillance programs and focussed on the buzz of activity across the room. As he concentrated on the leader, the auditory mush began to resolve itself into actual sense.

"....are they now?" the leader said.

"They've crossed the midrange marker and are getting closer," the one closest to the leader said. "They're walking, and the terrain gets worse as they get closer, so we should be able to get everything out as long as we don't waste any time."

Hope surged through Keene. Someone was on the way, Keene realized. And if he had to guess, he'd have put his money on it being Lexa-Blue and Ember. At least he hoped it was. For all he knew, it could be some rival with a grudge that would light the whole scene up with gunfire. *One problem at a time.*

He looked around, but at least one guard was devoted to watching him and Sindel while the others went about their tasks. And without actually knowing where they were, he'd be hard pressed to get them out of here, even if he could distract the guard enough to make a run for it. He couldn't even inform Sindel about what was going on without tipping his hand and letting their captors know he could understand what was being said.

They were stuck for now, hoping whoever was out there was friendly. And if they were, that they could get here before their captors could complete their bug out, taking them along for the ride.

And that is too many damn variables.

Ckuhraris looked up and saw them, his brows meeting in a scowl.

"Well, it seems as though your friends are smarter than I gave them credit for. We detected a ship entering the sector, and it's headed this way. They've likely landed."

"Looks like you're in for it now," Sindel said, her voice smug.

"Hardly," Ckurahris said. "Surely, you don't think that this pathetic base is all we have. And surely you remember how I brought you here. Our escape route is already planned."

Keene turned to see the only other person in the room not wearing a blur hunched over a console. And he didn't have to be an expert in body language to know something was not right.

"Wols," Ckurahris snapped. "Status?"

The man he called Wols looked up and shook his head. "We're still getting the same fluctuations. Sims all in the red."

"Looks like you're not going anywhere, eh?" Keene said, nudging Sindel away from her focus on their captor. A smile bloomed on her face as she took in what was happening. A sharp, mocking laugh burst from her.

"Looks like your fancy tech is broken, Astel," she said. "And your escape route is blocked."

A look of sheer hatred came over Ckurahris's face, and he strode furiously toward them. Keene tried to stand firm but felt Sindel flinch at his side. Ckurahris reached past him toward their escort.

Before he could think, he felt Ckurahris's hand gripping the back of his neck, and the cold metal of the stun baton dead centre of his forehead. At this range, the discharge would sear half his brain to ash. He heard Ckurahris's voice.

"Then it's a good thing I have someone here who can fix it."

∞

Lexa-Blue came to a stop in the shadow of the dome, hunkered down as low to the ground as she could get. She felt Ember slip into place at her side.

Schematics show a hatch about five meters along the wall, she said. *You ready?*

All set, Ember said, and she felt through his node as his hand went to the lockpick gear attached to his pressure suit at the waist.

Go. She stood, hugging close to the gentle upward curve of the dome wall, gun in each hand. *I'll cover.*

She advanced, each gun registering as a tingle of energy in her mind, each step precise and determined. The hatch was exactly where they expected. She took position, spreading her arms wide until one gun was pointed in each direction. She flicked her gaze back and forth, expanding the range of her node and taking advantage of Vrick's sensor array, even though ey was on the other side of the rocky ridges. As she absorbed the combined knowledge, she felt something at the edge of her consciousness, something that made her eye twitch.

What is that? she asked Vrick.

It feels like jamming of some kind, Vrick said. *You're on the edge of a blocker field, I think. Something inside is being used to selectively cut off outside signals. The focus is pretty narrow. If I was the betting sort, I'd wager someone inside is being kept from accessing Know-It-All.*

Makes sense if someone is trying to keep what's going on here a secret, Ember said, and Lexa-Blue could feel his hands moving as he worked the locking mechanism of the hatch.

Or if you're keeping someone hostage and you don't want them calling for help. I'd say that's pretty good evidence we're in the right place, Lexa-Blue agreed. *How's it coming with the door?*

Almost in, he said. *It's pretty sophisticated code. But definitely not the best I've ever seen.*

Just get me in there so I can shoot someone.

And…. done, Ember said, leaning back from the mechanism as the hatch began to open, a hiss of escaping atmosphere misting around them. He swiftly put his tools away and drew his own pistol.

I've got point, Lexa-Blue said, moving past him into the airlock. Ember followed, and she felt the vibration of the outer door closing behind them, then the change in pressure as atmosphere rushed into the small space once again, equalizing pressure. In front of her, the inner door slid open.

∞

Ckurahris pushed Sindel to the console at Wols's side. "Help him. Or all your friends will find here is your corpses."

With a look of pure hatred, Sindel went to work, conferring with Wols as they concentrated on the console's surface. Keene watched as she pulled open a panel and began rooting around inside it. At her direction, Wols stuck his hands into the opening alongside hers.

The buzz of activity kicked up to an even higher pitch as Keene observed their captors plan for their escape.

"They're inside," one of the blurred shapes said to Ckurahris.

"Trigger the internal defenses. Keep them occupied as long as possible. Get everything through to the other side as soon as the portal is open."

"I'm not sure we have enough time," Wols said, strain in his voice.

"Then stop talking and get moving." Ckurahris then turned to two others. "You two, get into position at the junction just past the living quarters. Hold there and wait for my orders."

The shape turned from them, and only Keene saw the fractional hesitation before the two moved to follow orders.

"Oh, for…" Keene heard Sindel say, feeling his guard tense at his side. The hard tip of the stun baton dug into his ribs at the sound of her outburst. "You can't run that much power through that kind of conduit. Here. Let me."

Wols pulled his hands free but remained close, handing her tools as she barked for them. Finally, she slammed the console shut. "There. Try that."

Wols hit the actuators and the console hummed back to life. "It's online. Powering up the portal now."

Portal?

Keene watched as Wols appeared to fine-tune settings on the console, then hit one final activation sequence.

On the far wall of the room, where their captors and their grav sleds were congregated, a spot began to glow. To Keene, it looked like someone was trying to burn through the wall from the other side, though anything powerful enough to do that would have given off heat, and he could feel no change in the room's ambient temperature.

As he and Sindel watched, the glow grew, becoming a circle filling most of the wall, even curving up onto the ceiling. The glowing energy reminded him of the energy of the Gates themselves, and he turned to Sindel, the question in his eyes. She must have picked up the resemblance herself, for she nodded sharply, her forehead creased in concern. When he turned back to the sight, the energy of the glow seemed to have stabilized, reaching its maximum size. But where the Gate energy was smooth and opalescent, this was more chaotic. It reminded Keene of marble, mostly pale, but veined with colour. Except in this case, the veining coursed through the background colour like lightning, sharp and fiery.

And the sound.

The air of the room filled with a deep vibration, jarring them to the bone with its resonances. Something powerful was happening, and Keene's instincts told him it was nothing good. Nothing good at all.

"Full power. Go," Wols said.

"Get everything through," Ckurahris barked. "Now."

Keene saw the others begin pushing the grav sleds forward, moving into that chaotic light with no hesitation. As he watched, he saw the leading edge of the cart hit the light, then seem to be consumed by it, disappearing by millimetres as it was pushed forward. It was almost as if the cart and its contents were being disintegrated, but Keene could tell by the nonchalance of the workers that something else was happening.

And from Sindel's wordless recognition and confirmation earlier, he had a pretty good idea what it was.

Within minutes, the carts and their cargo were gone, having been pushed through the portal. Only Ckurahris and four of the workers remained behind. Keene saw the leader turn to them and signal to them.

"Get them through," the leader said. "Stun them and drag them if you have to."

And they followed his command, two for Keene, two for Sindel, dragging them roughly to their feet and pushing them forward. He saw Sindel struggle against their grasp and remembered she wouldn't have heard the leader's willingness to knock them both out and drag them through like more cargo.

"Don't fight it," he said to her, seeing in her eyes she was more than ready to make this hard on their captors. "Trust me. It's easier this way."

Sindel's body remained tense as she was dragged forward, but then she relaxed and cooperated.

"A wise move," the leader said as they were dragged past them. Though Keene couldn't make out any facial detail behind the mask of his blur, he had a sudden creeping sensation the other one was watching him very carefully, appraising his every move. All too aware.

But then the moment passed, and he was pushed forward into the throbbing marbled portal. And was gone.

∞

You've got sniper bugs up ahead, Vrick informed them, es voice rising. ***And they're charging.***

The wave of tiny bots surged around the corner ahead of them, a seething mass along the walls. Fine centipede legs propelled the bugs forward, their backs bristling with pin beam generators.

High-Low 3, Lexa-Blue said. ***Go.***

Oh, sure, Ember said. ***I get to be the human shield.***

But he was already moving, sending commands to the gravity-warping skin field of his suit, leaping and spinning in midair. His feet came in contact with the wall at an absurd angle, almost upside down in relation to the floor, as he ran toward the armed drones. The display inside his helmet registered Lexa-Blue drawing her paired guns and opening fire, the bolts of energy coruscating past him. He focussed on the sniper bugs ahead, seeing one shatter in a gout of fragments and fire as its power cell ruptured.

Gah, I hate those things, Lexa-Blue said. *They make me jeebie.*

At least you're back there, Ember said. *They're even creepier when you're upside down.*

With his suit reacting to his thoughts, he spun and leapt, twisting in midair to evade a pin beam from one of the bugs, the soles of his boots slipping for a nanosecond before finding purchase on the opposite wall.

His suit's readings told him its upgraded plating was deflecting most of the pin beam's energy, but he didn't like the damage rates he was accruing. If they didn't handle the bots soon, one of those concentrated beams would certainly make it past the plating and carve through his flesh.

He dove and twisted again, almost losing his footing in the confined space of the hallway. He had adapted manoeuvres he was adept at on the ZeroBall court for close quarters situations like this, but even his best moves were hindered by the laws of motion. And in this kind of space, he only had so much range of motion to make the turns he needed to. But he was almost close enough now.

High and left in his vision, he saw one of the sniper bugs fragment from Lexa-Blue's gunfire, only to see another skitter past it, the bot's dozens of legs undulating almost faster than his eyes could register. Calculating his angles, he sent a flurry of commands to his suit, spiraling forward. A thought diverted the skin field's power up from his legs to his right fist, hardening the heavily plated gauntlet. One tight pulse of his suit's thrusters sent him forward in a surge of power, his fist aimed at the sniper bug as his display flashed vectors and timing at him.

Hope I got this right.

His gauntlet intersected with the oncoming bot, shredding its metal carapace with such force that it embedded what remained of the killer drone's chassis into the wall itself.

He pulled his hand free and adjusted the suit's thrusters and skin field, feeling himself turn in midair and shoot through the opening the sniper bugs were guarding, coming to rest with only the slightest of skids, facing back the way he came.

He settled just in time to see the last of the drones re-target on him, the pin beam emitters that lined their backs glowing sullen red.

Well, shit.

As he sent a desperate flurry of commands to his suit's shields and weapons, he saw the warnings in his HUD flash crimson with rage as the sniper bugs' targeting sensors locked into him. *Not going to make it.*

The sniper bug on his right tore apart in a gout of flame and fragments raining on the deck below it. The drone on his left managed to get off a shot but was hit by a blast of energy just like the one that had destroyed its partner, sending its aim off true. Ember cringed as the killing beam of violet light seared through the wall to his left and arced into the ceiling above his head.

Goss, I hate those things, he said. *What took you so long?*

Just stay out of the way, Lexa-Blue said, her heavy gauge blaster pistols at the ready as she joined him.

Fine, but don't cut it so close next time. I think I just flooded my sanitation system.

He turned back to the room, seeing a flash of movement and figures moving toward a smear of roiling light on the wall opposite them. And in that light, a familiar figure was being shoved into the vibrant sheen.

"Keene!" Ember shouted, the external speakers of his suit sending a blast of sound across the room.

At the sound of his name, the figure turned and locked eyes with Ember.

*Where is he?" Lexa-Blue shouted, unable to see past him. *You're in my way.*

Ember heard her heavy treads coming up behind him, reverberating through the floor into his suit. Ignoring her, he started forward, hoping desperately to catch Keene before whatever was happening whisked him away.

There, Ember called to her, sending his suit's visual to her as he surged forward to try and get to Keene before he disappeared into the maw of light.

Wait, there might be... Lexa-Blue called from behind him, and his suit's proximity system registered her gauntleted hand reaching for his shoulder to try and stop him. He felt it graze against his suit when the world exploded.

In an instant, they were hammered by sonic cannons so powerful they rippled the air in thick waves. Before either of them could react, their heavy suits were tossed back. Ember slammed into the wall behind him, and Lexa-Blue fell onto her back in the hall, among the remains of the sniper bugs.

His head ringing from the impact, Ember struggled to pull himself back up and clear his head. *What the hells was that?*

... traps, Lexa-Blue said, her voice seething. *I was going to say there might be booby traps, you idiot.*

Hey, I was trying to get to Keene before he disappeared.

And how did that work out for you? Lexa-Blue said. She was standing now, striding toward him, and when she reached his side, she leaned over and hauled him to his feet, using more of the suit's augmented strength than was properly necessary. Ember felt his shoulder was about to give way.

Easy there, slugger, he said, gritting his teeth against the aches all through his body.

We lost him, she said.

Trust me, I know, Ember said bitterly. He pointed at the anomaly splayed across the far wall. ***What is that thing, anyway?***

Lexa-Blue came to a halt beside him, and he sensed her slack-jawed gape through his node, knowing it matched his own. ***I have no rucking idea.***

Before them was the empty room, showing the evidence of their quarry's hasty retreat. But before them, the wall was a roil of colour and light, a sight that screamed its wrongness to them both. As the maw before them shrank, Ember keyed all of his suit's sensors to maximum, hoping to catch as much information as he could, but half of the readouts in his HUD showed nothing more than the disquieting word "Null" to indicate they were struggling to understand what was happening.

Vrick, are you getting this? Ember said. ***What are we seeing?***

Your guess is as good as mine, Vrick said, es voice thick with frustration.

A sudden pop and fizzle of electronics made them turn sharply, and they saw the console, the one remaining thing in the room, spouting sparks as the circuitry burned out.

It's melting down, Lexa-Blue said. ***Must have been rigged.***

As they watched, the console began to puddle into a pool of ceramic and metal slag.

Hang on, I'm going to nudge some more sensing power through your suit. This might sting a bit.

Ember stifled a gasp, feeling Lexa-Blue do the same, the inner interface membrane of the suit tingling with heat as Vrick pumped extra power through it.

Oh, yeah, Lexa-Blue said. ***Not liking this at all.***

Give me a minute, Vrick said. ***It's not going to hurt you. I think.***

As Ember watched the oozing pulse of sickly colours before them fade and shrink, he could see the sensor readings in his HUD strain to glean data from their surroundings, and his vision swam from both the heat inside his suit and the pulse of adrenaline in his system.

Tell me you're getting something from this, Ember heard Lexa-Blue say through clenched teeth.

One more minute, Vrick said. *Just hang on.*

Ember felt his head swimming, his vision greying out at the edges until two things happened. The phenomenon before them shrank to nothing, and the oppressive heat and buzz of energy that ran through his suit suddenly cut out. Breath pounded from his lungs at the sudden absence.

Don't ever do that again, Lexa-Blue said.

No promises, Vrick said, but as ey said it, Ember saw his own bio-monitors flood with reassuring data that confirmed neither one of them would suffer any ill effects from the sensor flood they had just endured.

So what the seven hells was that anyway? Lexa-Blue said.

Not a clue, Vrick said. *But I have some hunches. None of them good. I'm going to need some time to digest this data before I can draw any conclusions.*

Okay, while you do that, we can start picking this place apart, Ember said. *See what we can come up with.*

I've already dispatched evidence sweepers to your location, Vrick said.

Good, Lexa-Blue said. *I'm willing to take this place down to atoms if I have to. I want to know what the ruck was going on here.*

Chapter Six

They emerged from the portal into chaos. All around them, cloaked bodies rushed back and forth, the evacuation on the verge of panic. Keene lost his footing as the goon shoved him through the portal, and the stumble was made worse by a sudden physical disorientation that went all through him. Wherever they were now, everything was different. His node fluttered as all basic readings of his environment changed faster than should have been possible. Air pressure, temperature, ambient background noise. Everything had changed.

Then the world slammed shut as Know-It-All disappeared. *Another jammer.*

"Looks like you fixed it," he said to Sindel through clenched teeth, seeing from the expression on her face that she was as disoriented as he was.

"Three cheers for me," Sindel said, "but I did manage to learn a lot from getting my hands on it. They're having difficulty with the organic matter discriminators whenever they try to cross a dimensional boundary. They can get everything else through, but if it's human, plant, or animal, it turns to mush."

"Quiet," Ckurahris said as one of the blurred guards dragged Keene back to his feet.

"All right," Keene said, yanking his arm free. "Hands off the merchandise."

They stood in silence, watching as Ckurahris spoke intensely with Wols at a console that was a bigger, more complex version of the one they had seen on the other side of the portal.

"You've caused a stir," Keene said, nudging Sindel.

"They're probably trying to decide if I sabotaged it," she said, her voice soft and sour. "Or Astel is yelling at Wols for missing such an obvious fix to their problem."

"Dissension in the ranks might benefit us at some point," he answered quietly. "Keep your eyes open."

With a sudden slash of his hand, Ckurahris turned from Wols, his face shifting into a stony smile as he turned from his assistant to Sindel. "Well, it would seem that bringing you here was definitely a good call. No need for any more coercion."

He looked at Keene. "At least not yet."

"Take them to their quarters," he said to the guards. "Get them settled. We need to run some tests, and they'll need rest before we put them to work again."

He turned away as if they no longer mattered, and their guards nudged them toward the door.

"We've been dismissed," Keene said to her as the blurred human shapes moved into position, one ahead of them, one behind.

"So it would seem," Sindel answered. "Though not for long, I bet. If I know him, he had all the information from that other console dumped here and will be going over every detail, trying to see if the fix I used can be scaled up to his main system without frying every component."

"Do you think it will work?"

"It was a quick fix meant for that site-to-site portal. I'll bet you anything he has a much bigger version of it somewhere here. One that will jump him to his target dimensions. And that will need a lot more work than my little patch if he's having similar problems with it."

Keene was silent at her side a moment, taking in the corridor they were being marched through. Unlike where they had been held on the other side of the portal, everything here was in a far more advanced state of disrepair and decay. Wherever they were, it hadn't been used in a long time. And whoever had used it seemed to have stripped it when they left.

And another thing.

He took a deep breath in.

No doubt about it.

"Do you smell that?"

Sindel looked at him, confused. "What?"

Keene felt a sudden hard shove between his shoulder blades from the guard behind him.

"Quiet," the flat, toneless voice said from behind the blur.

They remained quiet as their guards led them through the dank, abandoned corridors before finally bringing them to a doorway. The guard in front raised a hand, and the door slid open. He ushered them in with a wave of his stun stick, and the door hissed shut behind them.

Unlike their previous accommodations, this room was much larger, with racks of bunks along one wall, ten in total. But where the last room had been clean, if sparse, this space was still mostly dirty and forgotten after years of neglect. While there had been a token effort to prepare for their arrival, it amounted to nothing more than one set of bunks being cleaned off for them in a corner of the space near the restroom. Other than that one neatened area, the rest of the room was a mess, as if it had been suddenly abandoned years before and ignored ever since.

"Charming," Sindel said, trying to clean off a chair enough to sit on it before just giving up and sitting on the edge of the one clean lower bunk. "Some kind of barracks or something? A prison, maybe?"

"I don't think so," Keene said, nosing around in drawers and cubbies. "Not miserable enough."

"Are you kidding? I've seen public toilets with more charm."

"No, I'm serious. Try to see past the dirt. It's communal, yes. But look."

He pointed to an entertainment unit, long dead, its screens ribboned with cracks and the emitters mostly missing their lenses. "This was set up for reasonable comfort. Look, there used to be privacy curtains on these bunks."

The rods now lay empty of anything but tattered, rotted shreds of fabric.

"Whoever set this up at least made some token effort at making it comfortable for its occupants."

"Maybe we can get them back to redecorate," she said. "What good does that do us?"

"Clues, my dear Sindel," Keene said as he continued to explore the room. "All clues as to where we might be."

"Speaking of that, what were you saying about the smell?" she asked.

"Wherever we were before, that was recycled, reprocessed air," he said. "Wherever this is, that's real atmosphere we're breathing."

"All I can smell is stale chemicals and neglect."

"Trust me. Even that tells us a lot. These smells would have been scrubbed out along with the CO_2 if we were still in a sealed environment. Once you've spent as much time breathing recycled air on ships as I have, you can always tell the difference. Somewhere out there, is real, honest to goss atmo."

"And that means?"

"It means that if we can ever figure out how to get outside, we won't asphyxiate. I don't know about you, but that kind of thing is important to me."

Sindel threw herself back onto her bunk with a groan. "Enough mysteries already."

"Too many questions, not enough answers," Keene agreed, dropping onto the other bunk, his head at Sindel's feet. "But someone went to an awful lot of trouble to get us here. And our sudden departure was definitely ahead of schedule, considering how rushed it all was. I have a hunch we'll find out more soon. Once our friends get settled again, we might finally get some answers."

∞

Vrick sent power to es atmospheric drive field, lifting emself up out of concealment, just high enough to clear the sharp grey crags of rock, and ey aimed for the habitat where the others waited.

The flight was only a few minutes, but they felt an eternity of frustration at having been so close to Keene and missing their chance at getting him back. Ey couldn't help but go over es records of everything they had done, trying to find some flaw, some mistake that had caused them to get to this airless rock pile too late to rescue their friend. Ey ran multiple alternate scenarios, altering a thousand variables at a time in parallel channels, searching for something they had done wrong, something that might improve their chances of success if they were so lucky as to get another shot at rescuing him.

That is if those two infantile meatbags could stop squabbling long enough.

As the habitat came into view, ey ran es scans and compared them to the building's plans, locating the best method of ingress to reach the others. There. The main ground level airlock. It was the right size to get the bots and equipment inside and was also close enough to where Lexa-Blue and Ember waited for em. Ey angled toward it, shifting into landing mode.

But it wasn't going to be that easy. Es landing terrain subroutines flared a warning, flooding es mind with elemental composition, topography, and size of the area outside the airlock. It was a small staging area designed for humans, not for landing vessels es size. Ey would never fit, and the dusty, rocky terrain was too uneven. If ey attempted to land as it was, ey would be at an incorrect angle to dock with the hab's airlock mechanism.

I do not have time for this.

Shifting power to es weapons grid, ey ran the calculations, variables flowing like water across es consciousness, then executed the targeting solution. Es underbelly flared with radiant, deadly light as ey fired on the terrain below in a precise, timed burst. Rock and dust boiled below, the flash of heat spiking across es sensor grid, the thermal energy dissipating into the frigid cold of the near airless moon. Temperature sensors precisely measured the burst of heat, and then the dissipation as the terrain cooled. The instant the temperature dropped enough and es sensor readings confirmed the ground had solidified, ey dropped the rest of the way to the surface, now smooth and glass-like, but still emitting trace heat. Ey knew the ventral surfaces of the landing struts would need to be checked and quite possibly re-laminated after, but ey didn't care.

Ey descended to a perfect landing, adjusting the landing struts to lower es hull into line with the hab's airlock, then extended es own docking cuff to connect to it. Its system chirped a disdainful alarm, but ey had no time for that either, extending fully into position, and then brute forcing the hab to unlock for em. The hab's lock system sputtered to silence, opening for em.

As ey had made the short flight, ey had already been reprogramming several of es maintenance bots for further evidence collection, lining them up in a queue at es airlock's inner chamber, filling their memory to capacity with the kind of specific scanning and recording ey needed them to do once they were inside. The interior bots rolled forward through the airlock on silent treads while the outer hull repair bots hummed forward on their grav fields, all in a precise and purposeful line, as if marching into battle.

Even as the bots moved forward, Vrick was rewriting subroutines for them and downloading them to their cores as fast as ey could.

What ey had managed to pull from Lexa-Blue and Ember's suit sensors was troubling and fascinating in equal measure, despite the limitations of just what those sensor arrays were capable of reading. There were dozens of half-formed theories floating around in es mind, all frustratingly incomplete, and ey wasn't even sure that with all the repurposed bots and new code, ey would be able to figure out just what they all had witnessed in that now empty room.

∞

Lexa-Blue skipped aside sharply out of the path of one of Vrick's bots as it hustled back and forth across the small bedroom, methodically searching for any and all clues. "Watch where you're going with those things."

Just stay out of their way, Vrick said, es voice sharp as a blade.

"Hey, we're on the same side, okay?" Lexa-Blue said.

Are we? Vrick retorted. *Because, honestly, right now I trust them far more than I trust either of you to be useful.*

"What did we do?" Ember asked. He looked to Lexa-Blue and saw her brow was as furrowed as his, but in her case more from anger at being spoken to that way.

You two have been at each other ever since Keene went missing. I've seen toddlers with better impulse control than you two have shown. This isn't some competition to show which one of you cares for him more. It's not a race to see who can get to him first.

They were both stunned into silence by Vrick's outburst.

You both need to shape up, get focussed, and stay on target. Our friend is still missing, and whatever is going on here is getting weirder by the minute. I swear on everything I hold dear in this universe, I will leave you both here and find new slabs of meat to take your place in a heartbeat if either of you continues to let your emotions get the better of you and get in the way of you working together. So, shape up or find a new ride home.

"Okay," Lexa-Blue said. "I feel like you have something on your mind you're holding back. I think you should just let it out."

At her side, Ember snorted with laughter, then stifled it, in case it set Vrick off on another rant.

For a moment, they weren't sure what was going to happen, but then Vrick spoke again.

I swear, you two are going to do me in once and for all. And I've been around for a very long time. Look, I know it's hard for you both, but it's hard for me too. I want him back as much as you do. And I can't find him without you.

"Not even with a coupla new meat sacks?" Lexa-Blue said.

I don't have time to break them in. Now get yourselves back here. My bots are done sweeping the place, and I have some information.

Lexa-Blue set out for the ship, but Ember hung back a moment, taking one last look.

He's gone, Vrick said gently on a private channel. *We have to keep looking.*

Ember didn't reply, just turned away and left the room.

∞

As soon as they were back on the ship, Vrick wasted no time in detaching the airlock, lifting off the cold, empty planetoid, and setting a course to get them far enough from the gravity well to shift into interspace. Once Ember and Lexa-Blue were out of their suits, ey already had coffee made.

"I've collated all the evidence the bots were able to pull together, and even if we missed them," Vrick said, es voice clearly frustrated by their failure to retrieve their friend, "we *do* know more than we did before."

"Hit us with it," Lexa-Blue said, pouring a cup of coffee. Sipping from the mug, she walked back to the lounge's main couch and took a seat beside Ember.

A spill of data filled the forward viewport, overlaid on the stars beyond.

"Keene was definitely there."

"I know. I saw him," Ember said.

Vrick paused, as if collecting es temper. "I know. But now we have concrete physical evidence. The bots did a detailed DNA sweep. Aside from a set of unidentified traces, one room was full of traces of both Keene and Sindel. Which confirms that whatever is going on, whoever is behind it, took them both."

"We knew that already." It was Lexa-Blue that interrupted this time.

"No, we *suspected* it, and it seemed likely," Vrick said, es voice sharp with forced patience. "Again, evidence. Which we now have."

"Sorry, junkpile. I'll be quiet now."

"If only I believed that," Vrick said, es voice gentler. "I have every speck of DNA and trace evidence we took from that dome, but I'm going to need access to some specialized databases before I can do any sort of identifications, and I can't get at them while we're in interspace. It will have to wait until we're back at Hub."

"Are you going to have any trouble getting access to these databases?" Lexa-Blue asked.

"No," Vrick said. "No, I'm not. One way or the other, I'm not."

"That's the answer I was looking for," she said.

"Seconded," Ember added. "What about that thing we saw?"

"That's where it gets odd," Vrick said, pushing the DNA results to the back of the display and pulling a new set to the forefront. Streams of numbers filled the display, equations stretching from one side to the other, graphs in various colours, along with waveforms that undulated to some unknown rhythm. Within seconds, the entire port was filled with a clash of colour and information.

"Whoa, whoa, whoa," Lexa-Blue said. "Easy there, champ. We're the tech-dumb pair, remember?"

"Trust me," Vrick said. "I'm aware. This is all high-level, bleeding edge multiplanar, interdimensional mathematics. None of this should even be possible."

"Dumb words, Vrick," Ember said. "We need dumb words."

"That room you found, the one with the light show on the wall, was filled with residual particle traces I've only ever seen in and around at Gate when it opens and closes. Opening the Einstein-Rosen Bridge…"

"Wormhole," Lexa-Blue said. "That much I remember."

"… Yes. Opening the wormhole produces cascades of exotic particles, none of them harmful to humans or ships, but they can show you exactly where the Gate has opened."

"If the giant metal, circular space station wasn't a clue," Ember said.

"But that's the thing," Vrick said. "That room was full of those particles, along with a whole other set I haven't seen before."

"Wait, are these other particles dangerous?" Lexa-Blue asked.

"Honestly, I have no idea. But you were both in your suits, and they're top of the line, rated for deep vacuum and radiation exposure, so my best guess is you were both safe."

"But what about Keene?" Ember asked. "I saw him pushed through that thing. To who knows where."

"All I can do is guess at this point," Vrick said, es voice clearly showing es frustration at the lack of solid data available. "And from what little I glean from the tests I can run on whatever these new particles are, and the fact that whoever took our friends didn't hesitate to use that… thing to make their escape, I feel like it's likely to be relatively safe."

"Not exactly a ringing endorsement," Ember said.

"Believe me, I know," Vrick said. "But there's one other thing. Aside from the standard Gate residue, those other particle traces remind me of something I've seen before."

A pane of information in the display split in two, flooding with two separate streams of data. Subatomic particles danced frantically in the images.

"Those are nothing alike," Lexa-Blue said, frustrated.

"No, look," Ember said. As he pointed, Vrick followed the angle of his finger and highlighted the various similarities he was indicating. "There. And there too. I have no idea what they mean, but I can see it."

"Right," Lexa-Blue said, her voice rising as she began to see the patterns. "Right. I see it now too. But what does it mean?"

"Those particles on the left are what I recorded in the vicinity of the breach that Rogan and his people came through."

Both Lexa-Blue and Ember gaped.

"Are you telling us Keene and Sindel have been kidnapped into another dimension?" Lexa-Blue asked.

"No, thankfully not," Vrick said. "Those new particles you recorded down there don't have the same vibrational patterns as the ones Sindel identified as coming from the interdimensional rift. But it's a portal of some kind. Leading somewhere. Which should not be possible without a structure the size of a Gate to harness all of the energies required."

"So, we have no idea where they went, and it's technically impossible that they went anywhere at all," Lexa-Blue said.

"Exactly," Vrick said. "But they did it. Which means there will be evidence. And that means we can figure out how they did it and where they are. And we can get Keene and Sindel back."

"There's only one problem," Ember said. "Wherever they went, they have a big head start."

"How?" Lexa-Blue asked.

"Think about it. If they used a portal, wherever they went, they likely got there instantaneously."

"And? We got here using the Gate."

"But there's no Gate here for us to get back."

"Gahdammit!" Lexa-Blue punched into the cushions beside her.

"We have to get back to Hub," Vrick said. "I need access to more information as soon as possible, and I need to pick Sei Li Ffiann's brain about what this particle residue might mean."

"Can't you do it over the tightline?" Ember asked.

"There's too much of it. I'm talking exabytes of information. The tightline infrastructure could never handle it. But I can get us back in just over three days, but I'll have to put you both under again to get the velocity I'll need."

Both Ember and Lexa-Blue groaned at the idea. They'd done it before. And hated every second. The technique Vrick described required them both to be sedated almost to the point of coma, while ey pushed the internal crash fields to maximum and powered es interspace drive to a speed that, under normal circumstances, humans wouldn't survive. They'd only done it once or twice before, and it was not a pleasant experience.

"What do you think, squib?" Lexa-Blue asked.

Ember didn't hesitate. "I want Keene and Sindel back. Whatever it takes."

"Do it."

∞

Once Ember and Lexa-Blue were under, Vrick slipped into interspace, feeling the texture of it against es hull. Once ey was sure nothing was out of the ordinary, one thought brought all the trace evidence Ember and Lexa-Blue had collected into Vrick's evaluation matrix. Data flooded es consciousness, swimming in a flow of information that ebbed and rose like an ocean.

Okay, let's do this.

Ey broke down the inventory of evidence into categories, sorting everything accordingly. Particulates here. Then energy and radiation traces there. And finally, all DNA traces. With the evidence sorted by type, ey launched three subroutines to compare and sort each sample within each category.

The radiation and energy trace sort ended first as there wasn't much out of the ordinary in those readings. Ey was able to eliminate all of the normal background radiation traces for the barren planetoid itself, comparing them to es own readings taken from the environment outside while ey had waited for es meat friends to complete their part of the mission. Once those baselines were eliminated, ey was able to identify and categorize all basic traces that were easily identifiable, like the portable generators and the independent power cells for the equipment their quarry had been using.

That left only the one, unrecognizable energy form. And it was quite the enigma. Ey ran it against everything ey had on file, having copious and detailed records covering es own life span. Whatever this final energy signature was, it permeated the hab dome, with the most potent traces centering on the portal they had seen.

There were some extremely specific similarities to the energy ey had recorded through es external sensors during Gate transition, but so much more concentrated. If the Gate was analogous to the light of a sun, then this was that sunlight concentrated into one fiery point by a magnifying lens or light concentrated through a laser. There were also similarities to the frequencies and energy states required for interspace entry and travel, again in such intense concentrations that ey found it hard to believe they hadn't punched a hole through the planet itself.

Ey bit back a curse, realizing none of the sensor equipment ey had deployed would have had a fraction of the power and scope necessary to read any potential damage this unknown radiation could have caused down any of the other dimensional interstices where the Gates and interspace intersected. That would have taken sensors so specialized that ey wouldn't even have known where to find them.

Pin it for now, ey thought, compiling the readings and all comparison data at hand into a file so ey could follow up with Hetri once the major review and basic analysis was complete.

With that done, ey turned es attention to the particulate review and analysis. What the subroutines had found so far was not encouraging. Everything the scans had found was completely routine. Minute food remnants consistent with various stasis-packed foodstuffs and prepared rations. Inorganic traces were all consistent either with familial metals or the standard range of recyclable or degradable polymers and ceramics used across the Pan Galactum. Any identifiable brands were easily traceable and so readily and easily available they could have been purchased on pretty much any Galactum world.

The hab's waste system yielded nothing other than recycled water. They must have cycled the system as they were leaving, sending any other waste matter into the power system as fuel. Atmospheric analysis was a dead end as well. In a planetary habitation module like that one, on a world without breathable atmosphere, the carbon dioxide filters and oxygen medium kept the air as close to pure as possible. There were no unusual trace elements in the scrubbed internal atmosphere that yielded any clues.

Well, that was a bust. Except…

There. So minute it barely registered, nothing more than a few grains of something at the base of the wall where the strange portal had opened. With the amount of air scrubbing and precision environmental maintenance required to keep inhabitants safe in a closed facility like this one, there would have been minimal intrusion beyond the artificial elements ey had already identified. But this was natural, not conforming to any of the others already identified. And more importantly, it didn't conform to the standard chemical and geological profile of the planetoid itself. Whatever it was, it was not native, and it had been deposited recently enough that the environment system hadn't purged it yet.

From the other side of that "doorway"?

Ey ran the sample through a full chemical and geo analysis, shunting the results into a new subroutine that would compare it against all known worlds, moons, or asteroids known to be inhabited by humans, setting the comparison to notify em with results.

Now. DNA.

This ey had confidence in, in terms of es ability to scan and sift through what the others had found. The DNA sniffers in es sensor package were top of the line because they often came in handy in their occasional forays into dealings with those who delved into the moral grey of the Pan Galactum's economy. And the evidence they had collected looked to be a gold mine.

Traces and comparisons flew across the subroutine, the colour and texture of the data flashing and flaring like a spray of shooting stars, as es code evaluated each full and partial sample against all the others. The sorting sequence seemed to Vrick to take forever, at least two or three minutes, before slotting into a configuration that reminded em of scattered constellations — a galaxy of genetic code.

The sortation subroutine had arranged the information in a neat pattern showing the number of distinct, verifiably individual traces.

Four. And two of those I recognize right off the bat. As to the other two, hold that thought.

There was also a wide range of incomplete and degraded fragments, but considering that the hab dome had history, it was no great surprise traces might be left behind. Ey ran what analysis ey could using a wide range of tools, and 89.76% of the traces came back as showing signs of vacuum degradation. And it was logical to assume the atmosphere in the hab dome had been either purged or stored after the last legitimate users had left it behind.

But the rest of those partial results, while inconclusive, showed no signs of vacuum or filtration degradation. There had been others there, but they had somehow managed to obscure or destroy their DNA traces. And ey had a short list of possibilities as to what had caused it.

A thought opened modelling code that was able to at least extrapolate some detail about the possessors of these specific genomes.

That left em with two unknown DNA traces, both XY. All ey needed now was access to the Galactum's genetic database.

And there's the rub.

Even with es advanced slicing skills, that database had the most sophisticated security protocols anywhere. The administrators of the Pan Galactum hadn't gone so far as to create any kind of genetic database of its citizens, being all too aware of the potential privacy and rights violations that could create. Not that ey wouldn't have sliced into it without the slightest moral qualm if it would have gotten them any closer to locating Keene and Sindel's kidnappers.

Galactum Security records might have DNA evidence on file, but it depended on whether any of these DNA traces belonged to someone who had committed crimes before. *Which is a pretty safe bet, considering the skill they seem to possess.* Not only were GalSec records notoriously hard to slice, but there were thousands of worlds with criminal evidentiary records to review. Without some way to narrow it down, even es formidable abilities wouldn't find them an answer in time.

If only I knew someone in close proximity to a GalSec station and advanced security clearance.

Oh, wait. I do.

But ey knew that was going to be a very dangerous pin to pull. And too big a decision to make on es own.

Chapter Seven

Vrick exploded out of interspace, practically on top of Hub's outer marker. Velocity sluiced from es drive field in a supernova of colour, flaring red to blue before finally fading to pastel wisps.

That will give the astronomers something to talk about.

A thought filed a flight plan in system to Hub's port, requesting a berth and landing clearance. Adjusting course for the most efficient trajectory, ey set es normal space drive for the best possible speed.

At the same time, ey concentrated on initiating the process of reviving Lexa-Blue and Ember.

Time to thaw the meat.

Ey was already raising es internal temperature back to optimal and taking the crash fields down to standard inertial dampening. Biosensor data flooded es consciousness, letting em know both Ember and Lexa-Blue were within safety zones as far as their response to the heavy sedation and accelerations. They were both a bit dehydrated, but that was to be expected. Ey sent a command to the auto-doc, and it prepared restorative solutions in the proper nutrient concentrations for their individual body chemistries. There was a soft, satisfying clink as the completed vials slotted into place, ready for distribution. Ey sent internal bots to retrieve the vials and deployed them, one to each of es meat colleagues' bedsides.

Against the sound of the small bots' motivators made as they trundled across es floors, ey heard the sound of a protracted and dramatic groan from Lexa-Blue's quarters.

And she wakes.

"Wakey wakey, soft and flakey," ey said through the vox in her room.

The only response was a burst of what sounded like a cross between gagging and coughing, as her lungs returned to full function. Ey dismissed a frisson of repulsion. *Flesh. Why?*

The bot in her room hummed forward, extending a manipulator with the vial of restorative held gently between its digits. Vrick watched her reach for it and press the tip against her neck. Her hiss of breath as she triggered the injector was in perfect syncopation with the sound it made as it released the cocktail of compounds into her system. She grunted and tossed the injector aside, bouncing it off the bot's dome onto the floor. The bot dutifully turned to retrieve it for disposal.

"Always so much drama with you," Vrick said. "Ember never gives me this much trouble."

And it was true, for ey was watching Ember's revival at exactly the same time. And he was stretching silently, accepting the flow of energy the restorative was giving him. He stretched his arms over his head and side to side, then stood, flexing his joints.

Lexa-Blue, on the other hand, had rolled over and stuffed her head under her pillow again.

Coffee. Definitely. And lots of it.

With a thought, ey added extra grounds to the brewer, right up to the limit that the intersection of their personal tastes would allow.

Ey allowed Lexa-Blue five minutes before unleashing the trumpeting of es alarm system.

∞

"I thought I told you to delete that audio file from your library," Lexa-Blue said as she came into the lounge.

"You did," Vrick said.

"So, why didn't you?"

"Is this the part where I remind you, for the 4,728th time that I don't take orders from you?" ey replied. "Half the time, I'm not actually even listening when you speak."

"Honestly, I'm pretty much the same," Ember said before taking a sip of his coffee. He'd already poured one for her and pushed it across the counter in her direction. She made a beeline for it and sighed beatifically at the first taste.

"This coffee is the only thing keeping me from killing you both," she said between sips.

"Isn't it cute that she thinks she could?" Vrick said to Ember. "Bless."

"You're safe," Ember said. "I might be concerned."

"She might be tough," Vrick said. "But you're sneakier."

Lexa-Blue slid her still three-quarters full mug across the counter in Ember's direction. "More, please. I promise not to kill you if you give me more."

"Where are we on the evidence we collected from that hab?" Ember said.

"I've been reviewing it all and organizing it the whole time we were in interspace," Vrick said. "DNA confirms Keene and Sindel were there, but other than that, only two confirmed samples."

"Wait," Ember said. "There were more of them there. We saw them going through. You had thermal traces of them."

"It was the blurs," Lexa-Blue said. "They don't just hide your identity visually. They destroy DNA traces too."

"Exactly," Vrick said. "For whatever reason, only two of them weren't wearing blurs, so they're the only ones who left any DNA behind. I'm guessing we surprised them, and they didn't have time to sterilize the scene before they left. I'll need some time in Hub's genetic databases to identify them, but it's something to go on."

"You need a warrant for that, don't you?" Ember asked, a sly grin on his face.

"Yes. Yes, I do," Vrick said. "And I will get right on that. What's giving me the most trouble is that thing you saw Keene and the others disappearing into. I've run the sensor data from your suits, but it's pretty limited in terms of what I'd need to really understand it."

"It looked an awful lot like a Gate, if you ask me," Lexa-Blue said, finally sounding cogent enough to be part of the conversation.

"That's it exactly," Ember agreed. "But that shouldn't even be possible, should it?"

"No, it shouldn't. But considering someone snatched Keene and Sindel out of ships transiting Gates, it's not a stretch to think they might have figured out something like what we all saw. Some kind of portal to another place," Vrick said. "I had my bots do a thorough scan when they went over that room. That was a solid wall with nothing beyond it other than what passes for atmosphere on that rock. There were some unusual radiation traces left behind, but nothing that made any sense. I compiled and transmitted them to Sei Li Ffiann as soon as we dropped back into normal space. He's working on them now and is expecting us once we land. Once we're in Hub's local sphere, it will be easier to slice into the databases we need to run the other evidence traces we found."

"What's our ETA?" Lexa-Blue asked.

"Thirty-two minutes, and we'll be on the pad," Vrick said. "Just after midday. Sei Li Ffiann has cleared his afternoon for us. I'm curious as to what he may have found. He sounded… distracted when I spoke with him."

"Just in time for a shower and something to eat before we land," she said.

"There are some leftover black ice noodles in stasis," Ember said. "Will those do?"

"Sold to the handsome thief," she said, heading aft to her quarters.

"Just put them in the cookbox," Vrick said. "I'll get them ready for you. Go make yourselves presentable. We have work ahead of us."

∞

When they arrived at Hetri Li Ffiann's office, his assistant ushered them in without even announcing them. They found him in the centre of the spacious office, surrounded by furiously dancing skeins of data that filled every corner of the room with lambent colours. As they watched, his eyes flicked from one stream of data to another, then back, the streams of information seeming to shift and recombine in response to his eye movements.

He looks completely swacked, Lexa-Blue said. *Last time I saw that look on someone's face, they were one stim away from the morgue.*

I'm afraid to disturb him, Ember said. *He looks like he'll go into shock if we interrupt.*

I'll send a nudge through his external comm, Vrick said. *Gently.*

Hetri's jittering motions calmed, and the dance of data stilled as he focussed his gaze on his guests for the first time and actually seemed to register their presence. His brows furrowed, still deep in thought.

"Where did you find all this?" he blurted.

"Nice to see you too," Lexa-Blue said.

Hetri shook his head. "I'm sorry. Thank you for coming. And thank you for bringing me this. Whatever it is."

"We were hoping you could tell us," Ember said.

"Some of it," Hetri said. "Maybe. There are elements I almost recognize, but they shouldn't be possible. Not on any scale this small. I mean, look at this."

Panes of data shifted, swirling, as three subsets enlarged while the others faded to a pale translucence.

"Your initial analysis was right. This looks an awful lot like the specific signature of Gate energy," Hetri said, coming closer to them. He extended one of his chair's manipulator arms, the fine digits at its end indicating specific readings. "This. And this. These are almost the same energy patterns we see as a Gate is powering up for transition."

"That makes sense," Ember said. "Considering we saw people using it to pretty much walk through a wall to who knows where."

"Yes, the harmonics are off. Just a bit," Hetri said. "It's definitely the same type of energy, but it has some very distinctive differences. Here. And here as well."

Streams of data highlighted and expanded even further.

"None of this should be possible," Hetri said. "Opening the Gates requires a huge amount of energy and a lot of mechanisms to ensure the targeting is precise and controlled. If this is some kind of down and dirty portal, it's a huge leap forward."

"If it works safely," Lexa-Blue said.

"Exactly," Hetri said. "If this is a legitimate advance of the tech, it needs to be tested. I mean, we're dealing with fundamental structures of spacetime here. Punching through them haphazardly without proper oversight and testing could do all kinds of irreparable harm to pretty much everything."

"Are we talking immediate danger?" Lexa-Blue asked.

"Not as far as I can tell, but I've never seen this before," Hetri said. "I can run some tests and some simulations, but I'm missing too much data to make any firm conclusions. It's all just theoretical at this point."

"It's not theoretical to Keene and Sindel," Lexa-Blue said, her voice sharp. "Whatever that thing is took them somewhere. And we've lost precious time getting here to try to get some answers as to where they might have ended up."

"If I might make a suggestion," Vrick said, accessing the office's internal system again.

"Please," Hetri said. "I'm at a loss as to how to proceed. I can run all the sims and variables I want, but there's so much going on here I have no idea where to start."

"The energy signatures are distinctive, correct?" Vrick said. "So, is it possible to search for instances of that particular resonance pattern? See where it's showing up or has shown up recently?"

Hetri blew air through his lips, crunching his face tight. The mechanisms that joined his manipulators to his chair rose and fell in a passable imitation of a shrug. "Maybe? I don't have to tell you how big the Pan Galactum is and how spread out all the worlds are. Any energy pattern you recorded would have started fading almost immediately."

"It was just a thought," Vrick said.

"I didn't say I couldn't try. I just said it's not going to be easy. The Gate network piggybacks a carrier signal along the same network of tightline relays that allows all the Galactum worlds to remain in touch without speed of light delays. I should be able to borrow some of the redundancy we have built into that system to at least search for instances of the energy pattern we're looking for. But it will take me some time to get everything calibrated properly and start the search. And the search is going to take time. But I have access to all the systems to make it happen. Sindel can take it out of my salary when we find her."

"Do it," Lexa-Blue said. "Even if it's a long shot, it's something."

"I'm on it," Hetri said. "I'll start putting the code together and send it to my best team."

His eyes closed, but they could see the rapid eye movements behind his eyelids as he used the motions to direct his interface to begin the preparations. Data pulsed with a new, throbbing rhythm across the displays that surrounded him. They watched him for a full minute or more, a thrum of tension connecting them as they waited for him to return his attention to them. Finally, his eyes opened. "Done. I've set up a feed to the search and any results it might turn up and subscribed you all to it."

"That was fast," Ember said.

"Yes, I am that good," Hetri replied. "I have a reputation as miracle worker to maintain."

Their nodes registered the new access point, giving them a warm, bright entry to the search and the data points already churning away within the newly created subroutine. Lexa-Blue shunted it to the side, but both Ember and Vrick touched the access point with a thought, opening the menu and testing what the interface offered them. In one corner, a progress meter shifted only slightly off of zero.

"I'm wondering something," Ember said. "Whatever this energy trace is, whatever we saw Keene be taken through, it must be complicated, right?"

"Very," Hetri said. "You've all seen how complex the machinery is for the Gates themselves. Whatever this is, there must be some kind of generator or machinery that's opening it."

"That's what I thought," Ember replied. "It requires tech to open the portal and generate whatever energy they're harnessing to get where they're going."

"Absolutely," Hetri said. "Even if they're ignoring every safety protocol in the book to punch open these portals, they'd definitely need equipment to do it."

"But where are they *getting* it?" Ember asked. "That's what I don't understand. This is specialized stuff we're talking about. You can't just pop out to the store and buy a portal machine."

"Which means whoever is behind this must know what they're doing," Vrick said.

"Exactly," Ember said. "And that goes a long way to narrow down our suspect pool. There can't be that many people in the Galactum with that kind of specialized knowledge."

"I'll start running down some names," Vrick said.

"And while you're at it, start looking for suppliers who could have provided the components needed to put this kind of thing together," Hetri said. "I'm sending you a list of things they'd probably need to pull this off."

"Don't limit yourself to suppliers either," Ember said. "Check for thefts, break-ins, hijacked shipments. Sales would be tracked, and anyone looking at the purchase orders might be able to put things together. And I doubt our friends are waiting for standard shipping. But if they're nicking them illegally, chances are the trails would be so diffuse and spread out, no one would be looking closely enough to draw the right conclusions."

"I knew keeping you around would come in handy," Lexa-Blue said. "You're sneaky."

"You think like a criminal," Hetri said. "Definitely a devious mind."

Ember exchanged a pointed glance with Lexa-Blue. "Just imaginative, I guess." He frowned. "Is there some way you can slice the GalSec databases? Get me criminal records of similar crimes? If I can see what's being stolen and where, I might be able to draw some conclusions. Or at least make some educated guesses."

"I am not hearing this," Hetri said. "I cannot be a person who is hearing this."

"Oh, relax, Bunky," Lexa-Blue said. "We'll make a felon out of you yet."

I think it's time to make that call, Vrick said privately to Ember and Lexa-Blue. ***I just hope he's willing and able to help.***

∞

After a few hours of rest and some more ration packs, Keene and Sindel had been pulled from the dusty barracks room and taken to what must have been the main mechanism room for Ckurahris's plans.

The room was huge, spreading out around them, and was packed with machinery unlike anything Keene had ever seen. When he looked to Sindel, her face showed no signs of the surprise he felt.

She noticed his expression. "I've seen tech like this before. It's definitely built off the Gate mechanisms. And I recognize the rest of it from the plans that got Astel fired. And the data packet he showed me when I got here. It's a monstrosity, but if he can get it working, it's going to do exactly what he says it will do."

"Lovely," Keene said, his tone indicating it was anything but.

"Here we go," Sindel said, then stepped into the room. "Astel. Where do you want me?"

With another of his snake smiles, Ckurahris summoned her over to the main bank of equipment and its access terminal.

Before she could join him, Keene laid his hand on her arm. "You sure about this?"

"If I don't do this, Ckurahris will hurt you. And he'll go on hurting you in ways I don't even want to think about. I will not have that on my conscience. And I certainly don't want to have to explain to Lexa-Blue why I let it happen."

"I can take care of myself."

"We are prisoners," she snapped back. "Who knows where? Surrounded by guards who have no compunction about hurting or killing either of us if their boss decides he wants it to happen. We both know Lexa-Blue and Ember are doing whatever they can to find us. Whether they do or not remains to be seen. And if they do, whether they do it in time. I am vamping for time here in the only way I know how. And at the very least, it helps me understand what Ckurahris is doing and how he's doing it. Because if we get very, very lucky and don't die, then maybe I'll know how to deal with it."

Keene looked at her, seeing the fire burn in her eye. "Are you finished?"

Sindel took a deep breath and released it. "For now."

Keene watched as Sindel joined the others and received a short, hushed briefing. He saw her nod curtly, then watched as she darted from projection to projection, running multiple simulations with the data from Ckurahris's machines. She moved with a fierce energy and focus that he recognized more from Lexa-Blue's descriptions than from personal experience.

There was nothing he could do but wait on the sidelines, guard at his side, the hard muzzle of a shock stick against his ribs.

After several minutes, Sindel began opening panels and access ports all over the machinery, digging into the vast machine's mechanical guts.

Suddenly, he saw a shower of sparks and heard her cursing. She pulled herself out of the opening she had been exploring sucking on her fingers.

"Astel!" she shouted.

He turned from his place across the room, scowling.

Oh, he did not like that.

"I need more hands here," she said, ignoring his attitude. "Keene has training with tech. He can help. You can still have one of your goons hover over us. But I need help."

Ckurahris stared at her a moment, then with a sneer and a flick of his hand, indicated Keene's guard to escort him over.

"Always winning people over," Keene said. "Okay, so what do you need me to do?"

"Here." She reached into the spread of holos around them and grasped a specific combination of dial and meter, pulling it toward him. "Hand," she demanded, and he raised his right hand into a similar position as hers. With a flick of her wrist, the pattern of light left her hand and surrounded his.

"Now, what?"

"Watch this," she said, indicating the meter. "If the reading moves out of this range, use the control until it's back. I need to run some sims to try and understand how this process even works, let alone what's going wrong with it."

For the next hour, Keene struggled to split his attention between the task he had been assigned and watching Sindel run simulation after simulation, the light of the holos blaring colours that filled every corner of the room.

"What... is that?" Keene asked.

"Focus!" Sindel barked at him, and he noticed the meter he was supposed to be monitoring had slipped out of the target range. He moved his hand and the readings stabilized.

"What it is," Sindel said, her voice even, if taut with concentration, "is multidimensional, interspatial nexus geometry. It makes spaceships go, and it makes the Gates work. And it seems it makes whatever the hells Ckurahris is doing work as well."

"I'm a tech guy. I have a pretty good understanding of the mechanisms of an interspace drive, and I even get the basics of how the Gate hardware works. But this..."

"I know," Sindel said. "Even when you have the right kind of mind and math to grasp it, it's pretty thrilling stuff. All the layers of substrate that underpin the tiny sliver of the universe we can perceive."

"Universes," Keene corrected.

Sindel turned from her displays and smiled at him. "I stand corrected. I suppose as one of the first people to encounter another universe, I should remember that."

"Especially if what Ckurahris said about what he's undertaking is true."

"Oh, from what I've been able to glean from all this" — Sindel waved a hand at the swirl of multihued data — "he has figured out how. And he's made the first steps. It's just up to us now to figure out how he can do it without liquefying himself and his goons."

"Do we really have to?"

Sindel barked out a harsh laugh. "Oh, how I wish we didn't have to. But that ship appears to have sailed."

"Hey, we're not done yet. Give us some credit. There's still time."

"I hope you're right," Sindel said, furrowing her brow as she concentrated on the displays again.

Keene turned his attention back to his own task, shifting his hand until the light of his controls went from amber back to green.

∞

"You need me to *what?*" Daevin said, slipping out of the meeting hall into the corridor beyond. As the door closed, the sound of the speaker went silent. He hoped he'd somehow misheard. Vrick's sigil, a swirl of nebula colours, hovered in the tightline link open in his field of vision as he stopped just out of the flow of traffic in the hallway.

"I just need you to get me access to the GalSec evidentiary database through that station on Scholus," Vrick said.

"That's what I thought you said," Daevin said, incredulous. "I'm flattered you think I have the power to somehow circumvent the chain of evidence, not to mention the dozens of privacy statutes that would violate. But that's not something I can do."

"I've formulated several methods of approach that show very high probability of success."

"It's not your skills I'm questioning here," Daevin said, rubbing the bridge of his nose. "There's a lot more to it than that. I'm a member of the Galactum Council. I can't just push my way through any law I please.

It goes against the oath I took. It goes against everything I'm supposed to stand for."

Vrick was silent, and the pulsing colours of es sigil stilled to a slow, pulsing turn. After a moment, ey spoke. "I suppose that's where we differ. I have no institutions to swear oaths to. I have only the beings that I love. My own Kith, and the humans I choose to call my friends. I would swear one of your human oaths to them. To protect them. To never rest if they needed my help. To do whatever I could to protect them from harm. But I don't have a 'position' to worry about. And I suppose I'm glad about that right now. I shall find another way, Councillor. Good day."

"Wait," Daevin said, cheeks burning with some potent combination of anger and embarrassment. "That was dirty dice you just threw there, old friend. Let me see what I can do."

"Thank you," Vrick said, sigil flashing in colours that Daevin could have sworn were full of affection somehow. "I'll do what I can to explore all possibilities until I hear from you."

"You'll hear from me soon," Daevin said, cutting the link. Behind him, he heard the door open and turned to see Rogan emerging, a quizzical look on his face.

"Come on," Daevin said. "I need some air."

He outlined Vrick's request to Rogan as they made their way out of the conference hall onto the street.

"That's quite a request," Rogan said as Daevin accessed Know-It-All to summon a taxi to take them back to the GalSec depot. He sent the confirmation and arrival time to Daevin, frowned at the offered arrival time, frustrated at the wait even though he knew it was perfectly reasonable given the time of day.

"That, my friend, is an understatement," Daevin said.

"I mean, this is Keene we're talking about though, right?" Rogan said, and Daevin could hear his own thoughts echoing back at him.

"Yes. It is."

"And you'd do pretty much anything for him, right?"

"Of course, I would." Daevin scrubbed his face with his hands. "Of course, I'm going to do what I can to help. This is just… so much to ask. I worked so hard to keep Brighter Light together. And I worked just as hard at my duties on the Council."

"And doing this means you could lose all of that."

"Exactly," Daevin said.

Rogan didn't respond, just looked at him.

"Not that it matters," Daevin said finally. "Whatever it is. For Keene, I'll do it. Come on, let's go."

The local innernet pinged to let them know their taxi had arrived, sending him the number of the car and where it would be waiting for them. Words tumbled through his mind as he tried to formulate some way of framing an argument convincing enough to get Chief Edneia to part with the information Vrick and the others needed.

As he stood at the curb, scanning for the cab, Rogan joined him, taking a position just to his left, but they didn't speak.

Finally, just as Daevin felt his skin begin to crawl with the wait, the ovoid capsule cab appeared at the end of the street, its registration number a neat overlay in the corner of his vision.

As he watched the cab manoeuvre through traffic, Daevin stepped even closer to the edge of the road, as if that would somehow shorten the trip, bringing him to Chief Edneia that much sooner. But as the cab pulled up to meet them, Rogan actually reached out and pulled him back a step, as he was within range of the cab's door striking him as it slid open.

"Thanks," he said, his hand resting on Rogan's a moment. Rogan's only response was a concerned smile.

Daevin sent their destination to the cab's LI, and it hummed out into traffic as soon as they were settled in their seats.

"What are you going to tell her?" Rogan asked as the buildings of Scholus's campus slid by them.

"I wish I knew," Daevin said. "I mean, I know why it's important to get the information. It's just about the most important thing in the world. To me, anyway. But to her? To anyone else but us? How do I justify handing this information over to people completely outside the legal system?"

"But that's the point, isn't it?" Rogan asked. "Everything they've done, all the times they've stopped terrible things from happening, they've been able because they were outside the system, outside the process. And you told me yourself that the Council and GalSec look the other way as much as they can because of the results that Keene, Lexa-Blue, Ember, and Vrick manage to bring. You even brought forth that motion to formally deputize them."

"Which failed spectacularly," Daevin said.

Rogan tilted his head with a small smile. "True."

"And cost me some allegiances on the Council that I'm still trying to mend."

"All of that may be true," Rogan countered. "But it was a good idea even if they couldn't see it."

"I can't deny the good they've done," Daevin said, staring out the cab's window.

"Neither can I," Rogan said, a smile in his voice. For it had been the Maverick Heart crew along with Daevin and Sindel who had saved him and his people when they had found themselves suddenly lost in the Pan Galactum.

Daevin turned to him, and the creases of worry smoothed for a moment, and he almost smiled. "I suppose we both have a lot to be grateful to them for."

"We do. And so do a lot of other people, even if they never know it. So, we do what we can." Rogan shifted in his seat. "That being said, if you can't convince them to give you the information legitimately, I may be able to get it for you another way."

Daevin's eyes widened, then he dropped his chin, rubbing the bridge of his nose. "Are you saying what I think you're saying?"

"I am. I may not be near the slicer Vrick is, but I got a good look at the systems this Sec outpost is using while I was taking those readings. And I'm pretty sure I can get around them if I have to."

"Don't tell me more. Please." Daevin ran his hands through his hair and sighed deeply. "I am literally supposed to oppose that kind of thing. It's in the oath I took when I joined the Council. But the number of times I've looked the other way…"

"Sometimes the thing that's right isn't the thing the rules tell you to do," Rogan said. "You're talking to someone that grew up in a community that had to scrape for every little trace of basic subsistence. We couldn't even have children unless someone died and made an opening. We did what we had to do to survive, to make lives for ourselves, and to make those lives mean anything at all. So, if me breaking some rules will save our friends' lives and stop whatever new crisis is looming, then I'll do it."

Daevin was quiet a moment, then laid his hand on Rogan's arm. "Stop it. You're making me look bad."

"Not yet," Rogan answered. "There's still time."

The cab pulled up outside the GalSec depot, and they stepped out, Daevin pinging Chief Edneia via Know-It-All as they crossed to enter the building, flagging it with his highest priority code.

As they entered, she was already emerging from the door leading to her office. Daevin was not encouraged by the look on her face that spoke of frustration and trepidation to be seeing him again so soon.

"Councillor Adisi," she said, her forehead creased into a frown. "How can I help?"

'How can I help?' sounds suspiciously like 'what the hells do you want now?'

"Chief, I have another favour to ask of you. And it's a big one."

∞

Ember strode up the ramp into the Maverick Heart, Lexa-Blue just behind him, a keen anticipation thrumming through him at the thought of having access to what might get him back in his element. With those case files, he might be able to use his own experience as a grifter to see a pattern that might lead to their quarry's method of obtaining the materials needed to pull off Keene and Sindel's kidnappings and whatever their endgame actually was.

He entered the ship's main lounge. "Do we have it?" he asked, knowing that if they did, Vrick would have already told him.

"It's just coming in," Vrick answered, not commenting on Ember's unnecessary question. "I have Daevin on the tightline now."

Daevin's holo image shimmered into the space at the fore of the lounge.

"You got it," Ember said.

"I did," Daevin said, his voice subdued.

Ember felt Lexa-Blue come up beside him. "But what did it cost you?" she asked.

At the tone in her voice, Ember really looked at Daevin, taking in his drawn and pale face. Getting them access to those files was definitely going to cost him.

"It doesn't matter," Daevin said. "Vrick should have everything I could get my hands on. I hope it helps. Let me know if there's anything I can do to help." He paused. "Anything at all."

"We will," Lexa-Blue said, and Ember heard the subdued note in her voice. The holo compressed and faded out as the tightline channel closed.

"The transfer is complete," Vrick said. "How do you want it?"

"Put it all up, please," Ember said. "I need to feel my way through it, see what stands out."

"You've got it," Vrick said, projecting the files into the empty air where Daevin's image had stood. The sheer volume of information filled the entire forward area of the lounge, collated in three dimensions. "Navigation and selection controls are here."

In Ember's vision, an overlay showed the basic information and how he could control and sort through the data. "Thanks, Vrick."

"I thought you were the smart one," Lexa-Blue said from the galley, where she was making coffee.

"Not for this," Vrick said. "This sort of thing is all Ember's sector of expertise. I can search it faster if I know the criteria, but it's as much instinct and experience as it is knowledge. He'll be able to see connections I would probably miss. He is our resident master thief, after all."

"That he is."

As Ember perused the volume of case data, familiarizing himself with the basic shape of it before starting his deep dive, he half listened to Lexa-Blue rummaging through the cupboards in the galley. In the beginnings of his hyperaware state, he recognized the sound of her taking a coffee mug out, then returning it and opening another cupboard. He heard the clink of a bottle against a glass.

"Snapwine?" Vrick said. "That's your contribution to the cause?"

Ember heard her pour a glass and take a swig, sighing with pleasure at the taste.

"Hey, like you said. This is his specialty. When you need muscle, I'll be ready."

Ember heard the coffee maker chirp, smelling the rich aroma. Then Lexa-Blue was at his side, putting the cup in his hand. As he took it, she rested her hand on his shoulder a moment.

"Dig deep, squib," she said, her voice soft. "We're running out of options."

He nodded grimly and turned his attention back to the daunting spread of data in front of him, its mass so great it curved the gravity of his virtual workspace.

Well, you wanted it all. Daevin was as good as his word. Here goes.

A command stripped away all misdemeanours and crimes unrelated to theft, while another brought up the list of the materials most likely needed for creation of the technology that seemed to be in play. In Ember's virtual workspace, data flowed like glowing water, reshaping into new patterns. He sorted again, this time to remove those GalSec had already solved, setting them aside for the moment.

Much more manageable. The trouble is a lot of the structural material is used in other projects too. And they're valuable. Which means there's probably a steady stream of them running through grey markets like Sombra.

Next, he cross-referenced the locations of the thefts with the star map of the Galactum, backdating the map to correspond with the dates of the crimes. Patterns shifted and moved, showing the relative galactic positions of the sites as spacetime itself expanded, shifting all of the stars and planets.

Vrick, can you run some interspace calculations against some destinations and dates? he said.

Of course. What am I looking for?

I want to know which of these thefts would have been in easy reach of Sombra and other markets like it. I'll include the list.

Hit me, Vrick said.

Ember compiled the data and pushed it over to Vrick, then turned his attention back to the list of other thefts, looking for any commonalities or patterns he could see.

Not even a minute later, Vrick sent him back the results of es search. Ember opened the results and scanned through them, then pushed them off to one side of the workspace.

Okay, I need another one. Can you take these locations and see if there are any common interspace vectors or lanes that would have made travel easier at the time?

On it.

Mere seconds passed this time. **What next?** Vrick asked.

Run them in terms of date and show me the planets that could have been reached by interspace in the time intervals between the crimes.

Ember had learned enough about the basics of interspace travel since living with Vrick and the others to know that the otherworldly hyper-realm, that had allowed humans to travel between the stars faster than the speed of light, was no calm thoroughfare. Eddies and currents and constantly shifting patterns sometimes left planets almost unreachable without careful calculations and piloting skills.

He lost track of time as he pulled and tweaked at the datasets, rearranging them in every combination he could think of. He tried flow after flow, combination after combination, trying to tease meaning from them, trying to fire his instincts, honed from so many years on the grift.

At some point, he became aware of a bowl in his hand, its contents half-eaten. The pungent, spicy scent tickled his nose. Rizotchki. One of his favourites, especially the way Lexa-Blue made it. He took a bite, then another, conscious this time of the rich mix of flavours, with a sharp tang of citrus aftertaste. The brief break — the rush to his senses — cleared his head, and he saw a new way to attack the data. He looked around for somewhere to put the bowl down, not wanting to move and break the flow of new inspiration coming to him. In an instant, Lexa-Blue was at his side, taking the bowl and then moving away without a word.

His hunger sated, he dove back into the work again, searching, reviewing, and rearranging the data in ever more complicated and intuitive ways.

And then he stopped, the panes around him going suddenly static around one highlighted set of planetary coordinates and routing data, the others ranked down in ever lower probabilities. He took in a deep breath, his neuropathy singing along his prosthetics. "This one."

Lexa-Blue came to his side again, taking it all in.

"Why not this one?" Lexa-Blue said, highlighting the next lower in priority. "This looks like a way better opportunity."

"You're thinking like me," Ember said. "If it was my score, I'd be all over that one. But whoever we're dealing with isn't like me. I was running grifts before I hit puberty. And whoever came up with this isn't a grifter. They're smart. Like Sindel smart. Someone that smart looks at the world and at probabilities in a whole different way. Running a good con is as much about instinct as it is about information. We're never going to find them if I think like me. I have to think like them."

"You're sure?"

"No. But everything inside me is saying that's the one."

Lexa-Blue regarded him silently for a moment. "Okay, then. That's good enough for me. And it's not like we have much choice in the matter."

"Thanks for the vote of confidence," Ember said, drily. "I appreciate it so—"

His voice was cut off by the shriek of an alarm.

Crash fields snapped up around Ember and Lexa-Blue, surrounding them with pliant, shock absorbing energy.

"Brace for impact," Vrick said, as Ember felt es hull thrum with the concussive energy, even through the crash fields. "Everybody hold on."

Chapter Eight

It was over in the slow blink of a human eye. Whatever had hit them had passed, moving off into the void beyond. As the crash fields dissipated, Vrick's interior was eerily quiet as es systems cycled back up to normal operations and ey ran through a litany of post-emergency diagnostics. At the same time, ey extended long-range sensors in both the direction the distortion wave had come from and the direction it was headed.

"What the ruck was that?" Lexa-Blue said, stretching her muscles after the sudden pressure of the crash fields.

"Some kind of space quake," Vrick said as data poured in through all of the various sensory inputs.

"Space… quake?" Lexa-Blue said. "Space can quake? Why is this the first time I'm hearing about this?"

"You'll have to forgive me if incredibly rare and theoretical spacetime catastrophes don't come up in conversation that often," Vrick said, es voice testy. "Give me a minute, all right? I'm as mystified as you are."

In the instant it took Lexa-Blue to form her response, Vrick sensed the network of micro-fractures along the starboard dorsal panels of es hull on the side that faced the spacetime disruption. No surprise there. At least the repair systems were already knitting the plating back together and were showing nothing unusual in terms of radiation or particulates.

Simultaneously, ey combed the quake's path for information on its trajectory and makeup. Data flooded into es mind, causing just as many questions as answers.

"Whenever you're ready to enlighten us, junkpile," Lexa-Blue said as she checked on Ember, who was rubbing the back of his neck.

"The good news is that I'm intact," Vrick said. "Or I will be once the repair nanites get done fixing my hull."

"And the bad news?" Ember asked.

"Well, from what I can gather, everyone else in a thousand light-year radius just got hit by a deep dimensional substrate shockwave."

"Which means what, exactly?" Lexa-Blue asked. "Dumb words, please."

"Some event exploded, for want of a better word, and rippled through about twelve different higher dimensions, causing a severe disruption to the basic structure of the universe."

"Different dimensions," Ember said. "Where did it start?"

The idea of other dimensions and realities was no longer that strange a thought for any of them to contemplate.

"I'm not sure. But it hit several other realities. At the same instant."

"What could have caused something like that?" Lexa-Blue asked.

"Your guess is as good as mine," Vrick said. "But if these readings I'm getting are correct, I'm reasonably sure of two things. One, it started here in this dimensional plane."

"Okay, that's bad," Lexa-Blue said.

"And two, there are distinct resonance trace commonalities to the readings you took back on that planet where we almost got Keene back. Traces which bear uncomfortable similarities to the energies of the Gates and the energy signatures of whatever was used to kidnap Keene and Sindel."

Lexa-Blue hissed through clenched teeth. "That is very bad. Did it actually come from there?"

"I'm running a trajectory scan in both directions, and I'm afraid so. It definitely originated from those galactic coordinates. And there's more."

"More?" Ember said.

"Have a look," Vrick said, activating the main holo display.

The holo filled with a black background of sparkling stars. Spinning and tumbling before them was a sea of jagged, rocky chunks. As they watched, fragments of debris caromed into each other, shattering even further in a slow, churning dance. Suffusing the debris field was a pulsing, yellow-orange energy. The depth of the destruction was staggering when they registered the flow of scale data skimming along the edge of the holo.

"Where's the planet?" Ember asked.

"That *is* the planet," Vrick said. "What's left of it. Whatever hit us erupted up into our dimension, along with several others, from inside it. Possibly somewhere on the surface."

"Holy macros," Lexa-Blue said. "Could it have been that portal thing we saw? The one they used to get away with Keene and Sindel?"

"Even with all my knowledge of upper dimensional astrophysics, I have no idea," Vrick said. "The readings are definitely similar. There's just a lot more of them. And the timing is highly suspect. If I was one to bet, I'd be pretty comfortable laying down my credits on it."

"Okay," Lexa-Blue said, as if that somehow made the information make sense. "We know where it came from and the direction it was headed. Which is basically, everywhere. How bad is it?"

"I've got reports coming in through Know-It-All from all across this quadrant. Ships reporting damage. But from what I can see, they're getting the help they need."

"What about the planets?" Ember asked. "Or the non-planetary habitats?"

"I'm seeing interference patterns on my long-range sensors," Vrick said. "The energy of the quake seems to be dissipating. In this dimension at least. I have no way of knowing how deep the extra-dimensional reverberations might go. And it looks like the planetary masses themselves are doing a good job protecting their populations. But if I had to guess, that is because that planetoid was so small and so isolated. If it had been closer or of greater mass, we wouldn't be so lucky."

"So, we definitely need to find Keene and Sindel as soon as possible," Lexa-Blue said. "If whoever has them keeps using that portal thing, and on one of the more populated inner worlds, things go to bollocks real fast."

"That's the conclusion I came to," Vrick said. "Though it's really no more than an educated guess right about now."

"It's the best we have to go on," Ember said. "And if you believe in my educated guesses, then I am ready to believe in yours."

"So, what do we do now?" Lexa-Blue asked.

"We go ahead with Ember's plan," Vrick said. "Being there when this gang of slugs makes their next theft is going to be the one thing we can do to get a little closer to catching them."

"I have to agree," Ember said. "I'd stake what little remains of my reputation on the fact that this is going to be where they hit."

He waved his hand, and the data on his conclusions appeared in a display.

"My gut tells me they'll hit this ship when it lands on Thesia. There's a massive delivery of raw materials and components expected there in four days' time. Procedures say it needs to be held in the free-trade zone for inspection before being officially allowed through customs into the main distribution terminal. That's where I'd hit it. The free-trade zone has separate security teams, but they're overworked contractors. There's a history of labour disputes. Which means the goods will be easier to get at because this is the one big shipment that will be on site. Everything else will either be processed through or won't arrive for at least another few days. There's a window that's the best opportunity to jack the goods before they disperse out into the system."

"Then that's where we hit them," Lexa-Blue said. "Have you got a plan?"

"The germ of one," Ember said. "I'm working out the details. I've got four days. Can you get us there in time, Vrick?"

In a moment too quick to be perceived by the humans, Vrick checked the repair status of es hull, and saw that all readings showed em ready for interspace.

"Just watch me."

∞

The conference on Scholus was finally winding down, and Daevin felt a deep fatigue as he finished his last session, peeling the microphone tab from his throat and handing it back to the moderator before leaving the stage.

His talk on advances in medical technology Brighter Light was about to implement after final testing, part of a larger presentation on medical innovations in general, had gone well. The question and answer period after had been thought-provoking. But it didn't really surprise him. The conference was known for the intelligence and curiosity it fostered in the innovation community.

But it had been hard to maintain concentration with the spectre of Keene's disappearance weighing so heavily on his mind. He'd done all he could, but after using his influence to get Ember, Lexa-Blue, and Vrick the data the needed, they'd gone silent. He'd heard nothing about what, if any, benefit they'd gleaned from what even he knew was an outrageous display of his own influence.

And, truth be told, on top of his ongoing worry, it stung.

He'd done everything he could to help them from where he was, right up to potentially damaging his own standing on the Council. He didn't doubt repercussions would be coming from how he had used his position on the Council to persuade Chief Edneia to give him access to GalSec files. He couldn't help but wonder if he'd still be a councillor when the dust settled.

He pushed the thoughts down, wending his way through the mass of people coming in and out of the meeting room as the crowd shifted into and out of the space for the next session. Outside in the hall, he took a moment to reorient himself, suddenly unsure of the layout of this section of the campus.

I am tired.

The exit to the quad was to his right and down one level to the lobby. Rather than wait with the crowd at the bank of lifts, he took the long, curving ramp that skirted the lobby area, emerging into the warm light of Scholus's primary sun.

His node pinged with Rogan's position, and he turned to see the other man seated on a bench, the predominant silver in his hair gleaming. As he approached, Rogan looked up.

"How did it go?"

Daevin shrugged. "It was fine. The audience listened. We talked. They asked questions."

"Intelligent questions, I hope," Rogan said, grinning.

"At this type of conference, they almost always are. Sometimes, I wish someone would come up with something completely off the wall."

"Be careful what you wish for. Is Moonshadow okay with you?"

Daevin nodded. They'd discovered the small café on the third day of the conference — one of those little hidden delights that combined ambience and a menu that was solid across the board. Whenever they managed to connect, which meant when Daevin wasn't in fancy official dinners or luncheons, they dined there.

The little café was busier than usual due to the increased crowds the conference had brought to the Scholus campus, but they were able to find a table along the side wall, moving through the press of people to hurriedly lay claim to it when they saw its occupants getting up to leave.

The daily menu appeared on the table's surface for their consideration. As they perused the day's offerings, a server brought them water with a beaming, if harried, greeting, then disappeared back into the crowd. Within a few minutes, they had both decided and submitted their order to the kitchen through the table's interface.

"You're still worried about Keene and Sindel aren't you?" Rogan said.

"How could I not be?" Daevin answered. "There's been no word since…" His voice trailed off.

"Since Lexa-Blue asked you for a favour that could ruin your entire career?" Rogan asked.

Daevin looked at him sharply, but there was no judgement or recrimination in Rogan's face.

Rogan lifted his hands, palms toward Daevin in a gesture of submission. "Hey, you won't get any criticism from me. And you won't hear me criticize her either."

"I know," Daevin said. "If the situation had been reversed, I'd have asked her for whatever it took to get Keene back."

"And she would do it. Hells, she probably is already doing it."

Daevin felt a sick tremor in his gut. Knowing Lexa-Blue and Ember, if the information he had provided them had any actual use, they were probably haring off in some half-cocked, incredibly dangerous plan to rescue Keene and Sindel, and that was why he hadn't heard from them.

"Hey," Rogan said, as if reading deep into Daevin's thoughts. "If anyone can get Keene and Sindel back, they can."

Daevin felt a kink between his shoulders loosen. It was true. He'd never have said it openly, but he trusted Lexa-Blue, Vrick, and Ember in this kind of situation far more than he trusted GalSec. When his own family was at stake, the rules could get sucked down a singularity.

"You're right. If anyone can untangle this, it's them. It's the waiting, the not knowing."

"But that can't be a new thing for you," Rogan said. "How many years have you led Brighter Light now? You know there are always going to be things out of your control, times you just have to wait for the answer to come to you. No matter how much you want it, you just have to let it ride."

In that moment, Daevin saw something in Rogan's eyes that he didn't reveal often. Something they both shared as leaders responsible for other people's lives. Leaders who had weathered crises and had paid their dividends in blood and lost lives. That ghost haunted Rogan sometimes, Daevin knew all too well. Even now, with Rogan's shipmates safe here, building new lives as part of the Pan Galactum, Daevin wondered if Rogan truly rested easy, truly trusted in his new life.

Daevin felt his anxiety ease somewhat. It still sat there, a restless bristle in his belly, but its voice quieted somewhat. All he could do was wait. Even his love for Keene, and in a different way, for Lexa-Blue, Vrick, and even Ember, couldn't change that.

"Chin up, my friend," Rogan said, resting a hand on Daevin's arm. "Have a little faith." He pulled his hand back and stood up. "Have to use the facilities and wash my hands. Be right back."

As he waited for the food and for Rogan's return, Daevin looked out through the panorama of the café's curving windows at the green space beyond, taking in the warmth of the sun, letting it nurture the hope and patience he was trying to cultivate down deep.

The concussion wave hit like a god-sized fist, impossibly seeming to come from all sides at once and hitting him deep within his cells. The café heaved in its wake, as did the planet beyond, wrenching through more dimensions than humans could perceive.

Followed by silence.

∞

"And how did you spend your summer vacation, Keene?" Keene said, holding his hand on a control and watching a readout at Sindel's request. She didn't even look up from her work. "Why, I helped a megalomaniac break reality. How about you?"

"I don't like it any more than you do, okay? If I don't help Ckurahris, you get more broken bones. Or worse. At least with our hands deep in his tech, we're both alive and well and have some time to think."

Her hands danced over the controls of the terminal, causing various readings to shift in rhythm. "Plus, the more I know about how the hells he plans on pulling off this plan of his, the better chance we have of maybe stopping him somewhere along the way."

She was barely paying attention to him, completely focussed on the instrumentation beneath her hands, and it worried him. While he definitely wasn't interested in getting any more bones broken, the thought of being used as a fulcrum against her to get her help with this outlandish scheme infuriated him. And it didn't help that he could see just how hard she was pushing herself. He couldn't help but wonder if part of her inquisitive, scientific brain was pushing her to solve the problem just for the sake of doing so.

"Sindel," he said, but she didn't even look up. Didn't even seem to have heard him at all, if he was honest with himself.

"You," she barked, snapping fingers at Ckurahris's assistant, Wols. "Watch that level. Increase the power flow and route it through the secondary buffer. Not the primary. Loop it through and see what that gives us. Now!"

Keene abandoned trying to get her attention for the moment. She was intent on her latest attempt to stabilize the quick fix she had used to facilitate their escape that had somehow kept them from all being turned into unstable molecular goo.

"Okay, these readings look good," Sindel said. "Bring the system online and set up the test run."

The Infinite Heist

Keene knew to stay out of the way while the test was running. As he watched, the techs powered up the system, the equipment that snaked around the room humming with life as energy poured through the tangle of linkages. As the power grew, he felt the deep subsonic vibration grow along with it, setting his teeth on edge.

"Align the sensors," Sindel said. "Open the portal on my mark. Three... two... one... mark."

The roiling, pearlescent energy spread across the wall like oil skimming across water, then settled into another portal, this time with a thickly bluish cast to it. Whatever was on the other side of it, Keene knew it was no longer a part of this universe.

"Sensors online and ready," one of the techs said.

"Initiate the tissue surrogate sensor and send it in," Sindel said, her voice tight.

A sinuous, multi-jointed armature extended from the equipment, reaching for the portal's energy. There was a flashing crackle of energy as the sensor module at the armature's tip touched the energy of the portal, but it flared and was gone.

"Sensor function nominal. Readings are starting to come in. Sim is showing positive cohesion on the other side," the tech said.

"Good start," Sindel said, her tense voice only a fraction calmer. "Give it a full cycle, then bring it back."

The room went silent as they waited, the glowing counter in the air above the portal counting down. The wait was excruciating.

Finally, the digits hit zero.

"Okay," Sindel said. "Bring it back."

The sensor armature retracted, folding in upon itself as it brought its payload back from whatever world lay beyond the portal. Sindel and the two techs at her side huddled over the sensor's monitor panel as the readings from it dumped data into the system's innernet.

"Pseudo-life sensor is showing point oh four four," Wols said, and Keene would have known from his tone the test wasn't successful even if Sindel hadn't briefed him on her target range.

Sindel swore. At least that's what Keene assumed, for the words were in a language he didn't recognize.

"That translates to—" the tech started to say, but she cut him off.

"Advanced molecular decay. Not total loss of cohesion, but bad enough. Whatever goes through would come back whole. At least on the outside. But not for long."

She sagged, and Keene saw the fatigue take her over. Whether she was just working to barter for their lives or if she'd just gotten caught up in the intellectual challenge of it all, she'd been working non-stop, and it had finally caught up with her.

He didn't have the heart to tell her that even if she managed to succeed, they were both as good as dead.

"Okay, bring up the full dataset and the last set up adjustments and we'll go again," she said, straightening up, a fierce determination in her eyes.

"No," Keene said, going to her side. "You are going to take a break. Get something to drink, get some food. Maybe a nap."

His two guards moved to intercept him before he could reach her, stun batons coming up to cover him.

"I can't," she said. "I'm so close."

Keene frowned at her, then cast a withering scowl at the blank shimmering faces of the cloaked guards. "Look. She's no good to you if you run her into the ground. She's exhausted. And if she doesn't take a break, she's going to start making mistakes. Tell your boss she's made enough progress for now. And if she's fed and has a chance to rest, she's that much more likely to actually get him what he wants."

The two blurred forms hesitated, but then a voice spoke to them from the air around them.

"Let them."

And of course, Ckurahris is watching. He probably has been the whole time.

"Listen to him," Keene said. "That's what you're paid for, isn't it?"

They moved out of the way, and Keene was able to get to Sindel's side. "Come on."

"But..." she started to say, but he cut her off. He saw the lines of fatigue around her eyes, warring with the drive to crack the problem, to somehow save them both.

"Sindel. Come on. It can wait while you recharge."

He laid a gentle hand on her arm and led her away from the console, heading out of the room toward their cell. The two guards, hidden behind their blurs, fell into step behind them.

∞

The instant of silence shattered into a sudden welter of noise.

Screams. Sirens. The sound of chaos.

Okay, not dead. That's good.

Where he lay on the floor of the ruined café, Daevin cautiously tried to move, gauging the various pains that played across his body.

He checked his node, receiving a thorough accounting of his injuries. Nothing but scrapes and bruises, except for a gash in his palm where his water glass had been shattered by whatever the hells had hit him. Stern warnings across his vision advised him to have it disinfected and sealed as soon as possible.

I'll get right on that.

He looked around, finding a napkin that was probably the cleanest thing available, and he wrapped it tightly around his bleeding hand, wincing at the sharp pain.

Around him, the café was a tangle of upturned tables and debris. The wide windows that had provided such a beautiful view were now spidered with cracks where they hadn't shattered outright. His table had upended and tipped over on him, but he was able to lift it up from where it rested across his thighs.

I am getting too old for this.

Free of the debris, he pulled himself up, muscles all over his body howling in protest. Upright, he could get a better idea of what he and the other patrons were dealing with.

The café was a ruin. Shelves behind the bar had collapsed, dumping supplies everywhere. Some kind of unidentifiable, multicoloured sludge was oozing from behind the service area.

From his now standing position, he could see people already helping each other as best they could. Everywhere was the spatter of blood and the painful human sound of aftermath. Sights and sounds he was all too familiar with.

He took a breath in to steady himself against the sudden triggering of his own planet's past, pushing aside the electric miasma of blood, burning, and dust, to take in the air beneath the clash of odours.

As close to calm as he was going to get, he moved through the debris, checking on the wounded and the helpers, dispensing what first-aid knowledge he had, assisting when needed.

Thankfully, there were no fatalities, though some would be spending substantial time in regen treatments before they'd be back on their feet. Relief coursed through his system to know that even in the worst cases, it seemed likely all would recover.

Rogan!

The thought stabbed through him, followed by a burn of shame that he had forgotten about his friend in the chaos. Ruthlessly shoving it down, he picked his way back through the rubble toward the back of the café where the restrooms were.

The storage room to his left had collapsed completely, blue sky visible through the crumbled ceiling. His stomach clenched as he carefully clambered over the spilled containers of goods to the back hallway. He cursed as he slipped on a thick spill of dark brown liquid from the storage room and braced himself against the damaged walls to clamber past it.

Turning the last corner, his heart surged with relief. There was Rogan, dishevelled but conscious, helping a dazed woman who had collapsed against one of the remaining walls. As Daevin watched, Rogan offered her sips of water from a dusty bottle he had retrieved from a case that had spilled from storage. Daevin saw the scarlet blaze of blood from a head wound, bright against Rogan's silver hair.

"Rogan," Daevin said, his voice heaving with concern.

Rogan looked up, and his shoulders sagged as tension fled his body. He stood and walked toward Daevin, pulling him into a short, hard embrace.

"Your head," Daevin said as they separated. He reached back to check the wound.

"It's nothing," Rogan said. "I'm fine."

"You're not fine. You're going to need that fused. Any nausea? Blurred vision? Headache?"

"I don't have a concussion," Rogan answered. "Just a knock on my hard head."

"Still, we need to get that gash closed up," Daevin said, looking past Rogan to the woman he had been helping.

Rogan looked as well, then shook his head. "She's just shaken up, I think. We can get her checked out when the medics arrive. What the hells happened?"

"I wish I knew. Come on."

They picked their way back through the café and out on the street. In every direction vehicles were abandoned and askew, the usual neat lines of traffic crumbled into chaos. Up the face of every building were shattered windows, and clouds of dust and smoke rose in lazy columns off into the distance. Sirens wailed over the sound of wounded, frightened people.

"Not just the café, then," Rogan said. "Earthquake?"

Daevin shook his head. "This part of the planet is supposed to be tectonically stable. And look at the ground."

Rogan looked in the direction he was pointing.

"The ground is undisturbed. No crevices, no cracks in the road surfaces or in ground cover in the park. Whatever it was, it didn't come from the planet itself."

"How is that possible?" Rogan asked. "Everything should be torn apart?"

"If it was an earthquake yes, but if it was some kind of interspace phenomena or sub quantum event," Daevin's voice trailed off. "I've never seen anything like it."

"What could even do something like that?"

"I wish I knew," Daevin said. "Come on. We need to find someone to tend to that head wound. And then maybe Chief Edneia has any idea what's going on."

∞

Twilight faded on the planet Thesia, becoming night. The ever-present chill in the air deepened, turning residual heat from the sprawling machinery to fog. The planet might have been prime real estate due to its access to multiple trade routes, but you'd never know it from out here on the edges of the massive complex of ports, warehouses, and administration complexes that ringed the planet.

Not here on the worst, coldest, furthest edge of the complex, nearest the poles. Not the spots where the newer, the smaller, the less wealthy were relegated to. The lowest on the rankings. Stuck out here with landing pad and warehouse assignment on the farthest edge of the complex, with nothing but tundra on one side of you, and a prohibitively high heating bill.

"You must have done something," Jeski Markstal said to his copilot. His fingers were becoming numb, even through the thermal gloves he was wearing. He was attaching the connectors that would purge and refill the blank matter tanks of the food synthesizers on his aging freighter. He locked the last connector in place and rubbed his hands together, feeling some of the deep numbness receding. He turned away from the landing pad's wall and saw again the pale, frigid blue of the sky arching over the frozen landscape. Beyond the edge of the pad, there was nothing man made. Not even the spars and construction bots that would indicate that new terminals were being built. Just… nothing.

"I didn't," Usseth Dé replied. "I swear."

"You can tell me. I won't be mad," Jeski said, the edge in his voice clearly showing he was lying. "I just want to know. If I know, then maybe I can fix it for next time, so we don't end up out here in the asshole of nowhere again."

Usseth pulled his head out from the open cowling where he had been making adjustments. "I *didn't*," he said emphatically. "What makes you think it wasn't something you did?"

"Because I'm the calm one," Jeski said, his voice tight and strident. "I'm the one everybody likes."

"Everybody likes me too."

"You keep telling yourself that," Jeski said. "And in the meantime, we'll die of frostbite out here on the edge of… that." He waved a hand at the emptiness beyond.

Usseth gave up the fight at that point. Jeski was clearly in one of his moods, and there was no point in arguing.

"It's weird though, right?" Jeski said. "You'd think a shipment of zylt crystals and cobaltium 23 would be given priority. Would be ushered right through the gates to the main concourse and the free-trade zone where they divvy it up and send it on. I mean, if it were third-rate deevee chips or plain old infrasteel, I could see it. That shit's common as grass. But this was supposed to be our big score. The one that gets us through the doors, gets us a seat at the table."

Usseth took in Jeski's monologue as he set the cowling back into place and resealed it. "I don't know what to tell you, cap. We were set for one of the central bays until we hit the system, then we got rerouted out here. I don't know why."

"Did you check to make sure it's legit?" Jeski said.

"Of course I did," Usseth said, his own voice hardening against the accusation. "I know how to do my job. And the central AI guided us out here. It's not like we can just fly wherever we want."

"I know, I know. Don't get janky. I just don't get it, all right?"

"I don't either, but we just have to live with it for now. Is everything set?"

"Yeah," Jeski said. "The unloaders just signalled their systems are ready to start emptying the holds. They don't need us for that."

"Fine," Usseth grumbled. "Let's go get something to eat. I heard there's actually a restaurant out here now."

"Oh, stellar," Jeski replied. "One whole restaurant. Ain't we lucky?" He checked his Link, brought up the restaurant's menu, and was instantly disappointed. "Okay, fine. At least we don't have to cook it. Let's go."

∞

Goss. How much longer do we have to listen to these two? Lexa-Blue said.

Oh, come on, Ember said. *If you'd gotten stuck out here, you'd have shot a hole through the dockmaster's door by now.*

Yeah, all right, she grudgingly agreed. *It is pretty much the ass end of nowhere.*

Look, Ember said, pointing at the two small figures far below them on the landing pad floor. *They're leaving.*

I pity the servers at that restaurant having to serve those two.

I can't say I blame them, having to set down out here. They got a raw deal, that's for sure.

And it was nothing they did, Vrick said. *I'm in the port's system and someone sliced in to change their docking assignment.*

Makes sense, Ember said. *Security is laxer out here on the fringes. Good way to isolate the shipment and make it easier for a snatch and grab. It's what I would have done.*

They were perched over the landing pad, high among the gantries and scaffolding that covered the ceiling of the open bay. Far below them, the scruffy but solid freighter sat silently as the unloading systems dispatched loader bots to remove the precious cargo from its holds.

How much longer are we going to have to wait up here? Lexa-Blue said, shifting her weight against the intersection of girders she'd wedged herself between.

I imagine they'll let the bots do the heavy lifting for now. Get everything out of the ship and onto the deck where they can find what they need more easily. He looked at her, the smooth matte of her face mirroring his.

They were both clad in augmented steelskins: the thin layer of non-reflective black armour reinforced at the joints and layered with all sorts of enhancements. Not nearly as bulky or lethal as their armoured battle suits, but far more suited for stealth in a full gravity and full atmosphere environment.

It's rucking cold up here.

You're imagining things, Ember told her. *That suit is insulated and heated. And it's no colder up here than it is down there. Quit complaining.*

I can't help it. This is how I prepare. I'm preparing. It's my process.

Far below, they could see the loader bots moving in and out of the *Sweet Baby Jake's* cargo hold, stacking the crates on the waiting conveyor tram.

I'm getting an energy spike in these new target emission bands, Vrick said. ***Heads up. It's showtime.***

There, below them on the landing bay floor, the air seemed to crease and fold, compressing in a disturbing way. Even through their steelskins, they felt the touch of a strange pressure crawling over their skin and through to their bones. Near the conveyor tram, in the middle of the floor and unsupported by anything, a pinhole of light appeared, opening rapidly into a roiling disc of opaline energy. It grew to around four metres across and stabilized.

Okay, that should have set off every alarm on the planet, Lexa-Blue said.

You're right, Vrick said. ***But they've got their fingers deep in the security algorithms and nothing is showing at all. Whoever is slicing for them, they're very good. One of the best I've ever seen.***

They're coming through, Ember said.

The disc of energy rippled and gave way and three figures came through, surrounded by a different sort of shifting light that clashed with the portal itself.

They're wearing blurs, Lexa-Blue said.

Sensible, Ember said. ***If anything goes wrong with their surveillance block, they're still not identifiable.***

As they watched, the cloaked figures below fanned out in the direction of the conveyor tram. With the blurs masking the details of their bodies, it was difficult to see what they were doing, but it looked like they were searching for the specific items they needed.

Okay, get ready, Ember said. ***On my mark. Go!***

∞

Ember launched himself from his perch, pulling his arms close to his sides and his legs tight to each other. As he fell, he activated his grav shifter's field to guide and shape his descent, twisting supplely in the air.

You take the one on the left, Lexa-Blue said. ***I'll take the other two.***

He glided on the shaped gravity fields, watching her trajectory across the tactical displays his node flashed across his vision. Per usual, she was taking a much blunter approach, descending like a cannonball, hitting the deck of the landing bay and already moving as his feet hit the deck. As she plowed into the reinforced metal, he could see it buckling beneath her, creating a heaving crater in its surface. She knocked her targets off their feet with the shockwave, their blurs sparking with angry energy.

Ember had no more time to think about her, as he shifted his body to make his own landing. *With a lot more finesse, I might add.*

Farther from Lexa-Blue's impact zone, Ember's target had been shaken by her landing, but remained on his feet. His attention was focussed on them rather than on the lithe body coming at them like a projectile.

Ember made a few quick adjustments to his grav field to increase his speed and angle of descent, plowing into the intruder's back. The impact took the other off its feet, while Ember used the grav controls to tuck and roll in the air and land in a precise combat stance.

But his target came back to his feet more quickly than Ember had expected, and he could tell right away his opponent had combat experience too. *Only fighters move like that.*

The sensors in his steelskin told Ember that while the intruder's blur provided disguise and some protection from weapons fire, there were no gravity enhancements installed.

Advantage: me.

Ember saw his target shift into attack mode, ready to pounce. Skills honed by years of practice playing ZeroBall kicked in. A thought shifted the gravity fields around him and he leapt. As soon as his feet left the decking, he turned his body sideways, suddenly parallel to the floor. He thought he saw shock in the other's stance, then moved on to the next part of his manoeuvre, executing a tight set of spins around his gravitic axis, his lower leg connecting hard across his target's midsection. As the other doubled over from the impact, Ember spun away, end over end to land once again on his feet.

That didn't feel right. The blow had not landed as it would have on flesh. What he had hit felt way more solid and unyielding. ***Heads up. They may have extra shielding built into those blurs.***

Got it.

Ember dove into a new set of manoeuvres, spinning up and round to go for the side of the neck.

∞

Lexa-Blue felt the impact of her landing go through her, both as a bone-deep vibration and as a wave of satisfaction.

We're going to have to pay for that damage, you know, Vrick said.

Nag, nag, nag, she said. ***Tell me later. I'm busy.***

With a practiced battle sense, she took in the sight of the splayed figures before her, stunned, but already rising to come for her. At the same time, she skimmed the sensor readings her node fed her, familiarizing herself with their capabilities.

One of them was up and was clumsily heading for her, a heavy stun baton in hand. She went into a crouch, settling her weight. Gravity tricks were Ember's thing, not hers. She preferred to feel the power of weight and momentum herself.

Her opponent was coming at her with the baton, greenish stun energy pulsing at its tip. She flashed a thought to the augment strips along her forearms and livid scarlet shield discs glowed to life, catching the baton's energy as she parried the blow.

She hissed within her cowl as some of the baton's energy leaked through her shield and resonated through her steelskin armour. *Well, that's not good.*

She realized the baton had way more charge in it than she had thought. *Note to self.*

Trying to avoid another shock from the swinging baton, she powered up the shield on her other arm, sending it as much power as she could. Using them almost as mauls, she waded toward her opponent, aiming to catch the arm holding the baton, rather than the weapon itself.

She felt several of her blows connect, which was deeply satisfying, but she still felt sizzles of energy bleeding through her attack and arcing through her steelskin.

Before she could formulate another attack plan, agony lanced up and down her back from a point just below her left shoulder.

Right. The other one. Forgot about him.

Pivoting, she twisted her torso out of range, swinging the energy shield on her right arm around in a savage arc. She heard it connect with the attacker's baton with an angry buzz like a swarm of fire hornets. Readings flashed across her vision, and she smiled behind her cowl. She'd managed to catch the attacker's baton at just the right angle to damage its casing and some of the circuitry. She saw its energy readings fluctuating wildly as the power cell drained.

Got 'em.

The Infinite Heist

Her satisfaction was short-lived, however, as her sensors showed the other coming back to take up the slack of her small success. She parried a flurry of blows as she sensed the second attacker recovering from the loss of their weapon.

Okay, enough subtlety.

While she was no match for Ember's skill with the gravity fields, she wasn't without a few tricks of her own.

Hold on, squib. Gonna go boom.

She had just enough time to register his surprise and know he was braced before she pulled the pin.

Gravitic energy pulsed out from her like the pressure wave of a bomb, sending her two attackers tumbling away from her.

"Okay, jerks," she said out loud, her voice amplified by the steelskin's comm gear. "Let's try that again."

∞

From es berth in the next landing pad, Vrick monitored the fight. Sliced into the complex's security system to keep it from sending every security person on the planet into the fray, ey had eyes on every angle, simultaneously running comparative combat algorithms to track when and if intervention may be needed.

Es engines were primed for a fast launch if it was needed to either weigh into the fight or provide an escape route if things truly went south. Knowing these types of operations, it was always good to have a backup plan.

I love them. But they do manage to get themselves into trouble.

With another part of es consciousness, ey kept a full sensor suite focussed on the writhing energies of the portal, trying to drink in all the information ey could. Ey had barely any time to scan and record the information about the previous iteration of it that had allowed Keene and Sindel's captors to escape along with es friends. This was a perfect opportunity to absorb as much information as ey could about the tech that made the portal possible, from its initial stages to its eventual closure.

What's a little life-threatening peril along the way?

As ey watched Ember and Lexa-Blue fight, ey could analyze each manoeuvre, observe it at a slower rate, evaluate the odds of success of each feint, punch, and kick. The raw physicality of it fascinated em, blunted even though it was by steelskins and blurs.

As ey watched, Ember executed another series of gravity defying twists, flips, and kicks. Overlaid in es visual sensors was a splay of data around both Ember and the blurred figure as they engaged. The data around Ember's image showed percentages with a higher accuracy index, while the other's data shifted wildly as es matrices recalculated from observations of their fighting style. Ey watched as the probable victory calculations shifted back and forth from one to the other.

In another feed, ey saw the other two interlopers recovering from Lexa-Blue's gravity pulse and coming in for another attack. Lexa-Blue's energy shield discs sparked angrily as blows rained on them. From the concerted way they were working together to assail her, ey deduced they were communicating with each other on some private channel. Ey scanned along all of the spectra used for communications systems and found it easily, though it was heavily shielded and encrypted.

I could break in, but it would take too much time.

Still, Lexa-Blue was more than holding her own, dealing more punishment than she was receiving.

She is definitely a scrapper, that one.

As ey watched, ey saw their communal strategy change. One drove forward, raining blows on Lexa-Blue's shields in a sudden, wild flurry. A percentage indicator in es vision shifted numbers as the attack confused the battle algorithm. But Vrick knew better.

The other slipped sideways out of Lexa-Blue's line of sight as her shielded forearms danced and deflected the rain of blows. Vrick saw the intruder duck behind and past her, running for the tram and the goods they had come here to steal.

Vrick watched as the cloaked figure swiftly scanned the cargo containers, searching for their specific target. When the search suddenly ended, ey saw the figure pull a device from inside the folded light of the blur and slap it against the crate.

Instantly, ey detected a spike on the gravitic sensors and saw the figure lift the heavy crate as if it were no heavier than a dinner plate. Without even sparing a look at the combat still raging behind, the figure darted toward the waiting portal.

Heads up, you two. We're in the endgame.

The figure gave the crate a powerful push and it glided on its localized gravitic field, skimming across the floor and through the portal. As it went through, ey caught a coded pulse on their communications channel and knew it was an evacuation signal.

Knowing these final moments were crucial, ey jammed es drive field to maximum — what would have been a perilous move if any human ground crew had been in the landing bay with em. But ey'd made sure no one was there to be hurt. Shaping the field, ey shot from the landing bay, swinging into a tight curve as soon as ey had cleared the boundary, swinging emself into position in the wide opening that showed a panorama of the chaos within.

I'm in position.

Ey felt Ember and Lexa-Blue acknowledge without words, then saw the resulting switch in battle tactics coming through the sensor feeds. The shift was subtle, just enough to give their individual opponents a sliver of opportunity.

Ey saw Ember knocked to the ground, es sensors showing how he had used his gravity fields to cushion his fall. Metres away, one of Lexa-Blue's energy shields collapsed in a glare of aching white light, and she had to alter her stance to give herself protection with her remaining shield.

Vrick saw the first intruder, the one who had managed to steal the crate, dive through the portal, and then the others abandoning their fights to run for the same goal.

And this is the tricky part.

Cranking es time sense down as much as possible, ey watched the two runners, measuring their distances to the portal as well as the distances between them, all the while running them against the timing and aiming co-ordinates.

Steady.

At the exact moment, ey fired a specifically modulated, low power pulse from es forward pulse-gun array. Just as the second intruder disappeared through the portal, the pulse hit, disrupting the dimensional matrix and collapsing it. The backlash of energy caught the last in line, lifting and tossing him back to land hard on the decking. Es sensors registered the heavy vibration of the thief striking the decking.

Over the open comm, Vrick heard the whoop of triumph from Lexa-Blue.

"And that," ey heard her say, "is how you do it."

∞

Keene heard the sound and risked a glance up from his work. There, framed by the eerie light of the portal, he saw a bound packing crate slide through the opening on a skim of antigrav. Two of the figures waiting for it moved forward to arrest its movement while still trying to stay out of the way of its mass.

"Eyes on your work," Sindel said from below.

"Something's up," Keene answered. "Look."

He was standing over the console, his hands splayed over controls, watching readings for Sindel who was on the floor on her back, her upper torso deep in the exposed guts of the machine.

"Give me a second," she said, and he heard the click as components slid back into place.

She had managed to keep the system running well enough for this latest jaunt through the portal, but it was still a temporary stopgap that left Ckurahris's goal of interdimensional doorways unattainable.

Keeping an eye on what was happening, Keene felt Sindel at his side, dusting herself off as she stood.

"What's going on?"

"Well, three went through. But only two came back," Keene said, pointing at where Ckurahris stood with the returning duo.

"That's not right," Sindel said, and Keene turned to her, something in her tone standing out.

"The portal," she said, indicating the circle of energy. "That harmonic looks wrong."

Keene followed her eye line and now that she had pointed it out, he could see the difference.

"Uh oh," Sindel said. "Here he comes."

Ckurahris was striding toward them, his face a thunderhead of rage. For a moment, Keene thought the raging man was about to strike him and had to fight to keep from stepping back. The last thing he wanted to do was show any weakness in front of their captor.

"Your friends are becoming quite—" Ckurahris started, then visibly reined himself in. "Bothersome."

Keene risked a slight sideways glance at Sindel, managing to keep a grin off his face. It wasn't hard to figure out which friends it was. Only Lexa-Blue could piss someone off that much.

"Progress report," Ckurahris demanded.

Keene saw Sindel's jaw tighten. She was definitely not used to being spoken to in that way, but more than that, he knew she was very close to resolving the issue, as much as it pained her to do so.

Again, out of habit, he reached for his node, intending to communicate with her directly, but was met with only the resounding emptiness in his head where Know-It-All should be. The feeling was not pleasant. In that moment, he had no way to communicate to her that this was their only option. That he understood she felt she had no choice but to complete the work, despite how much he had tried to reassure her his safety wasn't what she should be concerned about.

And she was right. If they were both whole, at least they had some slim chance of either stopping Ckurahris themselves or buying time until Lexa-Blue and Ember found them. But he saw the strain in her face as she spoke. Even though she was doing what she had to, she did not like it one bit.

"I need a couple of hours to run some final tests, but I think I have the matrix stable in the organic matter ranges. Once we confirm that, the system should be fully operational. And you can proceed with ripping reality apart."

You just couldn't resist, could you?

But Ckurahris smiled, the curve of his mouth sardonic, the expression of a man completely in control. "So melodramatic, Sei Kestra. You should have been on the stage. I fear you missed your true calling."

Keene felt Sindel bristle at his side but say nothing.

"Well, then," Ckurahris said. "Get it done. I have preparations to complete with my team."

He turned and swept away from them.

"That went well," Keene said drily.

"I didn't strangle him," Sindel replied. "Not sure how I think that's a win, but here we are."

"But what do we do now? If he has his system, he doesn't need us anymore."

"This infernal contraption he's built is held together with adhesive and megalomania," Sindel said. "I've gotten it to a point where people won't melt into goo when they go through the interdimensional portals, but that doesn't mean it's safe. I managed to engineer a few flaws into my repairs I think will keep them all guessing. And even if I hadn't, there are enough inherent issues in both the hardware and the extra-dimensional physics that he's going to need all the help he can get keeping it running."

"One for our team, I guess. But are we any closer to a plan to get ourselves out of here is the real question."

"Working on it, but it looks like we have to just give him what he wants for now," Sindel said, then sighed. "Run that organic matter simulation again, would you, please? I want to make some more adjustments."

"And see if there's a way we can maybe use it to our advantage?"

"Exactly."

Chapter Nine

"Get that blur switched off," Lexa-Blue said as she turned the unconscious body over on its back.

Careful, Vrick said, observing them through their nodes.

"No worries there," Ember said, pushing his hand through the taffy-like resistance of the blur. The defensive camouflage units were usually worn at the waist, and even with the glimmering field, he could tell the basic body shape. He felt along the waistline and found the control unit, pressing at controls he couldn't see.

"Doesn't seem to be booby-trapped," he said.

"Well, we're rucked if it is. You can tell just by touch?"

"You'd be amazed what these hands can do," he said. "Blurs are pretty standard. I've never heard of a case of them being rigged to blow. But these people went to a lot of trouble to hide who they are and what they're doing. I don't trust them not to have left us a nasty surprise."

"You're right. It only takes once," she said.

"Well, we'll find out soon enough."

Concentration furrowed his brow as he continued his exploration of the device. There was a small electronic chirp, and his face relaxed.

"Got it."

The field dissolved into crystalline particles of light which then winked out of existence, revealing what was hidden behind the layers of light.

"Huh," Lexa-Blue grunted. "Did not expect that."

Without the camouflage of the blur, what lay before them was a humanoid shape but fabricated from metal, ceramics, and tissue analogues.

"Wait," Ember said. "Is that one of those things you beat up when you're training?"

"No," Vrick said. "If the readings I'm getting are accurate, and they always are, that is a simulant. Similar construction, but with a bootleg AI core installed in it. Which is highly illegal, I might add."

"I mean, you hear rumours of them out in the Brink, but…"

"Makes sense when you think about it," Ember said.

"How so?" she answered.

"I always used to wonder how those villains in the old deevees found all those henchmen to do their bidding. I mean, how do you find all those people willing to just be a grunt helping to take over the world or whatever the grift was?"

"Some get paid," she said. "But a lot of the time, people don't need all that much encouragement to be the worst possible version of what passes for a human."

"True," he agreed. "But with these, you don't have to pay them. All you have to do is program them. No free will to make decisions for themselves that get in the way of the big plan. One big, completely obedient army. No one gets cold feet or has a sudden attack of morality."

"Which is exactly why human-shaped bots were banned back in the day," she said. "If it's something a human shape can do, then why not have a human do it? Seems to be the reasoning behind it. That and not having massive armies of programmable soldiers that can impersonate humans any time you want them to."

Must keep those smart machines in their place, Vrick said, but there was no edge in es voice, just a tickle of humour.

"What exactly is that?" she asked, pointing her pistol at the simulant's torso.

A thin plate of what looked like mechanism covered its chest, with a series of telltales blinking in a suddenly erratic rhythm.

Well, from the emissions it's giving off, I'd say it's a safe bet that's the mechanism that got our friend here in the first place, Vrick said. ***Can you get it off?***

"Probably," Ember said, leaning closer to examine the device more carefully. "But I'm betting that even if the blur wasn't rigged to blow, this thing might be."

"Can you defuse it?" Lexa-Blue asked.

"We'll find out soon enough," he said, unclipping a small tool kit from his waist. "There's definitely something here, just under this part of the casing. But whether it just slags the device or blows up everything in a five-metre radius, I don't know."

The motions of his hands were precise and practiced as he worked the mechanism. He was acutely aware of Lexa-Blue beside him, her body taut.

Finally, there was a slight click, and the main clasp on the unit popped open and released the straps. They both exhaled, the worst of the tension flowing out of their bodies.

Bag that thing and bring it to me.

"Got it," Ember said, slipping the device into a storage pouch on his steelskin.

No, I mean the whole thing.

"You need a new toy, junkpile?" Lexa-Blue said. "You getting bored with us?"

Well, you can't just leave it there. Who knows what use someone else might put it to. And we already have enough to explain to the port master without adding banned simulant tech to the mix.

"Fair point," Ember agreed. "But how are we going to move it? Mass readings are pretty high."

Just leave that to me. I can tweak your grav units to generate a synchronous field that should help you get it back to me.

Once Vrick had performed the required adjustments, they both felt their grav fields twinging together, like a physical pull between their steelskins.

"Okay, that feels weird," Lexa-Blue said.

"Very."

Always complaining, you two, Vrick said. ***Just get to it. Sooner you get out of there and get that thing back here, the sooner it's over.***

It took a few moments to figure out how to use the synced grav fields to lift the heavy simulant up from the decking and then finding the right position to keep it balanced between them. They took a few steps forward, and their burden seemed stable between them, so they kept moving.

"And what did you do at work today, honey?" Ember said, his breathing strained by the effort, even with the grav assist. "Oh, just took out some killer robots, nothing much."

"If it gets us any closer to finding this asshole, I'm good with it."

"Fair point. Let's get all this out of here. See what it can tell us. Ready for pickup, Vrick."

In the opening to the docking bay, Vrick edged es bow closer, nudging into the crowded space, as far as ey could, extending es ramp to touch gently against the decking.

∞

"Find me a vibrational target," Ckurahris said from where he stood in front of the portal, facing it down as if it was a foe in his way.

"Yes, sir. Scanning now," Wols said from his position at the console.

Keene and Sindel stood behind him, the imposing bulk of the machine humming with power around them.

"Eliminating targets without worlds at our home co-ordinates," the technician said. "Scanning the results for lyonite deposits." After a few moments, he said, "List of optimal targets is ready, sir."

In the air in front of them, a pane of ranked data appeared, and Ckurahris stepped away from the portal to take the information in.

"Okay," Keene whispered to Sindel, the thick background noise covering the sound of his voice. "How the hells did he manage that?"

"This system has some of the most sophisticated scanners I've ever seen," she replied. "I had a brief look at them as I was working on the repairs. We're talking a quantum leap beyond anything we have now. He's smart, I'll give him that."

"If unbalanced," Keene said.

"Be that as it may, this tech is revolutionary. If it wasn't so dangerous, I'd be impressed."

"Do you figure he can pull it off without ripping a hole through reality?" Keene asked.

"Thanks to me," Sindel said, her disgust evident, "probably. He'll be able to get through. But the long-term effects of this type of interdimensional rift, however controlled it is now, can't be foreseen."

"That one," Ckurahris said, indicating a string of multidimensional coordinates in the list. "Prepare for crossover."

The room exploded into activity as the team they were about to send across moved into position. Keene could see four of the guards in their blurs, now laden with portable mining gear. He saw them move a small floating cart into position as well, loaded with what looked like grav shifters and expandable crates. "They've thought this through."

"They have, indeed," Sindel whispered back. "This will be their proof of concept. If there's lyonite beyond that portal, they have everything they need to bring some of it back. And even if they only fill that small cart, they'll be richer than a lot of people walking around these days."

"Coordinates locked," Wols said. "Aligning the portal now."

Ripples of colour flickered across the portal's energy before settling to a milky blue-white.

"Portal connection is green," the technician announced. "Ready for passage."

"Go," Ckurahris said.

The incursion team moved forward, and a series of four panes opened up in the air, one for each.

"Body cams," Keene said. "Dimensionally quantum entangled by the looks of it."

"Of course," Sindel said with a sneer. "Ckurahris wants the experience but isn't willing to put himself on the line."

The panes swelled in size and fanned out around Ckurahris, but due to their position and resolution, Keene and Sindel were able to watch the entire operation as it happened.

"Dagger One reporting." A voice emanated from one of the panes rimmed with white light to show the viewpoint of the speaker. "We're through. Looks like some kind of ravine or valley. No signs of habitation, no activity on the standard EM bands. Atmo readings are thin, but nothing dangerous in it."

"Fascinating," Ckurahris said, his voice rapt with concentration. "A mirror copy of this world, but without humans. As if we never were."

So we're on one of the habitable worlds, Keene thought. *Not sure how to make use of that piece of information. Not yet, anyway.*

"Readings are strong in this direction," came another voice, as a different pane designated Dagger Two lit around the edges. "This way."

They watched as the four panes shifted direction, following the traces.

"Got it," Dagger One said, and Keene heard avarice in his voice. "Nice thick vein. We're setting up for extraction now."

The room was silent, the only sounds the clipped instructions of Dagger One as he and his team set up for their extraction of the lyonite ore from the rocky cliff face. Keene and Sindel watched, every bit as focussed on the operation as Ckurahris and his team.

In short order, the equipment was set up and light flooded the rock face. There, embedded in it, gleamed a thick vein of ore that gleamed in the light, the colour a glimmering mix of copper and blood.

"That is more lyonite in one place than has been on the market in the last decade," Sindel said to Keene.

"Quite the score for their first trip," Keene said. "Don't suppose they'll be happy with it, I guess."

"With a potentially infinite number of sources? I doubt it. And even if they somehow managed to mine all the possible sources of lyonite, there's any other number of valuable commodities out there they could harvest for money. They have an entire multiverse to exploit now."

"I'd say that is a most successful trial," Ckurahris said, his voice lush with satisfaction. He turned to the tech. "Tag the location for more extensive survey and prep the coordinates for the next sorties. I want team two suited up and ready to go as soon as we bring this team back in."

As soon as he finished speaking, the first small crate floated back through the portal, heaped with glistening copper ore. Despite the grav cushion, Keene felt something rumble through the floor for an instant.

Badly tuned grav shifters. Someone needs to pay closer attention to their work.

He turned to Sindel to comment but was brought up short by the knot of a frown on her face. Did she notice it too? Was it more than just bad grav equipment?

"Did you feel that?" she said. "Like a... tremor or something?"

He was about to open his mouth to answer her, but she shook her head.

"Never mind," she said. "It's nothing."

But he could tell from her face she didn't believe her own words. And it made him wonder too.

∞

"Put it in the sensor bay and let me have a look," Vrick said.

Ey extruded a flat surface from the decking of the lounge, shifting furniture out of the way to make room. Lexa-Blue and Ember wrestled the simulant onto it.

Across the sensor platform from her, Ember took the sensor he had used to take particulate readings and inserted it into a waiting data port. A pane opened, flooding with scan data.

"Particulates telling us anything?" Lexa-Blue said.

"Running comparisons against atmospheric, plant life, and particulate indices for every planet in the Galactum. Shouldn't take me more than a few minutes."

"I wish I could think that fast," Lexa-Blue said.

"As do I," Vrick retorted.

"What about the doohickey?" she asked Ember.

"Right here," Ember said, placing it on the opposite end of the scan platform.

Schematics formed in the air as Vrick's sensors played over the device, probing into its interior without penetrating the casing.

"I'm definitely getting a strong residual energy pulse that proves it's connected to those portals. Traces match up with what we found from Sindel's pod. The mechanism is complex. More so than anything I've seen built by humans before. Whoever made it is definitely an exemplary engineer."

"Can you figure out how it works?" Ember said. "Or at least show us where it's been?"

"Give a ship a bit of time to work," Vrick said. "There's a lot of new tech here."

"Okay, that's all the scan data they sent us on her clothes, her gear, and anything else she had with her on her trip," Lexa-Blue said. "What's next?"

"This one, I can do on my own," Ember said. He accessed his node, bringing up images of the simulant and its specs. A thought sent it to his innernet and simultaneously connected to Know-It-All. "A little bit of record checking might give us an idea where this thing came from."

A pane opened up, showing his scan of the simulant's basic construction, splitting into separate images of its shell, interior framework, and artificial muscles and nerves. Beside it, links to multiple databases expanded into view. Material and design comparisons flashed past their eyes in rapid succession.

"Is that a GalSec database?" Lexa-Blue said, mock astonished. "Should you have access to that? Isn't that a crime?"

"I've committed worse," Ember said. "And so have you."

The display chimed.

"Got it," Ember said, expanding the information with a wave of his hand. "The chassis is a pretty standard animate model, slightly newer than the ones you currently beat up while you're training."

"Remind me to buy some new ones after this is all over," Lexa-Blue said.

"But the artificial musculature has definitely been enhanced," Vrick said, zooming in on the artificial muscle fibres. "Far beyond the manufacturer's specs. Or the industry regulations. Someone planned for these to do some heavy lifting."

"And then there's this."

The image of the simulant's head split, exposing the AI processor core.

"That is definitely not standard issue," Ember said.

"Definitely not," Vrick agreed. "That model of core would allow extremely sophisticated actions and responses. It wouldn't be able to fly a ship or run a city, but it would definitely be able to do as it's told and adapt on the fly."

"Any idea where the unit might have come from?" Lexa-Blue asked.

"The serial numbers and maker's marks have been removed. I might be able to do some comparisons to existing companies and their inventories, but that won't tell us who made the modifications."

"Table it for now," she said. "What about the gizmo?"

They turned their attention back to the sensor platform and saw that Vrick had extended a filament probe into the device where it lay.

"Careful with that thing, junkpile," Lexa-Blue said. "It's not like we can just order a new one."

"I was, and am, exceedingly careful," Vrick said.

"What have you found out?" Ember asked.

"Well, the particulates weren't very enlightening. I suspect it underwent some kind of decontamination before it ended up coming through that portal. What little there is in terms of plant or mineral trace is all pretty bog standard and common to any number of worlds. I've compiled a list just in case even that little information might prove useful to compare to any other leads we have. But it's this that's really fascinating."

Light played over the harness the simulant had been wearing. Schematics and data streams flowed up from the sensor platform's surface.

"So, what's the skinny?" Lexa-Blue said.

"Well, it's pulsing with the same energy readings I took back on PD-785.3 before we lost Keene and Sindel."

"And it blew up," Ember added.

"In a very big way," Vrick agreed. "But I recorded a lot of sensor data before that portal closed, and this thing is definitely powered by the same energies. If it isn't designed to work with those systems, then I'm a garbage scow.

"The closest analogy I can make is that it's an anchor. There are some basic controls to it, and they aren't very sophisticated at all. If I had to make a guess, I'd say it keeps the wearer connected to the system. And there's a basic actuator I think would allow you to call up the portal again if it closed for some reason, then pull you back through to where you started from."

"Makes sense," Ember said. "If they're using these portals to get around, then they'd need some kind of method of either calling them up again or finding their way back to wherever they started from."

"Exactly," Vrick agreed.

"But when they were on Thesia, they just left the portal open for them," Ember said. "Surely the biggest energy expenditure is actually opening the portal. Like most machines, the powering up and down is what takes the most energy and causes the most wear and tear on the system."

"That's true," Vrick said. "But there's more microcircuitry in this thing than would be necessary for that task alone. And there are faint traces of energies that are way more complex than those used in the Gates for their wormhole transitions. I'm seeing traces of rare, higher dimensional energies, resonances far more similar to those we saw from that dimensional rift that brought Rogan and his people here."

"What are you saying?" Lexa-Blue asked.

"I think whoever has Keene and Sindel isn't just using this tech to punch through from location to location. I think they're using it to punch through from dimension to dimension. From reality to reality."

There was silence as Ember and Lexa-Blue took that in. He was the first to speak.

"That is… "

"The stupidest rucking thing I have ever heard," Lexa-Blue said, jumping into the pause he'd left.

"Pretty much," Vrick agreed. "And if what happened to PD-785.3 is any indication, dangerous beyond words."

"Whoever is doing this could blow apart any number of planets," Ember said. "What would make someone do something like that?"

"Greed," Lexa-Blue grunted. "It's pretty much always greed. There's something out there that he wants and wants a lot of."

"What?" Ember said. "Money? Think about it. Hard currency from another reality would be useless here. Not to mention credits or any kind of virtual currency."

He paused a moment.

"But what about precious metals? Jewels? Some kind of commodity that has some kind of hard value here? If you had access to other dimensions where there's a lot of it, you could make a killing. But what, I wonder?"

"I think I know," Vrick said. "In addition to the basic functions of this unit, there's a detector built in as well. Which, at the moment, has one setting programmed into it: lyonite."

"Should that mean something to me?" Lexa-Blue asked, but she turned to Ember when she heard his sharp, awed exhale.

"Back when I was on the grift," he said to her, "lyonite was the holy grail. There's almost none of it on the market, and all the sources on Galactum worlds have been mined out years ago. The price per gram must be astronomical."

"See for yourself," Vrick said, projecting the current per gram market value of lyonite in the display over the sensor platform.

Lexa-Blue let out a soft whistle of appreciation. "Greed. Definitely greed."

∞

"Is there any more of that?" Daevin asked, seeing the steaming cup Rogan held in his hands. "I don't even care what it is."

Rogan chuckled and gestured with his mug at the urn that stood on the counter. "Knock yourself out."

"Very funny."

Daevin poured himself a cup and held it to his lips, blowing on the sharp tangy steam that filled his nostrils. He still couldn't identify it, but the scent travelled right up into his brain, clearing away the fatigue momentarily. After a moment, he hazarded a sip. It was bitter on his tongue, some kind of spiced tea. But he didn't care. Just the smell and heat of it was enough.

"Better?" Rogan asked.

"Much. How's your head?"

Rogan reached up and pulled a spiky shock of hair aside to show off the livid pink of the new scar. "All good. Thanks for that."

"Don't mention it."

Rogan chuckled again. "I thought that poor medic was going to have a fit when you grabbed that wound sealer from his kit and used it yourself."

"He was busy. And he wasn't using it."

"He probably doesn't get many people helping themselves to his kit."

"Well, Brighter Light made the damn thing," Daevin said, taking another sip of his tea. "And I've had occasion to use one before."

"We both have too much experience with this kind of thing," Rogan agreed. "And speaking of which, do we have any idea what actually happened?"

Daevin topped up his mug and joined Rogan at one of the mess room's tables. "There are some theories already. It didn't just happen here. It happened all across the sector to varying degrees. Some kind of multidimensional shock or pressure wave originated on an empty rock of a planetoid which is now no longer there."

"Planets blowing up for no apparent reason is never good."

"Not at all," Daevin agreed. "Whatever caused it sent waves up and down through more dimensions than we perceive and possibly through more than we are even aware of. The readings coming in are showing the energy signature information Vrick sent us from Keene and Sindel's disappearances."

Rogan whistled a breath through his teeth, his eyes wide. "Do you think they're connected?"

"I can't see how they wouldn't be. That kind of event has only been theoretical up until now, so the chances of the sector experiencing it now, with everything else going on, are staggeringly small."

"How many planets were affected?" Rogan asked.

"Everything in a five thousand light-year sphere out from the point of origin, which was an uninhabited planetoid with nothing on it but an abandoned research station. Which just happened to be where Ember and Lexa-Blue almost found Keene and Sindel."

"No coincidence there, I'm guessing," Rogan said.

"Highly unlikely. Thankfully, most worlds weren't hit as hard, but any of the worlds with Gates that were powering up when the shock wave hit were caught in some kind of interference pattern."

"Which is what happened here."

"Exactly," Daevin agreed. "Just a ship was due to enter, so right at the peak of the power up cycle. Particularly nasty."

"Is the ship okay?" Rogan asked.

"Two dead. And the ship will be in drydock for a long time."

"What about planet side?"

"All the med centres are full. Twenty-seven dead. A lot of infrastructure damage."

Rogan was silent.

"I'd contact Vrick and the others to see if they know anything, but the main tightline transmitter network has been damaged. They're working on getting it up and running again, so hopefully it won't be long."

"Do you think they know more about this than we do?" Rogan asked.

"If this really does have something to do with everything that's going on, then they're out there in the middle of it."

"I hope they're okay," Rogan said.

"If anyone can survive all this and figure it out, they can."

"I hope you're right. Multidimensional shockwaves are pretty major."

"It could have been worse," Daevin said. "It could have taken out whole cities. Planets even. Believe it or not, we were lucky."

"True. But could it happen again?"

"It could. And this is just the attenuated edge of an event on a small planetoid," Daevin said. "If it happens again closer to a larger, more heavily populated world, it will be worse. A lot worse."

∞

Through swimming vision, Hetri Li Ffiann realized he was upside down.

Well, not completely. More at an awkward angle.

What is that? About forty-seven degrees or so?

Not the time, Hetri.

He'd been in his office when the shockwave had hit, no surprise there. He'd barely left, staring at the simulations and data analysis that had sprung up from Sindel and Keene's abductions. On top of that, he'd had his own work to do, with all of the Gates at various stages of development or implementation.

Since he'd provided the information on the various requirements they'd asked for, the Maverick Heart and es crew had gone silent, leaving him with no further idea about whether or not they'd found Sindel and Keene yet or if they were even any closer to doing so.

He'd done the only thing he knew to do: lose himself in work. He'd wrapped himself in the numbers and the science, poring over what little he knew, running simulations over and over, delegating much of the day-to-day operations of the Gate Project to his staff. They knew what they were doing and could handle it, though he set up several proxy algorithms that would monitor and let him know how it was all going.

So, he'd been in his office with all the strange scraps of data when the world seemed to turn inside out.

His chair had tumbled end over end, the manipulator arms automatically wrapping around him and going rigid to form a protective cage. The tumble had been quick and violent, leaving him in this unfamiliar and not particularly pleasant position.

Once the sudden motion had ceased, a quick check through his node showed nothing but a few minor bruises, a cut on his forehead that wasn't life threatening, and a diagnostic of the chair only showed a few minor dents in the casing. *Built to last.* More importantly, all of the required synaptic and physical connections between his body and the chair remained where they needed to be to keep him alive.

Now that he was certain he was unhurt, he craned his neck to get some idea of the state of his office. He couldn't see much from his position, but what he could see seemed as he had expected. The meager furniture he kept in his office had either overturned or been shattered. And there were disturbing cracks in his formerly pristine walls, taking out at least two square metres of viewscreen, though the ceiling seemed solid enough.

Okay, now what? Upright. Next goal is upright.

As he was still held in place by the chair itself, and his tumble had stopped, he could control the manipulators again. He was at rest on an angle, the left side of his body toward the floor, which impeded the range of motion of the left manipulator. He stopped and thought a moment, thinking in terms of leverage and directions of force.

Okay, I think I've got it.

Releasing the right manipulator from its protective position, he moved it across his body and aimed it down, spreading the palm of the artificial hand and planted it on the floor, pushing up and extending it to its full extent. It wasn't going to fully right him, but it was the first step. With just the small amount of space it provided him, he could move the left manipulator into a similar position, pulling it first into its shortest length, then planting its hand on the floor and pushing.

Then he lifted the right manipulator back over his body to the other side and aimed it at the floor, extending the servos to their fullest extent.

With full force, he jammed the manipulator down to the floor, digging its fingers into the damaged surface and gripping with its full strength.

He tested the grip, tensile numbers flowing through his node. *Not the best, but it should do.*

Okay, here we go.

With the one manipulator pulling and the other pushing, he accessed the grav controls and warped the field to add extra force. He managed to shift the overturned weight of the chair. With a disgruntled hum of the grav field, the chair fell back into the upright position, shimmying slightly on its gravs before steadying.

There. Now, let's see just how bad things are.

He accessed Know-It-All to check on the state of the complex as a whole, and what he saw disturbed him. Whatever had hit them, hit them hard. Reports of chaos and injuries flooded his node until he throttled back the flow of the data to a manageable level, rendering the gut punch tolerable.

But from what he could see, everyone was doing what they could to help each other. Senior staff was coordinating rescue efforts until help from outside the complex could arrive.

A thought opened his node beyond the complex itself, and his heart sank. Whatever it was had hit the entire planet. Reports flooded in from the farthest districts of Hub's main city. Even the newer, smaller outlying settlements far beyond the city itself were reporting damage and injuries from whatever had struck the planet. He steeled himself to look at the overall casualty numbers, running a quick calculation against the population as a whole, struggling to keep emotion out of the equation.

Could have been so much worse. Cities still standing. Lots of people still alive. Not that that is much of a consolation.

He turned his attention away from the details and concentrated on deciphering the cause.

The one major advantage of being in charge of one of the most advanced scientific and engineering projects known to the Galactum was having access to an extensive sensor and recording network that was almost always in use for one aspect of the project or another. Whatever had happened, it surely would have been noticed and recorded by the many pieces of equipment calibrated to read the fluctuations in the dimensional substrates that needed to be accessed and opened to make the Gates function.

Hetri opened panes and let the information flood into them, streams of sensor images, energy spikes, and data flowing across his vision.

Whatever it was that had hit them, it was particularly resonant with the energies of the Gate in orbit over Hub. One particular set of vibrational eddies centered on the massive ring itself, though, thankfully, the Gate had not been in its power down interval between transits when the dimensional tremor had hit. He quickly accessed the data on the other Gates, seeing that miraculously, none had been in use when whatever it was had hit. One had been in power down after a transit and had sustained some heavy damage, but it looked repairable.

I will take that miracle

He knew from the clashing clusters of numbers floating in the display that if the Gate had been powered up, or worse, actually mid-transit, those eddies would have been exponentially more intense. Simulations showed that if they had reached that full energetic potential, half of Hub might have been scoured clean when the dimensional membrane ruptured.

The algorithms pinged to draw his attention to the trajectory of the quake that had overtaken them. Star charts opened, showing him the epicentre of the expanding concussion sphere.

A nothing little planetoid. At least it used to be.

Know-It-All's star charts had only recently updated to show the planet's destruction.

If that update had been any more recent, I'd be seeing the words being spelled out letter by letter.

But it was also the planet Lexa-Blue and Ember had gone to seeking information on Keene and Sindel.

Surely they couldn't have blown up a planet?

A check for the Maverick Heart's transponder showed it pulsing strongly on the traffic grid, although it was out by Thesia at the moment. A quick cross-reference of their flight plans and movements showed they hadn't been near the planetoid when it had exploded, though he could see the quake would have intersected their course several hours earlier.

Relief washed over him. As glad as he was that they were still alive, he also was glad the evidence suggested they weren't directly responsible for the destruction of a planet, uninhabited though it might be. There are certain things one didn't want to have to explain to… well, anyone.

But even though they were alive, all the evidence said something related to Sindel and Keene's disappearance was directly responsible for this space quake and the devastation it had wrought across the Pan Galactum.

And his new friends were right in the middle of it.

∞

"There. Did you feel that?"

Keene looked up at Sindel from the readings he'd been monitoring. "What?" He could see the frustration underlying her expression but couldn't tell if it was something new or just a mirror of his own feelings about not having found a way out of their current situation.

"It's right there," she said. "Right there at the farthest edge of my peripheral vision."

"You're seeing sounds now? You really do need sleep."

He knew immediately it had been the wrong thing to say. Her face went stonily blank, and he'd seen her make that face around Lexa-Blue enough to know when she was truly angry.

"Okay, okay. I'm sorry. I'm exhausted too," he said, then he waved the cast on his arm at her. "And injured. What do you think it is?"

She clenched her fists, and he could see just how hard she was working to put the sensation into words.

"There," she said after a second. "There it is again."

This time, he felt it. A sudden odd pressure, not against him or their surroundings but rather a shift of the air around them like something rocketing off and leaving an absence in its place.

Sindel saw it in his face. "That."

"What the hell was it?" Keene asked.

"I have no idea. But it didn't feel… physical, somehow?"

Keene just stared at her.

"Like, I've felt earthquakes, tremors. But that... wasn't."

He nodded slowly, then looked around the room. "No cracks or stresses visible. I mean, it wasn't that strong, but if it had been a quake, you'd think it would have knocked something down or left a mark."

"It felt like... time?" Sindel said.

Keene looked at her skeptically. "You know what time feels like?"

"No, not exactly," Sindel said, visibly frustrated at not being able to find the right words. "But the Gates are all about spacetime. Opening two locations and connecting them. You spend enough time around the equipment needed to do that, and you get sensitive to what it feels like. The ripples, the undercurrents of reality."

"Okay, I can accept that, I guess."

Sindel looked around the room at the others. Wols manning the apparatus, the teams coming back and forth through the jagged wounds in the walls of the world, the teams sorting and evaluating the spoils as they accumulated. No one had seemed to notice anything untoward. "I doubt they'd notice if a bomb went off in here."

"Only insomuch as it would get in the way of the greed," Keene said with a sneer.

"But there is something going on," Sindel said. "And I can't say I'm surprised. This infernal machine is tearing through barriers that need to exist, that are fundamental to the very core of reality. All of the realities. I wouldn't be surprised if this is connected somehow."

"So, what do we do?"

Sindel moved to another section of the board. "I need to take some readings, do some digging. See if I can't find some trace of what's going on."

"But if you start messing with this thing, someone is going to notice. There's only so much you can do in the guise of making sure it keeps working."

"Don't you think I know that?" she hissed, trying not to attract any more attention. She moved her hands nonchalantly across the monitoring systems, making adjustments. "Just follow my lead."

Keene took a place by her side, glancing over at Ckurahris and his team. They were, so far, too deeply absorbed in the task of traversing the dimensional openings and bringing back their extremely valuable spoils.

"Switch that sensor packet over to this setting," Sindel said, indicating one she had just set herself. "Carefully. Too much energy diverted, and a bunch of alarms will go off."

Keene followed her lead, mimicking her movements. Thankfully, no alarms blared as they worked. The only sounds were the hum of the machinery and the crews industriously going about their work.

"There," Sindel said. "On the zeta band."

Keene looked at the sensor display she indicated but didn't see anything out of the ordinary. Then the gauge blipped ever so slightly. And he felt that strange, inside-out feeling again, just for a second.

"It's definitely radiating out from our location," Sindel said. "Like we're the eye of the hurricane. But there shouldn't be anything on that particular band at all."

As they watched, the sensor pattern flickered again, this time slightly more intensely. The problem was they were not the only ones to notice it. This time, the open portal had stuttered as well, sending sparks of energy off the handle of one of the grav lifts coming through. A handle that now lay, red hot, on the floor.

"You two. What have you done?" Ckurahris's voice cracked the air like a whip as he called to the two guards who were supposed to be watching them. "Get them away from there."

The one nearest Sindel moved in on her, grabbing her arm and sending her tumbling away from the console to the floor.

Keene started in her direction but was backhanded away by another guard. He went to the floor as well, a white-hot shard of pain running up his broken arm when he landed on it. His breath hissed out in a microsecond of agony before the splint shot him with a dose of painkiller.

His vision swam, but he was able to make out Ckurahris looming over them, his face purple with rage.

Chapter Ten

"Okay, so we know what they're doing and what they're after," Lexa-Blue said.

"I think *know* may be overstating the case just a bit," Ember said. "There's a lot of variables in this equation. It's a mound of guesswork mostly."

"Hey, squib. You know your stuff," she countered. "If this is what we have, this is what we have. And it gives us a place to start, at least."

"I know, but…"

"But nothing," Vrick said. "We both trust you. Keene would too if he were here."

"But he isn't," Ember said. "That's how we got to this monumental house of cards."

"And you were right about where they would strike next, which got us the inside skinny on what they're looking for. So, stow it, squib. Trust yourself or I'll smack you."

This brought a crooked grin to his face at least. "Okay, okay."

"Now that's settled, what's our next step?" Vrick asked.

Ember stretched to loosen his back. "All right. So, we know what they're looking for."

"The super valuable magic stuff," Lexa-Blue said.

"Lyonite," Vrick said, sharply.

"Whatever. And we know they're going to punch through to other realities where it hasn't been mined to… extinction or whatever."

"Minerals don't go extinct," Ember said. "Scarcity?"

"Fine, word guy," she shot back. "Whatever the word is, they can't find what they want here, so they're going to dig for it in places where it still exists."

"And they're causing potentially lethal space quakes in the process," Vrick said.

"Funny how ripping holes through dimensions that aren't supposed to touch will do that," Lexa-Blue said.

"So, in order to stop them, we have to find them," Vrick said. "How do we do that, Ember?"

He looked stricken a moment, then his face settled as he forcibly calmed himself. "Let's walk through it. Step at a time. They pulled Sindel and Keene off their transports using Sindel's trick of controlling what can and can't get through the Gates. Like she did with the Flense."

"Right," Lexa-Blue said. "And took them to that buttplug of a dead planet."

"Where we almost caught them."

"And then they blew the place up."

"Unintentionally," Ember said.

"Like that matters? Fact is, their messing with reality is what caused the place to go boom."

"Be that as it may," Vrick said, "we know they were able to hijack the Gates to get Keene and Sindel. Though Hetri assures me that vulnerability has been patched. And we know they have the ability to punch a door from one planet to another, which means they could strike from wherever they are to any other reality where lyonite is present."

"But that has to take a lot of energy, even with whatever advances they've made on the available tech," Ember said. "From what little I can understand of the tech, the place-to-place vectors are not the same as the dimension-to-dimension vectors."

"Simplified, but correct," Vrick said. "That's why the Gates don't randomly bounce people between dimensions, only between the specific spacetime coordinates."

"Okay, so without access to the Gates anymore, they're left with only their own tech," Ember said. "And with any operation like this, if it was me, I'd be keeping things as simple as possible."

"Which means what exactly?" Lexa-Blue asked.

"Think about it. You have access to an infinite number of realities where lyonite exists. And I assume, some way to at least check for it either before or after you go through."

"That lines up with the scans of the tech we liberated from our thief," Vrick said.

"So, why go from place to place in search of the treasure when you can stay in the same place and just take the same treasure over and over again," Ember said.

"That makes a lot of sense," Lexa-Blue said, the light dawning in her eyes.

"It does," Vrick agreed. "With an infinite number of dimensions, they must have plenty of sources to choose from."

"But how do we figure out where that is?" Lexa-Blue asked.

"Think about it," Ember said. "They're here in our universe, the only place they have any accurate information to work from."

"Yeah, but there's no lyonite here anymore," she said, frustration in her voice.

"But there used to be," Vrick said, understanding Ember's point.

"Exactly," Ember said. "Surely there's information in the records or even just in Know-It-All as to where the major deposits used to be. Because again, if it was me running this op, that's where I'd start."

"I'm on it," Vrick said. "Hold tight."

Ey was silent for almost thirty seconds, showing just how deeply es search was. When ey spoke again, es voice was troubled. "We have a problem."

"Another one?" Lexa-Blue asked.

"One more for the pile," Vrick said. "According to all records available, the greatest planetary source of lyonite found in any registry in the Pan Galactum was on Hub."

Lexa-Blue let out a whistle of impressed disappointment. Ember just shook his head in disbelief. "That's it," he said. "That's where I'd start if it was me."

"The capitol?" Lexa-Blue said, incredulous. "The most populous world in the Pan Galactum?"

"It makes sense," Ember persisted. "The population is mostly in the city proper. Only small outposts beyond that. And between the Gate in orbit and the Gate Project headquarters working on all kinds of research, not to mention all of the other industry and tech being developed there, hiding the extra energy readings in all that background noise wouldn't be that hard at all. Considering how similar the readings are to Gate Tech, it would likely blend right in."

"Grife," she said. "And if whoever is behind this unleashes another space quake or six, they could take out the whole planet."

"Not to mention any number of the other core worlds," Ember added.

"This is bad," said Lexa-Blue.

"Very bad," Vrick agreed. "What's our next step?"

While ey was unable to physically do so, Lexa-Blue turned her attention to Ember.

"Right, back to me then," he said. "Okay, Vrick. Dig through the info again. Look for any information on where the former mines were and rank them by the volume that came from them and where they are. That may give me some hints as to where they might be."

"I'm on it."

∞

Vrick transitioned to interspace on a course for Hub at the maximum velocity possible that Lexa-Blue and Ember could stand, while simultaneously running the search Ember had requested.

Normal space fell away, replaced by the hyperlight caress of the swirling realm against es hull. Even pushing es drives to their limits, it was going to take them almost four days to reach Hub. And there were already reports of more space quakes, though minor in comparison, spreading through the Galactum. *Aftershocks?* Ey could see the reports on the news streams, and even this first wave had caused damage and loss of life that tore em with sadness.

Four more days of this might be all it takes to bring the Galactum down.

Running a sim, ey saw an opportunity to push just a bit more speed out of the drive, nudging es internal fields up to compensate.

"Crikes, junkpile," Lexa-Blue said. "Give us a little warning next time."

Concern for them spiked. "Are you both all right?"

"I've been better," she said. "But we'll be okay."

Ey saw both of them sway unsteadily under the effects of the increased speed. "I've sent an order for Neurazoline shots to the autodoc. It should help without too much cognitive impairment."

"Impairment?" Ember said. "Keep an eye on her, then. It might be hard to tell if she gets any dumber."

"I don't even have the strength to hit you," she said. "Let's get those shots, pronto."

Once ey was sure the doses had been administered properly, ey turned es attention back to es course, using es sensors to maintain a close eye on trajectory and speed in case any opportunities presented themselves that might allow em to shorten their voyage at all.

Concerned by the reports coming through on the news streams, ey opened a tightline channel to Hub and flashed Hetri Li Ffiann's code.

When the channel connected, the immersive holo showed the administrator's office bearing witness to the strain of the recent quake, cracks ribboning the walls. The administrator himself showed the strain almost as much, his face bruised and a patch of synthetic skin across his forehead.

"Sei Li Ffiann," Vrick said. "Good to see you alive and well."

"Alive, yes," Hetri answered. "As to well… we'll have to see about that in time."

"I will take the one and hold hopes for the rest."

"And I will take those hopes gladly. How is the search faring?"

"We've made progress, but we still have a long way to go. And it seems to be leading right back to you."

Hetri's face showed stunned surprise.

"Our latest lead is bringing us back to Hub. It's a string of clues and guesswork at this point, but Ember's instincts for this sort of thing haven't led us wrong before."

"This sort of thing?" Hetri said. "Do I dare even ask?"

Vrick sent Hetri a pulse containing the data they had accumulated along with Ember's conclusions. Hetri responded with a blistering burst of profanity in multiple languages Vrick was sure singed the surfaces of es tightline array.

"Why is it always some asshole like this?" Hetri said.

"I wish I knew the answer to that question, my friend."

"Thank you for this information," Hetri said, visibly, but only slightly calmer. "There's a lot of data here I may be able to use. Let me send you what I have from all the planetary networks here. They absorbed a lot of information about the quake, as did the Gate in orbit and our main control and monitoring systems. I'm barely scratching the surface, but between us, we may be able to source something that gets us closer to stopping this bastichi in their tracks."

Vrick felt the tingle of Hetri's data packet arriving, and ey slid the information into the matrix ey had already created, alerting Ember and Lexa-Blue of the new information.

"Thank you for this. We will dig into it and pass on anything we come up with," Vrick said. "The problem is we're almost four days away from Hub at the very least. By that time, there could be nothing left of the planet but a debris field."

"And isn't *that* a cheery thought." Hetri's face screwed up tight with concentration. "Where are you now?"

Vrick sent a pulse through the link containing their coordinates.

"How quickly can you get to Aleph?"

Es astrogation core had the answer in the instant the planet's name was fully formed.

"If I push my drives, I can make it in less than twelve hours."

"Do it," Hetri said. "There's a Gate there that hasn't gone online yet. They're still doing construction on the superstructure, but the actual transfer system is in the final testing phase. Everything is testing in the top percentiles. If you can get there, I'll send word you're coming, and they'll get you here."

A thought altered their course through interspace towards Aleph as Vrick formulated es answer.

"Thank you," ey said. "That will bring us into orbit in 11.42 standard hours. Try and hold the planet together until we get there."

Hetri spread his manipulators wide, tightening their digits into a grasping position. "I shall do my damnedest."

∞

"What have you done?"

Despite the fury on Ckurahris's face, Keene saw Sindel's own anger burst forth to match his.

"What have *I* done? You're the one who's taken it upon himself to shred the fundamental structure of reality."

Keene saw Ckurahris's face flush purple, strangled with rage and disbelief.

"What I have done is create the greatest achievement science has ever seen. I have the power to access dimensions never seen, to penetrate the walls of the worlds. All worlds. Whenever I choose."

"And the only thing you can think of to do with it is become a common thief."

"Oh, I would say I have used it to become an exceptional thief. The greatest thief who ever existed."

As he spoke, Keene saw the crystalline glint of avarice in Ckurahris's eyes, as cold and hard as diamond. He'd seen that look before and knew it could not be talked back to reality — could not be convinced with logic to see the error of its ways. That specific combination of greed and megalomania had burned deep and long, fed by fires too intense to quench.

"There," Sindel cried as another of the strange pressure waves flowed out and away from them. "Do you think that's natural? That it's good? For all you know, those waves could be wreaking a dozen flavours of havoc on the worlds outside your little science project. Did you ever even stop to consider what might result from all this?"

"Come along, Sei Kestra. Surely you can't be that naive," Ckurahris said. "Everything dies. Every empire falls. This cosmos has never cared a whit for us or for the eye blinks that are our lives. Solar flares, black holes, magnetars. It is a miracle any planet exists for more than mere moments before our universe destroys them. We are nothing in the face of the forces aligned against us, nothing but what we take for ourselves from an indifferent universe, nothing but the reality we scrape together and mould for ourselves. And that is exactly what I am doing here and now."

Disgust slewed across Sindel's face. "There is nothing good about any of this. You could destroy the Galactum. You could destroy half the galaxy itself. Or worse, the effects could spread through all the known universe."

"And if I do, what remains will be mine. I'll have power unlike anyone has ever held in their hands before."

"You're evil. Pure evil."

"Evil," Ckurahris scoffed. "What does that even mean? What place does it have in discussions of science? Of discovery? What place does it have when we are talking about mastering the underlying forces of creation? I claim this power because I can. Because I was meant to. Because I *dare* to."

Sindel launched herself at him so fast that Keene couldn't stop her. She was on him like an animal, her open hand arcing viciously to leave a livid handprint on his face. Keene tried to intercede but felt a sudden hard grip on his arms, making the cast on the broken one sing with a sharp pain. Restrained, all he could do was watch as they pulled Sindel off Ckurahris and tossed her down. For a moment, Keene saw their captor's silken self-control slip, as a seething rage filled his eyes. He thought for sure in that moment Sindel was about to die or receive a severe beating at the very least. Held by two of the other henchmen, she would have been helpless. But Ckurahris's controlled, charming mask slipped back into place, if only barely.

"Get them out of here."

They were hastened back to their cell, shoved through the door, and locked inside. Sindel took the worst of it, stumbling into one of the beds and collapsing over it. Keene at least managed to stay upright.

"Are you okay?" he said, reaching to help her up.

She stood up on her own, waving his hand away. "How was my performance? I think Ckurahris was right. I could have a career on the stage if I wanted."

Keene gaped at her. "What?"

"I thought the slaps were just right. Enough to push him, but not too far. I mean, if I'd really wanted to, I could have put him down with one punch. But I needed him mad, not unconscious."

"Okay, was that really the smartest thing to do?" Keene asked. "There's not a lot we can accomplish in here."

"I wouldn't be so sure of that," she said, reaching into the folds of her tunic. "Maybe this will help."

She held out her hand, showing him one of the handheld terminals they'd been using, its polymer shell neatly folded. Keene took it and unfolded it, the display coming to life. "All we need now is to get our hands on a tool or two to make a few adjustments."

Keene chuckled and lifted the tails of his shirt. On each hip, tucked into the waistband of his trousers, were two microprobes he'd managed to grab during the day. "Great minds think alike."

"They do, indeed," Sindel said. "Let's see what we can get up to."

∞

"Okay, that was janky, right?" Lexa-Blue said. "It wasn't just me."

The light from their transition through the Gate had faded before the sentence was even finished.

"You're right," Vrick agreed. "I could feel the Gate compensating heavily for the localized spacetime distortions."

"Crikes," Lexa-Blue said. "Nice of Hetri to risk our lives like that."

"Oh, it was nothing that would have caused us any harm. But the systems were definitely straining. I've done this enough times to know the difference."

"Still, a warning would have been nice. Right, squib?" She turned to Ember but frowned when she saw the lines of strain creasing his face. His arms were crossed across his chest, and his entire stance was knotted tight.

Vrick? she said on a private channel.

I know. I see it.

She took a step closer to Ember. "You okay?"

It seemed to take him a second to register she was speaking and focus on her. "I'm fine."

"You sure?"

He frowned. "Vrick, how do my bio-signs look?"

"They're... acceptable," ey answered. "But not ideal. Did you actually sleep?"

"I said I'm fine."

"Well, you're one up on us then," she countered. "Because I'm not fine. Not until we get Keene and Sindel back. But I can see the signs. You're in a flare."

"I can manage."

"You're forgetting," Vrick said, "that I can read your bioscans. Every interface between your prostheses and your flesh is going off like a supernova. You need to rest."

"I'm fine," he insisted.

"Hold out your hands," she commanded.

He hissed out a breath and didn't comply.

"Ember, please," Vrick said.

Ember scowled but complied, hands flat out in front of him, palms down. A slight but noticeable tremor ran along the fingers of his left hand. He snatched them back and buried them in his armpits. "So, what now? You're going to try and bench me?"

"Like that would work," she scoffed. "I know I can't keep you out of this. But you need to be clear on where your body and mind are right now."

"There are a couple of options programmed into the auto-doc," Vrick said. "I would advise against using them regularly or for too long. But they'll take the edge off for now, providing we can wrap this up as quickly as we can. I can give you all the data on their effects when you're ready."

Ember scowled a moment, but his face softened. "Thanks."

"I need you in this with me, squib," Lexa-Blue said. "Okay?" She turned back to the main holo. "How are things down there?"

"See for yourself," Vrick said, grimly.

The surface of Hub rotated below them, bringing the urban sprawl of the planet's main cityscape into view. Ember's breath caught as he saw it.

What was normally a vast constellation of lights sparkling like stars was now patchy and broken. Gulfs of darkness yawned across the city, while in other areas, the dull sullen glow of fires seethed. Clouds of dark smoke rose high into Hub's atmosphere.

"It's not as bad as it looks, thankfully," Vrick said. "Mostly property damage. Safety systems took care of most of it."

"Mostly," Lexa-Blue said, as if the word was bitter on her tongue.

"Mostly," Vrick agreed.

"But it's not going to stay that way if we don't put an end to this," Ember said, his voice tight with a controlled rage.

"The safety systems and first responders are holding for now," Vrick said. "I've let Hetri know we're here and sent him the data we've managed to collect. He's expecting us."

"Good. We can pool our resources," Lexa-Blue said. "Deal with this once and for all."

"Agreed. I've had more than enough," Vrick said, descending through the smoky atmosphere to the wounded city below.

∞

Even with just the two microprobes, Keene had the casing of the handheld open in minutes and went to work.

"I should be able to get some relief from the node jammer. That should make things a bit easier," he said as he wielded the microprobes with deft, precise motions.

A moment later, they both felt the return of at least some sensation through their implanted nodes.

"Still no connection to Know-It-All," Sindel said.

"That's going to take some time," he answered. "This unit only has limited connectivity, and even that has some sophisticated alarm triggers tied into it. We use it as it is to access anything outside of its main functions, and it will start screaming at everyone."

Still, he could feel some of the simpler functions returning to his node. A thought allowed it to process visual input and make it easier to see the handheld terminal's inner workings in more detail. "Ah, now that's better."

As he worked, he talked to her, never looking up from the microcircuits. "Where exactly did you learn to pick pockets like that?"

"Me? What about you?"

They looked at each other and spoke simultaneously "Lexa-Blue."

"Not Ember?" she said.

"He'd never have sullied himself with something like that. He only cleans out accounts or safes. Never something as common as a pocket."

"The man has standards."

"What about you two? That's a mighty specific kink you have going on there. At least for me, it was for work."

"On our third date, she taught me how to shoot a gun," Sindel said.

"Yeah, that sounds about right," Keene said with a laugh. "Though it still sounds weird to hear she even went on dates. How did you talk her into it?"

"It wasn't easy," Sindel said, her expression turning thoughtful. "Nothing with her was."

"Sorry," he said. "Old wounds, I know. She's a complicated person. Has been ever since I met her."

"No, it's fine. The wounds have scabbed over. They're healing."

Sindel was silent a moment. "Still, I wouldn't be upset if that door opened and I saw her face."

"You and me both," Keene said, his face tight with concentration as he lightly probed at an alarm circuit. "And maybe we can make that happen. Just give me a couple of minutes."

Chapter Eleven

"If you have a berth at the port, you may as well stay there," Hetri said, visibly distracted. "The whole complex is deep in crisis and repair mode. We're still triaging the damage and working on getting the basic critical systems back to some semblance of normal. And that's just here. The streets are being cleared of anything but essential services. I doubt you'd be able to get transport here."

"We're down and safe," Vrick said. "This part of the port seems to be almost completely intact. Once I convinced the port master I wouldn't be any bother, they let us land. We can work virtually with you for the time being. No concerns there."

Hetri's holo nodded in agreement, only slightly blurred around the edges. A line of shuddering pixels crabbed its way through the image, roughly shoulder height. "Let's just hope these systems don't crash too."

"From what I can see, the grid is stable and getting better," Vrick assured him. "Plus, I have my ways."

"From your mouth to the universe's… whatever orifice it ignores us with," Hetri said.

"Have you had a chance to review the data we sent you?"

"I set some searches running as soon as it came in. There are a lot of historical records over at the Council compound, what with this being the Galactum capitol and all. But thankfully even the old stuff has been digitized."

"Well, don't keep us in suspense," Lexa-Blue said. "What have you found?"

"I set the search routines to comb through everything, including individual town histories prior to the amalgamation into this one city and mining and mineral records going back to the first landings here. Hub was one of the major sources of lyonite in the early days, which is partly why the planet ended up being chosen as capitol. The mining companies and the traders wanted to be as close to the action as they could to keep their costs down. When the lodes ran dry, the planet was so entrenched as the centre of government, it made no sense to move all that bureaucracy elsewhere."

"Inertia," Vrick said. "One of the biggest factors in so many human decisions."

"No doubt about that. There was enough commerce and government adjacent to the lyonite trade that the behemoth was too much to wake. And here we are."

"So, what do the records tell us?" Ember asked, an edge of impatience in his voice.

"Well, there are old lyonite mining facilities all over the uninhabited areas of the planet," Hetri said, and an image of the planet appeared in the holo beside him. The main, sprawling city of Hub, where almost all of the planet's population was centred, took up most of the temperate region of the largest of the three continents, and glowed in a soft, luminous blue. Other dots of the same colour, merely pinpricks, showed the various smaller communities across the continent. They all knew that those communities were usually dedicated to scientific research or just didn't want to be part of the sprawling seat of government.

"You can see the lyonite mines here," Hetri continued.

Spots and splotches of bright scarlet appeared, spattered across the globe, the concentrations as livid as wounds. "The bigger mines were on the main continent close to where the city grew up, but there were locations all across the globe at one point."

They could see the concentrations of red thin out into a mist of fine pinpricks of light, the faintest traces on Hub's two smaller continents.

"It's amazing there's anything of the planet left," Ember said. "It's like they were eating it alive."

"Yes," Hetri agreed. "It's sad, but thankfully, lyonite mining was relatively safe and didn't have any toxic by-products. And it was centred in the rockiest, least fertile spots."

"It was also a long time ago," Vrick said. "There's been time for the ecosystem to start balancing back out."

"Do the records show which areas had the biggest yields?"

"There were pretty conscientious records kept because of all the money at play, so yes. Here's the information on where the biggest lodes were found and the facilities with the greatest lifetime output," Hetri said, and an icon indicating a new file transfer appeared in the holo.

"Got it," Vrick said. "I'm adding it to the data we already have and the sensor traces we took from the thief's equipment and running some comparison algorithms."

"Do you really think that's going to tell you where they are now?" Hetri asked.

Ember shrugged. "It's the best data we have to go on. If we're theorizing this clown has their sights on concentrations of lyonite, and they can punch their way through to alternate dimensions, it stands to reason there might be a whole slew of worlds where the concentrations of it might be similar to this reality."

Hetri nodded in agreement. "That makes a lot of sense. You're good at this."

"I try," Ember said, a small grim smile on his face. "Like I said, it's the best we have to go on. And with an infinite number of realities available to them, they'd have to start planning somewhere. Whenever you're on a heist, you need to make as many things as easy as possible. Everything else gets complicated real fast."

"Just for the record," Hetri said. "I don't own anything valuable. Just in case you were getting ideas."

Ember laughed. "I never steal from friends."

"Good to know. Keep me posted on what's happening and let me know if you need me. Now, if you'll excuse me, I have a network of wormholes to keep from imploding. Hetri out."

∞

"Got it," Keene said.

"Is it too much to hope you've taken complete control of every system in this gossforsaken place?"

He let out a bitter hiss of a laugh. "Just a bit. But at least I've gotten through the final layer of security on this thing. Now I'll see just how much access I actually do have."

He snapped the cover of the terminal back in place and unfolded it again. The holo that formed over the imaging surface was fuzzy with static and jittered before settling into a relatively stable image.

"Well, that's not optimal," he said, "but it's better than we had before. And it should be invisible to their grid."

He laid the open terminal on the table again and made several gestures with his hand that the grainy holo sluggishly reacted to. He carefully worked his way through the options.

"Well, how does it look?" Sindel asked.

"The masking I implemented seems to be holding. Even if we were to link it to the room's main interface, I doubt it would get us noticed. But I'm not going to risk it if I don't have to."

"Smart," Sindel agreed. "So, we can't shut down their dimension disruption tech, but what can we do?"

Keene gestured into the interface a few more times, shifting the colours of the holo again. "Well, so far, I can access the diagnostics for the atmospheric controls. And the waste disposal system."

"Great. Maybe we can get this place to shit us out."

"Give me a minute," Keene said with mock indignation. "The master is only getting started."

"Lead on, O Great One. I await your next trick."

"With a bit of luck, I should be able to at least figure out where we are."

After a few more motions of his hand, a scowl clouded his face. "Oh for…."

"What is it?"

With a turning of his hand, he shifted the display so she could read it. When she registered the information, she cursed vividly. "Hub? We've been on Hub this whole time?"

"At least potential rescue is nearby," he said, "if I can find a way to get through the encryption and stealth shields Ckurahris has set up around everything and get a message out."

"How difficult do you think that will be?"

"Hard to say. I have to give him credit. His work is good. This would be a challenge for the best slicers out there. Which I am not. I'm a tinkerer not a code wrangler."

"Just get us something," Sindel said. "Just some way of getting word or slowing him down or anything that might give us an advantage or help us out of here."

"Working on it," Keene said, concentrating. "With this thing hidden from the main systems, there's not a lot I can do. And neither atmo nor waste systems are going to be much good to us."

He paused, a thought forming in his eyes.

"Wait," he said, his fingers weaving patterns in the interface holo. "Wait, wait, wait."

"Tell me."

"The few diagnostic routines I can see are going to give me access to some others. Including those that run in the background of the cloaking systems."

"Okay," Sindel said, clearly not getting it. "How does that help us?"

"Hear me out. The cloaking system uses a distorter field to mask the radiation output of whatever it's trying to hide, even the wavelengths humans can't see."

"With you so far."

"And that distorter field has to be reactive. It has to constantly adjust to whatever's hitting it at any given time. With access to the diagnostics, I should theoretically be able to introduce some non-random fluctuations. Like old school Morse Code only hidden in the field variations."

He closed his eyes a moment as he fugued, using his node to run some coded messages and convert them into the pulses of the cloaking field's natural variances. He opened his eyes and focussed on Sindel.

"What do you think? Your ident, mine, Vrick's, and then tell them we're here?"

"You can hide all that in the cloak?"

"Once I know the words, I can just have my node convert it into the harmonics. For a human, it would take hours to register even a few words. But if Vrick is listening, and I have a hunch ey is, then ey will register the pattern within about a second."

Sindel's shoulders relaxed. "I'd take that bet. Not that I have much choice. Do it."

Keene input the instructions that would access the cloak's diagnostics and fed the translated message directly into it from his node. They held their collective breath as the progress indicator showed the upload, waiting for any sign of detection.

But the alarms remained silent.

∞

"Okay, squib. Where do we go?"

Once again, they were in front of the main holo display, data flowing, as Ember tried to sift through the geographical and historical data Hetri had provided them with. Lexa-Blue stood at his side, wound as tight as grav coil, her hands restlessly playing over the pistols strapped to her thighs.

And that energy is not helping. At all.

"Okay, if we're using the same train of logic that we've used so far..."

His voice trailed off as he concentrated.

"It hasn't steered us wrong so far," Vrick said, coaxing gently.

Ember swiped a set of datapoints away. "Forget these. Too small. If it was me, I'd be concentrating on the biggest potential scores. Shoot for the parallels where the concentrations of lyonite are similar but haven't been mined out by the locals of that reality. Several of the old mine sites have been repurposed, so too many people would be around for secret crime ops. That leaves only the fully abandoned ones."

"So, what does your mojo tell you?" Lexa-Blue said, an edge of impatience cutting through the words. "Time is ticking."

"It's not an exact science," Ember snapped back, though he knew he was just as impatient as she was. "I've been guessing this entire time. We've gotten lucky so far. And I don't know how much further it's going to get us."

"I swear, you two," Vrick said. "Best friends one second, mortal enemies the next. You'd give me whiplash if I had anything that could whip. Ember, take your meds. Lexa-Blue, step back and let him work."

Lexa-Blue was silent but some of the wire-like tautness in her body eased. She grabbed Ember's med case and handed it to him.

"Auto-doc says half dose now," Vrick said. "Save the last doses for when you go into action. Anymore, and you'll end up in a real hospital."

Ember took one of the smaller patches from the case and pressed it against his neck. Within seconds, he felt the neuropathy ease at least somewhat, allowing him to concentrate again. He knew it was just a stopgap to get him through the fatigue, but he was happy to take it.

I can sleep when this is over.

With his mind clear again, he swiped away more locations that didn't make sense within the framework of him trying to put himself in their quarry's mindset. Finally, the image in front of him resisted any more manipulation. He hit a wall in terms of the suppositions he could make. The remaining results were too closely similar to call.

"There. Best I can do."

"That's still seven options," Lexa-Blue said. "And I'm guessing wherever they are, they're cloaked. Or someone would have seen traces of them so far. What about it, junkpile? Any sensor hoodoo you can pull out of your thrusters to narrow it down a little more?"

"As soon as Ember indicated those locations, I pulled up any data available in the public sectors of Know-It-All. And I'm just configuring some full spectrum drone sensors to see what I can see from orbit."

Ey paused. "And done. Launching now."

Ember barely felt the vibration as the drones launched. A new pane opened in the holo, tracking the drone launcher as it shot up and through the atmosphere to the edge of space. As it hit the apex of its course, the trace image split into seven smaller lights. They silently watched them disperse and position themselves over the already marked areas. Data flowed back through them, filling the pane even more.

Minutes passed.

"Nothing unusual on the primary scans," Vrick said, es voice pensive. "Let me dig a little deeper."

Ember saw no real change in the display, despite the scanning energies Vrick was dropping like rain on the targeted sites.

"Well, well. Will you look at that," Vrick said with a chuckle. "I think I may have found something."

In the holo, one particular reading expanded, showing energy spikes that, to the human eye, were only mildly different from those showing for the other sites.

"Enlighten me," Lexa-Blue said. "I don't speak squiggle."

"That particular reading is of a minor energy flux on the arteron-zeta axis. But when you scrub it, run it through the translator and turn those pulses into language…"

The peaks and troughs of the energy reading dissolved into sparkles of light, then reformed into words:

WHAT'S TAKING YOU SO LONG? K&S.

Chapter Twelve

"It's a bog standard, out of the box mining facility by the looks of it," Lexa-Blue said. "Not enough of anything else worth mining to keep it open. And it's too remote to be useful for anything else. That whole area is just sand, rocks, and more ruins like this one."

The main section of the holo was filled with a high-res image of the location captured by one of Vrick's drones. Around the image was all the publicly available information on the site. Archival photos showed the facility when it had been in full operation, machinery shining and buildings clean and new. Later images showed the area as the elements had done their work, wearing away at what had been left behind when the mine had been abandoned. Rust bled down the chipped, eroded walls of the core buildings that remained standing. All around, dry sands played through the compound, dancing on the wind.

"That's definitely where the signal is coming from," Vrick said.

"Are you able to narrow it down more precisely?" Ember said. "Can you tell which building they're in?"

"Not from here," ey said. "The cloak is still mostly intact except for the small gap that let the signal through. If I was closer, then maybe. But the best way to find them will be to get inside the perimeter of their shielding."

"By the looks of these ruins, there's not much space for a big butch ship like you to land," Lexa-Blue said. "Let alone get close enough for the type of scan you'd need to do to get a precise fix on Keene and Sindel."

"Which means we're going to have to just go in and search from there," Ember said.

"Getting a fix on them from inside should be no problem," Vrick said.

"Yeah, once we're inside, you can use all our suit sensors to track them down," Ember said. "And we'll have a better idea of what defenses they have."

"So, what's our plan to get in?" Lexa-Blue asked. "You're the brains at this stuff. I'm just the muscle. If it gets in our way, I shoot it. But you're the one that points me in the right direction."

Ember pushed all of the outdated images of the mining facility away, leaving only the image of how it looked right now. He peered intently at the image, rotating it to get a good look from all sides.

"Okay, most logical places for scanners are here, here, here, and here," he said, the indicated points glowing with hard white light as he touched them. "But even the best system on the market is only going to get you so far. There are a couple of natural bottlenecks that will bounce the sensor data around too much to get accurate readings. If there's anything moving in the dead zones, here and here, they'll be getting sensor ghosts too confusing and frequent to act on."

He indicated the specific narrow gaps in the rock of the mesa that shielded the mine on one side.

"These wadis must have been cut back when this part of the planet got more rain. But they're so tight, it would be almost impossible to get sensors placed in there."

"Are we going to be able to get through?" Lexa-Blue asked. "I mean, it looks like we could fit through without any gear, but we are not heading in there without at least the augmented steelskins if we can't use full suit."

"Full armor is definitely out of the question," Ember said. "Even if we could get through there wearing it, it's probably going to be close quarters in there. We need to be able to move with a little bit of stealth."

"Stealth is my middle name," Lexa-Blue said.

"Mayhem is your middle name," Ember said. "And there will be plenty of opportunities for that, too."

"So, what's the plan, then? Vrick can't take us in, but we need to get to those channels before we can get close enough to scan for Keene and Sindel."

"We're going to need some form of transport across those plains," Ember said, indicating the vast swaths of dunes and grasslands surrounding the facility. "There's a lot of empty space around the compound in pretty much all directions. Even on the side with the mesa, there's nothing for kilometres. But that whole side of the mesa facing the dunes is the perfect place for full on scans. If we go in on anything with too big a power signature, we'll set off all the alarms."

"Alarms, bad."

"Very bad, but something we can live with if we have to." He was quiet a moment. "What we really need is something fast but with almost no motive power or electronics. Any ideas?"

"Actually, I do," she said, her trademark lopsided grin forming on her face. "Are the local comms still working?"

"Everything is currently stable. You've got an open channel," Vrick said.

She pushed em the ident and after two short rings, someone answered. An image filled the screen, jowly, wind burned, and garrulous.

Friend of yours? Ember asked.

Friend might be pushing it. But he owes me. At least I think it's his turn. Hush.

"Ipana, how's it hanging, you old boot?" she said as the image broke into a grin of recognition.

"The world is falling apart," Ipana said. "Same as always. Just trying to get through the day."

"You and Feysi okay?"

"Well, the walls haven't fallen in on us yet, so I guess it's a good day. The big boom dinged up a couple of my babies, but I can buff it out. You up to your neck in this gaszhik as usual?"

"Would you believe me if I said no?" Lexa-Blue said, grinning.

"Not a chance. Is the sky really falling?"

"It's bad, speeder. And it's about Keene."

Ipana's face took on a grave expression. "How can I help?"

"Can I borrow the *Scream*?"

"I've had her battened down since the quakes started. I'll have my crew bring her over."

"Here's my coordinates," she said, flashing their berth information to him. "Thanks. I owe you one."

"Just get your boy home safe," he said. "And maybe stop the universe from exploding."

"You know I'll give it my best shot," she said. "Love to Feysi. You two stay safe and hang in there. We've got this."

With a nod from Ipana, the holo cut out, and the view of the mine complex returned.

"The *Scream*?" Ember said. "Should I be worried?"

"Come on, squib," she said. "This is us. If you're not worried already, you're not paying attention."

Despite the chaos that engulfed Hub, Ipana's crew arrived within the hour towing a grav trailer behind a heavy hauler. With a bare minimum of words, they had transferred their cargo to Vrick's bay where it now lay uncrated and ready for them.

"What... is it?"

"That, my dear squib, is the *Solar Scream*," Lexa-Blue said. "Fastest solar racer this end of the circuit."

Ember just stared at it, stunned. It didn't look like much: a cross between a cylinder and an arrowhead, emblazoned in gaudy, ferocious colours, with a single spar extending more than a metre from the craft's nose.

"It's not exactly made for stealth, is it?" Ember said, obviously concerned.

"No, but she's fast. She'll get us where we need to go without setting off those alarms you're worried about."

"But is it going to get us all the way from the port out to the mine?" Ember asked, unconvinced.

"It shouldn't have to. Vrick can get us as close as possible without tripping any local sensor nets, then we slip the rest of the way in the *Scream*."

"How... does it even work?" Ember asked.

Lexa-Blue indicated the spar jutting from the craft's nose. "That is the most efficient ambient energy collector ever invented. Solar, sound waves, wind, you name it. Pulls it in and converts into raw motive power for the drive field."

"Wait, so someone invented a collector like that and it's not being used everywhere? I mean, Keene would have been raving about that if he'd heard about it."

"Yeah, well, it works super well at this small scale and in high-speed, high-energy demand conditions, but that's it," Lexa-Blue explained. "Engineers have tried to scale it up for general use, but it never works. Besides, the inventor has made a fortune off of licensing it for racers."

"Is it safe?"

"Ipana is the best driver in this racket, and his team is top notch. I trust him. The *Scream* will get us there."

"All right then. Let's do it."

"Come on, squib. We need to figure out what to wear to this party. We've got a galaxy and some friends to save."

∞

The door's lock panel sparked angrily, sending pinpricks of pain across Keene's hand.

"No luck?" Sindel asked, turning from her seat at the cell's terminal.

"Not so far." Keene rubbed the edge of his hand, then held it to his mouth. "Even if I had Ember's skill with locks, this one would be a challenge. Ckurahris really doesn't want us getting out of here. How's it going over there?"

Sindel had the handheld Keene had cracked propped up on the terminal's top, working the keypad in between input gestures at the floating display before her. "It's still sluggish, but I'm getting a little bit of info from the outside world."

"Anything we can use?" Keene asked, gingerly exploring the lock's internal mechanism with the two stolen microprobes.

"I'm working on it. Most I've gotten so far is information on those disturbances I felt."

Something in her tone caught Keene's attention, and his hands went still. He turned to her. "Tell me."

Sindel let out a frustrated breath. "Well, remember that first place we were held? That was a rogue planet. *Was* being the operative word."

"That can't be good."

"It isn't. Not at all. After Ckurahris and his goons dragged us through that portal, that whole ball of rock blew up."

"Blew up?"

"Dimensional stresses ripped it apart and spread out in concentric spheres out from the epicentre. Covered almost four sectors before they faded."

"How bad was it?"

Sindel reached into the display and captured the data, then flicked it to his node. The numbers flashed across his vision, accompanied by news footage and images of the damage.

"Crikes," he said, scrolling through the lists of dead and injured. A thought spiked his heart, and he selected the lists for Scholus, searching for two names in particular. Relief shot through him. "Daevin and Rogan are okay."

"Praise the cosmic singer," Sindel said, fervently. "But that could change at any moment."

"What do you mean?"

"I've got some limited access to the scientific feeds from the teams researching the waves. And even from what little I can see, this is definitely originating here, from those damned portals Ckurahris is tearing open."

"But surely there would have been more of them by now. Wouldn't they coincide with the opening and closing of the portals?"

"It's not that simple," Sindel said with a weary, frustrated shake of her head. "It's more elastic than that. It's not single portals causing individual quakes. It's more of a cumulative reaction. They must have used that other portal any number of times to work out kinks and run tests. The combined energy distortion caused by the rips between the realities builds, stretching and stretching until it reaches the extent of what the fabric of the universe can stand, then bam. Once that point is reached, that energy is released, just like ordinary tectonic plate pressures release in earthquakes."

"And with the number of portals he's been using indiscriminately…" Keene said.

"When it goes, it's going to be a whopper. Centred here on Hub."

Keene's face went slack with shock. "Hub has the biggest population density of any world in the whole Galactum. The loss of life would be worse than anything we've seen in our lifetimes."

"Not to mention the ripple effects outward. Hub would be the epicentre of the effect, but it would still take heavy damage. The quake would radiate out through the core worlds, way farther than it did the last time. It could bring the entire Galactum to its knees."

"Can you predict when it's coming?" Keene asked.

Sindel scoffed. "With a sliced handheld and a mostly locked down terminal? I mean, if you don't mind a possible date range of about a hundred years or so, maybe."

"All the more reason for me to get this door open and get us out of here."

Concentration furrowed his forehead as he went at the locking mechanism once more.

"And I'll keep at this data, such as it is," Sindel said, turning her attention back to the flickering display. "Anything I can wrench out of this half-cooked data is going to be better than where we are now."

"See if you can find any schematics of this place," Keene said. "Once I get this door open, it will help to know where to go next."

"On it. Come on, little data pixels. Come to Mama."

∞

Off to one side of the Maverick Heart's main cargo bay was a room maintained just for such occasions as this. While they each kept their basic steel-skin in their quarters when they weren't wearing them, this space carried garb for more specialized situations. Racked pressure suits, colour coded for each of them, were in one section, while the more advanced, tactical augments that could be worn along with the steelskins were kept in another. There was even a space reserved for the hardcore battle suits that Vrick's old friend, the sentient warship Makhai Rampant, had given them, though most of that space was taken up by Lexa-Blue's full-on heavy duty Thunkbuster unit — the biggest and baddest hardware of the bunch. As they entered the room, she ran her hand along its thick armour plating wistfully.

"Do you need a moment alone?" Ember asked. "Sorry, but as much as we could use the firepower, you'd never get into the *Scream* wearing it. Not to mention stealth is going to be the key word once we're inside."

"I know, but a girl can dream, can't she?" she said. With a sigh, she patted the shoulder of the battle armour. "Next time, sweetness. Next time."

"I'm thinking the high-end augment packs over the standard steelskins should be about right," Ember said.

"With extra guns," Lexa-Blue said.

"That works," Ember said. "I feel like doing some shooting myself."

"Wow. Mark the day on the calendar. Sometimes, you just gotta shoot something—that's what I always say."

"The augment packs have been kept serviced and ready," Vrick said. A cabinet opened, revealing a rack that expanded out in front of them.

Without a word, they both stripped off their shipsuits, Ember hanging his on a hook, Lexa-Blue tossing hers into a heap on the bench. Beneath the casual, one-piece garments, the steelskins covered their bodies like a microthin layer of chrome, only their heads and hands visible.

Beneath their feet, the deck thrummed as Vrick lifted off from the port. "I've calculated the course that will get us as close as possible, hopefully without tripping any security scanners. Flight time is twenty minutes."

A countdown display materialized in the air, ticking down.

"Got it," Lexa-Blue said, reaching into the racks of augment packs. "I'm thinking bracers for sure."

She tossed a pack to Ember, and he cracked the seal, pressing it to his chest. Rivulets of silver flowed from it, reacting with the steelskin and slithering across it to reinforce critical points like joints and major organs.

"Atmo packs too," Ember said. "In case they try to gas us or something. Can't hurt to be extra careful."

"Yeah," Lexa-Blue said, tossing him another pack and opening one herself. Holding the contents over her shoulder, the thin atmosphere recycler slid down into place on her back, affixing itself there. "Especially when going after a bona fide megalo who can portal you to who knows where."

"Grav shifters too," Ember added. "Might as well gear up right."

"Done," she said, tossing him one to add to the waist of his steelskin as well. "And now, for the real fun stuff."

"Your accessories, milady," Vrick said, as ey opened another cabinet with many sophisticated weaponry options.

"You do know how to make one feel pretty," Ember said. "And by pretty, I mean prepped for mayhem."

He reached into the cabinet and pulled out two medium weight pistols, strapping their holsters to his thighs.

"Ah, the Proteus 5," Lexa-Blue said, reaching over to slide one from its holster. She held it up and aimed along the sight. Giving it a twirl around her finger, she handed it back. "Good choice. Light, well built, and with the stopping power of a gun twice its size. You're learning."

"And I've been practicing too," Ember said, adjusting the holster straps.

"Now me, I like something with a little more heft," she said, reaching in and pulling out a pair of matching pistols for herself. These, however, were almost twice the size and weight of Ember's choice. "The Ekta Two. Can stop a cargo hauler in its tracks if you hit the grav field just right."

"Subtle," Ember said. "But ever so stylish."

"Not done yet," she said, making sure the Ekta pistols were secured to her thighs. When she was sure of the fit, she reached back into the cabinet again and pulled out a long barrelled sonic rifle and clamped it on her back over the bump of her atmo pack. Seeing Ember's look, she said, "Sometimes you just need to make some noise and break a few bones."

"Duly noted," he said.

But there was more. Another foray into the cabinet led to her having two flechette-loaded mini railguns attached to her forearms. Ember just raised an eyebrow.

"This assface has two people I care about as hostages," she said. "I'm not taking any chances."

"No arguments from me there," Ember said. "You set?"

"Yep," she said, patting her various armaments down. "Good to go."

"Perfect. The two of us will fit in the *Scream* with room to spare."

"Three," Vrick said.

They both looked up confused.

"When I said getting a fix on them from the inside would be easy, I wasn't talking about through your suits. I'm going in with you."

"We went over this. There's nowhere for you to land, and I'll bet they have some kind of security system that would see you coming half the desert away."

"I'm not going in as me. I'm going in with the two of you in the *Scream*."

"What the ruck are you talking about, junkpile? Have you sprained a processor?"

Across the room from the racks of equipment, a door to a closed workshop opened. They gazed in slack-jawed shock at what came through.

"I made a few modifications," Vrick said.

Before them was the simulant they had captured on Thesia, albeit heavily modified. It was clothed in a spare steelskin, and Vrick had liberally applied reinforced armour packs all over it, as many as the unit could take from the looks of it. It still looked sleek compared to the full suits of combat armour on the racks, but its litheness spoke of power waiting to be unleashed. The dark traceries of a blaster net ran over the arms and torso, its power pack on the back where the atmo pack would have been if it had been necessary.

"I scrubbed the code and downloaded a somewhat limited copy of myself with some combat subroutines added," Vrick said. "As long as you don't need me to calculate any interspatial trajectories or slice into any hypercomplex systems, I should be okay."

"Look, Vrick..." Ember began.

"They're my friends too," Vrick said.

"Yes, they are, junkpile," Lexa-Blue said, quietly. "Yes, they are. Okay, let's get the *Scream* prepped and ready. We are go in... fifteen minutes and twenty-three seconds."

∞

Rogan stepped out of the hotel lobby, grateful for the fresh air. In the aftermath of the strange quake that had hit Scholus, the hotel had been commandeered for emergency accommodations. He and Daevin had been moved from their suite to a simpler two-bed room, something they had both been more than willing to do. But the hotel now seemed to vibrate with the residual trauma the campus planet had undergone. Hallways that had once been quiet had been filled with emergency beds. There was a constant, low-level rumble of sound, a pitch of fear and uncertainty. The whole complex seemed to thrum with it.

He had needed air, even the air of an evening full of the sounds of a wounded city filling all of the empty spaces.

But, honestly, he had to admit this was all somehow familiar. The feel of a community on the edge was almost comfortable to him. Even after the time spent becoming a part of the Pan Galactum and residing on Orb, he had never been far from the memories of his youth on Frostbite, or on the Spearhead, and their constant, precarious flight in search of some kind of safety.

The parts of the Galactum he had seen had always seemed too clean, too safe, too perfect somehow, though he knew that not to be true. *All relative, I guess.*

He was discomfited by how much more comfortable he felt in the wake of this disaster. How much more real it seemed to him somehow.

In the distance, sirens called.

"Excuse me, sei," a voice said hesitantly from the twilight.

He turned and saw a young woman wearing one of the reflective vests of the volunteers.

"Yes?" he said, taking her in. She was slight and scuffed. *Young, too. A student maybe?* Her eyes shone at him from the dim light caused by the still rolling blackouts that blanketed this part of the campus.

"I'm sorry, sei, but this area is under curfew, and it begins in a few minutes. I'm going to need you to go back inside. Please." Her voice almost cracked as she relayed the instruction, and there was something pleading, yet determined in her gaze. Please don't give me trouble, it said.

"Of course," he said, a part of him wanting to tell her he had seen so much worse in his time. "Thank you for letting me know. Take care of yourself out here."

Relief radiated from her slim frame. "Thank you. You as well."

He turned away with one last nod and went back into the lobby.

He did his best to skirt the main area, where the furniture had been turned into yet another sleeping area. He stopped for a moment at a supply station where rations and beverages had been laid out, pouring a cup of tea from a large dented urn, then he took the elevator back to the room.

He heard Daevin's raised voice through the door, unable to make out the words, but absolutely certain of the blazing urgency. He waved his Link over the lock and entered.

"I don't care what you have to do," Daevin shouted into an archaic handheld comm device that they were all reduced to due to an overload of the local comm network. "I need a ship. It doesn't matter what size or shape. It could be a maintenance skiff for all I care. As long as it has thrusters and an oxygen supply, I'll take it."

He turned slightly and registered Rogan had returned, watching him with a concerned curiosity in his eyes. With a flick of his hand, Daevin turned a holo projection so Rogan could see the data it contained.

"I have already checked on that. The Gate is functioning again and ready for transit. It's one quick transit to Hub. All I have to do is get to orbit, which is where you come in." He paused as whoever was on the other end of the line responded. When he spoke again, Rogan was sure the temperature in the room had gone down several degrees. "Yes, I am quite aware of what the planet has gone through. I was here. I experienced it just like you did."

Rogan felt sorry for whoever was on the other end of that line, but he tore his attention away from the call to concentrate on the data. Skimming through it, he was suddenly unsure where to look. The ident showed it was from Vrick. And it was astounding. Rogan felt as if the floor swayed under his feet, and he had to convince himself they weren't experiencing a full-on aftershock. *Do space quakes have aftershocks? Focus, Rogan. Focus.*

Vrick had apparently sent all they had discovered. The dimensional rips and their causal relationship to the catastrophe outside these walls. Keene and Sindel on Hub. The rescue plans that were in place.

And the fate that suddenly rested on the shoulders of the Maverick Heart and es crew.

"Incompetence!" Daevin cursed, holding his hand over the comm's mic. "I'm on hold. How long do you need to pack? Or you can stay here. Whatever you want."

"Daevin, slow down," Rogan said. "Fill me in."

"Fill you in?" Daevin gaped at him. "It's all there. Keene and Sindel are on Hub. That's where all of this chaos has come from."

"I can see that. But what do you expect to do? Surely Vrick and the others have it in hand."

"I don't know," Daevin said, his voice strangled with emotion. "But I can't sit here while all this is going on. If nothing else, I need to get back to the Council. And I need to be there if Keene..."

"I know. I get it," Rogan said, thinking of his dead love, Nathe, gone for so long now. "I'll pack. You just find us a ride up to the Gate."

Relief sagged Daevin's shoulders a moment before he straightened again, and Rogan knew whoever he had been talking to had come back on the line.

"Yes, I'm still here. You have something for me? Thank you! Where and when?" A pause. "Got it. We'll be there."

Daevin disconnected the call and tossed the antique handset on the bed. "There's a work drone at a hangar at the port. The last time it was out helping move rubble, the manipulators were damaged, and they don't have the parts needed to fix it. But all the atmosphere seals are intact. It's space worthy."

"But how do we get there?"

"One hurdle at a time, my friend," Daevin said, beginning to gather what he could to take with him. "One hurdle at a time."

Chapter Thirteen

Vrick came in low, es altitude far below the standard minimum flight path. The veldt sped by below.

"Careful there, junkpile," Lexa-Blue said. "You'll scrape your paint."

"I don't tell you who to shoot," Vrick replied, "so don't tell me how to fly. I have my grav field at minimum safe intensity and my altitude below standard aviation scanner range. I can always get my hull repainted if I need to."

Beyond the main port, the horizon dipped as ey made a course correction. "You'd better get back to the *Scream* and strap in. We're almost there."

Back in the cargo hold, they found the simulant Vrick had copied emself into waiting by the smaller vehicle. As they approached, it spoke.

"I've rerun all the diagnostics and everything is optimal. The *Scream* is ready for us."

"Okay, that's still weird," Ember said.

"Hey, you lived with a copy of em for how long before we met you on Weald and saved the first Gate?" Lexa-Blue said.

"And I didn't know about it at the time. Ey was pretending to be a simple AI brainbox. I feel em having limbs and a head is a slightly different thing."

"It's quite easy for someone like me to do," Vrick said, not from the simulant but from the walls of the bay.

"You get used to em doing weird shit, believe me," Lexa-Blue said, simultaneously shaking her head no.

"I can see that," Vrick said. "Both of us can see it."

"Okay, that's enough," Ember said. "Let's get this bird flying."

"Let's do it," Lexa-Blue said, popping the *Scream's* canopy and sliding it back.

"You sure we're all going to fit in there?" Ember asked.

"I did an accurate scan of the interior and compared it to our various masses and the flexibility of your bodies, as well as this simulant," the humanoid version of Vrick said. "It won't be all that comfortable, but it should work."

"Okay, Vrickbot, that's not weird or anything," Lexa-Blue said. "You first. Bend yourself as small as you can and squeeze into that cargo spot behind the second seat."

"Oh. I'm stuck with that name now, aren't I?" Vrickbot said.

"Oh, yes. Most definitely. Now… In."

The simulant lifted itself over the lip of the small cockpit and levered itself into the last seat, tightening into a rounded shape no human would have ever been able to accomplish.

"You next, squib."

Ember followed suit, settling into the second seat, designed for the navigator. Once seated, he strapped himself in and tested the seat's gimbals. "Good shock absorption. In case you crash."

"In your dreams," Lexa-Blue answered. "I have yet to find anything I can't fly. With a bit of practice."

"And just how much practice have you had flying this thing?" Ember asked.

"None. But how hard can it be?" she asked as she settled into the pilot's seat and pulled the canopy closed. "We'll find out soon enough, I guess."

"We're at the landing site," Vrickbot said, es voice echoing in the cramped crew cabin. "I'm taking us down."

"So weird," Ember muttered.

They heard Vrick's drive field change pitch as ey landed at the designated coordinates, and they felt the slight change in sensation as the grav field died away. Beyond the *Scream's* spar, the cargo bay ramp lowered, filling the space with brilliant sunlight.

"Good day for it," Lexa-Blue said, her hands sure on the controls. "Thrusters up."

The *Scream* hummed with contained power.

"Taking us out."

The small, sleek craft hummed forward, angling down as it reached the ramp, then evening out on the dry terrain below.

"Powering up the spar," Lexa-Blue said, flipping a control switch on the dashboard.

In the narrow window at the front of the tiny craft, they could see the throb of violet energy course across the spar, growing steadily.

"Spar is powered up and stable. Course laid in and confirmed. Hang on, kids. This thing kicks."

Lexa-Blue jammed both of the control grips forward, and the *Scream* lived up to its name, air howling across its hull as the sailskip shot forth like it had been fired from a railgun. Behind her, Ember was slammed back against his seat. In the back of the compartment, Vrickbot was too well wedged in to shift more than a centimetre or two.

"Crikes, this thing moves," Ember managed to squeeze out.

"Doesn't it?" Lexa-Blue said, her voice ringing with joy. "I gotta get me one of these."

Outside the cockpit, the wide empty landscape sped past, all detail nothing but a smear of colour.

"First course change coming up in fifteen seconds… and mark," Lexa-Blue said, her voice tight with concentration.

A rock formation came toward them, seemingly too fast for a human pilot to react, but just in time, Lexa-Blue jammed the controls hard to port. The *Scream* slued to one side, its keel almost perpendicular to the ground before slipping back down into an even attitude.

Ember thought to open his mouth to complain about the ridiculous manoeuvre, but he didn't think she'd hear him. She was too busy whooping like a child as they bore down on the next obstacle in their way.

∞

With a whisper of a click, Keene felt the lock give way. "Got it."

He faced Sindel. "Can you get eyes on the corridor? Won't do us much good to get the door open only to find out there's a guard patrol out there."

"One minute," she said, concentrating on the panel. "No, we're clear. Ckurahris has every available body going through the portals and bringing back more lyonite."

"What about the impending quakes? Any more info on the timeline we're looking at?"

"Oh, you mean the death of all life in this galaxy? I can see some of the energy indices growing, but this terminal can't do much. We need to get our hands on some more sophisticated equipment before I can hazard a better guess as to how much time we have."

"Any idea where we find it?"

With a gesture, she flung a schematic of the mining complex into the air between them. "This is the portal room. And this is the power plant."

The space she indicated was in a different wing, two floors down.

"If we can get there, I'll have access to some much better sensors."

"Not to mention we can blow the reactor if we have to. That should shut Ckurahris down pretty fast."

"True," Sindel agreed. "But those portals are literally ripping through the walls between universes. If we just click the off switch, we could bring about the exact catastrophic spacetime disruption we're trying to prevent."

"Just lovely," Keene said, rubbing a hand across his face. "What about a controlled power down?"

"Maybe. That might regulate the power flux enough to keep the universe from ripping apart. But first, we have to get there."

∞

"Hang tight, you two," Lexa-Blue said. "I've got the compound on the scopes, and we're on our final approach. This last stretch is straightaway. No cover. So I'm gonna floor it and hope there are no guns trained on the flat. Or else we're splinters."

Impossibly, the sailskip sped up even more, and they could hear the sound of the power cells straining as they pushed the last reservoirs of power to the drive field. Dust flew up around the craft as it sped on to its destination.

"There it is," she added, sending an image to the rear seat for Ember and Vrickbot.

The facility was a scar on the horizon, dark corroded metal rising from the ground, burnt and baked by years of exposure to the elements.

"Cutting power to the spar, going to take us in on momentum only," Lexa-Blue informed them. "Less chance of any of the scanners reading our power output that way."

The sailskip went suddenly quiet, only the sound of the air outside murmuring over the hull.

"Powering down. We should be hitting the perimeter in two minutes."

None of them spoke as the sailskip skimmed across the remaining distance, their own silence matching the emptiness of the long-abandoned mine. Around the perimeter, they could see the smaller outbuildings had borne the worst of wear, crumbling down to bare support girders in some spots, merely piles of stone and 'crete in others.

Lexa-Blue coasted the *Scream* to a soundless halt in the shadows of one of the domes in the middle ring of structures, using the thrusters to tuck it in against a ruined wall.

"And we're here," Lexa-Blue said. "Powering down the rest of the systems." *Go silent.*

She popped the canopy of the sailskip open and the vast silence from the abandoned mine rushed in to engulf them.

There is a special kind of silence in the empty places, Ember said softly.

Lexa-Blue grunted. *Poetry, squib? Just remember, it ain't that empty. There's probably at least some security standing between us and our friends. Stay frosty.*

Grabbing the sides of the open cockpit, she levered herself out, pulling her pistols as soon as her hands were free. *Form up on me and helmet up.*

Ember and the Vrickbot formed a triangle with her at the apex and in the lead. As usual, she was the wedge, the battering ram. As they took their first steps, the collar of all three of their steelskins softened and slid up to cover their heads completely, leaving only featureless, reflective silver.

Breather check in the green, she said.

Mine too, Ember responded.

What do the scans tell you, VB? she asked, scanning the ruins around them.

Initiating wide beam scanning for the energy signatures we received before, Vrickbot said. *No surprise, it's all centred on that main building housing the drill systems and processing.*

Then that's where we're headed, she said, already moving in that direction. *You keep focussed on those readings. Try and get us a fix on life signs that might be Keene and Sindel. Ember, you and I will scan for sentries, automated or otherwise. Syncing my eye with your imagers.*

The heightened spectra visible to her sensor eye flooded Ember's node, and it translated the input into a full field of vision piped into his optic nerve.

They moved forward, the only sound the light skiff of the drifting sands under their feet. As they neared the massive hulk of the mine's main complex, they skimmed their path, avoiding the clots of scrub and dry, crawling moss that had found a foothold in this abandoned place.

There's a jammer field somewhere close by, Vrickbot said. *Designed to block your nodes from accessing Know-It-All by the looks of it.*

Yeah, I can feel it, Ember said. *Fuzziness around the edge.*

It's affecting my eye as well, Lexa-Blue said. *Hard to get a fix on what we're walking into.*

Give me a second, and I should be able to compensate. My connection to my other self should be enough to anchor a decent relay connection.

The blurriness of the signal dissipated suddenly.

There. That should do it.

I've got an access point up ahead, Lexa-Blue said, sending the tactical data to the others.

Got it, Ember said. *Lead on.*

Within moments, they were in front of a wide, high cargo door in the side of the main building at the centre of the complex. It was one of a series extending off to their right.

Looks like a loading dock of some kind, Ember observed. *Can you see a locking mechanism anywhere?*

She holstered one of her pistols and reached for a battered access panel, the formerly shiny surface scoured cloudy by decades of dust and grit. *Got it. But I wouldn't count on it opening easily.*

Let me have a go at it, Ember said, stepping around her. He knelt at the scarred panel and probed at the edges, seeking some way to get at the inner workings. *It's wedged on pretty tight.*

He searched the ground for something to use as a lever. Off to one side, several shards of metal jutted from the dirt. The intervening years had left them unidentifiable, but Ember sifted through them, tossing aside the ones in the worst shape, finally settling on one, flexing it to gauge its remaining strength. Satisfied, he wedged it under the edge of the panel and pulled.

The panel snapped open with a sharp, metallic clank that ricocheted through the silent compound and made them freeze in place. The sound died out with no sign anyone had heard it. Ember went back to probing the interior of the locking mechanism, only to be rewarded with a sudden rush of spejders that had obviously taken up residence in the wiring. Their seven legs left fine trails in the dust covering the wall as they skittered away.

No luck. They've eaten or torn their way through most of the mechanisms.

Okay, then, Lexa-Blue said. *Plan B. Stand back.*

She took up a position a few paces back from the panel and activated the sound cannon on her back. It gimballed out on its armature and aimed over her shoulder, drawing a bead on the door's latching mechanism. *Power to minimum. Just to give it a little nudge. Firing in three... two... one."

∞

Keene looked up from the cell door's locking mechanism, shaking his head slightly at the sudden rush of sensation back to his node. "Was that you?"

Sindel looked up from the panel she was working on, just as confused as he was. "I don't think so."

"I'm not imagining it, though, right? We just got our nodes back. Fully."

She nodded. "Yes, the jamming is down. I took out most of the security measures, but that one wasn't me. I looped them in on themselves, so they're all seeing the same input from the last twelve hours. The data should keep self-scrubbing for at least that long. That might have taken the jamming out too somehow."

"Whatever. I'm not taking the gift for granted," Keene said. "Can you see if the hallway is clear?"

She pored over the security feeds for a moment then looked back at him. "Clear."

Keene made one precise motion with his probes, and the locking mechanism clicked. "And there we are. Let's see if we can get this thing open."

Though the lock was no longer engaged, the sliding door remained in place. Between them, they were able to get just enough purchase on the smooth surface. Heaving together, they opened it just enough to get their hands around the edge for a better grip.

"Where to now?" he asked.

Sindel transferred the schematics she'd pulled up from the security system from her node to Keene's. "It's an old, abandoned lyonite mine complex. Looks like this is the only building left standing."

A glow of light pulsed in one wing of the building. "This is where Ckurahris has his portal generator, linked directly into the mine's old reactor. Here."

A second location, two levels down and closer to the centre of the building, glowed as well.

"Why does an abandoned mine still have a usable reactor?"

"Well, when the lyonite bust happened, they'd have pulled out with anything they could to recoup the loss. But those old mine reactors are twitchy. Once they're tapped down into the planet, they're really hard to spin down and remove without causing major tectonic instability. Mostly, they just write them off. Costs too much in fines and liabilities if something goes wrong."

"Leaving them behind for any old, diabolical mastermind that comes along."

"Usually, there are safeguards in place, but I wouldn't put it past Ckurahris to be able to find a way around them all."

"No doubt. Would scrambling or powering down the reactor close the portal generators?"

Sindel paused. "Yes. But like I said, interfering with it could tear a hole in this whole continent."

"But it would be localized here, wouldn't it? It's not going to spread across the galaxy and destroy civilization, right?"

Sindel sighed. "I see where this is going. No, you're right. It might shake some foundations, but it won't end civilization."

"But it will take us out," Keene said.

"Almost certainly," Sindel said, her usually lively expression suddenly downcast.

"Well, if you've gotta go, saving the galaxy is a pretty good way to do it."

"It is at that," she agreed, her smile sad.

Keene reached out and took her hand for a moment, squeezing it before letting it drop. "So, which way do we go?"

∞

Vrickbot stepped around them to the now buckled edge of the door frame, using the strength of the simulant's body to wrench the ruined metal aside. The shrieking echoed through the empty interior.

Well, if there's anyone in there, they know we're here now, Lexa-Blue said, shouldering past Ember and Vrickbot to cover their entry. Once through the opening, she snapped her head to one side, then the other, her pistols at the ready and the sonic rifle sweeping back and forth. *Clear.*

Ember followed with Vrickbot holding at the rear.

Where to now? she asked. *Got any floor plans in that brainpan of yours, VB?*

Downloaded them before we even left, ey said, transferring the details to their nodes.

It's a rucking maze in here, she said. *Any idea where we start?*

Well, the whole complex is pretty much dead except for two power sources, Vrickbot said. *Here. And here.*

Ey illuminated the two energy sources in their maps, a twisting line leading from one to the other. *This one is the old reactor. And this one is reading just like those energy spikes the portals give off.*

Any life signs? Ember asked.

Two heading in the direction of the reactor core. And two at the portal site. But I'm also picking up several signals on the same band that this simulant gives off there.

Which could be a problem for us if they're armed or our nemesis decides to use them as a shield.

Yes, Lexa-Blue agreed. *And two life signs heading in the opposite direction could very well be Sindel and Keene.*

I say we head for them, Ember said. *I'll bet you anything they're headed there to mess with the reactor.*

It's what I'd do, Lexa-Blue agreed. *No power, no portals. VB, find us the fastest path to get there.*

Done. The route appeared before them on their tactical displays.

I'm trying to hail them both, but I'm not getting anything back, Ember said.

It's the energy signatures from those portal initiators interfering, is my guess, Vrickbot said. *The three of us can tightbeam because of our proximity. Much farther than about ten metres and nothing.*

Good thing we're gonna get closer, then, Lexa-Blue said. *Come on. And keep an eye out for any killer bots. If it's metal and it moves, shoot it.*

∞

"This way," Sindel said, pointing down a hall that branched off the junction ahead of them.

They'd worked their way through the long, empty halls of the building, skirting debris left from the facility's abandonment.

"This is like some bad horror sensie," she said as she led the way. "Are we sure there aren't any shombies lurking in the shadows?"

"Number one: shombies don't exist," Keene said. "And number two: don't borrow trouble. We have enough on our plate with only one possible horrifying death."

"Can't argue that. This way."

The corridor widened ahead of them, ending in a pair of heavy crosswire gates. Though covered in warning signs, the gates hung open and forgotten.

"Through here," Sindel said. "There's a gantry that should lead us around to the main reactor access."

Slipping through the gap in the gates, they saw they were in the main mine entrance. Before them hung a massive drill easily four metres across. Its surface was scabrous with rust and fungus, and it plunged into the chasm below, tapering to a vanishing point deep in the planet's crust. Cowed by the massive metal tube, they traversed the gantry in silence, hugging the wall until they reached the opening they were searching for.

"Here it is," Sindel said, stepping to another abandoned, no longer secure gate. "Reactor control should be through here."

"I still can't believe they left a reactor just lying around," Keene said.

"Well, aside from the potential dangers I told you about, these pinpoint reactors are easy to manufacture and don't cost all that much. No real practical reason to salvage them. And they just sit in neutral until they get fired up again."

"Yeah, by some asshole who doesn't mind blowing up the galaxy. I'm gonna have to have a talk with Daevin about this. I can't imagine the Council won't want to do something about it."

"Well, let's see if we can get out of this in one piece first," Sindel said. "Then I'll help."

They walked on for a while after that, a sad quiet between them, knowing Keene's crusade against rogue reactors would likely not make it beyond the doors ahead.

As they neared, they were distracted from their melancholy by thick, twining conduits, each cluster thicker than a human torso, wedging the door to the reactor room open. From deep in the reactor chamber, the writhe of conduits led off down a side corridor. When they stopped to look down it, they saw the power couplings twist sharply up to disappear in a jagged hole in the ceiling.

"We must be almost below the portal chamber," Keene said.

"Map has it…" Sindel said, referring to their map and pointing left and up. "… right around there. Don't suppose we can just saw through one of these things and cut power that way? Would shut the portals down right quick."

Keene knelt by the thick conduit and had a closer look. He shook his head. "No such luck. This stuff is rated so high, it would take a diamond blade to get through it. And even if we had one, with the amount of power coursing through it, the second it broke the insulation layers, you'd be a pile of ash on the floor."

"Oh, well," Sindel said, the faint flicker of hope fading, leaving her resigned once more. "In we go."

"Hey," Keene said, standing up to catch her arm. Their eyes met and he saw her fear.

"This is who we are. Who she is. This stuff happens. And we just do what has to be done. Because no one else will. But sometimes it's shitty."

She rested her hand on his. "I know. But it's not easy watching you fly off to do it. Especially those times I wish I was flying off with you."

"I don't imagine it is," he said. "Shall we?"

They followed the serpentine coils of conduit through the door into the reactor chamber, seeing them wind off to one side where the makeshift interface of the portal equipment connected to the massive power source.

There in the centre of the vast, three-storey space was the pinpoint reactor — a gently glowing sphere. Even with the facility in ruins, the cool white glow of it shone in the debris that littered the floor in the wake of the mine's abandonment. It rotated peacefully in the antigravs of its containment bottle, as if content with its place in the universe, sure in its power.

They were rapt a moment, the reactor's light somehow reassuring, but the danger was not so ignorable.

"Over here," Sindel said, leading the way to where the interface mechanism penetrated the power transfer linkages. "Crude but effective. Can you check the reactor status board?"

"Looks like the reactor is holding steady," Keene said, his face lit by the readouts. "And they're drawing pretty much its entire output. It was in stasis mode when they got here, but they've had it running pretty much at full output ever since. I'm amazed it hasn't blown up already."

"These things are sturdy," Sindel said. "They can run at full output for centuries without any problems as long as the maintenance is kept up. If it was in stasis mode when they got here, it would have been fine for decades before needing service."

"Until we muck it up," Keene said.

"Seems to be our specialty today," Sindel said.

"Do you see a way in?" Keene asked. "Any ideas as to how we set it off?"

"Give a girl a minute," she responded, her fear making her words both sharp and teasing.

"Just tell me what you need me to do."

Sindel brought up the diagnostics on the nearest terminal, filling the air with panes of information. Glowing data streams illuminated her face as she concentrated, her hands swiping through the flood of readings. All Keene could do for the moment was watch her.

"Okay, I think I have something," she finally said, maximizing a data stream and sending the others to the background. "But we have a problem."

Chapter Fourteen

Their path through the derelict facility led them through the massive sorting and packing room, machinery as big as houses looming on either side. Long conveyers spanned the space, their antigravs silent for decades.

It's just all so... empty, Ember said.

Industries rise and fall, Vrickbot said. *Same as civilizations. Planets and stars too. Everything ends.*

But maybe if we keep our minds on task, they won't end today, Lexa-Blue said pointedly.

Ember exchanged a glance with Vrickbot and shrugged, though his expression was hidden by the steelskin.

We've got company, she said, snapping her arm out to arrest their movement. *Fade back.*

They shifted back into the shadow of a hulking boxy machine — one of the main components of the conveyor line. Its massive shadow provided more than enough cover for the moment.

With a precise, slow movement, Lexa-Blue eased out from concealment just enough to train her vision on the whisper of movement she had seen. A flick of her left hand indicated the space high above. *Looks like they have patrols after all.*

They all looked up to the network of gantries crisscrossing the upper space of the loading room, catching the motion amplified by her sensor eye. *I've got two. Looks like they're wearing blurs.*

No life signs, Vrickbot said. *I'm guessing they're simulants too. This close, even with blurs, I'd be able to catch some indication on one of the bands.*

The suspicion was confirmed as one of the blurred shapes walked to the edge of a gantry, casually climbed the railing, and dropped to the floor two storeys below. Impossible for a human being, it flexed its legs and took the weight of the descent easily.

Show-off, Lexa-Blue said, then hissed when she saw the simulant turn in their direction. ***Ruck. It's coming this way. Get ready. We might not get out of this unnoticed after all.***

At her side, Ember drew his own pistols, as she silently swung her rifle out to target the simulant in the distance.

It's not putting out anything but low-level scans, Vrickbot said. ***I don't think it knows we're here.***

But it will, Lexa-Blue said. ***Even low-level scans will pick us up if it gets any closer.***

Maybe it will keep on going, Ember said.

Across the floor, the simulant paused a moment, then turned in their direction, the smeared light of its blur coming closer as it began to move toward them.

Or not, Ember said.

Get ready, Lexa-Blue said, flashing a plan to Ember and Vrickbot, who shifted position to follow her lead.

Now.

She stepped out of the shadow, swinging the sonic rifle to bear on the simulant. She fired a low-level blast, and the air rippled as the fist of energy slammed dead centre in the simulant's chest. Its body curled around the impact, its feet screaming like overheated metal as it skidded backward.

Ember ducked around her, his own pistols blazing. The simulant's blur shattered like a prism, revealing its metallic torso in the instant before it tore apart into slag.

In the moment Ember fired, Lexa-Blue had already swung the rifle up toward the simulant's companion, having zeroed on the sound of its feet clanging on another of the gantries, below and left. The metal walkway howled in protest as the full power sonic blast rocked it, sending it twisting and straining at all its anchor points. As the shock wave travelled through the grating, she brought up her forearm railguns, shredding the railing on either side of the second simulant. She was already striding forward as it toppled from the walkway, the blur sparking a riot of colour as it hit the sorting room floor.

One of its arms shattered on impact, but it struggled to rise, legs bent at inhuman angles. Using one of her railguns, she fired again, the energy from her gun shearing through the simulant's head in a chromatic splatter.

The others caught up to her, Ember with his pistols at the ready.

That will have attracted attention, she said. *We need to move. Now. What's our fastest route from here to the others?*

Vrickbot flashed the route to their nodes.

It will be tight, she said. *But we can make it if we hustle. Keep your eyes open. Let's go.*

∞

"Of course there's a problem," Keene said with a sigh. "Just once it would be nice if it all went smoothly. What are we looking at?"

Sindel indicated the pane of data. "I can initiate a reactor shutdown from here. Or at least I could under normal circumstances. But Ckurahris has rigged a fail-safe up in the portal room. He's routed the controls up there and shut out access to these terminals."

"Wonderful," Keene said. "Which means we have to go back up there. To a room full of goons. With no weapons."

"I don't like it much either," Sindel agreed, "but it's either that or let the spillover energy from those damn portals rip the galaxy to shreds."

"Can you at least set things up from here? We won't have much time when we get up there. If we can at least set it in motion from down here, the less we'll have to do up there."

"I think so," Sindel said. "The mains are down here anyway. I can prime the shutdown sequence, do almost everything from this room. It's just the final steps that would need to be done from his fail-safe station."

"Well, we'd better get to it, then," Keene said. "What do you need me to do?"

"That panel there," she said, pointing it out. "Watch the field strength and let me know if it changes."

"Got it."

She went to work at her terminal, hunched with concentration as she ran through the reactor shutdown sequence steps from the system itself, familiarizing herself with the peculiarities of this model. Finally, she went into action, her hands moving through the panes of the interface. "Any change?"

"No, it's holding," Keene said. "Slight dip in the energy output, but the fields are steady."

"Okay," she grumbled. "Good to know our plan to blow ourselves up is going well."

"Wait…" Keene said, his whole body suddenly alert. "Did you hear that?"

"Hear what?"

After a moment, there was definitely a sound, faint and far off, from somewhere in the halls outside the reactor. If there had been any background noise other than the murmur of the reactor, they'd never have heard it.

"Can you keep going if I check that out?" Keene asked.

"Go," she said, swiping her hand to open the sensor feed he'd been watching for her. "I've got it."

Keene crossed to the door, first trying to get a look at the corridor beyond through the gap made by the conduits on the floor, but the space was too narrow to get a good look. Seeing no alternative, he gripped the edge of the door and gently pushed it open, trying to stay as quiet as possible.

There, at the edge of hearing, he caught the sound again, the metallic sharp energy crack of gunfire. And it was getting closer.

Just. Great.

He ducked back and called quietly to Sindel, keeping his voice as low as he could. "We've got company. Company with guns. And they're headed this way."

Sindel's face was a mask somehow mixing shock and hope. "But who's shooting at who?"

"No idea, but I'm hoping at least one of those parties is on our side. Or, at least, less of an immediate threat than Ckurahris."

"From your mouth to the universe's ears. I'm almost done here. If they get any closer, stall them."

"With what? The power of my brain?"

"You're a creative boy. And you do this shit for a living. Think of something."

Keene looked around, scanning for anything he might be able to use as a weapon. The best he could come up with was a weighty section of loose pipe from one of the reactor chamber's walls. He hesitated a moment before grabbing it, concerned it might have some purpose, but he saw it was only connected at one end and was cold to the touch. Bracing himself against the wall, he was able to pry it free of its mountings. There was a heavy elbow joint at one end. *That should do some damage. If I can get close enough without getting shot.*

With his makeshift cudgel in hand, he slipped back through the door, facing the source of the gunfire, his back to the conduit leading to the portal room. Bracing his stance, he lifted his weapon to the ready.

About twenty metres farther down the corridor, there was a junction. Now that the sounds were getting closer, he could tell they were coming from somewhere off to the left branch of the intersection.

He almost jumped out of his skin when the sound of a particularly close blast echoed through the corridor, and a body flew through the air into the junction, slamming hard into the floor. He recognized the scintilla of light as that of a blur losing power, and knew it was one of Ckurahris's goons there.

Except, without the blur, the body reflected light off copper bronze skin. *That is… not what I was expecting.*

He had only just enough time to swing his weapon up when he saw another flash of shimmering metal come around the corner, brandishing two pistols and some kind of back mounted long gun as well. But this particular colouration, at least, he recognized.

A steelskin.

He dropped his club.

"Blue?"

The chrome hood of her steelskin melted back from her head, and joy exploded across her face.

"Keene!"

She holstered her pistols and ran toward him, her steelskin boots ringing across the plating of the floor.

∞

"Broken arm," Keene said through clenched teeth as she lifted him in the air. "Broken arm!"

"Whatever," she said. "Shoot some more pain meds out of that splint."

But she put him down right away, hiding a twinge of guilt.

"How is it?" she asked, examining the splint to check its readouts. She'd only just gotten him back, and she wasn't planning on anything else happening to him.

Unless the world ends. But at least we're together.

"It's fine," Keene said. "When it's not being crushed."

"Excuse me," Ember said. "Mind if I cut in?"

Almost unwillingly, she stepped aside to make space. *We may be partners. Family even. But he's not just mine. Which is stupid. But here we are.*

She saw Ember fold Keene into his arms, mindful of the splint, and kiss him with quiet relief. Giving them time, she stepped away from their embrace.

Now, the hard part.

Sindel was hunched over the terminal concentrating, though Lexa-Blue could tell at least part of that was a front. She moved closer, keeping her movements slow and easy, as if approaching a skittish and potentially dangerous animal. *Which is not unreasonable considering how we left things.*

"Hey," she said, feeling a backlog of so many words pressing against her throat.

"You found us," Sindel said, not looking up.

"We did. And it wasn't easy, let me tell you."

Sindel was silent an awkward moment that stretched the space between them. Finally, she looked up. "I know you came because of him. But… thank you." The words came out all angles and sharp edges.

"Is that what you think?"

Sindel's eyes dropped, her fingers playing with the terminal's edge.

"I would have come for you, Sindel. I came for you both."

"I know, I know," Sindel said, unable to make eye contact again. "I'm sorry. You might be used to this freaky, world ending shit. But I'm not."

Lexa-Blue grinned at the flash of fire in Sindel's voice. *I'll take snarky Sindel over mournful Sindel any day.*

"Speaking of which, what the ruck is going on and how do we stop it?"

Sindel laid it out for her in her familiar crisp, concise style, starting with Ckurahris and who he was, and ending with her and Keene's plan to stop the reactor and blow themselves up in the process.

"Yeah, we're not doing that," she said. "We're shutting this dickfritz down and closing these portals once and for all. And we're all getting out of here. I want a plan B."

"Look, I'm sure you do, but…" Sindel started to say, but Lexa-Blue cut her off with a wave of her hand.

She turned to the others. "VB. Front and centre."

Vrickbot came forward, and es hood retracted, revealing the simulant's smooth, metallic head. Ey peered at the reactor control panel, seeing the flow of data through the terminal's display panes.

Sindel gaped at the sight of the simulant and turned to Lexa-Blue for an explanation.

"Vrick is in there," Lexa-Blue said to Sindel "Fill em in."

"No need," Vrick said, reaching for the terminal. Ey interfaced with it directly, absorbing the data and programming Sindel had put in place. "A solid plan. How were you planning to reach minimum safe distance when the reactor destabilizes?"

Sindel paused for just a second. "We weren't. Aren't."

"Well, I'd prefer to come up with another option."

"Which is why you're here," Lexa-Blue said. "Use that big brain. There must be some other way."

"I shall put my mind to it," ey said. "But if it comes down to it, you can get the others out and I can trigger it here myself."

"No," Lexa-Blue said, clamping her mind shut against the possibility.

"Lexali, this isn't me. It's a copy in a shell. It's expendable."

No. I will not. Not even like this.

"Last resort, then," she said out loud. "But we try any and all other options first."

Vrick nodded, the simulant's face blank even without the steelskin helmet in place. "All right."

A shrill, frantic cheeping burst from the terminal that showed Sindel's work.

"Oh, that is not good," Sindel said, gesturing frantically at the holo interface.

"What is it?" Keene asked.

"Some kind of alarm. I must have triggered it while I was working. If I'm reading this correctly, Ckurahris knows I'm here and knows what I'm trying. He's locking me out."

"Which means we need to get up there, now," Lexa-Blue said. She turned to Keene and offered him one of her guns. "You're gonna need this."

"You keep it," Ember said, handing one of his own pistols to Keene, then turned to Lexa-Blue. "You're a way better shot than me any day."

Even with his arm in the splint, Keene wedged his makeshift cudgel in the back of his belt, cocked the gun, sighted down it, and checked the charge before holding it at the ready.

Lexa-Blue turned to offer the gun to Sindel, who shook her head adamantly. "Don't look at me. I hate those things. I just about shot my foot off the one time I tried."

Lexa-Blue shrugged. "More fun for me. We need to move out now. I'm on point, then Ember, Keene, Sindel, and Vrick at the rear."

She turned her attention to Vrick. "Do you have everything you need?"

"I do. I'm running calculations. I should have options by the time we get there."

"Good. Let's go."

∞

The simulants attacked at a chokepoint one level up, the blurs vibrating against each other in a chaotic clash of colours as they spilled into the corridor from an empty utility shaft.

"Everyone back," Lexa-Blue called, urging the others back around the corner.

"How many?" Keene asked.

"Hard to tell with those blurs flaring."

"Scans show ten," Vrick said from the rear.

"I've had worse odds," Lexa-Blue said, aiming the sonic rifle and firing a blast into the oncoming swarm of colours.

The sonic blast hit the group dead centre, scattering them. The two on the outer edge of the formation slammed into the walls and went down. When they rose, both had damaged limbs, but they inexorably continued down the passage.

"Persistent little buggers, aren't they?" Keene said through gritted teeth. He fired, shearing off one of the simulant's arms, its blur collapsing in disjointed pastel fragments hovering over its body.

"Very," Lexa-Blue agreed, switching from her pistols to the railgun, taking another one out with a blast to its torso. "But even with bits missing, they'll do a lot of damage if they get to us. And they're keeping us from that portal room."

"I have an idea," Ember said. "Can I have that gun back for a sec?"

Keene handed it back to him without question.

"Keep them occupied for me, would you?" Ember said to Lexa-Blue.

"You got it, squib. Just say when."

Ember scanned the hallway, then focussed back on the advancing simulants, his intense concentration on his plan. "Now."

Lexa-Blue stepped forward, unleashing a barrage at the advancing horde with the railgun and the sonic rifle. The second she fired, Ember ducked out and ran at the wall to his left. His grav shifter rippled to life. When he leaped into the air, the field took hold of him and twisted his body, bringing his feet to rest on the wall at its highest point just below the high ceiling. As soon as his feet touched, he was off again, running along the wall, perpendicular to the floor. As he neared the throng of simulants, he leapt again, his body twisting in the air, his momentum augmented by the grav shifter. As he turned, his twin pistols blazed fire down at his targets. Three of the simulants' heads burst in ripe explosions of hue and cybernetic fluids.

He completed his arc over them, his feet coming into contact again, one on the wall, the other on the ceiling. But he only rested there a moment before pushing off again in a wide trajectory over the remaining simulants. At the last minute, he twisted one more time and cut power to the grav shifter, landing on the floor directly behind the metal mob. He fired both pistols with full intensity, shearing through the backs of the four simulants at the rear of the pack. They jerked at ripped, awkward angles and collapsed.

This was all Keene and Lexa-Blue needed to push their final frontal assault. Blaster fire and sonic booms hammered the remaining simulants into fragments, while Keene swung his pipe cudgel back and forth, finishing the last one off as it dragged itself, scraping, across the floor toward them. One final blow drove the end of the pipe through its metal skull.

The corridor was suddenly quiet again.

"That was fun," Lexa-Blue said.

Ember stepped over the metal ruins and handed one pistol back to Keene. "Thank you, good sir."

"What's mine is yours," Keene said with a courtly bow.

"You two," Lexa-Blue said. "You're gonna make me bortch."

"I'm getting increased power levels from the portal room," Vrick said.

"Show me," Sindel said, her face radiating concern.

Vrick piped the data to their nodes, and a three-dimensional representation of the readings filled their vision.

"Those are the portal targeting signatures," Sindel said. "He's closing his current portal and preparing to open another."

"He could be heading anywhere," Keene said, his voice sharp with alarm.

"How long?" Lexa-Blue asked.

"The power down and re-task will take ten minutes at most."

"Then we'd better move."

They carefully picked their way past the simulant debris and mechanical ichor to the junction beyond.

"This way," Sindel said. "The elevator is jammed, but there are stairs that we used to get down from that level."

She led them to the stairwell and pushed the door open, revealing stark emergency lighting casting cut glass shadows. They entered and began to climb.

∞

The staircase let them out into the hallway outside the room where Ckurahris had set up his portals. To their right, they could see the twisting conduits that supplied the power leading into the room. The steady thrum of the mechanism vibrated through the very structure of the building.

That's it, Keene said. *Portal itself is in the far-left corner of the room. Only other human we saw in there was Ckurahris's assistant, Wols. He's probably at the console if they're preparing to retarget the portal generator. I don't know how many more of those killer bots he's got in there.*

I'm only reading two humans present, Vrick said. *I think he sent all the simulants to take us out.*

Bad tactical move, Lexa-Blue said. *Shouldn't be hard to take him down.*

Don't get too cocky, Sindel said. *You shoot the wrong thing in there, and the cascade failure will not only blow the reactor, but it will also set off the next space quake and take half the galaxy along with it.*

Shoot carefully, Lexa-Blue said with a grin. *Got it.*

If that's the best you can manage, I'll take it, Sindel said.

Will the gizmo stand up to a low-level stun charge? Lexa-Blue asked her.

Your guess is as good as mine. I'd say probably, but I'd keep it as low as possible. We're talking about some pretty radical and unstable tech here.

Just great, Lexa-Blue said.

Vrick, do you have a fix on where those two life signs are? Ember asked. *I have an idea.*

Here. And here.

Positional data flowed into their nodes, showing one figure at the console as Keene had predicted, and the other over near the writhe of energy that was the portal itself.

If you can cover this one, Ember said, indicating the figure near the portal, *I can use my grav shifter to take out the one at the console.* A line appeared over the tactical plot, showing his potential trajectory, using the surfaces inside the room to ricochet himself into the figure at the console.

I can work with that, Lexa-Blue said. *Keene covers from the door. Sindel, you and VB stay out of the line of fire until Ember takes out his target, then head straight for that console. You're the only ones with a chance of getting that gizmo under control. Set it up, squib.*

One by one, they took the positions Ember laid out for them: Keene and Lexa-Blue at the doors, ready to burst in and clear the path.

On my mark, Ember said, flexing his knees. ***Three... two... one. Go!***

Lexa-Blue and Keene fired precisely metred low-level blasts at the doors, just enough power to knock them off the hinges. In that moment, they took in the seething portal embedded in the wall, with Ckurahris readying himself before it, and Wols gaping at the sudden intrusion from the control panel.

Ember dove through the gap the others had opened for him, pinwheeling in the air to carom off the wall into Wols, dropping the stunned man to the floor.

"Don't move!" Lexa-Blue called to Ckurahris, both her pistols trained on him.

"Oh, well done," he said, a smug smile spreading across his face as he buckled the harness around his torso. "But we both know you can't shoot me. Too much risk you'll set your precious galaxy alight."

"I'm a pretty amazing shot," Lexa-Blue said. "Wanna try me?"

"As tempting as that sounds, I do have other plans."

He turned and dove for the portal, swallowed by its light.

"Damn it," Keene said.

"Let him go," Lexa-Blue said. "He can be some other universe's problem now."

"That's cold," Ember said. "Practical. But cold."

"I don't like the idea of him being free to wreak this havoc on another universe," Vrick said.

"Sad when the robot has more conscience than you, eh, Blue?" Keene said.

Her retort was cut off by the sound of Sindel's voice.

"Hold on," Sindel said, examining the portal's control mechanisms. "There are some new modules uploaded here. And I can see the power routing protocols too. If I'm reading this right, I think I can use the power from stopping the reactor to set up a counter wave that will cancel out most of the energy build-up from the portals. But it won't work as long as he's out there wearing that harness."

"So, we have no choice but to go after him," said Lexa-Blue.

"I'm coming too," Keene said.

"No," Sindel barked from the console. "I need you here working this console. And we have no idea what environments he might be heading to or through. The others are at least wearing some protection."

"She's right, Junior," Lexa-Blue said. "And you know it."

"But I don't have to like it." He rejoined Sindel, pulling Ember in for a kiss along the way.

"You and me again, kiddo," Sindel said to Keene. "Keep an eye on the dimensional variance readings while I input these new parameters. I just need one more second to lock in on him," Sindel said. "Each of you get one of those stabilizer harnesses on. I'm syncing Vrick's locators to his, and it should be readable to you as well, so wherever his system takes him, yours will follow. Just need to zero in on him to make the final connection."

She entered a flurry of commands, both on the physical interface and the holos above.

"Got it. But you're going to have to move. You have about thirty seconds before I lose his signal."

"One sec," Lexa-Blue said. "Vrick."

The armoured simulant turned to her. "Yes?"

"No, not you." She turned and looked up, directing her attention to the ship. "Other you."

"Okay," Vrick said, answering in a voice with just the slightest hint of distortion from the commo link. "I'm listening."

"If it comes down to it, and we can't stop this, you blast for orbit and get as far away as you can."

"I'm not leaving you."

"You might have to. We all know this is a crapshoot. We don't know if this gizmo will even work to neutralize the waves and heal the ruptures."

"If the waves crest, there's no way to know if I'll even get far enough away to survive them."

"Well, I know you, junkpile. And if I was betting on anyone to survive this, it would be you."

"She's right, Vrick," Ember said. "And you know it. Give us a good shot at fixing it, but if the clock runs out, go. Save yourself."

Vrick hesitated. "I will. If it comes to that."

"Okay," Lexa-Blue said, her steelskin flowing over her face again. "Let's end this once and for all."

She turned and ran for the portal, Vrick and Ember at her heels. In quick succession, they were swallowed by the swirling light of the portal and were gone.

CHAPTER FIFTEEN

Blink

∞

The mine around them was suddenly alive again. The long dormant machines they had seen now screamed, howling like thunder and shaking the foundations below. Acrid fumes even their breathers couldn't fully filter clung to the air, so noxious that Ember gagged at the sudden stench.

Trust me, squib. You do not want to bortch inside that helmet, Lexa-Blue said, running. Ckurahris's contact trace shone in her mind as she tried to translate the ever-shifting picture of their surroundings her node kept feeding her.

I'm fine, Ember responded, though it didn't sound that way. *I'm fine. What is that smell?*

Lyonite smelting, Vrick said. *The process relies on heavy acids to break the ore out of surrounding rock and clean it off. Nasty stuff.*

Yeah, I noticed, Ember said. *Where are we? This doesn't look anything like the room we were in.*

I've linked myself into the harness, and it looks like he's jumping spatially as well as dimensionally. There's limited range, but if Sindel hadn't synced our gear to his, we'd have no idea where he is.

I see him, Lexa-Blue said. *Come on.*

Her legs pistoned faster as she sprang forward, her guns in hand and the sonic rifle slung tight to her back. Ember kept pace, and the sound of their breathing echoed inside the steelskin masks, which let air through to their lungs. At the rear, Vrick loped effortlessly.

All around them, miners and support crew drew back as they passed, gawking at the spectacle of three chrome apparitions chasing a man through their midst.

He's going for the catwalk, Lexa-Blue said. ***Squib, do your thing.***

Ember scanned the area as he ran, his brain running through scenarios and trajectory possibilities, looking for an option that wouldn't get him killed.

Time is ticking, Lexa-Blue called. ***We're losing him.***

With a quick prayer to the universe, Ember leapt, twisting to bounce off the sheer metal wall of a sorting machine into the arm of a crane. He dimly registered that the distorted gravity of his impact had jostled the bell full of white-hot slag, spilling the molten cargo to the floor. He heard shouts below, but thankfully, no screams.

Didn't kill or maim anyone. Good to know.

With the gantry approaching, he shot his arm out and grabbed the railing, using the grav shifter to plant his feet firmly on the walkway. In a flash, he had his pistol out and fired. But the blast squealed off metal, and Ckurahris was gone around the corner.

I've still got a fix on him. Get up here now.

Alarms wailed through the complex, set off by his weapon, and the air flushed with crimson emergency lighting.

I rucking hate gravity shit, he heard Lexa-Blue say, but then felt both her and Vrick grav shifting to leap and follow him. Before they had even landed, they were moving again.

Through there, Ember said, indicating the high galleries where the upper mechanisms of the mining facilities opened for repair and maintenance access. The trace on Ckurahris glowed like a star in their helmet displays as he ran above them in the murk and darkness of the rafters and gantries. Fumes and smoke clogged the air, and every surface had an oily sheen.

I liked this place better as a ruin, Ember said, his steelskin smeared with the greasy film where he'd touched the railing.

I don't think we're going to be here for long, Vrick said. ***Energy readings show he's going to…***

∞

Blink

∞

...shift.

They emerged into oppressive silence in the dim red glow of a swollen, aged star that filled a ruddy brown sky. All around lay parched sand the colour of long dried blood. There was no sign of the factory here. Not a single girder or scrap remained.

They almost lost their footing in the shifting, sucking sand they now stood on. They heard the breathers in their steelskins hum to a higher setting as they registered an unbreathable atmosphere.

Where do you figure we are now? Ember asked.

Wherever it is, Vrick said, *there's almost no atmosphere. And what little there is would kill you in less than a minute. The star has aged, obviously a lot faster than the one in our universe.*

Ey pointed up, where the doleful crimson eye of the star stared down at them, taking up almost a third of the sky.

Good thing we came equipped.

Numbers flashed across their vision, giving their approximate amount of time before their breathers gave out.

Okay, so we have just under two hours before we have to get out of here.

If I can't take him down in two hours, I'll turn in my pistols, Lexa-Blue said. *But I'd like to know how he's managing to breathe here.*

These harnesses have a limited emergency bubble field. We weren't the only ones who came prepared, Vrick said. *He's got a bubble of air, but it won't last him more than around ten minutes or so.*

Let's find him then, Lexa-Blue said, struggling forward as the sand sucked at her legs.

Can you get a bead on him, Vrick? Ember asked.

It's not easy. That star is pumping out a lot of radiation that's interfering with my sensors.

We in any danger from it? Lexa-Blue said, scrambling for purchase on a slope of rock that jutted from the pull of the sand.

Debatable. If we were here long term, definitely. But I doubt we'll be here long enough for it to make much difference.

Let's get this asshole, then, and get ourselves out of here.

I'm getting something from over that ridge. Vrick indicated a scrub-covered, rocky ridge about a hundred metres away.

Best lead we have so far. Lexa-Blue skirted along the tumble of rocks that formed a broken path to the ridge Vrick had indicated. ***Come on.***

They followed her as she tread carefully, Ember using his grav shifter to keep his steps even, while Vrick hopped nimbly from rock to rock.

Show-off, Lexa-Blue grumbled, then promptly lost her footing. Vrick's arm shot out and caught her by the mount of the sonic rifle, keeping her from tumbling into the dirt.

You're welcome, Vrick said brightly, turning back to the path ahead.

I've got movement, Ember said, leaping to a higher vantage point. ***Over there. In the gap between those rocks.***

Sure enough, the sere, limp branches of the desert bushes rustled as if moved by wind, though the thin atmosphere around them was still and heavy.

Got it, Lexa-Blue said, swinging the sonic rifle out from her back as she targeted with her pistol as well. Before she could fire, a shape burst from the dry sedge, shimmying up into the gaps in the rock behind. She fired, but her blaster merely tore into the rock face, sending debris flying.

He's moving again, Vrick said.

Yeah, thanks. I noticed, she said through gritted teeth. ***Can you get a fix?***

Still too much interference, Vrick said. ***Those rock formations are bouncing the signals even more. Trying to compensate.***

Come on, squib. Looks like we're climbing.

Ember fell into formation just behind her as she swept an opening in the vegetation to search for Ckurahris's path.

Here, she said, flashing an image of footprints to his node. ***He's fast for a genocidal maniac.***

Let me have a look, Ember said, retuning his grav shifter and leaping up to a position on the rock face perpendicular to her. ***He's moving fast, too. He's almost to the other edge of this formation.***

We need to move then, she said, speeding up.

He followed her, bouncing back and forth between the orange, ochre rocks. But two twists in the path ahead, the trail of footprints ended.

Ruck, Lexa-Blue said, kicking up a storm of dirt and dust in frustration. ***Can you see anything from up there?***

Nothing. It's like he disappeared, he said, dropping back down beside her.

A sudden grinding roar split the eerie quiet, the rock faces around them rumbling with a heavy thrum.

Above you! Vrick shouted from behind. Their eyes snapping up, they saw a boulder loosed from some ledge overhead, hurtling down to crush them.

Hit it with everything! she commanded.

Lexa-Blue snapped her sonic rifle into position, unleashing a full power blast augmented by her and Ember's pistols flaring with energy. The fusillade tore the boulder apart in a blaze of furious light and sound. The canyon echoed with the force of their assault, but the boulder shattered into a hail of stones that pummelled down on them.

The sounds trailed off into the thin quiet atmosphere, as Vrick approached the clog of stone before em.

You two okay in there?

Nothing broken as far as I can tell, Ember said.

Me neither, Lexa-Blue agreed. *Give us a second to lever ourselves out of here.*

As ey watched, the pile of stone began to shift from within as they squirmed to free themselves. Finally, the air rippled with another sonic blast that took the top off the pile. Ember and Lexa-Blue emerged from the stone pile, their steelskins dulled by the reddish dirt.

That's gonna leave a mark, Ember said, levering himself out from the rocks. As he stood, he dusted himself off.

Be glad that's all it did, Vrick said. *You're both lucky you weren't... Hold on. Energy readings spiking again. He's going to...*

∞

Blink

∞

They fell into an explosive smear of colour that suddenly overwhelmed their vision until the suits' visual sensors adjusted. The silent red world was replaced in an instant with the sudden, riotous noise of a city at twilight, the planet's primary star that dipped toward the ring of structures now youthful and golden.

They stood in an intersection of several major streets, still covered in the dust of another universe. They took stock of their surroundings, though no one seemed to even notice their sudden appearance or be at all concerned by three faceless silver figures on their street.

At first glance, they could tell the city was at a technological level at least as advanced as their own. Sleek, graceful spires rose into the sky on all sides of the square where they found themselves. But there, the resemblance ended. The surface of every building, no matter the size, was smeared with gaudy imagery and animated holos screaming out at them.

An arm the size of a car, made of light, thrust toward them, holding out a massive fizzstick. Huge curls of holographic smoke twined up into the sky. Text around the image blared in slashes of colour.

PRIMO VEND!

From another angle, an image of a gigantic tope bottle pushed out, facets of the sculptural shape reflecting their faces back at them. As they watched, it tipped, sending a rainbow of illusionary liquid flowing in waves over them into the street beyond.

SUPRA BESTO!

From another angle, a woman's face, too perfect to be real, looked down at them, light glinting from exquisite jewelry at her throat and ears, and the diadem around her forehead. Languidly, the hologram face turned its neck in slow motions designed to show off the adornments it wore.

A-1 GLITZKRIEG!

From around a corner, a holo of a car, all sharp angles and reined-in power, sped in an arc, coming toward them. They flinched as it bore down on them, only to have it spread like smoke as it engulfed them and pass on.

NANTI CREDS PRIMO!

Mute viz, Lexa-Blue said between breaths, and the blistering intensity of the colours faded almost to greyscale.

Good idea, Ember said, following suit. *What the hell is all that kack anyway?*

Even without the sound of the demanding voices, the imagery kept on coming. Products ever more outlandish howled for their attention, a miasma of colour and light that assaulted the senses.

I believe they call it… advertising? Vrick said, a note of disgust in es voice.

Whatever the ruck it is, how do they live like this? Lexa-Blue asked.

I have no idea, Ember answered. *Maybe they get used to it, though I can't see how.*

I have a fix on Ckurahris, Vrick said. *This way.*

The path shone for them, and they moved forward as a group into the seething ocean of hue and cry that filled every metre of the spaces of the city.

The Infinite Heist

I think he may think he got rid of us, Vrick said. *I don't think he realized yet that we're synced to him. He doesn't seem to be in a rush to get anywhere.*

Good, Lexa-Blue said. *Maybe we can get the jump on him.*

She surged ahead into the crowd, none too gently.

Hey, careful, Ember said. *You're going to hurt someone.*

If this goss damned kack doesn't ease off, I might hurt them all, she said.

Wait… Vrick said. *I think I have a reading on him.*

Crosshairs formed in their vision, picking out one bobbing head in the attention-numbed crowd.

Got him, Lexa-Blue said, surging forward again.

They were approaching an intersection, Ckurahris just stepping out of the street on the other side.

Lexa-Blue stepped off the curb, registering the shape of a shimmering car bearing down on her in another smear of light and sound. *Rucking holos.*

But the car was suddenly solid and real, its cushion field scooping her up from the pavement and rolling her across the hood in a splay of chrome-coloured limbs before she rolled back off and hit the hard street. A scream rose in the air, shrill enough to pierce even the unyielding demands of the advert holos. Across the sea of faces, Ember saw Ckurahris's head snap around and register their presence.

He's made us.

Ember and Vrick shoved roughly through the gathering crowd to her side. Her curses were almost drowned out.

Don't move until I do a scan, Vrick said, es hand out but not making contact until ey was sure she was unhurt.

Forget me, she hissed through a clench of pain. *Focus on him.*

Don't tell me how to do my job, ey said. *You have a couple of greenstick fractures. But your steelskin is already tightening up to keep them from moving. But it's going to hurt.*

Just keep an eye on him.

I've got him, Ember said, as Vrick helped Lexa-Blue to her feet. *He's heading into an alley. Maybe we can…*

∞

Blink

∞

The wind hit them like a fist of stone, tearing Ember's words away as bitter cold crushed against them. The heaters in their suits, which were designed for the depths of space, wheezed under the sudden shift in temperature. Around them, the world was white.

Oh, for… Lexa-Blue said, a soft edge to her voice as her node pumped her system with painkillers for her fractures. ***Where the ruck are we now?***

Definitely not the beach, Ember said as he tried to get his bearings in the shapeless, frigid white.

At least there's no radiation to worry about, Vrick said. ***My sensor's readings are clearer. I'm cataloguing the local lifeforms so I can get a fix on Ckurahris.***

There are lifeforms here? Lexa-Blue said, incredulous. ***What could live here? Ice cubes?***

Anomalous reading that way, Vrick said, pointing off to their left and sending the fix to their nodes.

Yep. Got it, she said, using her sensor eye to see heat patterns and flashing the data back to them. ***I've got a reading in the shape of a murdering monster.***

"Ckurahris!" she yelled into the swirling storm, but her words were taken by the wind. Using the transmitter in her steelskin, she jammed the volume of the speaker to full. Her voice boomed out across the ice field. "HEY, ASSHOLE. I'M TALKING TO YOU."

For a moment there was nothing but the howl of the wind, then his voice boomed back. "THE NAME IS ASTEL. HOW KIND OF YOU TO JOIN ME."

With a sharp curse, Lexa-Blue aimed her pistol and fired into the swirling snow, her aim precise even in her anger. A spot just to the left of Ckurahris's thermal shape exploded up into the air. The heat of the blast melted the top layer of ice into a splash of superheated water that froze immediately and fell to the ground as a rain of glittering ice crystals.

"DO I HAVE YOUR ATTENTION NOW?"

"YOU DO. BUT IT'S NOT MY ATTENTION YOU NEED TO WORRY ABOUT."

From out in the swirl of snow came a terrifying sound, raw and animal, rising above even the din of the storm. A sound of rage, power, and hunger. The sound of a predator.

What the ruck is that? Lexa-Blue asked.

Bad, Ember said. *Bad is what it is.*

The creature began to emerge from the featureless landscape ahead, off to the right from where Ckurahris stood. Its shape was massive and slow as it lumbered toward them on four legs, every motion showing coiled energy ready to strike. Just from the hints they could see, it clearly massed more than 150 kilos.

Crikes, Ember managed to say. *What the hell is that thing?*

Sensors are showing both ursine and feline characteristics, Vrick said. *Apex predator by the looks of it.*

No shit, Lexa-Blue said, trying to watch the advancing shape and cover Ckurahris as well.

A sudden lull in the wind-sheared snow brought the animal into full view as it stalked ever closer to them. Now that they could get a good look at it, they could see the sheer mass of its body, pelted in a swirling pattern of white and grey. While the body resembled a leaner version of a bear, its face was definitely more feline in nature, with two fiery amber-gold eyes that fixed on them with seething hunger and bloodlust. But the most disturbing feature was the tusks that sprouted from the upper jaw, curved upward like two razor sharp scimitars.

"Good kitty," Ember said, though the words were lost as a whisper to the wind.

Watch out for those tusks, Vrick said. *That thing can generate enough force to shred your steelskin like paper.*

The beast roared once more, the sound ripping from its throat — its hot breath a cloud of condensation in the frigid air. As the sound echoed around them, it reared back on its hind legs, brandishing paws bigger than a human head, tipped with deadly pointed black claws.

Ckurahris is on the move, Vrick said.

Can you blame him? Lexa-Blue shouted back, keeping her eyes on the snow creature's threatening stance. *Tell me we're at least still synced to him.*

We are. When he jumps, we will too.

If we don't end up as dinner first, Ember said. *Look out!*

The creature lunged for them with a speed that belied its hulking size. Ember dove down into the layer of snow over the ice below, rolling to one side. Lexa-Blue ran and ducked in the other direction, turning to fire but losing her shot as one of the beast's paws swung at her like a maul. She felt one of the claws rake along her shoulder, squealing as it sparked across her steelskin without puncturing it. Warnings flashed across her suit's HUD. But the momentum of the blow knocked her down, sending white-hot pain through her existing injuries.

As he came to his feet, Ember drew his own guns and fired, scoring two hits on the creature's side, burnt and blackened. Red blood splattered on snow, but still less damage than he'd anticipated. The creature screamed with rage, whipping its head back and forth.

What is that thing made of? he said, trying to get another clear shot. *That blast should have gone clear through it.*

I have no idea, but I'd rather not kill it if we don't have to. We're the intruders here, remember?

The beast roared again, this time with rage and pain, fixing its gaze in Ember's direction. Ember saw ruthless intelligence in those narrowed amber eyes, and the animal turned slowly to stalk closer to him.

We need to move. Now! Vrick called, at Lexa-Blue's side helping her to stand.

Yeah, thanks, Ember said, firing over his shoulder as he ran. *The thought had crossed my mind.*

His mind raced as the enraged beast moved ever nearer. He knew if he moved either left or right to try to get around it, the beast would be on him in a moment. One swipe of a paw and he'd be down. Or impaled on one of those tusks. Would his steelskin be able to stand up to that? He didn't want to find out.

If you can't go around, go through.

He called on all of his ZeroBall skills and ran calculations as best he could on a frozen ice field in the middle of a raging blizzard with a slavering murder beast about to eat him.

I need a distraction. On your left, he called, flashing his plans to Lexa-Blue and Vrick.

Are you nuts? she responded. *Okay, I'm ready. Say when.*
Now!

He heard the sound of her blaster fire and ran forward, having just enough distance between him and the creature. At least he hoped so.

He'd been right. With Lexa-Blue firing to the animal's left, it had swung its head in that direction. Keying the grav shifter, he leapt, its field lifting him farther and higher than his legs could have. He spun in the air, reaching for the highest point of the beast's back. His hands made contact with the thick, mottled fur and gave him just the momentum boost to fly the rest of the way up and over the predator.

Contracting his body into a ball, he tweaked the grav field one last time to bring him into position to land. But a gust of bitter wind caught him, sending him careening to one side. The ground came up at him suddenly and he hit the ice, losing his footing and coming down hard.

Shaking his head to clear it, he saw he was only about a metre from Lexa-Blue and Vrick.

But the creature had turned to follow the arc of his flight and was advancing on them again.

That asshole better jump soon, Lexa-Blue said. *Or we're...*

∞

Blink

∞

Once again, they were met with a profound, echoing silence, though the star above their heads was as faded as the landscape around them. It hung low to the horizon, its warm yellow light breaking into watercolour washes of orange and pink as it set. In the sudden warmth, a halo of steam rose from their steelskins.

But the city that had once existed on the site had fallen decades, if not centuries ago. All that was left were abandoned husks of its buildings, jagged and skeletal against the paleness of the sky. All around them was the stink of decay.

He certainly took his sweet ass time, Ember said.

The bastard was probably waiting for that thing to eat the three of us, Lexa-Blue said as she picked herself up to survey their surroundings.

I'm not sure we're any better off here, Vrick said. *I'm getting alarms on all the biological hazard sensors. The air here is seething. Biologicals. Nerve agents. Ionizing radiation, you name it. If it kills living tissue, it's here.*

Well, isn't that rucking lovely, Lexa-Blue said. *How dead are we?*

Your breathers and steelskins, along with the harness field, should handle it, as will his gear. But I'll feel better the sooner we're out of here.

Problem is, we ain't the ones doing the driving, she grunted.

Which begs the question, how do we get back once we have him? Ember asked.

I break bones until he hits the right button.

Looks like you can tell him that for yourself, Ember said, pointing beyond her.

Their quarry stood at the end of the street, surrounded in the glow of his emergency force field. But he was not alone.

All around him were the natives of the broken city, staring and shambling aimlessly. Gaunt and clad in filthy tatters, their skin spoke of their residence in the fields of poison. Burnt, scarred, and covered in sores and wounds that had never been given a chance to heal properly, they moved in a restless, shifting mass around him.

Crikes, Ember said, his voice soaked in horror. *How are these people even alive?*

They aren't, Vrick said. *The levels of toxins in the atmosphere will finish them off within a year.*

And he's using them as a shield, Lexa-Blue said, her rage like a blade.

"Don't move, asshole," she said, advancing on him, her pistol aimed at him.

"As I mentioned before, the name is Astel," he said, a smug smile on his face. "Would you be so kind as to put that gun away? You wouldn't want to hurt one of these poor unfortunates, now, would you?"

"I could take you down without even giving one of them a contact burn," she said, stepping closer. "And it's not like I need this anyway."

She launched into such a vivid description of what she planned to do to him that even Ember was disturbed by it.

"Take one step closer, and I open a portal to send these people through to the centre of Hub's most populous neighbourhood. And send every pathogen they carry along with them."

"You would, too, wouldn't you?" Ember asked. "What's a few thousand, a few million more?"

"I would do what I have to," Ckurahris said with a shrug. "I have broken through the walls between the worlds, something no one before me has ever accomplished. The power is mine because I wrestled it from the gods themselves. What I do with it is up to me. It is my right."

"But at what cost?" Ember said. "Opening these portals is breaking down the fabric of space itself. That planetoid you were using blew up. And the shockwaves hit all the core worlds. Is that what you want? Look around you. This world is dead. They just don't know it yet. This is the kind of devastation you'll leave behind if you keep ripping those portals open."

"And for every dead world, there will be a billion, billion more." For a moment, Ckurahris's eyes burned with a hungry, power-mad look like the creature they had narrowly escaped on the ice world. "Worlds to conquer. To take. All of them laid bare at my feet. Think of it. Open your tiny minds for once in your hopelessly mundane lives. An infinity of worlds. More possibilities than any human could even imagine. And open to us by the power of my mind. My will. Open for the taking because of my work."

"And what happens to them when they're torn apart? When this toy of yours sends more quakes through more realities?"

"Then there will be more. And more after that. Worlds enough and time. And all of them mine."

Lexa-Blue surged forward, taking two urgent steps and aiming at him again, but he had already moved back into the crowd of lost, dying natives.

Hold on, Ember said. ***You might make the shot, but what if you don't?***

Stall him, Vrick said. ***Keep him talking. I may have a plan.***

She unleashed a stream of curses and stepped back, lowering her gun hand. But only slightly.

"That's a good girl," Ckurahris said. "Behave. We wouldn't want any of these poor people to suffer further now, would we?"

"Oh, believe me," she said. "The suffering is all reserved for you."

"Now, now," Ckurahris replied. "A little respect. If it's not too much trouble."

He touched the controls on his harness, and a portal popped open to the right of the crowd, swallowing five of the diseased natives in its light. In a second, the light faded, and they were gone.

"You sick bastard," Lexa-Blue said, aiming her gun at him again. "Where have you sent them?"

Ckurahris shrugged again. "Who knows? It's an adventure! Should we follow? Watch them bring a new civilization to its knees? Or maybe they'll be cured? It's a mystery."

I've got it, Vrick said. ***I've sent a pulse back through my link to his equipment. He shouldn't be able to take any of them with him when we jump the next time. But we need to get out of here.***

Okay, my turn then, Lexa-Blue said. ***Get ready and follow my lead.***

Her plans flowed from her node to the others.

She aimed the sonic rifle on her back over the heads of the crowd ahead, firing a diffuse blast into the air. Taking advantage of the distraction, Ember drew and fired at the same time, aiming for the ruined buildings lining the street. In the sudden cacophony of noise, the terrified crowd of ragged survivors panicked and ran for shelter. The sudden, seething mass of motion made it impossible for Lexa-Blue to aim at him again.

Ckurahris was suddenly alone in the street, bathed in the lambent light of his harness and protective field. But his hand was already at the controls of the portal mechanism on his harness.

"Oh, bravo," he said. "Well played. Aren't you all clever?"

His hand moved ever so slightly on the controls, and the glow around him began to brighten again.

Lexa-Blue aimed for him.

No! Vrick yelled. ***If you hit him while in the middle of that power surge, you'll unleash all of that energy at once.*__

With a hiss of rage, she dropped her gun again.

The glow around Ckurahris blazed higher, obscuring him. For a moment they thought they heard him laughing, then caught his parting shot thrown at them as the portal opened.

"What do you think we'll find on our next stop? Let's find out, shall we?"

∞

Blink

∞

The rusted, jagged spires of the ruined city were gone, replaced by the lights and sounds of a vibrant, living city. But though the city was alive, a quick glance showed it was still not their home — not the world they had known.

Where even the ruins on the last world had hinted at lost beauty, the architecture here was angry and brutalist, its hard grey angles showing no softness or inviting curves. All around them, actinic spotlights played aggressively across the streets, bathing them in harsh white light.

They were in some kind of square or open space. Banners hung all around them, their jagged, unrecognizable symbols blood red on black. As the light of the portal faded, they heard a chant from the crowd around them, the language guttural and full of rage, dropping away as the crowd registered their presence. Along the front lines of the crowd, guards in black uniforms, accented with the same insignia as the banners, turned, training their weapons on the trio that had suddenly appeared in their presence.

Where the ruck are we now? Lexa-Blue asked.

I don't know specifically, Ember said. *But I've seen this story before. It never ends well.*

A metre off to their left, they saw Ckurahris kneeling on the hard, rough ground. Though he was obviously winded by their transit here, he flashed them a wild grin. "And here we are!"

The lull brought on by their sudden appearance lasted only until someone in the crowd pointed and shouted. The call was taken up by the crowd, becoming an oppressive wave of sound. The bright spotlights illuminated masks of hate.

Okay, I don't need to know the language to know they aren't complimenting our outfits, Lexa-Blue said.

One of the guards surged forward, shining black leather straps crisscrossing the sharp lines of his tunic, matching the patina of his well-shined boots. He waved his weapon and barked at them, more unintelligible words.

Stay calm, Vrick said. *We do not need this to turn into another firefight.*

The guard moved cautiously closer, a vicious looking weapon in his hands. But as he came within touching range of them, his face suddenly contorted and he staggered back, unable to breathe.

My sensors are giving off a contagion alarm, Vrick said. *We must have pulled something along with us when we came through.*

So, how do we keep from killing everyone here? Ember said.

Your guns, these settings. Shoot us all. Quickly.

Lexa-Blue recognized the power and dispersion numbers and acted, hauling out both pistols and firing at Ember and Vrick, then swinging her arm to fire at Ckurahris as well. The guns gave off a pale, wide-beam light that bathed them all and caused a shocked, violent roar from the crowd around them. She had just enough time to turn the weapons on herself before they heard a shocked command, and a deep thrum of energy bathed the square, making their teeth vibrate. Lexa-Blue felt her guns go dead in her hand, and felt Ember signal the same. She sent a command to the sonic on her back, but it lay folded neatly in its mount.

Weapon damper, Vrick said. *The whole square is lined with them.*

And I'm betting it doesn't affect their guns at all, Ember said.

I don't need a weapon to finish this, Lexa-Blue said, sliding her pistols back into their holsters and glancing sideways at Ckurahris. *I might even enjoy it more.*

They were surrounded now, uniformed guards in a ring, their black garb soaking up light.

And what are we going to do about them? Ember asked.

Give me a minute.

Around them, the guards advanced, ugly metal manacles in their hands as they levelled their weapons to cover the intruders.

Stay down. Whatever happens, Vrick said. *Just remember. This isn't me. I'll see you soon.*

Wait... Lexa-Blue said, but ey was already moving.

The simulant body moved almost faster than they could track. Vrick leapt from es crouch, taking out the nearest guards with a sweep of es arm. Though ey took out three at once, more surged forward to fill the gap. Ignoring them, the simulant ran for Ckurahris.

Down! Ember grabbed for Lexa-Blue as she moved to rise and follow Vrick's path.

The guard brought their weapons to bear on Vrick and fired, sending the burning chemical stink of projectile weapons in the air. All Ember and Lexa-Blue could do was watch as the hail of bullets hammered into es back, their force denting the metal body of the simulant beneath. Their eyes flew open as the projectiles somehow managed to tear through the steelskin, ripping into the simulant beneath.

As Vrick staggered forward, the harness around em began to glow with portal energy. Step by step, ey moved ever closer to Ckurahris, whose eyes showed sudden, real fear.

The guards stopped firing a moment, as if shocked by the metal being before them and not wanting to harm the human it was approaching.

When Vrick reached es target, Ember and Lexa-Blue heard Vrick's voice through their nodes, es audible words to Ckurahris lost in the growing swirl of energy.

*This ends *now*.*

The broken remains of Vrick ripped the harness from Ckurahris's chest. Coruscating, blinding energy exploded around him. With a sound somewhere between a scream and a maniacal laugh, Ckurahris's body tore apart on the waves of light.

The security force fired as one, the fusillade sparking like lightning across Vrick's steelskin, and tearing into es exposed skull. For a moment, the gouges they made in es skull made a grotesque mockery of a face. But even as the hail of projectiles tore through es body and sent em to es knees, es hands flew over the surface of Ckurahris's harness. With one final triumphant motion, the simulant turned to Ember and Lexa-Blue. The waves of dimensional energy compressed down to a dot that burned like the heart of a star...

Blink

Chapter Sixteen

"Patch this into the reactor override bus," Sindel said. "No, not there. There."

Keene followed her finger and snapped the cable into place, giving it a twist to lock it tight. "Okay, what's next?"

"Run the power load diagnostic to make sure the linkages are secure and can handle what we're going to shove through them."

Keene worked the panel, seeing the readings all glow green. "We're good. Looks like everything is working."

"Good," she said from her position on the floor, once again deep in the insides of the machine. She pulled out a circuit board and swapped it with another, pushing the translucent veined polymer into place. "I just have to reroute a couple more of these circuits, and we should be ready."

"And then we can blow ourselves up," Keene said drily.

"Yeah, it doesn't quite sound like as much of an achievement when you put it like that."

"Well, keep your brain on it. We still might think of something," Keene said, watching the power flow indicators as Sindel made the final swaps to the inner mechanisms of the console.

"There," she said. "Ready."

"Uh, Sindel," Keene said, wariness in his voice. "You might want to have a look at this."

"I do not like the sound of that," she said, levering herself up from the floor. "What is it?"

Her jaw went slack as she stood beside him.

The portal had swollen out from the wall, distended and pulsing. Its once pearly white surface now swirled with sickly yellow-green veining as it grew like a blister.

"Is it supposed to be doing that?" Keene said.

"You're asking me? How should I know?"

She looked down at the readings that had tracked Ckurahris's progress and kept Vrick synced with him to allow them to follow. She paled. "I've lost the signal. Ckurahris and Vrick are gone."

"Gone? How? What about Blue and Ember?"

"I have no idea. The trace wasn't routed through their gear."

"Can they even get back if something has happened to Vrick or Ckurahris?"

"Your guess is as good as mine," she said. "But that thing looks like it's about to burst, and it's the one doorway to wherever the hell they are, so let's hope whatever's happening works in our favour."

The blister of writhing light spread out in one last paroxysm of growth, burst in a shower of sickly light, and faded.

There on the floor before the now blank wall lay Ember and Lexa-Blue, their steelskins streaked with scorch marks. Their hoods folded back, exposing their faces as they gulped in air.

"Please... tell me.... you can shut... this shit down," Lexa-Blue said between ragged breaths. "I never want to do that again."

Ember nodded his head vigorously, without adding any words.

Keene and Sindel ran from the terminal to their sides, helping them rise.

"What happened?" Keene said, his arm around Ember's shoulder. "Where's Vrick?"

Ember didn't answer, instead looking over at Lexa-Blue, whose face slammed shut. "Ey's out beyond the dunes. The simulant took out Ckurahris and his portal gear," she said flatly. "And we got shoved through what felt like a keyhole. Sideways," Lexa-Blue said. "Now let's get the ruck out of here and blow this place into quarks."

"It's all ready," Sindel said. "You should have enough time to get to your vehicle and get out of here. I can trigger the reaction from here once I know you're clear."

"No," Keene said. "We are *all* getting out of here."

"Someone has to trigger the reaction to nullify the damage the portal has already caused and prevent the next space quake."

"And this has to be you?" Keene asked. "Set a remote trigger or a timer or something."

"You know that our best chance at stopping this is—"

"Forget it," Keene said, striding back to the console. He snatched up the handheld he'd liberated earlier, keying commands into it as he held it over the console and transferred settings to it. With a flourish, he handed it back to her.

"Now that the tech he was wearing is gone, you have a remote trigger. Complete with countdown until the space quake energy gets too strong to stop. No excuses. Now can we go, please?"

"Just one more second. I need to check this."

Lexa-Blue shouldered past Keene to Sindel's side. "Sindel, I swear if you do not move that beautiful ass of yours, I will knock you out, carry you down the stairs, and drag you behind the sailskip by a rope tied to your ankle. No one else is dying here today. Now, move!"

"Uh, everyone," Ember said. "We have another problem."

"What now?" Lexa-Blue said.

Ember merely pointed at the spot on the floor where Ckurahris's aide, Wols, lay unconscious.

"Oh, for…." Lexa-Blue muttered. She looked around, spotting a first aid kit attached to a wall. She opened it and rifled through the contents, finally pulling out an injector. She stomped back to Wols and knelt beside him, jamming it into his arm.

He gasped and bolted upright into a sitting position, his eyes wide as the stimulant hit his system.

"Welcome back, asshole," Lexa-Blue said. "This is your lucky day. I don't have time or the energy to drag your ass out of here with us. So unless you want to be blasted into ooze, I'd suggest you run. Fast."

Wols looked at her a moment, confused.

"NOW!" she shouted right in his face. He scrambled up and was out the door like a shot.

"Okay, can we go now?" she asked.

∞

They ran from the room, jumping over the twisted conduits that fed the energy from the reactor to their improvised bomb.

The empty mine stood silent around them as they ran, their footsteps echoing down through the rows of silent, massive machines.

"The sailskip is this way," Lexa-Blue said. "Come on."

She led them through the dusty, debris ridden lanes of the complex until they reached the spot where the vehicle remained.

"Uh, I hate to be that guy, but how do we all fit?" Keene said.

"Ruck!" Lexa-Blue swore, kicking a curved chunk of metal out of her path. "It only has two seats."

Junkpile, she called, linking the others in. *We need pickup at our current location.*

Vrick's voice sounded anguished. *The dimensional waves are starting to build up around your device, and they're playing hob with my core systems. If I could land right at your position, I might be able to get out. It's like the eye of the hurricane. I'd have to land outside, but if I did, then chances are I'd never make it back in the air before I lost all propulsion and nav. You're going to have to get out of the blast radius yourselves. I'll wait for you.*

No, Lexa-Blue said. *Remember what I said before. You save yourself.*

"Uh, I hate to bring this up, but what's the blast radius going to be?" Ember asked.

"Too far," Sindel said. "I'm going to have to trigger the reaction within the next five minutes or this whole sector is space dust. We're not going to make it clear before it blows."

"No. This is not happening," Lexa-Blue said, her voice sharply desperate. "You're smart. We need a solution. Think."

They heard it at the same time, the whine of a grav drive starting up.

"Wols. He must have access to a vehicle," Keene said. "He can take some of us."

"Too late," Ember said. "Look."

In the direction he pointed, a capsule car shot up from the ruins of the mine, arcing up and away into the distance.

"If we get out of this, I am going to find that man and punch him. Repeatedly," Lexa-Blue said.

I have his ident and am tracking him, Vrick said. *We'll be able to find him again.*

Still no exit plan, though, Lexa-Blue said. "I'm not hearing ideas, people."

Ember exchanged a look with Keene and held out his hand. "You and Sindel take the sailskip. We'll figure something out."

"No," she said, her voice strangled. "No."

"There might be some other vehicle here we can jumpstart. We'll be fine."

She was about to open her mouth to argue, when they all heard the sound of a grav field being pushed to its limits high above them. They all craned their necks to see if they could identify the source.

"There!" Keene said, pointing. "Is that a work pod?"

It came out of the sun's glare, arcing down in what looked suspiciously like a death dive.

"Yes," Sindel said. "Yes, it is. We use those for Gate construction all the time."

"Whatever," Lexa-Blue said. "It's a ride, and that's all I care about."

She drew her pistol and adjusted the settings through her node, aiming into the sky. When she fired, the energy shot up like a flare.

The pod altered course, wagging its stubby fins to indicate the pilot had seen their flare.

"When that thing lands," Lexa-Blue said to Keene. "You get on it. Shoot the pilot if they don't want to give you a ride. But you get on that pod and get out of here. I'll take the sailskip and meet you on the other side."

The pod came in for a sharp landing about a hundred metres down the laneway, just fitting between the wreckage of the buildings. As the dust settled, they could finally see the pilot.

"Hey, there," Daevin said, using the pod's external mic as he waved from the pilot seat. "Just happened to be in the neighbourhood. Thought I'd drop in."

∞

Daevin slapped the control for the pod's hatch. "Get them on board. We need to get out of here fast," he called to Rogan. "I don't like the readings I'm getting from this place."

"Ready," Rogan said, holding on to the grab bar at the rear of the pod.

Dusty hot air filled the pod's cabin as the hatch opened. Keene and Sindel ducked in under the raised hatch.

"Welcome aboard," Rogan said. "Strap in, and we'll get you out of here."

"One second," Keene said, walking forward to where Daevin sat. He leaned over and wrapped an arm around Daevin, still strapped into the pilot seat. "I have no idea why you are here, but I'm glad you are."

"Wait, where are the others?" Daevin asked.

"They've got their own ride." He kissed Daevin's temple fiercely and let him go. "Now get us the hells out of here."

Keene opened one of the folding seats and strapped himself in across from Sindel. Rogan passed them, heading to the seat beside Daevin.

"Hatch is secured, Captain," Rogan said, cheeky despite the gravity of the situation.

"Hold on, everyone," Daevin said. "This might get rough."

He jammed the pod's controls forward, and the grav field screamed, sending the small craft straight up past the walls around it. As soon as they were clear, he banked hard to port and accelerated as high as the pod's engines could go.

The tiny vehicle shot from the abandoned facility out over the dry scrubland beyond, aiming for the city in the far distance.

"Okay, I don't want to alarm anyone," Rogan said. "But those weird energy readings are spiking again."

"That would be me," Sindel said, pulling out the handheld and opening it. "Just have to make sure we're all far enough away."

"How close are we cutting it?" Keene asked over the howl of the pod's engines.

"Too damn close," Sindel said. "Can you see the others?"

"Hold on," Daevin said. "Checking for them now. Nothing on my side. Rogan, have you got them?"

"Not yet," Rogan said, scanning the land below. "Wait! There. I've got a dust plume matching our course. Thirty degrees off the starboard side."

"I've got visual," Daevin said. "Not sure what they're riding, but it's going like nothing I've seen before."

Keene sagged with relief in his seat. "Okay, now all we have to do is hope we can make it far enough away that we don't get blown to subatomic bits."

"Working on it," Sindel said tightly, keeping her eyes on the readings. Not looking up, she called out to Daevin. "Just get us as far away as you can as fast as you can."

On her screen, the axes that indicated the projected safe distance and the point when the space quake became inevitable moved ever closer.

∞

Pushing the others toward the pod, Lexa-Blue turned and ran for the sailskip. But she quickly became aware of another set of footsteps running beside her.

"I told you to get on that pod," she said.

"We started this together," Ember said. "We finish it together."

"Fine, but don't blame me if we get flitzed by Sindel's gizmo in there."

"If we do end up dead, I'll go easy on you."

"Sure, you say that now," she said, slapping the release for the cockpit of the sailskip, sending it sliding back along the vehicle's hull.

She grabbed the sides of the cockpit and lifted herself into the pilot seat, slapping at the power-up controls to bring the sailskip back online. She heard Ember drop into the seat behind her. "Watch your hands."

She hit a button and the cockpit slid closed, the sleek craft rising once again on its field generators. At the sailskip's bow, the spar glowed to life.

Gripping the sailskip's stick, Lexa-Blue nudged the craft from its spot out into the laneway again, then hit the impellers and sent them forward with a burst of speed.

"Do you know how to get us out of this maze?" Ember asked.

"I mapped the route we took coming in, and I've got the schematics up. I should be able to figure it out one way or another."

She sped the sailskip up, shooting down the laneway and then banking high on a crumbling wall and around the first bend.

"No, no. That's fine," Ember said through clenched teeth. "Didn't need those organs anyway."

"No backseat driving."

Their speed increased as she deftly steered them through the twisted warren of wreckage.

Suddenly, Lexa-Blue's control board chirped politely but insistently.

"Okay, it might be a good thing you're here after all," Lexa-Blue said. "I'm getting some nasty shimmy on the lateral stabilizers."

"Is that bad?"

"Well, if you want to get out of here without becoming a black smear on one of these walls, then yes."

"Let's not do that, then. What can I do?"

Lexa-Blue tapped another control, and an auxiliary control board unfolded from the back of her seat into Ember's lap. "Okay, see those two readouts?"

Two displays with control pads beneath them glowed with a soft pink light.

"Got 'em," Ember said.

"Okay, these are the ranges I need you to keep the stabilizers in." The numbers dropped into his node, and he recognized them on the displays themselves. "Just keep the numbers within that range, and we should be okay."

The Infinite Heist

Ember put his hands on the control surfaces, feeling the minute tremor go through the sailskip's hull as she yielded control of the subsystem to him. With slight movements of his hands, he got the feel for the control pads, making slight changes in the reading and correlating the feel of the system with the feel of the sailskip itself.

"Okay, I think I've got it," he said.

"Then hang on," she said. "It's time to get the ruck out of here."

She jammed the accelerator forward, maxing out the sailskip's speed. Ember gasped behind her at the sudden rush of speed and its subsequent pull on the stabilizers he was controlling.

Controlling the craft together, they shot through the laneways of the long-forgotten mining facility until they came to the main exit from the ruins out onto the dusty plain ahead.

"We're almost out of time," Sindel called, simultaneously transmitting through her node to Ember and Lexa-Blue far below them on the surface. "If I don't trigger it within the next minute, it will be too late."

"I'm flat out up here," Daevin said. "Fast as I can go."

At his side, Rogan closed his eyes.

Same down here, Lexa-Blue said. ***Ready as I'll ever be.***

Ember sent only wordless assent.

Across from her, Keene gripped the edge of his seat. "Do it."

With a breath and a prayer, Sindel triggered her device.

Through the tightline transmission circuit, Sindel's jerry-rigged device clicked to life, cross circuiting panels throughout the portal device's mainframe and architecture, inverting the mammoth energy signatures that could open the doors between worlds. In the blink of a human eye, the energy propagated through the interspace substrates across the sector. The building space quake collapsed in upon itself and, in a way imperceptible to human senses, the galaxy was suddenly quiet.

There on the surface of Hub, far out in the empty plains beyond the city, in a forgotten husk of metal and stone, reality split apart.

For a moment, the universe seemed to collapse around them as the mining facility's core shut down, releasing its energies into the portal matrices, sealing them shut forever. Arcs of blinding white fire shot into the air from the void where the ruins had suddenly ceased to exist, buffeting the two tiny vehicles that sped from the epicentre of the blast.

Around those fleeing vehicles, light seemed to bend, refracting at wrong angles, until, finally, the air was quiet once more.

And two tiny crafts, one in the air, one on the surface, sped on.

Epilogue

Once the shockwave of the detonation had faded, the salt flat was quiet as they sped across it. It was pretty much a straight line to the city now, so Ember's work on the stabilizers was unnecessary. He was silent in the back seat. Reaching out with her node, she found him in a light doze. Lexa-Blue wondered how much his prosthetics were hurting but kept the thought to herself. Let him have the silence. They'd be back with Vrick soon. He could rest there. They all could.

For now. Until the next time the world falls apart.

She saw em in the sky before she heard es call through her node, the brilliant splay of sunset colours across es hull in the distance. She adjusted their course slightly to intersect the coordinates she'd been given.

And there in the distance, she saw em turn in a graceful curve and come in to land, rear cargo ramp opening for them.

She cut her speed to almost nothing, letting their built-up velocity take them the rest of the way. The cargo hatch loomed, an inviting shape of light against the gathering dark.

Home.

She manoeuvred into final position, slid up the ramp into place, and braked, bringing them to rest.

She sat in that stillness a moment as the sailskip's systems cycled down. She needed a moment to breathe, to adjust. Finally, she popped the hatch open and slid it back, breathing in the familiar air of Vrick's interior with its smells of cooking and play and recycled air and all the traces of their life here.

"Come on, squib," she said as she levered herself out of the cockpit to stand beside the sailskip. "We're home."

Ember opened his eyes with a start and looked around blankly. "I'm awake."

"I know you are," she said, indulgently, peeling back the gloves of her steelskin and unsealing the main seam down the front. "Come on."

"Looks like we scratched the paint. Is your friend going to be pissed?"

She stopped and looked at the battered sailskip. "Keene will help him fix it. I'll get him drunk. He'll forgive us."

She turned and strode out of the cargo bay, stopping a moment at the hatch leading into the main lounge in the bow. She just looked at it a moment, taking it in. Without really stopping to think why, she reached out, her hand touching the curve of the wall where it opened out into the common area. The ceramic and metal were cool against her palm, but there was something else. She realized they had taken off. Beneath her palm, she felt the pulse of Vrick.

Of Vrick alive.

The sudden sickening flare of light replayed in her mind, and she closed her eyes against it.

It wasn't em.

Ember came up behind her and patted her shoulder, causing her to jump, but she covered it quickly.

"Honey, we're home," Ember said, jaunty through the definite note of fatigue in his voice.

"And just what time do you call this, young man?" Vrick retorted.

"Sorry, got caught up saving the galaxy again and lost track of time."

"Well, you're grounded. No life-threatening adventures for at least a month."

She heard Ember laugh, and a pang shot through her.

"I'm going to get out of this steelskin and have a shower," Ember said. "And maybe a nap."

She saw him stretch, his eyes closed, and she knew he was hurting.

"Don't take too long," Vrick said. "We're off to meet up with the others."

"Got it," Ember said, exiting the room.

Is everything okay? Vrick said through her node, intimate even though they were alone.

Yeah, just tired.

I notice there's only two of you, Vrick said softly.

Don't you know what happened?

I lost contact with the simulant the moment you went through the portal. I have no record of anything that happened while you were out of range.

You did great. I mean, ey did great. I mean... she said, fumbling the words. *I'll tell you all about it sometime.*

I look forward to it.

Ey was quiet a moment.

You know that wasn't me, right? It was just a sim. A tool.

That's just what the other you said.

Ey was smart. You should listen to em.

Es words eased the knot in her chest. *I do. Thank you.*

Go get cleaned up. We'll be there shortly.

∞

The pod was sitting there on the pad when they arrived, as Vrick descended from the sky. Blazing lights illuminated the landing area holding the night at bay, great swaths of the city still plunged in darkness as workers struggled to restore power.

Vrick settled into a space beside the pod, and Ember could see Keene waiting there. He'd risked a dose of the meds, feeling it was pretty safe to dull his awareness at this point as it mixed with his fatigue. At least it stilled the ache in his leg and side. And there would be sleep soon.

Ember was already at the ramp, ready as it lowered, striding down it before the edge had even fully extended.

And Keene was there, Ember's arms tight around him.

They just held each other in silence, taking comfort in what would likely be a fleeting moment of safety.

After a time, they split apart, just looking at each other.

"So," Ember said. "What have you been up to?"

Keene laughed, the sound deep and throaty with tension release. "Oh, you know. This and that."

Ember laughed too, and just that shared moment sent a rush through him, pushing the pain down.

"Hey, can I get in on this?" Daevin said, coming up from behind Keene's left shoulder. He laid an arm around Keene's shoulder but reached forward to place his hand on the back of Ember's neck, pulling him close until their foreheads touched. Ember revelled in the warmth of Daevin's skin against his.

"Thank you," Daevin said softly, then kissed Ember lightly on the cheek. "Okay, you two rest. You've earned it. I need to check in with the Council. See if I still have a job after all the strings I've pulled in the last few days."

He kissed Keene and turned away, walking off with Rogan.

"Is he going to be okay, do you think?" Ember asked. "We asked a lot of him, and he put everything on the line to help."

"He'll land on his feet," Keene said, pulling Ember against him again. "And wait… were you just nice to him? Actually… concerned?"

"Shut up. I'm tired. It will pass."

"No, no. I like it," Keene said, grinning. "It's nice to have the two men I love not hissing at each other like ratcats."

Ember swatted him in the arm. "Shut up and kiss me."

∞

Lexa-Blue saw Sindel standing across the pad, deep in intense conversation with Hetri.

Imagine being in a room with those two going at it. All that brain stuff. And all that temper.

Lexa-Blue hesitated, unsure of whether to approach or hang back, not knowing how important the conversation was. But she was close enough to hear when Hetri raised his voice.

"All I'm saying is you can take a break, have a rest," he was saying, the heat of his voice blistering even from a distance. "You were kidnapped, for crikes sake. There was shooting. And explosions. No one would begrudge you taking some time. And whether you believe it or not, I can handle things in your absence."

"I know there was shooting," Sindel said, her own voice rising to meet his. "I was there. But that space quake caused damage all through the core systems. We have to make sure everything is safe on every one of the Gates before we proceed."

"Which is exactly what I've been doing," Hetri said, biting off the words.

"Okay, you two," Lexa-Blue said, stepping forward with her hands out to hopefully pacify them. "Back to your corners. Round One is over. Everybody breathe."

They both started in again.

"But he won't listen—"

"She's being unreasonable—"

"Enough!" Lexa-Blue yelled. "I am tired and cranky and I will shoot you both."

They both went quiet, stunned by her outburst. Then Sindel chuckled. "She will too."

Hetri grinned at her. "Oh, please. I barely know her and I know she will. Look, trust me. Everything is on track. Get some rest. We can talk about it tomorrow, okay?"

"Deal," Sindel said.

"All right," Hetri said, turning his chair toward the entrance to the complex. "You two play nice. We have work to do in the morning. Like… a lot of work."

And they were alone. For the first time in months.

"So," Sindel said after a flat, strange silence. "Thanks for saving my life and everything."

Lexa-Blue laughed. "You're welcome. Even if things are… You know. You still get life saving privileges."

"Good to know. Hopefully, I won't have to invoke them again any time soon."

"Well, this is me after all," Lexa-Blue said.

"Yeah," Sindel said, subdued. "And that's the thing, isn't it? Sooner or later, there's the shooting and the chasing and the explosions. It never really ends."

"No," Lexa-Blue said. "It doesn't. And I never pretended it doesn't."

"No, you didn't. But I really just want to spend my life building things."

Lexa-Blue's face broke out in a lopsided grin that Sindel knew all too well. One that still made her heart race a little. "Of course, I could point out that this time, it was you building things that started the whole mess off."

Sindel's face screwed up into a scowl. "Damn. You're right. I'll try to only build safe things from now on."

"Yeah. Get right on that," Lexa-Blue said.

They were silent a moment.

"So," Lexa-Blue said. "Dinner tomorrow night?"

"Deal."

They were quiet again, both staring out at the wounded city of Hub.

Far off in the distance, one of the dark areas of the city sputtered with the sudden flickers of light as power was restored, pushing the darkness back just a little.

Acknowledgments

The Infinite Heist was my pandemic book. The one that I'd just started when the world shut down. And though you'd think that all that time alone in my apartment would have been perfect writing time. If not for the depth of the collective trauma we were all living through as the world coped with this mysterious new illness. There were fits and starts, bursts of incredible productivity and then months long droughts. So, first of all, a huge thank you to all my writing community on social media who kept me going, who understood what so many of us were going through with our projects. Who nudged and poked, but never judged, and always supported. It took me a while, but I got here.

As always, a big thank you to Renaissance Press for believing in the Maverick Heart books and giving them a home when they were orphaned.

Eternal gratitude to Jerry L. Wheeler for being the first editor to have a go at it, before I'd even submitted.

Much love and gratitude to my Beta readers: Troy Anthony Young, Andrew Deobald, and Michael White. I will gladly trade you sneak peeks in return for the encouragement I needed to keep going in that long solitude of writing it all down.

Thanks to my editors at Renaissance Press, Alex, Alec, and Max, for shepherding me through and seeing the things I couldn't.

Thanks to my cover designer, Nathan Fréchette, for taking the rough, shaggy idea in my head and making it pretty.

To my dear sistren, Linda King and Jennifer Saemann, and to our lost fourth, Sue Brooks who missed out on this one. Thanks for always being there, my constant North stars.

And of course, thank you to anyone who has bought a copy of any of my books, who joined on the journey, who laughed and cried and thrilled along with me. I'm so glad you came along with us. You've always been members of the crew.

ABOUT THE AUTHOR

Stephen Graham King (He/They) is a disabled survivor of metastatic synovial sarcoma, a story chronicled in the memoir, Just Breathe: My Journey Through Cancer and Back. Since then, he has concentrated on writing speculative fiction, in particular, queer-themed space opera, and his short fiction has appeared in the anthologies North of Infinity II, Desolate Places, Ruins Metropolis, and the Aurora Award winning Nothing Without Us Too. His first novel, Chasing Cold, was released in 2012, followed by the books in the Maverick Heart Cycle: Soul's Blood (2016), Gatecrasher (2017), A Congress of Ships (2019) and in 2022, Ghost Light Burn. He has been a frequent guest on podcasts and panels, passionately advocating for lived experience queer and disability narratives in stories of the future. They are also an avid black and white photographer, with two of their photos appearing in an installation at the Art Gallery of Ontario. They are also working on a book compiling their intimate and immediate photos captured on the streets of Toronto, where they currently reside.

About Renaissance

Renaissance was founded in May 2013 by a group of authors and designers who wanted to publish and market those stories which don't always fit neatly in a genre, or a niche, or a demographic. Like the happy panbibliophiles we are, we opened our submissions, with no other guideline than finding a Canadian book we would fall in love with.

Today, this is still very true; however, we've also noticed an interesting trend in what we like to publish. It turns out that we are naturally drawn to the voices of those who are members of a marginalized group, and these are the voices we want to continue to uplift.

At Renaissance, we do things differently. We are passionate about books, and we care as much about our authors enjoying the publishing process as we do about our readers enjoying a great Canadian read on the platform they prefer.

pressesrenaissancepress.ca

pressesrenaissancepress@gmail.com